METRO
2034

Also by Dmitry Glukhovsky from Gollancz:

METRO 2033

METRO 2034

DMITRY GLUKHOVSKY

Original text copyright © Dmitry Glukhovsky 2009
English translation copyright © Andrew Bromfield 2013
All rights reserved.

First published in Great Britain in 2014
by Gollancz
An imprint of the Orion Publishing Group
Orion House, 5 Upper St Martin's Lane, London WC2H 9EA
An Hachette UK Company

This edition published in Great Britain in 2014 by Gollancz

10

A CIP catalogue record for this book is available
from the British Library.

ISBN 978 1 473 20430 0

Typeset at The Spartan Press Ltd,
Lymington, Hants

Printed in Great Britain by Clays Ltd,
Elcograf S.p.A

The Orion Publishing Group's policy is to use papers that
are natural, renewable and recyclable products and made
from wood grown in sustainable forests. The logging and
manufacturing processes are expected to conform to the
environmental regulations of the country of origin.

www.nibbe-wiedling.de
www.orionbooks.co.uk
www.gollancz.co.uk

The World of Metro 2034

The entire world lies in ruins. The human race has been almost completely wiped out. Radiation renders half-ruined cities uninhabitable, and rumours say that beyond the city limits there is nothing but boundless expanses of scorched desert and dense thickets of mutated forest. But no one knows what really is out there.

As civilisation draws its final, shuddering breaths, memories of humankind's former glory are already obscured by a thick fog of fantasy and fiction. More than twenty years have passed since the day when the final plane took off. Corroded, rust-pitted railway tracks lead off into nowhere. The great construction projects of the final great age lie in ruins, destined never to be completed. The airwaves are empty, and when radio operators tune in, for the millionth time, to the frequencies on which New York, Paris, Tokyo and Buenos Aires once used to broadcast, all they hear is a vague, distant howling.

It is only twenty years since it happened. But man is no longer the master of the earth. New creatures born of the radiation are far better adapted to this new world than human beings. The human era is almost over. Those who refuse to believe it are very few, numbering mere tens of thousands. They do not know if anyone else has been saved, or if they are the last people left on the planet. They live in the Moscow Metro – the largest nuclear bomb-shelter ever built; in the final refuge of the human race.

On *that day* they were all in the Metro, and that was what saved their lives. Now hermetic seals protect them against radiation and monsters from the surface, decrepit but functional filters purify their water and air, dynamos built by amateur engineers generate electricity, underground farms cultivate mushrooms and breed pigs. But the central control system of the Metro disintegrated long ago, and its stations have become dwarf states, each with a population united by its own ideology and religion – or merely by loyalty to the water filters.

This is a world without any tomorrow. There is no place in it for dreams, plans and hopes. Here instincts take priority over feelings, and the most powerful instinct of all is survival. Survival at any price.

What happened before the events recounted in this book is described in the novel *Metro 2033*.

CHAPTER 1

The Defence of Sebastopol

They didn't come back on Tuesday or Wednesday, or even Thursday, which had been set as the final deadline. Armoured checkpoint number one was on twenty-four-hour alert, and if the men on watch had caught even a faint echo of appeals for help or spotted even a pale glimmer of light on the dark, damp walls of the tunnel, a search and rescue unit would have been dispatched immediately in the direction of Nakhimov Prospect.

With every hour that passed the tension grew more palpable. The finest combat troops, superbly equipped and specially trained for exactly this kind of mission, hadn't grabbed a single moment of shuteye all night long. The deck of cards that was used to while away the time from one alert to the next had been gathering dust in a drawer of the duty-room desk for almost two days. The usual joshing and banter had first given way to uneasy conversations in low voices and then to heavy silence, every man hoping to be the first to hear the echoing footsteps of the returning convoy: far too much depended on it.

Everyone at Sebastopol could handle a weapon, from a five-year-old boy to the very oldest man. The inhabitants of the station had transformed it into an impregnable bastion, bristling with machine-gun nests, coils of prickly barbed wire and even anti-tank hedgehogs, welded together out of rails. But this fortress-station, which seemed so invulnerable, could fall at any moment.

Its Achilles' heel was a chronic shortage of ammunition.

Faced with what the inhabitants of Sebastopol had to endure on a daily basis, the inhabitants of any other station wouldn't even have thought of defending it, they would have fled from the place, like

1

rats from a flooding tunnel. After tallying up the costs involved, probably not even mighty Hansa – the alliance of stations on the Circle Line – would have chosen to commit the forces required to defend Sebastopol Station. Despite its undeniable strategic significance, the price was far too high.

But electric power was very expensive, expensive enough for the Sebastopolites, who had constructed one of the largest hydroelectric stations in the Metro, to order ammunition by the crate with the income earned from supplying power to Hansa and still remain in profit. For many of them, however, the price paid for this was counted, not only in cartridges, but in their own crippled and shortened lives.

Ground waters were the blessing and the curse of Sebastopol Station, flowing round it on all sides, like the waters of the Styx round Charon's fragile bark. They turned the blades of dozens of water mills constructed by self-taught engineers in tunnels, caverns and underground watercourses – everywhere that the engineering exploration teams could reach – generating light and warmth for the station itself, and also for a good third of the Circle.

These same waters incessantly eroded support structures and gnawed away at cement joints, murmuring drowsily just behind the walls of the main hall, trying to lull the inhabitants into a false sense of security. And they also made it impossible to blow up the superfluous, unused side tunnels, from out of which hordes of nightmare creatures advanced on Sebastopol Station like an endless millipede creeping into a meat grinder.

The inhabitants of the station, the crew of this ghostly frigate hurtling through the nether regions of the Underworld, were doomed eternally to seek out and patch over new breaches in the hull of their vessel. It had begun springing leaks long ago, but there was no safe haven where it could rest in peace from its labours.

And at the same time they had to repel attempt after attempt to board their vessel by monsters from the Chertanovo and Nakhimov Prospect stations, creeping out of ventilation shafts, percolating through drains with rapid streams of turbid water, erupting out of the southern tunnels.

The whole world seemed to have ganged up against the Sebastopolites in a bitter determination to wipe their home off the map of the Metro. And yet they clung to their station obdurately, as if it were all that remained of the universe.

But no matter how skilful the engineers of Sebastopol Station were, no matter how experienced and pitiless the soldiers trained there might be, they could not effectively defend their home without ammunition, without bulbs for the floodlights, without antibiotics and bandages. Yes, the station generated electric power, and Hansa was willing to pay a good price for it, but the Circle had other suppliers too, and resources of its own, whereas the Sebastopolites could hardly have held out a month without a flow of supplies from the outside. And the most frightening prospect of all was to be left without ammunition. Heavily guarded convoys set out to Serpukhov Station every week to purchase everything that was needed, using the credit arranged with Hansa merchants, and then, without delaying a single hour more than necessary, they set off back home again. And as long as the World kept on turning and the underground rivers flowed and the vaults erected by the Metro's builders held up, the order of things was expected to continue unchanged. But the latest convoy had been delayed – delayed beyond any reasonable limit, long enough for the realisation to dawn that this time something terrible and unforeseen had happened, something against which not even heavily-armed, battle-hardened guards and a relationship built up over the years with the leadership of Hansa had been able to protect it.

And all this would not have been so bad, if only the lines of communication were functioning. But something had happened to the telephone line that led to the Circle. Contact had been broken off on Monday, and the team sent out to search for the break had drawn a blank.

The lamp with the broad green shade hung down low over the round table, illuminating yellowed pieces of paper with graphs and diagrams drawn in pencil. The little bulb was weak, only forty watts, not because of any need to save electric power, but because the occupant of the office was not fond of bright light. The ashtray, overflowing with stubs from the atrocious local hand-rolled cigarettes, exuded an acrid, bluish smoke that gathered in viscous clouds, stirring lazily under the ceiling.

The station commandant rubbed his forehead, then jerked his

hand away and glanced at the dial of the clock with his only eye, for the fifth time in the last half-hour. He cracked his finger joints and rose ponderously to his feet.

'We have to decide. No point in putting it off any longer.'

The robust-looking old man sitting opposite him in a military camouflage jacket and threadbare sky-blue beret, opened his mouth to speak, but instantly started coughing. He drove away the smoke with a sharp flap of his hand, frowned in annoyance and replied:

'Then let me tell you again, Vladimir Ivanovich: we can't take anyone off the south side. The guard posts are already struggling to hold out under this kind of pressure. In the last week alone they've had three men wounded, one critically – and that's despite the reinforcements. I won't let you weaken the south side. And apart from that, they need two teams of three scouts to patrol the shafts and connecting tunnels. And as for the north, apart from the soldiers from the reception team, we don't have any men to spare, I'm sorry. You'll have to find them somewhere else.'

'You're the commanding officer of the perimeter, you find them,' snapped the station commandant. 'And I'll handle my own business. But the team has to set out in one hour. What you need to grasp is that we're thinking in different categories here. We have to look beyond solving the immediate problems! What if it's something really serious out there?'

'I think you're getting ahead of yourself, Vladimir Ivanovich. We've got two unopened crates of 5.45 calibre in the arsenal, that's enough for a week and a half, for certain. And I've got more lying around under my pillow at home.' The old man laughed, baring his strong, yellow teeth. 'I can scrape together a crate, for sure. The problem's not the ammunition, it's the men.'

'I'll tell you what the problem is. We've got two weeks to get our supplies in order before we have to close the hermetic doors in the southern tunnels, because we won't be able to hold them without ammunition. That means we won't be able to inspect and repair two-thirds of our mills. A week after that they'll start breaking down. Nobody will be happy about disruptions in the power supply to Hansa. If we're lucky, they'll just start looking for other suppliers. And if we're not . . . But the power's not the worst of it! The tunnels have been totally deserted for almost five days now – nobody, not

4

a single man! What if there's been a cave-in? What if we've been cut off?'

'Ah, come on! The power cables are in good order. The little numbers are spinning on the meters, the current's flowing, Hansa's consuming it. If there was a cave-in, you'd know straight away. Even supposing it was sabotage, they'd have cut our cables, not the phone. And as for the tunnels – who's going to come down them now? Even in good times no one's ever strolled down here just to be sociable. Nakhimov Prospect is bad enough, without throwing all the rest in. No one can get through it on his own, the merchants from other stations don't stick their noses in here any longer. And the bandits obviously know about us. We did the right thing, letting one go alive every time. I'm telling you, don't panic.'

'It's easy for you to talk,' growled Vladimir Ivanovich, lifting the bandage off his empty eye socket and wiping away the sweat that had sprung out on his forehead.

'I'll give you a team of three men. Honestly, I simply can't give you any more yet,' the old man said, speaking more calmly now. 'And stop smoking, will you! You know I can't breathe that stuff, and you're poisoning yourself! Why don't you just get us some tea?'

'That's something we can always manage,' said the commandant, rubbing his hands together. 'Istomin here,' he growled into the telephone receiver. 'Tea for me and the colonel.'

'And summon the duty officer,' said the perimeter commander, taking the beret off his head. 'I'll give the instructions about those three men.'

Istomin's tea was always the same, from the Economic Achievements Station – a special, select variety. Not many could afford that sort of thing – delivered from the far side of the Metro and charged duty three times along the way by Hansa's customs posts, the commandant's beloved beverage was getting to be so expensive, even he would have stopped indulging his weakness, if not for his old contacts at Dobrynin Station. He once fought side by side with someone there, and ever since then, every month, without fail, the commander of the convoy returning from Hansa had brought a bright-coloured bundle, which Istomin came to collect in person.

A year ago, however, supplies of the tea had become unreliable. Alarming rumours reached Sebastopol Station of a terrible new danger menacing the Economic Achievements Station, perhaps

5

even the entire Orange Line: new mutants of a type never seen before had come down from the surface, and supposedly they could read people's thoughts, were almost invisible and, even worse, virtually impossible to kill. Some said the station had fallen and Hansa, fearing an incursion, had blown up the tunnel beyond Peace Prospect Station. The prices for tea soared, and then it disappeared completely, and Istomin had been seriously alarmed. But a few weeks later the frenzy subsided, and the convoys returning to Sebastopol Station with ammunition and electric light bulbs started delivering the aromatic beverage again – and what could possibly be more important than that?

As he poured the perimeter commander's tea into a china cup with a chipped gold border, Istomin squeezed his eyes shut for an instant, breathing in the fragrant steam. Then he strained some tea out for himself, sat down heavily on his chair and stirred in a tablet of saccharin, tinkling his little silver spoon.

Neither of them spoke, and for thirty seconds or so this melancholy tinkling was the only sound to be heard in the dark office, wreathed in tobacco smoke. But suddenly the tinkling was drowned out by a different sound, in almost exactly the same rhythm, that came hurtling out of the tunnel – the jangling of the alarm bell.

'The alarm!'

The perimeter commander leapt up off his chair with incredible agility for a man of his age and darted out of the room. Somewhere in the distance there was the crack of a single rifle shot, immediately overtaken by the chatter of machine-guns – one, two, three of them. Metal-tipped soldiers' boots clattered along the platform and from somewhere far away came the bass rumble of the colonel's voice barking out orders.

Istomin also reached for the gleaming militia machine-gun that was hanging by the cupboard, but then he gasped and clutched at his waist, flapped his hand helplessly, went back to the table and took a sip of tea. The perimeter commander's abandoned cup was standing there, cooling, on the table in front of him, with the light-blue beret lying beside it, forgotten in the colonel's haste. The station commandant grinned sourly at the beret and started arguing in a low voice with the commander who had bolted, coming back again and again to the same old topics with new arguments that he hadn't thought of while they were wrangling face to face.

It was a constant subject of sombre jokes at Sebastopol – the similarity of the next station's name, Chertanovo, to the Russian word for a demon, 'chert'. The watermill generators were scattered deep into the tunnels between the two Metro stations, but nobody even dreamed of making things more convenient by occupying and developing vacant Chertanovo, in the same way as Kakhovka Station, adjacent to Sebastopol, had been annexed. The undercover engineering teams who crept closest to it, in order to install and inspect the more distant generators, didn't dare approach within a hundred metres of the platform. Apart from the most hard-bitten atheists, almost all the men setting out on an expedition like that crossed themselves furtively, and some even said goodbye to their families, just in case.

There was something bad about that station, and everyone who came within half a kilometre could sense it. The heavily armed detachments that the Sebastopolites, in their ignorance, dispatched to Chertanovo when they were still hoping to expand their territory, had sometimes returned battered and crushed, with their numbers reduced by half, but most often they hadn't returned at all. Some battle-hardened soldiers had come back so badly frightened that they hiccupped and drooled and trembled uncontrollably, even sitting so close to the campfire that their clothes began to smoulder. They struggled to recall what they had been through, but one man's recollection was never like another's.

The generally accepted explanation was that somewhere beyond Chertanovo Station the side branches of the main tunnels dived downwards, weaving their way into a colossal labyrinth of natural caves, rumoured to be teeming with all sorts of loathsome creatures. At the station this place was referred to provisionally as the Gates – only provisionally, because none of the living inhabitants of Sebastopol Station had ever seen it. There was, of course, the well-known incident in the early days, when the line was still being explored and the Gates were apparently discovered by a large reconnaissance team that had managed to get through Chertanovo Station. They were carrying a communications device, something like a land-line telephone. On this device, the signal officer reported to Sebastopol Station that the scouts were standing at the entrance to a wide corridor that descended in an almost vertical incline. His voice was cut off before he could add anything else, but for several minutes after that, until the cable was snapped, the commanding officers of Sebastopol Station huddled round the intercom, listening as the soldiers of the reconnaissance team screamed in diabolical horror and agony – until one by one their screams were cut short. Nobody even attempted to fire, as if every one of the dying men realised that ordinary weapons couldn't possibly protect them. The last one to fall silent was the commanding officer of the group, a cutthroat Chinese mercenary from Kitai Gorod Station who collected the little fingers of his dead enemies. He was evidently some distance away from the telephone receiver dropped by the signal officer, and it was hard to make out what he was saying. But, concentrating hard on the man's sobbing as he died, the station commandant recognised a prayer – the simple, naïve kind of prayer that parents who believe teach their little children to say.

After that incident they had abandoned all attempts to push beyond Chertanovo Station and were even planning to abandon Sebastopol and join Hansa. But the accursed Chertanovo seemed to be the frontier post marking the precise outer boundary of the human domain in the Metro. Creatures that infiltrated beyond it were a cause of serious annoyance to the Sebastopolites, but at least they could be killed, and with a properly organised defence these attacks could be repelled relatively easily and almost without human bloodshed – provided there was enough ammunition.

The monsters that crept up to the sentry posts were sometimes so large that they could only be stopped with explosive bullets and high-voltage discharge traps. But most of the time the sentries had to deal with beasts that were less frightening, although they were extremely dangerous. These beasts had been given the name of a vampire monster out of a book by Gogol, a word that sounded almost affectionate, like the name of a household pet – 'upyr'.

'There's another one! Up on top, in the third pipe!'

The searchlight, torn off its ceiling anchors, dangled jerkily on a single wire, flooding the space in front of the guard post with harsh white light, picking out the contorted figures of the mutants who were lurking in the shadows, then plunging them back into impenetrable gloom, then glaring blindingly into the eyes of the sentries. Blurred, quivering shadows heaved and surged on all sides, shrinking back and springing forward, slanting and twisting: men cast shadows like fiends, fiends cast shadows like men.

The guard post was very conveniently located at a point where the tunnels converged: shortly before the Final War, the Metro Construction concern had launched a renovation programme that was never completed. At this node the Sebastopolites had set up a genuine little fortress: two machine-gun positions, a barricade of sandbags that was a metre and a half thick, anti-tank hedgehogs and booms on the tracks, electrical traps on the close approaches and a carefully planned signalling system. But when the mutants advanced en masse as they did on that day, it seemed that with just a little more pressure, the defences would collapse.

A machine-gunner stared in amazement at his scarlet-soaked hands, breathing out bubbles of blood through his nose and muttering something in a vague, monotonous tone: the air round his jammed 'Pecheneg' was quivering with heat haze. He snorted briefly and fell quiet, nestling his face trustingly against the shoulder of the next man, a massive warrior wearing an enclosed titanium helmet. The next second a blood-curdling shriek rang out ahead of them as an upyr launched into the attack.

The warrior in the helmet rose up above the parapet, pushing aside the bloodied machine-gunner who had tumbled onto him, flung up his sub-machine-gun and fired a long burst. The repulsive, sinewy, matt-grey beast had already flung itself forward, stretching out its knotty front limbs and gliding downwards on taut-stretched folds of skin. The upyrs moved with incredible speed and anyone who hesitated had absolutely no chance – only men with the nimblest feet and fastest hands stood duty on this watch.

The whiplash of lead cut the shriek short, but the dead creature continued falling by inertia and its hundred-kilogramme carcass slammed into the barricade with a dull thud, throwing up a cloud of dust from the sandbags.

'Looks like that's it.'

Only two minutes ago the torrent of gruesome creatures gushing out of the immense sawn-off pipes suspended under the ceiling had seemed endless, but now it had dried up. The sentries started cautiously picking their way out from behind the defences.

'Get a stretcher! A doctor! Get him to the station quick!'

The husky fighter who had killed the final upyr attached a

bayonet to the barrel of his automatic weapon and started walking unhurriedly round the dead and wounded creatures littering the battlefield, giving each one a kick in its toothy jaw with the toe of his boot and thrusting the bayonet swiftly and deftly into its eye. Finally, when he'd finished, he leaned back wearily against the sandbags, raised the visor of his helmet and pressed a flask to his lips.

Reinforcements arrived from the station after it was all over. The commander of the perimeter also arrived, with his private's monkey jacket unbuttoned, breathing hard and cursing his old aches and pains.

'So where am I supposed to find him three men? Rip them out of my own flesh?'

'What are you talking about, Denis Mikhailovich?' asked one of the sentries, peering into his commander's face incredulously.

'Istomin insists we send a team of three scouts to Serpukhov. He's worried about the convoy. But where am I going to get three men for him? Especially right now...'

'So there's still no news about the convoy?' asked the large man who was quenching his thirst, without turning round.

'Not a word,' the old man confirmed. 'But it hasn't really been all that long yet. Which is more dangerous, when you really get down to it? If we strip the south naked today, in a week's time there'll be no one left to meet that convoy!'

The husky warrior swayed his head without speaking. And he didn't respond when the commander carried on muttering for a few minutes and asked the sentries at the post if anyone wanted to volunteer for the team he would have to assign to an expedition to Serpukhov Station, otherwise the station commandant – damn him to hell – would have the old man's bald head.

There were no problems with selecting volunteers; many of the sentries were already tired of being stuck here, and it was hard for them to imagine anything more dangerous than defending the southern tunnels.

Of the six men who put themselves forward for the expedition, the colonel selected those who, in his opinion, Sebastopol needed least. And this turned out to be a good choice, because none of the three men who were dispatched to Serpukhov ever returned to the station.

*

For three days now, ever since the scouts had set out in search of the convoy, the colonel had imagined whispering behind his back and sidelong glances from all directions. Even the most animated conversations broke off when he walked by. And in the tense silence that fell wherever he appeared, he seemed to hear an unspoken demand to explain and justify himself.

He was simply doing his job: maintaining the security of the defensive perimeter of Sebastopol Station. He was a tactician, not a strategist. When every soldier counted, the colonel had no right to squander men by sending them out on missions that were dubious, or even entirely pointless.

Three days ago the colonel had been absolutely convinced of that. But now, when he could feel on his own back the lash of every frightened, disapproving, doubting look, his certainty had been shaken. Travelling light, the team should have taken less than twenty-four hours to cover the distance to Hansa and back – even allowing for any possible skirmishes and waits at the borders of independent way stations. And that meant...

Giving orders for no one to be allowed in, the colonel locked himself in his little room and started muttering, going over for the hundredth time all the possible versions of what could have happened to the traders and the scouts.

At Sebastopol they weren't afraid of people – apart from the Hansa army, that is. The station's bad reputation, the stories of the price its inhabitants paid for survival, first told by a few eyewitnesses, then taken up and exaggerated over and over in the telling by shuttle traders and people who liked to listen to their tall tales, had spread right through the Metro and done their work. Quick to realise the usefulness of this kind of reputation, the station's commanders had done their best to reinforce it. Agents, travellers, members of convoys and diplomats were given an official blessing to lie in the most terrible terms possible about Sebastopol Station – and in general about everything that came after the Serpukhov stretch of the line.

Only a few individuals were capable of seeing though this smoke-screen to perceive the station's appeal and genuine significance. In recent years there had only been one or two attacks by ignorant bandits attempting to force their way in past the guard posts, and the superbly well-tuned Sebastopol war machine had decimated the isolated bands without the slightest difficulty.

Nevertheless, before setting off on its reconnaissance mission, the three-man team had been clearly instructed that if any threat of danger arose, they should not engage the enemy, but come back as quickly as possible. Of course, there was Nagornaya Station, a less malign place than Chertanovo, but still very dangerous and sinister. And Nakhimov Prospect Station, with its upper hermetic doors stuck open, which meant it couldn't be completely closed off against infiltration from the surface. The Sebastopolites didn't want to detonate the exits there – Nakhimov Prospect's 'ascent' was used by the local stalkers. No one would ever venture to make his way alone through 'the Prospect', as it was known at the station, but there had never been a case when a team of three men had been unable to repel the beasts they encountered there

A cave-in? A groundwater breach? Sabotage? Undeclared war with Hansa? Now it was the colonel, and not Istomin, who had to give answers to the wives of the scouts who had disappeared, when they came to him, gazing into his eyes with weary yearning, like abandoned dogs, seeking for some kind of promise or consolation in those eyes. He had to explain everything to the garrison soldiers, who never asked unnecessary questions, while they still believed in him. He had to reassure all the alarmed people who gathered in the evening, after work, by the station clock that had noted the precise time of the convoy's departure.

Istomin said that in the last few days people kept asking him again and again why the lights had been dimmed at the station and demanding that the lamps be turned back up as bright as before. But in fact no one had even thought of reducing the voltage, and the lamps were burning at full power. The gathering darkness was not in the station, but in people's hearts, and not even the very brightest mercury lamps could dispel it.

Telephone communications with Serpukhov still hadn't been restored, and during the week that had passed since the convoy left, the colonel, like many other Sebastopolites, had lost a very important feeling, one that was rare for inhabitants of the Metro – the sense of close companionship with other people.

As long as the lines of communication functioned, as long as convoys travelled to and fro regularly and the journey to Hansa took less than a day, everyone living at Sebastopol Station had been free to leave or to stay, everyone knew that only five stops away from their station lay the beginning of the genuine Metro, civilisation ... The human race.

It was probably the way polar explorers used to feel, abandoned in the Arctic after voluntarily condemning themselves to long months of battling the cold and loneliness for the sake of scientific research or high pay. The mainland was thousands of kilometres away, but somehow it was still close, as long as the radio worked and every month the rumbling of a plane's engines could be heard overhead and crates of canned meat came floating down on parachutes.

But now the ice floe on which their station stood had broken away, and with every hour that passed it was being swept further and further out into an icy blizzard in a black ocean, into the void of the unknown.

The waiting dragged on, and the colonel's vague concern for the fate of the scouts sent to Serpukhov was gradually transformed into the sombre certainty that he would never see those men again. He simply couldn't afford to take three more soldiers off the defensive perimeter and fling them after the others to face the same unknown danger and, most likely, certain death. But the idea of closing the hermetic doors, cutting off the southern tunnels and assembling a large strike force still seemed premature to him. If only someone else would make the decision now ... Any decision was foredoomed to prove wrong.

The perimeter commander sighed, opened the door slightly, looked around furtively and called over a sentry.

'How about letting me have a cigarette? But this is the last one, don't give me any more, not even if I beg you. And don't tell anyone, all right?'

Nadya, a thickset, talkative woman in a fluffy dress with holes in it and a dirty apron, brought a hot casserole of meat and vegetables, and the sentries livened up a bit. Potatoes, cucumbers and tomatoes were regarded as very great delicacies here: apart from Sebastopol Station, the only places where you could feast on vegetables were one or two of the finest restaurants of the Circle or the Polis. It wasn't just a matter of the complicated hydroponic equipment required to grow the seeds that had been saved, there was also the fact that not many stations in the Metro could afford to spend kilowatts of energy on varying their soldiers' diet.

Even the top command's tables were only graced with vegetables on holidays, usually the children were the only ones who were pampered like that. It had cost Istomin a serious quarrel with the chefs to get them to add boiled potatoes and a tomato to each of the portions of pork that were due on uneven dates – in order to keep up the soldiers' morale.

The trick worked: the moment that Nadya, with typical female awkwardness, dropped the sub-machine-gun off her shoulder in order to lift the lid of the casserole, the sentries' wrinkled faces started relaxing and smoothing out. No one wanted to spoil a supper like this with sour, tedious talk about the convoy that had disappeared and the overdue reconnaissance team.

'I don't know why, but I've been thinking about Komsomol Station all day today,' said a grey-haired old man wearing a quilted jacket with Moscow Metro shoulder badges, as he squished potatoes in his aluminium bowl. 'If I could just get there and take a look . . . The mosaics they have there! To my mind, it's the most beautiful station in Moscow.'

'Ah, drop it, Homer, you probably used to live there, and you still love it to this day,' retorted a fat, unshaven man in a cap with earflaps. 'What about the stained glass at Novoslobodskaya? And those light, airy columns at Mayakovsky Station, with the frescoes on the ceiling?'

'I like Revolution Square best,' a sniper confessed shyly – he was a quiet, serious man, getting on in years. 'I know it's all stupid nonsense, but those stern-looking sailors and airmen, those border guards with their dogs. I've adored that station ever since I was a kid.'

'What's so stupid about it? There are some very nice-looking men depicted in bronze there,' Nadya said, backing him up in as she scraped the remains off the bottom of the casserole. 'Hey, Brigadier, look sharp, or you'll be left with no supper!'

The tall, broad-shouldered warrior, who had been sitting apart from the others, strolled over unhurriedly to the campfire, took his serving and went back to his spot – closer to the tunnel, as far away as possible from the men.

'Does he ever show up at the station?' the fat man asked in a whisper, nodding in the direction of the massively broad back, half-hidden in the semi-darkness.

'He hasn't moved from this place for more than a week now,' the sniper replied in an equally quiet voice. 'Spends the night in a sleeping bag. I don't know how his nerves can stand it. Or maybe he just enjoys the whole thing. Three days ago, when the upyrs almost did for Rinat, he went round afterwards and finished them off. By hand. Took about fifteen minutes doing it. Came back with his boots covered in blood . . . Delighted with himself.'

'He's a machine, not a man,' a lanky machine-gunner put in. 'I'm afraid even to sleep beside him. Have you seen what a mess his face is? I don't even want to look in his eyes.'

'But I only feel calm when I'm with him,' the old man called Homer said with shrug. 'What are you running him down for? He's a good man, just got maimed, that's all. It's only the stations that need to be beautiful. And that Novoslobodskaya of yours, by the way, is just plain tawdry, bad taste. There's no way you can look at all that coloured glass unless you're drunk. Stained-glass rubbish!'

'And collective farm mosaics, covering half the ceiling, aren't in bad taste then?'

'Where did you find any pictures like that at Komsomol Station?'

'Why, all that damn Soviet art is about collective farm life or heroic airmen!' said the fat man, starting to get heated.

'Seryozha, you lay off the airmen!' the sniper warned him.

'Komsomol Station's garbage, and Novoslobodskaya's shit,' they heard a dull, low voice say.

The fat man was so surprised, he choked on the words that were already on the tip of his tongue and gaped at the brigadier. The others immediately fell silent too, waiting to see what would come next: the brigadier almost never joined in their conversations, he even answered direct questions curtly or didn't bother to answer at all.

He was still sitting with his back to them, with his eyes fixed on the gaping mouth of the tunnel.

'The vaults at Komsomol are too high, and the columns are too thin, the entire platform can be raked with fire from the tracks, it's wide open, and closing off the pedestrian passages is too tricky. And at Novoslobodskaya the walls are a mass of cracks, no matter how hard they try to plaster over them. One grenade would be enough to bring the whole station down. And there haven't been any stained-glass panels there for ages. They're all broken. That stuff's too fragile.'

No one dared to object. The brigadier paused for a moment and blurted out:

'I'm going to the station. And I'm taking Homer with me. The watch will change in an hour. Arthur's in charge here.'

The sniper jumped to his feet and nodded, even though the brigadier couldn't see it. The old man also got up and started bustling about, collecting his scattered bits and pieces into his knapsack, without even finishing his potatoes. The warrior walked up to the campfire, fully kitted out for an expedition, with his eternal helmet and a bulky knapsack behind his shoulders.

'Good luck.'

Watching the two figures as they receded – the brigadier's mighty frame and Homer's skinny one – the sniper rubbed his hands together, as if he felt cold, and cringed.

'It's getting a bit chilly. Throw on a bit of coal, will you?'

The brigadier didn't utter a single word all the way, apart from asking if it was true that Homer used to be an engine driver's mate, and before that a simple track-walker. The old man gave him a suspicious glance, but he didn't try to deny it, even though he had always told everyone at Sebastopol that he had risen to the rank of engine driver, and preferred not to dwell on the fact that he used to be a track-walker, believing it wasn't really worth mentioning.

The brigadier walked into the station commandant's office without knocking, saluting the sentries stiffly as they moved aside. Istomin and the colonel – both looking tired, dishevelled, and bewildered – got up from the desk in surprise when he entered. Homer halted timidly in the door, shifting from one foot to the other.

The brigadier pulled off his helmet and set it down on Istomin's papers, then ran one hand over the clean-shaven back of his head. The light of the lamp revealed how terribly his face was mutilated: the left cheek was furrowed and twisted into a huge scar, as if it had been burned, the eye had been reduced to a narrow slit and a thick, purple weal squirmed its way down from his ear to the corner of his mouth. Homer thought he had grown used to this face, but looking at it now he felt the same chilly, repulsive prickling sensation as the first time.

'I'll go to the Circle,' the brigadier blurted out, dispensing with any kind of greeting.

A heavy silence descended on the room. Homer had heard the brigadier was on special terms with the command of the station because he was so irreplaceable in combat. But only now did the realisation dawn that, unlike all the other Sebastopolites, this man didn't seem to defer to the commanders at all.

And at this moment he didn't seem to be waiting for the approval of these two elderly, jaded men, but simply giving them an order that they were obliged to carry out, which made Homer wonder yet again just who this man was.

The perimeter commander exchanged glances with his superior and frowned, about to object, but instead merely gestured helplessly.

'You decide for yourself, Hunter, it's pointless trying to argue with you.'

CHAPTER 2

The Return

The old man hovering by the door pricked up his ears: he hadn't heard that name before at Sebastopol Station. Not even a name, but a nickname, like he had – he wasn't really called Homer, of course, he was just common or garden Nikolai Ivanovich, who had been named after the Greek teller of myths here at the station, for his irrepressible love of all sorts of stories and rumours.

'Your new brigadier,' the colonel had said to the watchmen, who were examining with morose curiosity this broad-shouldered new-comer clad in Kevlar and a heavy helmet. Ignoring basic courtesy, he turned away indifferently: the tunnel and the fortifications seemed to interest him far more than the men entrusted to his command. He shook the hands of his new subordinates when they came up to make his acquaintance, but he didn't introduce himself, nodding without speaking, committing each new nickname to memory, and puffing out bluish, acrid cigarette smoke into their faces to demarcate the limits of closeness. In the shadow of the raised visor his narrow gun-slit eye, framed by scars, had a ghastly, lack-lustre gleam to it. None of the watchmen had dared to insist on knowing his name, either then or later, and so for two months now they had been calling him simply 'Brigadier'. They decided the station must have shelled out for one of those expensive mercenaries who could manage perfectly well without a past or a name.

Hunter. Homer silently worked the strange un-Russian word around on his tongue. Better suited for a Central Asian Shepherd Dog than a man. He smiled gently to himself: well, well, so he still remembered that there used to be dogs like that. Where did all this stuff in his head come from? A fighting breed with a short docked tail and ears clipped right in close to the head. Nothing superfluous.

And the name, if he kept repeating it to himself for a while, started sounding vaguely familiar. Where could he have heard it before? Borne along on an endless stream of gossip and tall stories, it had snagged his attention somehow and then settled on the very bottom of his memory. And now it was overlaid with a thick layer of silt: names, facts, rumours, numbers – all that useless information about other people's lives that Homer listened to with such avid curiosity and tried so zealously to remember.

Hunter . . . maybe some jailbird with a reward from Hansa on his head? The old man tossed the idea like a stone into the deep millpond of his amnesia and listened. No, nothing. A stalker? He didn't seem like one. A warlord? More like it. And a legendary one, apparently . . .

Homer cast another stealthy glance at the brigadier's face, so impassive that it seemed almost paralysed. That dog's name suited him remarkably well.

'I need a team of three men. I'll take Homer, he knows the tunnels around here,' the brigadier went on, without even turning towards the old man or asking his permission. 'You can give me another man you think will suit. A runner, a courier. I'll set out today.'

Istomin jerked his head hastily in approval before he gathered his wits and raised his eyes enquiringly to look at the colonel. The colonel frowned and muttered gruffly that he had no objections either, although for days he had been battling desperately with the station commandant for every free soldier. It seemed like no one intended to consult Homer, but he didn't even think of arguing: despite his age, the old man had never refused this kind of assignment. And he had his reasons for that.

The brigadier snatched his immensely heavy helmet up off the desk and headed towards the exit. Lingering in the doorway for a moment, he said brusquely to Homer:

'Say goodbye to your family. Pack for a long journey. Don't bring any bullets, I'll give you those . . .' And he disappeared through the opening.

The old man set off after him, hoping to hear at least some basic explanation about what he should expect on this expedition. But when he emerged onto the platform, Hunter was already way ahead,

20

ten of his massive strides away, and Homer didn't even try to catch up with him, but just shook his head and watched him go.

Contrary to his usual habit, the brigadier had left his head uncovered: perhaps, lost in thoughts of other things, he had forgotten, or perhaps he was feeling a need for air right now. He passed a gaggle of young women – pig herders idling away their lunch break – and there was a whisper of disgust behind his back: 'Ooh girls, my God, what a repulsive freak!'

'Where the hell did you dig him up from?' asked Istomin, slumping back limply in his chair in relief and reaching out his plump hand to a pile of cut cigarette papers.

People said the leaves that were smoked with such relish at the station were gathered by the stalkers at some spot on the surface almost as far away as Bitsevsky Park. Once, for a joke, the colonel had held a radiation dosimeter to a packet of 'tobacco', and it had started chattering away menacingly. The old man had given up smoking on the spot, and the cough that had been tormenting him at night, terrifying him with thoughts of lung cancer, had gradually started to ease. But Istomin had refused to believe the story of the radioactive leaves, reminding Denis Mikhailovich, with good reason, that in the Metro absolutely anything you picked up was more or less 'hot'.

'We're old acquaintances,' the colonel replied reluctantly; then he paused and threw in: 'He didn't used to be like this. Something happened to him.'

'That's for sure, if his face is anything to go by, something definitely happened to him,' the commandant snorted, and immediately glanced towards the door, as if Hunter could have been loitering there and overheard him by chance.

The commander of the defensive perimeter had no right to grumble about the brigadier's unexpected return from out of the cold mists of the past. From the moment he showed up at the station, he had effectively become the backbone of the perimeter's defence. But even now Denis Mikhailovich couldn't entirely believe that he *had* come back.

The news of Hunter's strange and terrible death had flashed round the Metro the previous year, like an echo racing through the tunnels. And when Hunter turned up on the doorstep of the colonel's little room two months ago, the colonel had hastily crossed himself before opening the door. The suspicious ease with which the resurrected man had passed through the guard posts – as if he had walked straight through the soldiers there – made the colonel doubt that this miracle was entirely benign.

Through the steamed-up spyhole of the door he saw what seemed to be a familiar profile: a bull neck, a cranium scraped so smooth that it shone, a slightly flattened nose. But for some reason the nocturnal visitor had frozen in semi-profile, with his head lowered, and he didn't make any attempt to lighten the heavy silence. Casting a reproachful glance at the large, open bottle of home-brew beer standing on the table, the colonel heaved a deep sigh and pulled back the bolt. The honour code required him to help his own, and it drew no distinctions between the living and the dead.

When the door swung open Hunter looked up from the floor, making it clear why he had been hiding the other half of his face. He was afraid the other man simply wouldn't recognise him. Even a hardboiled veteran like the old colonel, for whom the command of the Sebastopol garrison was like honorary retirement on a pension, compared with the turbulent years that came before it, winced when he saw that face, as if he had burned his fingers, and then started laughing guiltily – he couldn't help himself.

His visitor didn't even smile in reply. Over the months the terrible scars that mutilated his face had healed over slightly, but even so almost nothing about him reminded the colonel of the old Hunter. He flatly refused to explain his miraculous escape or why he had been missing for so long, and simply didn't answer any of the colonel's questions, as if he hadn't even heard them. And worst of all, Hunter presented Denis Mikhailovich with an old debt for repayment and made him promise not to tell anyone that he had shown up. The colonel had been obliged to leave Hunter in peace and stifle his own commonsense reaction, which cried out for him to inform his commander immediately.

The old man had, however, made some cautious enquiries. His visitor was not implicated in anything shady and no one was look-ing for him any more after his funeral rites had been read so long ago. His body, admittedly, had never been found, but if Hunter had survived, someone would certainly have heard from him, the colonel was confidently informed. Definitely, he agreed.

On the other hand, as often happens when people disappear without a trace, Hunter, or rather, his simultaneously blurred and embellished image, had surfaced in at least a dozen myths and legends that had the ring of half-truth about them. Apparently this role suited him just fine, and he was in no hurry at all to disabuse the comrades who had buried him so prematurely.

Bearing in mind his unpaid debts and drawing the appropriate conclusions, Denis Mikhailovich had kept his mouth shut and even started playing along: he avoided calling Hunter by name in the presence of outsiders and let Istomin in on the secret, but without going into detail. It was basically all the same to Istomin: the brigadier earned his issue of rations in spades, spending all his time, day and night, on the front line in the southern tunnels. He was hardly ever spotted at the station where he put in an appearance once a week, on his bath day. And even if he had only jumped into this hellhole so that he could hide there from unknown pursuers, that didn't bother Istomin, who had never been squeamish about employing the services of legionaries with dark pasts. Just as long as he was a fighter – and there were no problems on that score.

The soldiers of the watch had grumbled among themselves about their new commander, but they stopped after the first engagement. Once they saw the cold, methodical, inhuman euphoria with which he annihilated everything they were supposed to annihilate, they all understood his true value. No one tried to make friends with the unsociable brigadier any longer, but they obeyed him implicitly, so he never needed to raise his dull, cracked voice. There was something hypnotic about that voice, even the station commandant started nodding dutifully every time Hunter spoke to him, without even waiting for him to finish, for no special reason, it was simply an automatic response.

For the first time in recent days it felt easier to breathe in Istomin's office, as if a silent thunderstorm had swept through it, relieving the tension in the air and bringing welcome release. There was nothing left to argue about. There was no finer warrior than Hunter – if he disappeared in the tunnels, the Sebastopolites would be left with only one choice.

'Shall I give instructions to prepare for the operation?' asked the colonel, bringing up the subject first, because he knew the station commandant would want to talk about it anyway.

'Three days ought to be enough for you,' said Istomin, clicking his cigarette lighter and screwing up his eyes. 'We won't be able to wait for them any longer than that. How many men will we need, what do you think?'

'We've got one assault brigade awaiting orders, I can handle the other men, there's another twenty or so. If by the day after tomorrow we haven't heard anything about them—' the colonel jerked his head in the direction of the door '—declare a general mobilisation. We'll break out.'

Istomin raised his eyebrows, but instead of objecting, he took a deep drag on his cigarette, which crackled faintly. Denis Mikhailovich raked together several well-scribbled sheets of paper that were lying around on the desk, leaned down over them shortsightedly and started sketching mysterious diagrams, writing surnames and nicknames inside little circles.

Break out? The station commandant looked through the drifting tobacco smoke, over the back of the colonel's head, at the large schematic map of the Metro hanging behind the old man's back. Yellowed and greasy, covered with markings in ink – arrows for forced marches, rings for ambushes, little stars for guard posts and exclamation marks for forbidden zones – the map was a chronicle of the last decade. Ten years, during which not a single day had passed peacefully.

Below Sebastopol the marks broke off immediately beyond Southern Station: Istomin couldn't remember anyone ever coming back from there. The line crept on downwards like a long, branching root, immaculately chaste all the way. The Serpukhov line had proved too tough a nut for the Sebastopolites to crack; even if the entire toothless, radiation-sick human population combined its most desperate efforts, it probably wouldn't be enough down there.

And now a white, swirling fog of uncertainty had obscured the stub end of their line that reached obstinately northwards, to Hansa, to the human race. Tomorrow none of the men that the colonel ordered to prepare for battle would refuse to fight. The war for the extinction or survival of humankind, begun more than two decades ago, had never stopped for a moment at Sebastopol. When you live by side with death for many years, the fear of dying gives way to indifference, fatalism, superstitions, protective amulets and animal instincts. But who knew what was waiting for them up ahead, between the Nakhimov Prospect and Serpukhov stations? Who knew if it was even possible to break through this mysterious barrier – and if there was anywhere to break through to?

He recalled his latest trip to Serpukhov Station: market stalls, tramps' makeshift beds and dilapidated screens behind which the slightly better-off inhabitants slept and made love to each other. They didn't produce any food of their own, there were no hothouse chambers for growing plants, no pens for cattle. The nimble-footed, light-fingered Serpukhovites fed themselves from profiteering, reselling old surplus goods picked up for a song from convoy merchants who were running behind schedule, and by providing citizens of the Circle Line with services for which those citizens would have faced trial at home. Not a station, but a fungus, a parasitic growth on the mighty trunk of Hansa.

The alliance of rich trading stations on the Circle Line, aptly dubbed 'Hansa' in memory of its Teutonic prototype, was an enduring bulwark of civilisation in a Metro that was sinking into a swamp of barbarity and poverty. Hansa was a regular army, electric lighting even at the poorest way station and a guaranteed crust of bread for everyone whose passport contained the coveted stamp of citizenship. On the black market passports like that cost an absolute fortune, but if Hanseatic border guards discovered anyone with a counterfeit, the price he paid was his head.

Of course, Hansa owed its wealth and power to its location: the Circle Line ringed the central tangle of radial lines, with its transfer stations allowing access to all of them and harnessing them together. Shuttle traders carrying tea from the Economic Achievements Station and trolleys delivering ammunition from the arms factories at Bauman Station preferred to offload their goods at the closest Hansa post and go back home. Better to let the goods go cheap than set off right round the Metro in pursuit of profit, on a journey that could be cut short at any moment.

Hansa had annexed some of the adjacent radial line stations, but most of them had been left to themselves and became transformed, with Hansa's connivance, into grey areas, where people conducted the kind of business in which the disdainful bosses of Hansa preferred not to be implicated.

Naturally, the radial transfer stations were flooded with Hansa's spies and they had been bought, lock, stock and barrel, by its merchants, but they remained nominally independent. Serpukhov Station was one of these. A train had halted forever in one of the stretches of line leading from it, after failing to reach the next station, Tula. Rendered habitable by the Protestant sectarian believers who now occupied it, the train was indicated on Istomin's map with a laconic Latin cross: it had become an isolated homestead, lost in a black wasteland. If not for the missionaries roaming round the neighbouring stations, with their insatiable greed for lost souls, Istomin wouldn't have had any complaints about the sectarians. But in any case these sheepdogs of God didn't roam as far as Sebastopol, and they didn't cause any particular hindrance to passing travellers, except perhaps by delaying them slightly with their intense conversations about salvation. And apart from that, the other tunnel from Tula to Serpukhov was entirely clear, so the local convoys used that one.

Istomin ran his glance down the line again. Tula Station? A settlement gradually running to seed, picking up the crumbs dropped by Sebastopolite convoys marching through and the sly traders from Serpukhov. The people lived on whatever they could turn their hand to: some mended various sorts of mechanical junk, some went to the Hansa border to look for work, squatting on their haunches for days at a time, waiting for the next foreman with the high-handed manners of a slave driver. 'They live poorly too, but they don't have that slippery, villainous Serpukhov look in their eyes,' thought Istomin. 'And there's a lot more order there. It's probably the danger that binds them together.'

The next station, Nagatino, was marked on his map with a short stroke of the pen – empty. A half-truth: no one loitered there for long, but sometimes there was a motley swarm of rabble at the station, leading a subhuman, twilight existence. Couples who had fled from prying eyes twined their limbs together in the pitch darkness. Sometimes the glow of a feeble little campfire sprang up among the columns, with the shadows of tunnel bandits and murderers swarming around it. But only the ignorant or the ab-solutely desperate stayed here overnight – by no means all the station's visitors were human. If you stared hard into the trembling, whispering gloom that filled Nagatino, you could sometimes glimpse silhouettes straight out of a nightmare. And every now and then the homeless vagabonds scattered, if only briefly, when a bloodcurdling howl rang through the stale air as some poor soul was dragged off into a lair to be devoured at leisure.

The tramps didn't dare set foot beyond Nagatino, and from there all the way to the defensive boundaries of Sebastopol, it was 'no-man's-land'. A strictly notional name – of course, the area had its own masters, who guarded its boundaries, and even the Sebastopolite reconnaissance teams preferred not to come up against them.

But now something new had appeared in the tunnels. Something unprecedented, swallowing up everyone who tried to follow a route that supposedly had been thoroughly explored long ago. And who knew if Istomin's station, even if it called on every inhabitant who was fit to bear arms, would be able to marshal a force strong enough to overcome it. Istomin got up laboriously off his chair, shuffled over to the map and marked with an indelible pencil the stretch of line running from the point labelled 'Serpukhov' to the point labelled 'Nakhimov Prospect'. He drew a thick question mark beside it. He meant to put it beside the Prospect, but it ended up right beside Sebastopol.

At first glance Sebastopol Station appeared deserted. On the platform there was no sign of the familiar army tents in which people usually lived at other stations. There were only forms vaguely perceived by the light of a few dim bulbs, the anthill profiles of machine-gun emplacements, built out of sandbags, but the firing positions were empty, and dust lay thick on the slim square columns. Everything was arranged to make sure that if an outsider found his way in here, he would be certain to think the station had been abandoned long ago.

However, if the uninvited guest got the idea of lingering here, even for a short while, he risked staying forever. The machine-gun squads and snipers on twenty-four-hour duty in adjacent Kakhovka Station occupied their positions in those emplacements in a matter of seconds and the weak light was drowned in the pitiless glare of mercury lamps on the ceiling, searing the retinal nerves of men and monsters accustomed to the darkness of the tunnels.

The platform was the Sebastopolites' final, most comprehensively planned line of defence. Their homes were located in the belly of this stage-set, in the technical area under the platform. Below the granite slabs of the floor, hidden away from the prying eyes of strangers, was another storey, with a floor area as large as the main hall, but divided up into numerous compartments. Well-lit, dry, warm rooms, smoothly humming machines for purifying air and water, hydroponic hothouses... When they retreated down here, even further underground, the station's inhabitants were enfolded in a sense of security and comfort.

Homer knew the decisive battle he would face was not in the northern tunnels, but at home. He made his way along the narrow corridor, past the half-open doors of other people's apartments, dragging his feet slower and slower as he approached his own door. He needed to think through his tactics one more time and rehearse his lines: he was running out of time.

'What can I do about it? It's an order. You know what the situation's like. They didn't even bother to ask me. Stop acting like a little child! That's just plain ridiculous! Of course I didn't ask to be taken! I can't do that. What are you saying? Of course I can't. Refuse? That's desertion!' he mumbled to himself, switching between determined outrage and a wheedling, cajoling, affectionate tone.

When he reached the doorway of his room, he started mumbling it all over again. No, there was no way tears could be avoided, but he wasn't going to back down. The old man pulled his head into his shoulders, readying himself for battle, and turned down the door handle.

Nine and a half square metres of floor space – a great luxury that he had spent five years waiting in line for, shifting about from one dormitory to another. Two square metres were taken up by a two-tier army bunkbed and one by a dining table, covered with an elegant tablecloth. Another three were occupied by a huge heap of newspapers, reaching right up to the ceiling. If he had been a solitary bachelor, then one fine day this mountain would certainly have collapsed, burying him underneath it. But fifteen years earlier he had met a woman who was not only prepared to tolerate this huge pile of dusty junk in her tiny home, but even willing to keep it neat and tidy, so that it wouldn't transform her domestic nest into a paper Pompeii.

She was prepared to tolerate very many things. The interminable newspaper cuttings with alarming headlines like 'Arms Race Heats Up', 'Americans Test New Anti-Rocket Defence', 'Our Nuclear

Shield is Growing Stronger', 'Provocative Acts Continue' and 'Our Patience is Exhausted', which covered the walls of the little room, like wallpaper, from top to bottom. His all-night sessions, hunched over a heap of school exercise books with a well-chewed ballpoint pen in his hand and the electric light burning – with a heap of paper like that in their home, candles were completely out of the question. His humorous, clownish nickname, which he bore with pride and others spoke with a condescending smile.

Very many things, but not everything. Not his juvenile urge to plunge into the epicentre of the hurricane every time, in order to see what things were really like in there – and this at the age of almost sixty! And not the frivolity with which he accepted any assignment from his superiors, forgetting that he had barely escaped with his life and managed to scramble back home after one of his recent expeditions.

Not the thought that she might lose him and be left all alone again. After seeing Homer off to the watch – his turn to stand duty came round once a week – she never stayed at home. To escape from her distressing thoughts, she called on neighbours, or went to work even when it wasn't her shift. The male indifference to death seemed stupid, egotistic and criminal to her.

It was pure chance that he found her at home: she had dropped in to change after work, and now she froze just as she was, with her arms threaded into the sleeves of her darned woollen sweater. Her dark hair, visibly streaked with grey – although she wasn't even fifty yet – was tangled, her brown eyes were bright with fear.

'Kolya, has something happened? Aren't you on duty until late?'

Homer suddenly lost all desire to tell her about the decision that had been taken. He hesitated: maybe if he just calmed her down for the time being, he could slip the news into the talk over dinner?

'Only don't you even think of lying,' she warned him, catching his wandering gaze.

'You know, Lena ... The thing is ...' he began.

'Has someone ... ?' – she asked the most important question immediately, about the most terrible thing of all, not wishing even to pronounce the word 'died', as if she believed her dark thoughts might materialise as reality.

'No! No,' said Homer with a shake of his head. 'They just took me off duty. They're sending me to Serpukhov,' he added in a matter-of-fact voice.

'But isn't it...?' Elena said and faltered. 'Isn't that... Have they come back then? That's where...'

'Oh, come on, it's all a load of nonsense. There's nothing there,' he said hastily.

Elena turned away, walked over to the table, shifted the salt-cellar from one spot to another and straightened out a fold in the tablecloth.

'I had a dream,' she said and coughed to clear the hoarseness out of her voice.

'You have them all the time.'

'A bad dream,' she went on stubbornly and suddenly broke into pitiful sobs.

'Oh come on, now. What can I do? It's an order,' he mumbled, stroking her fingers and floundering as he realised his entire well-prepared speech wasn't worth a damn.

'Let that one-eyed bastard go himself,' she yelled furiously through her tears, jerking her hand away. 'Let that other fiend go, in his little beret! All they ever do is give orders. What does he care? All his life he's slept with a machine-gun beside him instead of a woman. What does he know?'

Once you've reduced a woman to tears, you can only demean yourself by turning round and trying to console her. Homer felt ashamed, and genuinely sorry for Elena, but it would have been all too easy now to break down, promise to refuse the assignment, reassure her and dry her tears, only to regret later missing his chance – this chance that had fallen to him, which could be the last one in a life that was already unusually long by today's standards.

So he said nothing.

It was already time to go, gather the officers together and brief them, but the colonel carried on sitting in Istomin's office, taking no notice of the cigarette smoke that usually irritated and tempted him so badly.

While the station commandant whispered something thoughtfully, running one finger over his battle-scarred map of the Metro, Denis Mikhailovich kept trying to understand why Hunter wanted to do this. There could be only one thing behind his mysterious appearance at Sebastopol, his desire to settle here and even the cautious way in which the brigadier almost always showed up at the station wearing his helmet to conceal his face: Istomin must be right, Hunter was on the run from someone after all. In order to earn extra points, he had made the southern guard post his base: by doing the work of an entire brigade, he was gradually making himself indispensable. At this stage, no matter who demanded that they hand him over, no matter what reward they offered for his head, neither Istomin nor the colonel would even think of letting them have him.

He had chosen the perfect place to hide. There were no outsiders at Sebastopol and, unlike the garrulous shuttle traders from other stations, the local convoy merchants weren't loose-tongued, they never gossiped when they got out into the Greater Metro. In this little Sparta, clinging to its patch of earth at the very end of the world, the qualities valued most highly were reliability and ferocity in battle. And people here knew how to keep secrets.

But then why would Hunter abandon everything, volunteer for this expedition and set out for Hansa, risking being recognised? Even Istomin wouldn't have had the heart to assign him a sortie like this. Somehow the colonel didn't believe the brigadier was really alarmed about the fate of the missing scouts. And he wasn't fighting for Sebastopol out of love for the station, but for reasons of his own, known only to him.

Maybe he was on a mission? That would explain a lot: his sudden arrival, his secrecy, the obstinacy with which he spent the nights in a sleeping bag in the tunnels, his decision to set out for Serpukhov Station immediately. But then why had he asked the colonel not to let anyone else know? Who could have sent him, if not *them*?

Who else?

The colonel forced himself to ignore the desire to take a drag from Istomin's cigarette. No, it was impossible. Hunter – one of the pillars of *The Order*? The man to whom tens, maybe hundreds of them owed their lives, including Denis Mikhailovich himself?

'*That* man couldn't...' he objected cautiously to himself. 'But was the Hunter who returned from the abyss still *that* man?' And if he was acting on instructions from someone... Could he have received some kind of signal now? Did this mean that the disappearance of the armaments convoys and the three scouts was no coincidence, but part of a carefully planned operation? But then what part was the brigadier playing in it?

The colonel shook his head briskly to and fro, as if he were trying to toss off the leeches of doubt that had fastened onto it and were rapidly swelling up with blood. How could he think like this about a man who had saved his life? Especially since, so far, Hunter had served the station impeccably and given no reason at all to doubt him. And Denis Mikhailovich, refusing to label the man a 'spy' or a 'saboteur' even in his thoughts, took a decision.

'Let's have a cup of tea, and then I'll go to and talk to the men,' he declared with exaggerated cheerfulness, cracking his knuckles. Istomin tore himself away from the map and gave a weary smile. He was just reaching out to his ancient disc-dial phone to summon his orderly when the phone started ringing. The two men glanced sharply at each other, startled – it was a week since they had heard that sound: if the duty orderly wanted to report something, he always knocked at the door, and no one else at the station could call the commandant directly.

'Istomin here,' he said warily.

'Vladimir Ivanovich, I've got Tula Station on the line,' the operator jabbered. 'Only it's very hard to hear anything. I think it's our men but the connection . . .'

'Just put it through, will you?' the commandant roared, slamming his fist down hard on the desk and setting the telephone jangling pitifully.

The startled operator fell silent and Istomin heard crackling and rustling sounds in the earpiece, and a distant voice, distorted beyond recognition.

Elena turned away to the wall, hiding her tears. What more could she do to hold him back? Why was he so glad to grab the first opportunity to get away from the station, using that moth-eaten old excuse about orders from the command and punishment for desertion? What had she failed to give him, what else should she have done in all these fifteen years, in order to tame him? But here he was, longing to get back into the tunnels again, as if he hoped to find something out there, apart from darkness, emptiness and death. What was it he was looking for?

Homer could hear her reproaches in his own head as clearly as if she were speaking out loud. He felt mean and shabby, but it was too late to retreat now. He almost opened his mouth to apologise, to speak warm, tender words, but he choked, realising that every word would only throw more fuel on the flames.

And above Elena's head Moscow cried – hanging on the wall, lovingly set in a little frame, was a colour photograph of Tver Street in a transparent shower of summer rain, cut out of an old glossy calendar. At one time, a long time ago, during his old wanderings round the Metro, Homer had owned nothing but his clothes and that photo. Other men's pockets held crumpled pages with photos of naked beauties, torn out of men's magazines, but for Homer they couldn't take the place of a real, live woman, even for a few brief, shameful minutes. That photo reminded him of something that was infinitely important, inexpressibly beautiful . . . And lost forever.

With an awkward whisper – 'I'm sorry' – he edged out into the corridor, carefully closed the door behind him and squatted down, absolutely drained. The neighbours' door was ajar, and two puny, pasty-faced little children, a boy and a girl, were playing in the opening. Catching sight of the old man, they froze: the crudely sewn bear stuffed with rags that they had just been arguing over flopped to the floor, forgotten.

'Uncle Kolya! Tell us a story! You promised you'd tell us one when you got back!' they exclaimed, dashing at Homer.

'Which one do you want?' he asked, unable to refuse.

'About the mootants with no heads!' the little boy howled gleefully.

'No! I don't want a story about mootants!' the little girl exclaimed sulkily. 'They're frightening, I'm afraid!'

'So which story do you want, Taniusha?' the old man sighed.

'In that case, the one about the fascists! And the partisans!' the little boy interrupted.

'No . . . I like the one about the Emerald City . . .' Tanya said with a gap-toothed grin.

'But I told you that one only yesterday. Maybe the one about how Hansa fought the Reds?'

'The Emerald City, the Emerald City!' they both clamoured.

'Oh, all right,' the old man agreed. 'Somewhere far, far away on the Sokolniki Line, out beyond seven empty stations, out beyond three ruined Metro bridges, a thousand, thousand sleepers away from here, lies a magical underground city. This city is enchanted and ordinary people can't get into it. Magicians live there, and only they can come out through the gates of the city and go back in again. And up on the surface of the ground is a huge, mighty castle with towers, where these wise magicians used to live. This castle is called...'

'The Versity!' the little boy called out, giving his sister a triumphant look.

'The University,' Homer confirmed. 'When the Great War happened and the nuclear missiles started raining down, the magicians withdrew into their city and put a spell on the entrance, so the wicked people who started the war wouldn't get in. And they live...' He gagged and stopped.

Elena was standing there, leaning against the doorpost and listening to him: Homer hadn't noticed her coming out into the corridor.

'I'll pack your knapsack,' she said in a hoarse voice.

The old man walked up to Elena and took her by the hand. She put her arms round him awkwardly, feeling shy in front of the neighbours' children, and asked:

'Will you come back soon? Will you be all right?'

And Homer, astounded for the thousandth time in his long life by the invincible female love of promises, regardless of whether it was possible to keep them or not, said: 'Everything will be just fine.'

'You're so old already, but you kiss like you were a young couple,' said the little girl, making a spiteful face.

'And our dad said it isn't true, there isn't any Emerald City,' the little boy said in a surly voice, just to round things off.

'Maybe there isn't,' Homer said with a shrug. 'It's just a story. But how can we get by here without stories?'

It was appallingly difficult to hear anything. The voice forcing its way through the crackling and rustling sounded vaguely familiar to Istomin – a bit like one of the team of three scouts sent to Serpukhov.

'At Tula Station... We can't... Tula...' said the voice, straining to communicate something important.

'I understand that you're at Tula!' Istomin shouted into the receiver. 'What happened? Why don't you come back?'

'Tula Station! Here ... Don't ... It's very important ... don't ..' But the end of the phrase was swallowed up by the damned interference.

'Don't what? Say again, don't what?'

'You mustn't storm it! Whatever you do, don't storm it,' the receiver suddenly said quite clearly and distinctly.

'Why? What the devil is going on there? What's happening?' the commandant yelled impatiently.

But he couldn't hear the voice any more; it was drowned in a massive surge of noise, and then the receiver went dead. But Istomin refused to believe it and he wouldn't hang up.

'What's happening?'

CHAPTER 3

After Life

Homer thought he would never forget the look he got from the sentry who said goodbye to them at the most northerly guard post. It was the same look people give the body of a fallen hero as the honour guard fires that final volley in salute: a mournful, melancholy kind of look. Saying goodbye forever.

Looks like that aren't meant for the living. Homer felt like he was climbing up a flimsy ladder into the cabin of a tiny plane that could take off but never land again, because devious Japanese engineers had converted it into a machine from hell. The imperial banner fluttered in the salty wind, mechanics bustled about on the airfield, engines hummed and sprang to life, and a potbellied general held his fingers tight up against the peak of his cap, his puffy eyes glittering with samurai envy...

'What's got you in such a cheerful mood?' Ahmed asked, shattering the old man's daydream.

Unlike Homer, he felt no urge to be first to discover what was going on at Serpukhov Station. He had left his wife behind on the platform, brooding silently as she clutched their first child's little hand in her left hand and cradled their second child in her right arm, cautiously nestling the mewling bundle against her breast.

'It's like drawing yourself up to your full height – and launching yourself into the attack, charging the machine-guns. The same feeling of reckless elation. We'll face a hail of deadly fire up ahead,' Homer tried to explain.

'What you have is a different kind of attack,' Ahmed muttered, looking back towards the little patch of light at the end of the tunnel. 'Custom-made for psychos like you. No sane man would voluntarily go up against a machine-gun. Who needs dumb heroics like that?'

'Well you see, it's like this,' the old man replied after a brief pause. 'When you feel your time coming, you start thinking: Have I really done anything? Will I be remembered?'

'I don't know about you, but I've got children. They'll remember me all right ... The oldest, at least,' Ahmed added gravely after pondering for a moment.

Homer was stung by that, and felt he should make a sharp retort, but Ahmed's final words had blunted his battle fervour. It was true: it was easy enough for an old man like him, with no children, to risk his moth-eaten skin, but the young man still had a long life ahead of him – too long to be concerned about immortality.

They moved beyond the final lamp – a glass jar with a little electric bulb inside it, set in a frame of thin metal rods. It was full of singed flies and flying cockroaches. The chitinous mass was heaving slightly: some of the insects were still alive and trying to crawl out, like condemned prisoners who had fallen into the common trench with everyone else who was shot, but hadn't been finished off.

Homer paused involuntarily for an instant in the spot of light that this lamp-grave wrung out of itself – weak and yellow, flickering on the point of extinction. Then he filled his lungs with air and plunged on after the others into the ink-black gloom that extended from the boundary of Sebastopol all the way to the approaches to Tula – if, of course, any station with that name still existed.

She wasn't alone, that sombre woman with two little children, standing rooted to the granite slabs, the platform wasn't entirely deserted. A fat man with one eye and wrestler's shoulders was standing motionless some distance away, watching as the soldiers left, and one step behind him stood a sinewy old man in a private's pea jacket, talking quietly to an orderly.

'All we can do now is wait,' Istomin declared, absentmindedly switching a dead cigarette end from one corner of his mouth to the other.

'You wait, I'll get on with my job,' the colonel retorted obstinately. 'I tell you, that was Andrei. The leader of the team we sent out,' said Istomin. He listened once again to the telephone-receiver voice still clamouring insistently in his head.

'So now what? Maybe they forced him to say that under torture. The specialists know all sorts of different methods,' said the old man, raising one eyebrow.

'It didn't seem like that,' said the commandant, shaking his head thoughtfully. 'You should have heard the way he said it. There's something else going on there, something inexplicable. Something we can't fix with a brisk cavalry sortie...'

'I'll give you an explanation as quick as a wink,' the colonel assured him. 'Tula's been captured by bandits. They set up an ambush and killed our men or took some as hostages. They don't cut off the power, because they use it themselves, and they don't want to get on the wrong side of Hansa. But they cut off the phone. What weird sort of business is that – a phone that sometimes works and sometimes doesn't?'

'But his voice, the way it sounded...' said Istomin, sticking to his point.

'What way did it sound?' the colonel exploded, making the orderly move back a few steps. 'Stick pins under your nails, and we'll see what your voice sounds like! And with a simple pair of pliers you can change a bass to a falsetto for the rest of a man's life!'

Everything was already clear to him, he had made his choice. And having resolved all his doubts, he felt as if he were back on his steed, and his cavalryman's hand was itching for the sabre, no matter how dismally Istomin might whinge.

The commandant took his time before answering, giving the colonel a chance to cool off.

'We'll wait,' he said at last, amicably but firmly.

'Two days,' said the old man, crossing his arms.

'Two days,' said Istomin, nodding.

The colonel spun round on the spot and tramped off to the barracks: he wasn't going to waste the precious hours ahead. The commanders of the assault units had been waiting for him at HQ for the best part of an hour, lined up along both flanks of the long planking table. The only empty chairs were at the opposite ends: his and Istomin's. But this time they would have to start without the commandant.

39

The station commandant didn't notice that Denis Mikhailovich had gone.

'It's amusing, the way our roles have switched over, isn't it?' said Istomin, perhaps talking to himself, perhaps to the colonel.

Swinging round without waiting for a reply, he encountered the orderly's embarrassed glance and waved his arm to dismiss him. 'I don't recognise the same colonel who refused to let me have a single extra man,' the commandant thought. 'The old war dog has scented something. But is that nose of his leading him astray?'

Istomin's own gut feeling told him something quite different: Lie low. Wait. The strange phone call had only intensified his dark premonition: at Tula their heavy infantry would come face to face with a mysterious, invincible adversary.

Vladimir Ivanovich rummaged through his pockets, found a cigarette lighter and struck a spark. And while the ragged smoke rings still rose into the air above his head, he stayed there, rooted to the spot, with his eyes riveted to the dark cavity of the tunnel, gazing spellbound at it, like a rabbit staring into the beckoning jaws of a boa constrictor. When he finished the cigarette, he shook his head again and set off to his office. The orderly emerged out of the shadows and followed him at a respectful distance.

A dull click – and the ribbed vaulting of the tunnel was illuminated for a good fifty metres ahead. Hunter's flashlight was so large and powerful, it was more like a searchlight. Homer breathed a silent sigh of relief – for the last few minutes he had been tormented by the stupid idea that the brigadier wouldn't switch on the light, because his eyes could manage perfectly well without it.

Once he set foot in the dark stretch of tunnel, the brigadier had started looking even less like an ordinary man, or any kind of man at all. His movements had acquired a graceful, impetuous, animal quality. It seemed as if he had switched on the flashlight for his companions, but he himself was relying on different senses. He often took off his helmet and turned one ear towards the tunnel, listening carefully, and even bolstered Homer's suspicions by stopping dead now and then to draw in the rusty-smelling air through his nose.

Hunter glided along soundlessly several steps ahead of the others, without looking round at them, as if he had forgotten they even existed. Ahmed was baffled – he didn't often stand watch at the southern frontier post and he wasn't used to the brigadier's eccentricities. He prodded Homer in the side, as if to ask: What's wrong with him? The old man just shrugged – how could he explain that in a couple of words.

What did Hunter need them for anyway? He was the one who had cast Homer in the role of native guide, but he seemed far more at home in these tunnels than the old man. Of course, if he were asked, Homer could have told him a lot about the places around here, tall tales and true ones – which were sometimes far more fantastic and terrifying than the most incredible yarns spun by bored sentries sitting round a lonely campfire. He had his own map of the Metro in his head, nothing at all like Istomin's. Where the station commandant's map had yawning gaps, Homer could have filled all the blank space with his own markings and explanations. Vertical shafts, service facilities standing open or closed up and mothballed, spiderwebs of connecting tunnels between the main lines. On his map, along the stretch of tunnel between Chertanovo and Southern, just two stations down from Sebastopol, a branch line budded off and merged into the gigantic bulge of the Warsaw Metro Depot, criss-crossed with the fine veins of dozens of dead-ends and drainage tunnels. For Homer, with his reverential awe of trains, the depot was an eerie and mystical place, like an elephants' graveyard. The old man could talk about it for hours at a time – if only he could find listeners willing to believe him.

Homer regarded the line between Sebastopol and Nakhimov Prospect as very tricky. The rules of safety and plain common sense required them to stick together, moving slowly and cautiously, examining the walls and the floor ahead of them closely. Even in this stretch of tunnel, where all the hatches and cracks had been bricked up and triple-sealed by engineering teams from Sebastopol, on no account could they afford to leave their rear uncovered. The darkness sliced open by the beam of the flashlight closed up again right behind their backs, the echoes of their footsteps fractured as they were reflected off the reinforcing ribs of countless sections of tunnel lining, and somewhere in the distance the wind howled, trapped in the ventilation shafts. Large, viscous drops gathered in cracks in the ceiling and fell – perhaps they were just water, but Homer tried to dodge them. Not for any particular reason – just in case.

In olden times, when the bloated monster of a city on the surface still lived its own feverish life, and the restless city-dwellers still thought of the Metro as a soulless transport system – back in those days the youthful Homer, who everyone still called Kolya, used to wander through its tunnels with a flashlight and a metal toolbox.

Entry to those places was barred to ordinary mortals, whose access was restricted to the 150 or so marble halls, polished to a high gleam, and the congested carriages, pasted with bright-coloured advertisements. The millions of people who spent two or three hours in the rumbling, swaying trains every day were unaware that they were only permitted to see a mere tenth of this incredibly vast underground kingdom that extended far and wide below the surface. And to make sure they didn't start speculating about its true size and where all those inconspicuous little doors and iron shutters led to, or where the dark little branch-lines and connecting passages closed for never-ending repairs actually went, they were distracted by pictures bright enough to dazzle their eyes, provocatively stupid slogans and wooden-voiced commercials that prevented them from relaxing on the escalators. At least, that was how it seemed to Kolya after he first started penetrating the secrets of this state within a state. The frivolous rainbow-coloured schematic of the metro that hung in the carriages was intended to convince the curious that they were looking at an exclusively civilian system. But in reality its cheerfully coloured lines were intertwined with the invisible branches of secret tunnels, from which military and state bunkers dangled like bunches of grapes – and some stretches of tunnel linked up with the tangled catacombs dug under the city by ancient pagans.

During the early days of Kolya's youth, when his country was too poor to vie with the power and ambition of others, Judgement Day had seemed very far off, and the bunkers and shelters built in anticipation of its arrival had gathered dust. But money brought the return of former arrogance and, with it, of enemies. The rust-coated, multi-ton doors of cast iron were opened again with a rasping creak, the stocks of food and medications were renewed, the air and water filters were rendered fully operational.

And all just in the nick of time.

For Kolya, a poor young man from out of town, to be accepted for a job in the Metro was like joining a Masonic lodge. It transformed him from an unemployed reject into a member of a powerful organisation that paid generously for the modest services he was able to provide and promised to initiate him into the arcane mysteries of the universe. The wages offered in the job announcement seemed very tempting to Kolya, and almost no requirements were specified for would-be trackwalkers.

It was some time before he began to understand, from the reluctant explanations of his new colleagues, just why the Metropolitan was obliged to entice employees with high salaries and bonus payments for occupational hazards. It wasn't a matter of a heavy schedule, or the voluntary renunciation of daylight. No, it had to do with dangers of an entirely different kind.

Homer had a sceptical mind, he didn't believe in the ever-present dark rumours of ghosts and ghouls. But one day his friend failed to return from checking a short dead-end stretch of tunnel, and for some reason they didn't bother to search for him – the shift foreman just shrugged helplessly. And his friend's disappearance was followed by the disappearance of all the documents testifying that he had ever worked in the Metro. Kolya was the only one still so young and naïve that he refused to accept this disappearance and eventually one of his senior colleagues whispered in his ear, gazing around as he did it, that his friend had been 'taken'. So who, if not Homer, should know that bad things used to happen in Moscow's subterranean depths long before life in the megalopolis died, scorched by the withering breath of Armageddon.

After losing his friend and being initiated into forbidden know-ledge like that, Kolya could have taken fright and run, abandoned this job and found another. But instead, his marriage of convenience with the Metro developed into a passionate love affair. When he'd had his fill of wandering around the tunnels on foot, he underwent the rites of initiation as a driver's mate and established himself in a more solid position in the complex hierarchy of the Metropolitan.

And the better he got to know this unacknowledged wonder of the world, this labyrinth with a nostalgic yen for antiquity, this ownerless, cyclopean city that was an inverted reflection in the brown Moscow earth of its prototype up above, the more deeply and selflessly he fell in love with it. This man-made Tartarus was indisputably worthy of the poetry of the genuine Homer, or at least the fleet pen of Swift, who would have seen it as a greater joke than Laputa. But the man who became its secret admirer and artless singer was Kolya – plain, simple Nikolai Ivanovich Nikolaev.

It was absurd.

Anyone reading the Russian folk tale *The Stone Flower* might feel that he could love the Mistress of the Copper Mountain – but love the Copper Mountain itself? And yet the day came when Kolya's love was requited with a jealous passion that took away his family, but saved his life.

Hunter froze abruptly on the spot and Homer, hunkered down under his snug feather quilt of memories, had no time to pull back: the old man ran into the brigadier's back at full tilt. Without making a sound, the brigadier flung him aside and froze again, lowering his head and turning his mutilated ear towards the tunnel. Like a bat mapping out space in its blindness, he was picking up wavelengths that only he could hear.

But Homer picked up something else: the smell of Nakhimov Prospect, a smell that was impossible to confuse with any other. They'd certainly got here quickly. He just hoped they wouldn't be made to pay for the ease with which they'd been let through. As if he could hear Homer's thoughts, Ahmed shrugged the sub-machine-gun off his shoulder and clicked off the safety catch.

'Who's that up there?' Hunter suddenly boomed, turning to the old man.

Homer chuckled to himself: who could tell what hellish beasts they might find? The wide-open gates of Nakhimov Prospect were like a funnel, sucking in from above creatures that defied the imagination. But the station had its permanent residents too.

'Small ... With no hair,' said the brigadier, trying to describe them, and that was enough for Homer. It was them.

'Corpse-eaters,' he said in a low voice.

From Sebastopol to Tula, and maybe in other parts of the Metro as well, this old, clichéd Russian insult now had a different, new meaning. A literal one.

'Predators?' asked Hunter.

'Scavengers,' the old man replied indecisively.

These repulsive creatures that simultaneously resembled spiders and primates never risked openly attacking human beings and fed

44

on carrion dragged down from the surface to the station they had made their own. A large herd of them nested at the Prospect, and all the tunnels nearby were filled with the sickly-sweet stench of decomposition. At the station itself the sheer pressure of it made men feel dizzy, and many of them found it so unbearable that they pulled on their gas masks on the approaches to the station.

Homer, who remembered this distinctive feature of Nakhimov Prospect only too well, hastily pulled the mask of his respirator out of his knapsack and put it on. Ahmed, who had packed hurriedly, gave Homer an envious glance and covered his face with his sleeve: the repugnant vapours emanating from the station gradually enveloped them, spurring them to move on quickly.

But Hunter didn't seem to smell anything.

'Something poisonous? Spores?' he asked Homer.

'The smell,' Homer mumbled through his mask and wrinkled up his face.

The brigadier examined the old man searchingly, as if trying to work out if Homer was making fun of him, then shrugged his massive, broad shoulders.

'The usual,' he said and turned away.

He shifted his grip on his short automatic, beckoned for them to follow him and moved on ahead, stepping softly. About fifty steps further on, the hideous stench was joined by an obscure murmuring. Homer wiped away the perspiration that had started streaming down his forehead and tried to curb the galloping pace of his heartbeat. They were really close now.

The groping flashlight beam finally found something. It swept the darkness off broken headlights peering blindly into nowhere, off the glass of dusty windscreens cobwebbed with cracks, off light-blue metal panelling that stubbornly refused to rust. There ahead of them was the first carriage of a train that blocked the throat of the tunnel like a gigantic cork.

The train had died ages ago, it was beyond all hope, but every time he saw it Homer felt like a little boy, he wanted to climb into the devastated cabin, caress the keys and switches of the instrument panel, close his eyes and pretend that once again he was dashing through the tunnels at full speed, pulling behind him a string of brightly lit carriages filled with people – reading, dozing, gazing at advertisements or struggling to make conversation above the rumble of the engines.

'If the alarm signal "ATOM" is given, drive to the nearest station, stop there and open the doors. Assist the efforts of civil defence units and the army to evacuate the injured and seal off the stations of the Metropolitan...'

The instructions on what train drivers should do on Judgement Day were precise and simple. Wherever it was possible, they were carried out. Most of the trains that froze at the platforms of the stations had fallen into a lethargic sleep and gradually been cannibalised for spare parts by the inhabitants of the Metro, who, instead of spending a few weeks in this refuge, as promised, had been detained here for all eternity. In a few places the trains had been preserved and converted into homes, but that seemed blasphemous to Homer, who had always seen trains as possessing a distinctly animate essence – it was like having your favourite pet cat stuffed and mounted. In places that were unfit for human habitation, like Nakhimov Prospect, the trains stood, gnawed on by time and vandals, but still intact.

Homer simply couldn't take his eyes off the carriage. A phantom alarm signal wailed in his ears, drowning out the ever-louder rustling and hissing sounds from the station, and a deep, low siren blasted out the signal that had never been heard before that day: one long blast and two short ones: 'ATOM'!

A lingering clang of brakes and a bewildered announcement in all the carriages 'Ladies and gentlemen, for technical reasons this train will not proceed any further.' It was too soon yet for the driver mumbling into the microphone, or Homer, his mate, to grasp the anguished hopelessness of those hackneyed words. The rasping sound of hermetic doors straining shut, separating off the world of the living from the world of the dead forever... According to instructions, the gates had to be finally locked no later than six minutes after the alarm was sounded, no matter how many people were left on the other side. If anyone tried to prevent the gates closing, the recommendation was to shoot at them.

Would a little police sergeant, who guarded his station against homeless bums and drunks, be able to shoot a man in the stomach because he was trying to hold back the immense metal behemoth, in order to give his wife, who had broken her heel, time to run inside? Would a high-handed turnstile-woman in a round uniform cap, who had spent her thirty-year career in the Metro perfecting two skills – not letting people through and blowing her whistle – be able to refuse entrance to a desperately panting old man with a pathetic row of medal ribbons? The instructions gave them only six minutes to change from a human being into a machine. Or a monster.

Women squealing, men clamouring indignantly, children sobbing desperately. The staccato popping of pistol shots and rumbling bursts of automatic fire. Recorded appeals to remain calm, relayed through every speaker in a metallic, passionless voice – they had to be recorded, because no human being, knowing what was happening, could possibly have kept his presence of mind and simply said it like that, indifferently: 'Do not panic...'

Tears, prayers...

More shooting.

And precisely six minutes after the alarm, one minute before Armageddon – the rumbling funereal clang as sections of hermetic doors lock together. The reverberating clicks of the bolts. Silence.

The silence of the crypt.

They had to walk along the wall past the carriage. The driver had braked too late – perhaps he had been distracted by what was happening at that moment on the platform... They clambered up a cast-iron ladder and a moment later they were standing in an amazingly spacious hall. No columns, just the half-cylinder of a single semi-circular vault, with egg-shaped recesses behind the lamps. An immense vault, arching over the platform and both tracks, together with the trains standing on them. The structure is incredibly elegant – simple, divinely light and uncluttered. Only don't look down at your feet, at the floor ahead of you. Don't let yourself see what the station has been turned into now. This grotesque graveyard, where no rest could possibly be found, this macabre meat market, piled high with gnawed skeletons, rotten carcasses, chunks ripped off someone's trunk. The vile creatures have greedily dragged in here everything they could grab anywhere within their extensive domain, more than they can devour immediately, reserves for future use. These reserves putrefy and decompose, but the brutes carry on accumulating them incessantly.

In defiance of the laws of nature, the heaps of dead meat moved

47

as if they were breathing, and a repulsive scraping sound could be heard on all sides. The beam of light picked out one of the strange figures: long, knotty limbs; flabby, grey, hairless skin, hanging down in folds; a crooked spine, dull eyes blinking weakly, immense ears moving as if they had a life of their own.

One creature gave a hoarse cry and trudged unhurriedly to the open doors of a carriage, stepping with all four of its arm-legs. Other corpse-eaters started climbing down off other heaps in the same lazy fashion, hissing indignantly, sniffling, baring their teeth and snarling at the travellers.

Standing erect, they barely came up to Homer's chest, and he was short. He also knew perfectly well that the beasts were cowardly, that they were unlikely to attack a strong, healthy man. But the irrational horror that Homer felt at the sight of the creatures was rooted in nightmares, in which he lay all alone, exhausted and abandoned in a deserted station, and the beasts were creeping ever closer. Like sharks in the ocean, who can scent a drop of blood from kilometres away, these creatures could sense the approach of death, and they hurried to be there when it arrived.

Senile anxiety, Homer told himself contemptuously – he had once read a whole raft of text books on applied psychology. But that wasn't much help to him now.

The corpse-eaters weren't afraid of people: using up ammunition on the repulsive but apparently harmless devourers of carrion would have been regarded as criminal waste at Sebastopol. The convoys passing through tried not to take any notice of them, although sometimes the corpse-eaters behaved provocatively.

They had bred in huge numbers here, and as the three men moved further in, crushing someone's small bones under their boots with a sickening crunch at every step, more and more of the beasts reluctantly tore themselves away from their feasting and wandered off into cover. Their nests were in the trains, and Homer loathed them even more for that.

The hermetic doors at Nakhimov Prospect were open. It was believed that if you moved through the station quickly, the small dose of radiation you received was no danger to health, but it was forbidden to halt here. That was why both of the trains were relatively well preserved: the windows were all in place, the stained and soiled seats could be seen through the open doors, the light-blue paint showed no signs of peeling off the metal flanks.

Towering up in the middle of the hall was a genuine burial mound, built from the twisted skeletons of unknown creatures. As he drew level with it, Hunter suddenly stopped. Ahmed and Homer glanced at each other in alarm, trying to work out where any danger could come from. But the reason for the halt turned out to be something different. At the foot of the mound two small corpse-eaters were stripping a dog's skeleton, champing and growling with relish as they ate. They hadn't hidden in time: either they were too absorbed in their meal and didn't notice the signals from other members of their tribe, or they simply hadn't been able to control their greed.

They screwed up their eyes in the glare of the brigadier's flash-light and carried 'on chewing, starting to withdraw slowly in the direction of the nearest carriage, but suddenly, one after another, they somersaulted backwards and flopped down onto the floor, like empty sacks.

Homer gazed in amazement at Hunter, who was putting a heavy army pistol with a long cylindrical silencer back in his shoulder holster. His face was as inscrutable and lifeless as ever.

'They must have been very hungry, I suppose,' Ahmed muttered under his breath, examining the dark puddles spreading out from under the dead beasts' smashed skulls with squeamish interest.

'So am I,' the brigadier responded incomprehensibly, making Homer shudder.

Hunter moved on without looking round at the others and old Homer thought he could hear that low, greedy growling again. What an effort it cost him every time to resist the temptation to put a bullet into these vermin! He had to coax himself, calm himself down, and eventually he got the upper hand and demonstrated to himself that he was a mature individual who could tame his nightmares, who refused to let them drive him insane. But Hunter apparently had no intention of even trying to fight his impulsive desires.

Only what were those desires?

The silent demise of two members of the herd galvanised the other corpse-eaters: scenting fresh death, even the boldest and the laziest of them moved off the platforms, wheezing and whining faintly. They crammed into both trains and fell silent, lined up at the windows and crowding in the doors of the carriages. These creatures didn't show any rage or desire for revenge. Once the team left the station, they would immediately devour their own dead relatives. 'Aggression is a quality of hunters,' thought Homer. 'Those who feed on carrion don't need it, just as they don't need to kill. Everything living dies sooner or later, it will all become their food anyway. All they have to do is wait.'

The beam of the flashlight revealed the repulsive faces pressed up against the other side of the dirty, greenish panes of glass, the misshapen bodies, the clawed hands groping restlessly at the inside of the satanic fish tank. In total silence, hundreds of pairs of dull eyes doggedly followed the movement of the team as it walked by, the creatures' heads turning uncannily in precise synchronisation, watching intently as the men moved away. The little freaks sealed in flasks of formalin at the Kunstkamera Museum would have watched the visitors like that, if their eyelids hadn't prudently been sewn shut.

Despite the approaching hour of reckoning for his godlessness, Homer still couldn't bring himself to believe in either the Lord or the Devil. But if Purgatory did exist, this was exactly how it would have looked for the old man. Sisyphus was doomed to battle against gravity, Tantalus was condemned to the torment of unquenchable thirst. But waiting for Homer at the station of his death was a train driver's jacket and this bloodcurdling ghost train, with its monstrous gargoyle passengers: the mockery of vengeful gods. And on leaving the platform, the train would drive straight into one of the old legends of the Metro, with the tunnel looping round into a Möbius strip, a dragon devouring its own tail.

Hunter had lost interest in the station and its inhabitants and the team crossed the rest of the hall at a brisk pace: Ahmed and Homer could hardly keep up with the brigadier's impetuous stride.

The old man felt the urge to turn round, shout, fire – to scatter these insolent freaks and banish his own painful thoughts. But instead he trudged on with his head lowered, concentrating hard to avoid stepping on anybody's rotting remains. Ahmed hung his head too, absorbed in his own thoughts. And in their hasty flight from Nakhimov Prospect, no one thought of looking round any longer.

The patch of light from Hunter's flashlight scurried rapidly from side to side, as if it were following an invisible gymnast under the dome of this baleful circus, but even the brigadier was no longer taking any notice of what it picked out.

A set of fresh bones and a half-gnawed skull – clearly human – glinted briefly in the beam and immediately disappeared back into the gloom, unnoticed by anyone. Lying beside them like a useless shell were a steel army helmet and a bulletproof vest.

Over the peeling green paint of the helmet a single word had been stencilled in white: 'Sebastopol'.

CHAPTER 4

Tangled Knots

'Dad ... Dad, it's me, Sasha!'

She carefully loosened the tight canvas strap restraining the terribly bloated chin and removed her father's helmet. Thrusting her fingers into his sweat-soaked hair, she hooked out the strip of rubber, pulled off his gas mask and flung it aside like a ghastly, shrivelled grey scalp. His chest heaved painfully, his fingers scrabbled at the granite floor and his watery eyes stared at her without blinking, but he didn't answer. Sasha put the knapsack under his head and dashed to the door. Bracing her skinny shoulder against the enormous panel of metal, she took a deep, deep breath and gritted her teeth. The massive slab yielded reluctantly and scraped into place with a low grunt. Sasha clanged the bolt home and slid down onto the floor. A minute, just one little minute to catch her breath, and then she'd go straight back to him.

Every new expedition drained more of her father's strength, and the meagre pickings he came back with couldn't compensate for the loss. These sallies were draining away what was left of his life not by the day, but whole weeks and months at a time. An exorbitant price that had to be paid: if they didn't have anything to sell, they'd have no choice left but to eat their tame rat – the only one in this God-forsaken death-trap of a station – and then shoot themselves.

Sasha wanted to take her father's place. So many times she had asked him for the respirator, so that she could go up there, but he was adamant. Probably he knew the filters on the leaky gas mask had been blocked for so long, it was no more use now than any other good luck charm. But he never admitted that to her. He lied about knowing how to clean the filters, he lied about feeling fine after an hour's 'stroll', he lied about simply wanting to be alone, when he was afraid that she would see him vomiting blood.

Sasha was powerless to change anything. They had driven her father and her into this corner and if they hadn't finished them off, it was more out of contemptuous curiosity than pity. They hadn't expected the two of them to last more than a week, but her father's willpower and sheer grit had kept them going for years. Although they were hated and despised, they were given food regularly – but not, of course, for free.

In the breaks between expeditions, in those rare moments when the two of them sat together beside the stunted, smoky little camp-fire, her father liked to tell her about the way things used to be before. He had realised years ago that there was no point in lying to himself any longer: he had no future. But no one could take away his past. 'I used to have eyes the same colour as yours,' he told her. 'The colour of the sky.' And Sasha thought she could remember those days too – the days before the gigantic tumour swelled up on his neck, before his eyes faded and turned colourless, when they were still as bright as her own were now.

When her father said 'the colour of the sky', of course he meant the azure sky that lived on in his memory, not the crimson sky that eddied and swirled above him when he went up *there* at night.

He hadn't seen daylight for more than twenty years. Sasha had never seen it. Except in her dreams – but how could she be sure the way she imagined it was right? Is the world that people blind from birth see in their dreams like ours? And do they see at all, even in their dreams?

When little children squeeze their eyes shut, they think darkness has swallowed up the entire world. They think everyone else around them is as blind as they are at that moment. 'In the tunnels, a man is as helpless and naïve as those children,' thought Homer. 'He can click his flashlight on and off as much as he likes, imagining that he's the master of light and darkness, but even the very blackest darkness around him can be full of seeing eyes.'

This thought haunted Homer now, after their brush with the scavengers. He had to take his mind off it somehow, distract himself. 'Strange that Hunter didn't know what to expect at Nakhi-mov Prospect,' he thought. When the brigadier first appeared at

Sebastopol two months earlier, none of the sentries could explain how a man with such a massive figure could have slipped past all the guard posts set up in the northern tunnels without being noticed. Thankfully, the perimeter commander hadn't asked the duty sentries for any explanations.

But if he didn't come through Nakhimov Prospect, how had Hunter got to Sebastopol? The other routes to the Greater Metro had been cut off ages ago. The only exception was the abandoned Kakhovka line, where no living creature had been seen in the tunnels for many years – and for good reason. Chertanovo? It was ridiculous to suppose that even such a skilled and ruthless warrior could have made his way alone through that cursed station – and it was impossible to get to it without showing up at Sebastopol first.

If the north and the south were excluded, Homer could only assume their mysterious visitor had reached the station from above. Naturally, all the known ways in from the surface and back out to it were thoroughly sealed off and guarded, but still... Could he, for instance, have opened a blocked ventilation shaft? The Sebastopolites thought there was no way the scorched ruins of the concrete-slab high-rises could still throw up someone intelligent enough to disconnect their alarm system. The boundless patchwork chessboard of residential districts was carved apart by fragments of the warheads that fell on the city, and it had been empty for a long, long time. The last human players had abandoned it decades ago, and the horrific, malformed chess figures that roamed across its surface now were playing a new game, by their own rules. Man couldn't even dream of getting a return match.

Brief excursions in search of anything valuable that hadn't rotted away in more than twenty years – hasty and humiliating attempts to pillage their own homes – that was all people had the strength for now. Encased in their anti-radiation armour, the stalkers went up there to ransack the skeletons of the nearby low, Khruschev-era buildings for the hundredth time, but they shied away from decisive combat with the new landlords. The most they could do was fire a snarling burst of automatic fire and sit it out in the apartments polluted with rat droppings until the danger had passed – then make a headlong dash for the underground.

The old maps of the capital had lost all resemblance to reality a long time ago. Where once there were wide avenues choked with traffic jams several kilometres long, now there might be gaping precipices or dark, impassable forest thickets. Entire residential areas had been swallowed up by swamps or scorched bald patches. The most reckless stalkers investigated the surface within a radius of up to one kilometre from their home burrows: others were far less ambitious.

The stations that followed Nakhimov Prospect – Nagornaya, Nagatino and Tula – had no exits of their own, and in any case the people living at two of them were too timid to go up onto the surface. It was a mystery to Homer where a living man could have come from in the middle of this wasteland. But he would still have liked to think that Hunter came to their station from the surface. Because there was one other, final possibility for the route the brigadier had followed to reach them. And this possibility came creeping into the godless old man's mind against his will, while he was trying to control his panting breath and keep up with that dark silhouette rushing ahead so furiously that its feet didn't even seem to touch the ground.

From below?

'I've got a bad feeling about this,' Ahmed murmured slowly – just loud enough for Homer to make out his words, but too softly for the brigadier, who had pulled ahead slightly, to hear. 'We've picked the wrong time. Believe me, I've been in plenty of convoys here – this is a bad day at Nagornaya.'

It was a long time since the bands of petty robbers, who rested from their plunder at dark way stations as far away as possible from the Circle, had dared to come anywhere near the Sebastopol convoys. When they heard the regular tramping of metal-tipped boots announce the heavy infantry's approach, the only thought in their minds was how to get out of the way as quickly as possible.

No, they weren't the reason why the convoys were always so well-guarded, and it wasn't because of the four-handed scavengers at Nakhimov Prospect either. Iron discipline and audacious courage, with the ability to close ranks into a wall of steel in seconds and exterminate any tangible threat with a withering hail of fire would have made the Sebastopol convoys masters of the tunnels from their own guard posts all the way to Serpukhov ... If not for Nagornaya.

Nakhimov Prospect and all its horrors were behind them now, but neither Homer nor Ahmed felt even a moment's relief.

Nagornaya Station, so plain and unassuming, had been the end of the line for many travellers who failed to take it seriously enough. The poor souls at the next station, Nagatino, huddled as far away as possible from the greedy jaws of the tunnel that led south, to Nagornaya. As if that could protect them ... As if what crept out of the southern tunnel to garner its harvest wouldn't bother to prowl a little further in search of prey that suited its taste.

Travelling through Nagornaya Station, you always had to trust to luck, the place was so capricious and inconsistent. Sometimes it let travellers pass, merely frightening them with the bloody stains on its walls and fluted steel columns – as if someone had tried to escape by climbing up them. But the reception it gave the next group, literally only minutes later, would make the survivors think the loss of only half their comrades was a victory. It could never be sated. It had no favourites. It defied observation and study. For the inhabitants of all the stations around it, Nagornaya embodied the whim of fate. And it was the greatest ordeal of all for men who set out on the journey from Sebastopol to the Circle and back.

'Nagornaya couldn't have done it all on its own ...' Ahmed was superstitious, like many of the Sebastopolites, and he always spoke about this station as a living creature.

Homer didn't need to ask what he meant – he had also been wondering how Nagornaya Station could have swallowed up the convoys that had disappeared and all the scouts sent out to search for them. 'All sorts of things have happened, but for so many men to disappear at once,' he agreed, 'it would have choked on them .'

'Don't talk like that!' Ahmed exclaimed, clicking his tongue angrily at Homer and flinging his hands up in alarm – or perhaps he was holding back the slap that the old man was obviously asking for. 'It won't choke on you, that's for sure!'

Homer let that go and reined in his resentment. He didn't believe Nagornaya could hear what they said and hold it against them. Not at this distance, anyway. Superstition, it was sheer superstition! If you tried to pay homage to all the idols of the underworld, you were bound to fail, you couldn't avoid offending someone. Homer had stopped worrying about that kind of thing long ago, but Ahmed thought differently. He pulled a set of prayer beads – made of blunt pistol bullets – out of the pocket of his uniform jacket pocket and started twirling the string of lead through his dirty hands and fluttering his lips, praying in his own language to atone for Homer's offences against Nagornaya. But the station didn't seem to understand him, or perhaps it was already too late for apologies.

Hunter detected something with his supernatural sense of smell and waved his gloved hand, killing the pace. He sank down slowly onto the ground. 'There's fog up there,' he said curtly. 'What's that?'

Homer and Ahmed exchanged glances. They both understood what it meant: the hunt was on, and now they would need all their luck to reach the northern limits of Nagornaya alive.

'How can I put it?' Ahmed replied reluctantly. 'It's breathing.'

'What is?' the brigadier asked him coolly and shook his knapsack off his shoulders, evidently planning to select the appropriate calibre from his arsenal.

'Nagornaya Station,' said Ahmed, switching to a whisper.

'We'll see about that,' Hunter said with a contemptuous, crooked grin.

But no, Homer had only imagined the brigadier's mutilated face coming to life: it had remained as immobile as ever – the grin was only a trick of the light.

A hundred metres further on the other two saw it: a heavy white mist creeping over the ground towards them, first licking at their boots, then twining round their knees, then flooding the tunnel waist-high. It was as if they were slowly walking into a cold, hostile, ghostly sea, sinking deeper and deeper with every step they took across its deceptively sloping bottom, until they were totally submerged in its murky waters.

They couldn't see a thing. The flashlight beams got stuck in this strange mist like flies in a cobweb: they forced their way a few steps forward, then ran out of strength, went limp and hung there in mid-air – feeble, submissive captives. Sounds were hard to make out, as if they were forcing their way through a feather mattress, and it even became harder to move, as if the team really was walking over a silty sea bed, not a line of railway sleepers.

It got harder to breathe too, but not because of the humidity – it was the unusual, tart aroma that had appeared in the air. The men felt reluctant to let it into their lungs, it made them feel as if they were drawing into themselves the breath of some huge, alien creature that had already extracted all the oxygen from the air and saturated it with poisonous exhalations.

To be on the safe side, Homer pulled his respirator back over his face. Hunter gave him a quick glance, then lowered his hand into the canvas bag hanging under his shoulder, tugged open a strap and slapped a new, rubber mask over his usual one. Ahmed was the only one left without a gas mask – he had either forgotten it in his haste or decided not to bother.

The brigadier froze again, pointing his tattered ear towards Nagornaya, but in the dense white murk he couldn't make out the snatches of sound coming from the station clearly enough to assemble them into a complete picture. Something really massive seemed to tumble over with a crash, someone gave a long whoop on a note too low for a man – or for any kind of animal. There was a hysterical scraping of metal, as if a hand was tying one of the thick pipes running along the wall into a knot.

Hunter tossed his head, as if he were throwing off some kind of dirt that was sticking to it, and the short automatic pistol in his hand was replaced by a military Kalashnikov with twin clips and an under-barrel grenade launcher. 'At last,' he murmured to himself.

They reached the station without even realising it. Nagornaya was flooded with fog as thick as pig's milk: gazing at it through the misted lenses of his gas mask, Homer felt like a scuba-diver who had swum into a sunken ocean liner.

The similarity was emphasised by the embossed panels decorating the walls: seagulls imprinted into metal by a crude, artless Soviet stamp. More than anything else they resembled the imprints of fossilised organisms exposed on the ruptured surfaces of rock strata. 'Fossilisation – that's the fate of man and his creations,' Homer thought briefly. 'But who'll dig them up?'

The miasma filling the air around them was alive – it flowed and quivered. Sometimes patches of darkness condensed out of it – at first Homer thought he saw a mangled and twisted carriage or a rusty sentry box, and then it was the scaly body or head of some mythical monster. He was afraid even to imagine who might have occupied the crew's quarters and settled into the first-class cabins in the decades that had passed since the shipwreck. He'd heard a lot about things that had happened at Nagornaya, but he'd never come face to face with . . .

'There it is. Over there, on the right!' yelled Ahmed, tugging the old man by the sleeve.

There was the muffled pop of a shot fired through a homemade silencer.

Homer swung round at a speed that was impossible with his rheumatism, but his blunted flashlight lit up nothing except a section of column faced with ribbed metal

'Behind us! There, behind us!' Ahmed fired a short burst, but his bullets merely crumbled the remnants of marble slabs that had once covered the walls of the station. Whatever features Ahmed had spotted in the trembling mirage, their owner had dissolved back into it unharmed.

'He's breathed too much of this stuff,' thought Homer.

And then, out of the very corner of his eye, he saw something... Gigantic, hunched over – because the station's fifteen-foot ceiling was too low for it – something unbelievably agile for its immense size, breaking out of the fog on the very boundary of visibility and swaying back in again before the old man could train his automatic on it.

Homer looked round helplessly for the brigadier. He was nowhere to be seen.

'Okay. Okay. Don't worry,' her father reassured her, halting to rest between the words. 'You know... somewhere in the Metro right now there are people who are far more afraid...'

He tried to smile, but it turned out terrifying, like a skull with a jaw that has come adrift. Sasha smiled back, but a salty dewdrop crept down across her sharp, soot-stained cheekbone. At least her father had come round – and the few hours that seemed so long had given her time to think everything through again.

'A real failure this time, I'm so sorry,' he said. 'I decided to go to the garages after all. But it turned out to be too far. I found one completely untouched. A stainless steel castle, covered in oil. I couldn't break in, so I attached a charge, the last one. I was hoping there'd be a car inside, spare parts. And when I blasted it opened, it was empty. Nothing at all. So why did they lock it, the bastards? And that thunderous noise... I was praying no one would hear. Then I walked out of the garage and I was surrounded by dogs on all sides. I thought that was it... I thought I was done for...'

Her father lowered his eyelids and stopped talking. Feeling alarmed, Sasha grabbed hold of his hand, but he just swayed his head gently, without opening his eyes, as if to tell her: Don't worry, everything's okay. He was too weak even to speak, but he wanted to tell her how it happened, he needed to explain why he'd come back empty-handed, why they would have a tough week now until he got back on his feet. But sleep overcame him before he could tell her.

Sasha checked the bandage wrapped round his torn calf – it was soaked through with black blood – and changed the compress that was already hot. She straightened up, went over to the rat's little house and opened the tiny door a crack. The little beast peeped out warily and hid again, but then it did what Sasha was hoping for and scrabbled out onto the platform to stretch its legs. The rat's intuition never let it down: the tunnels were quiet. Reassured, the girl went back to the stretcher bed.

'You will definitely get up, you'll walk again,' she whispered to her father. 'And you'll find a garage with an entire car in it, all in one piece. And we'll go up there together, get into it and drive far away from here. Ten, fifteen stations away. To where no one knows us, where we'll be strangers. Where no one will hate us. If there is a place like that anywhere...'

She was telling him the same magical fairytale that she had heard from him so often, repeating it word for word, and now, as she recited this old mantra of her father's, she believed in it a hundred times more powerfully. She would nurse him back to health, she would cure him. There *was* a place in this world where no one could give a damn about them. A place where they could be happy.

'There it is! There! It's looking at me!'

Ahmed squealed as if he had already been seized and dragged away, he screamed as he had never allowed himself to scream before. His automatic roared again, then stuttered and choked. Ahmed's usual composure deserted him completely and he trembled violently as he tried to insert a full clip into the slot.

'It's chosen me... Me.'

Somewhere nearby another automatic barked briefly, fell silent for a second and then chattered again in clipped, three-shot bursts. Hunter was still alive after all, so there was still hope. The chattering moved away and then came closer, but it was impossible to tell if the bullets had found their mark. Homer strained his ears in vain for the furious roar of a wounded monster. The station was enveloped in oppressive silence; its mysterious residents seemed to be either immaterial or invulnerable.

Now the brigadier was waging his strange battle at the far end of the platform, where fiery strings of tracer bullets repeatedly flared up and faded away. Enthralled by his fight with phantoms, he had abandoned his men to their fate. Homer took a deep breath and looked up, cautiously giving in to the desire that had been tormenting him for several long moments already. He could feel that gaze all too clearly with his skin, the top of his head, the fine hairs on his neck – a cold, leaden, crushing gaze – and he couldn't fight his foreboding any longer.

Right up under the ceiling, high above their heads, another head was hovering in the fog. A head so immense that at first Homer didn't realise what he was looking at. The titanic creature's body remained hidden in the dense gloom of the station, leaving its monstrous face suspended, swaying in the air above the tiny little men brandishing their useless weapons: strangely, it seemed in no hurry to attack, allowing them a brief respite.

Numb with horror, the old man sank to his knees, resigned to his fate, and the automatic rifle tumbled out of his hands, clanking pitifully against a rail. Ahmed howled and screeched hideously. The creature shifted forward effortlessly, and all the space in front of them was blotted out by its dark body, as huge as a cliff. Homer closed his eyes, readying himself, saying goodbye ... He had only one thought left, one regret – a bitter thought searing through his mind: 'I haven't finished yet!'

And at that very moment the grenade launcher spat fire and the pressure wave slammed into his ears, deafening them, leaving behind a subtle whistling sound that went on and on. Gobbets of burnt flesh came showering down. Ahmed, the first to gather his wits, tugged the old man to his feet by the scruff of his neck and dragged him away. They ran forward, stumbling over sleepers and getting up again without feeling any pain. They clung to each other, because it was impossible to make out anything through the milky haze even at arm's length. They raced along as if it was not mere death pursuing them, but something infinitely more terrible – the final extinction and utter annihilation of their bodies and souls.

Demons pursued them, invisible and almost completely silent, but only one step behind, escorting them without attacking, toying with them, allowing them the illusion of escape.

Then the chipped marble walls gave way to the lining of the tunnel: they'd made it through Nagornaya! And the guardians of the station were left behind, as if they had reached the limit of the chains to which they were attached. But it was still too soon to stop. Ahmed strode on in front, feeling for the pipes on the walls, groping for the way ahead and goading on the old man, who was stumbling along, and kept trying to sit down.

'What happened to the brigadier?' Homer croaked, tearing off his stifling gas mask as he walked.

'When the fog ends, we'll stop and wait. That must be soon now, very soon! Only another two hundred metres... Get out of the fog. The important thing is to get out of the fog,' Ahmed kept intoning. 'I'm going to count the steps...'

But after two hundred steps, and even after three hundred, the haze enveloping them was still as dense as ever. 'What if it's spread all the way to Nagatino?' thought Homer. 'What if it's already gobbled up Tula and Nakhimov Prospect?'

'It's not possible... I must... Not far to go now...' Ahmed mumbled for the hundredth time and suddenly froze on the spot. Homer ran into him and they both tumbled to the ground.

'There's no more wall,' said Ahmed, stroking the sleepers, the rails, the rough, damp concrete of the floor in dumb bewilderment, as if afraid that any moment now the ground would treacherously slip away from under his feet in the same way as his other support had vanished.

'Here it is, what's wrong with you?' said Homer groping around for the slope of a tunnel liner, then grabbing hold of it and cautiously getting to his feet.

'Sorry,' said Ahmed and paused, gathering his thoughts. 'You know, back there at the station... I thought I'd never get away from the place. The way it was looking at me... Looking at me, you know. It had decided to take me. I thought I'd be left there forever. And never buried.'

He had to struggle to force the words out, he didn't want to let them out for a long time – he was ashamed of screaming like a woman. He wanted to make excuses – and he knew there couldn't be any excuses. Homer shook his head.

'Drop it. I pissed my pants, and it's not bothering me any. Come on, we must be almost there now.'

The pursuit had been called off, they could get their breath back. They couldn't run any longer in any case, and they wandered along, clutching at the walls as blindly as ever. Advancing towards deliverance step by step. The worst of the terror was behind them, and although the murk was still not receding, sooner or later the predatory draughts of the tunnels would bite into it, shred it and drag the shreds into the ventilation shafts. Sooner or later they would reach a place where there were people and wait there for their delayed commander.

It happened sooner than they could possibly have hoped – maybe because time and space were both distorted in the fog. A cast-iron ladder appeared, running up the wall onto a platform, the round cross-section of the tunnel gave way to a right-angled one and a hollow appeared between the rails – a safe refuge for passengers who fell onto the track.

'Look at that,' whispered Homer. 'It looks like a station! A station!

'Hey, is there anyone there?' Ahmed yelled as loud as he could. 'Hey lads! Is anyone there?' he yelled, overwhelmed by senseless, triumphant laughter.

The yellowish, exhausted beams of their flashlights picked slabs of marble, gnawed away by time and people, out of the hazy gloom. Not one of the bright-coloured mosaics – the pride and joy of Nagatino – had survived. And what had become of the stone-faced columns? Could this really be...?

No one answered Ahmed, but he didn't despair and carried on calling cheerfully: it was obvious enough, the people had taken fright at the fog and run off – but they couldn't fool him like that! Meanwhile Homer kept searching anxiously for something on the walls, licking at them with his fading beam of light, while suspicion chilled his blood.

And then at last he found it – iron letters screwed into the cracked marble: NAGORNAYA.

Her father believed it was never accidental when people went back to a place. They returned in order to change something, in order to put something right. Sometimes, he believed, God himself takes us by the scruff of the neck and brings us back to the spot where we accidentally escaped his watchful eye, in order to enforce his sentence – or give us a second chance. That was why, he explained, he would never be able to return from exile to their native station. He had no strength left to take revenge, to struggle, to prove anything. He had long ago stopped wanting anyone's contrition or remorse. In the old story that had cost him his former life and almost ended his life completely, everyone had got what they deserved, he said. As things turned out, they had been condemned to eternal exile – Sasha's father didn't want to put anything right, and in any case the Lord never called into this station.

The rescue plan – to find a car that hadn't rotted away in over two decades, repair it, fuel it and break out of the narrow circle in which fate had imprisoned them – that plan had been no more than a bedtime story for a long time already.

For Sasha there was another way back to the Greater Metro. When she went down to the bridge on the set day to exchange the clumsily repaired devices, blackened jewellery and mouldy books for food and a few cartridges, sometimes they offered her a lot more.

Training the trolley's searchlight on her slightly angular, boyish figure, the shuttle traders winked at each other and smacked their lips, beckoning to her and shouting promises. The little girl seemed wild – she glowered at them with her head down, tensed up like a spring, concealing a long-bladed knife behind her back. The loose-fitting man's overalls couldn't blur the bold, clear lines of her body. The mud and engine oil on her face only made her blue eyes shine even more brightly, so brightly that some men turned their own eyes away. The white hair, artlessly trimmed with the same knife that was always clutched in her right hand, barely covered her ears, the gnawed lips never smiled.

Soon realising that petty gifts were poor bait for taming a wild wolf, the men on the trolley tried to bribe her with freedom, but she never answered them even once. They decided the girl must be dumb. It was easier like that. Sasha knew perfectly well that no matter what she agreed to, she could never buy two places on the trolley. People had too many accounts for her father to settle, and they couldn't possibly be paid.

Faceless and with adenoidal voices in their black military gas masks, they weren't simply enemies to her – she couldn't see anything human about them, not a single thing that could have set her dreaming, not even at night, even in her dreams.

And so she simply set the telephones, irons and kettles down on the sleepers, moved back ten steps and waited for the shuttle traders to take the goods, fling the bundles of dried pork down on the track and toss her a handful of cartridges, deliberately scattering them out of spite, so they could watch as she collected them, crawling on her hands and knees.

Then the trolley slowly sailed off into a different world and Sasha turned round and went home, where a heap of broken household appliances was waiting for her, along with a screwdriver, a soldering iron and an old bicycle converted into a generator. She mounted it, closed her eyes and hurtled away, far off into the distance, almost managing to forget that she could never move from the spot. And the fact that she had made her own decision to reject the offer of pardon lent her strength.

What the hell? How had they ended up back here? Homer feverishly racked his brains for an explanation. Ahmed suddenly shut up when he saw where Homer was shining his flashlight.

'This station won't let me go,' he said in a hoarse, low voice.

The fog enveloping them had grown so thick, they could barely see each other. Nagornaya had slumbered while the men were away, but it had awoken now: the heavy air fluctuated subtly in response to their words and vague shadows stirred in its depths. And not a single sign of Hunter . . . There was no way a creature of flesh and blood could win a battle against phantoms. As soon as the station was weary of toying with them, it had shrouded them in its acrid breath and swallowed them alive.

'You go,' Ahmed gasped despairingly. 'I'm the one it wants. You don't know, you almost never come here.'

'Stop talking drivel!' the old man snapped, surprising even himself with the loudness of his voice. 'We just lost our way in the fog. Let's go back!'

'We can't leave. Run as hard as you like, you'll end up back here, if you're with me. You can break out on your own. Please, go.'

'Stop it, that's enough!' Homer grabbed hold of Ahmed's wrist and dragged him towards the tunnel. 'You'll thank me for this in an hour!'

'Tell my Gulya...' Ahmed began.

An incredible, monstrously powerful force tore his hand out of Homer's hand, jerking it upwards into the fog, into extinction. He had no time to cry out, he simply disappeared, as if he had instantaneously disintegrated into atoms, as if he had never existed. The old man screamed and howled for him, spinning round on the spot as if he'd lost his mind, wasting clip after clip of precious cartridges. Then a crushing blow that could only have been struck by one of the local demons landed on the back of his head and the universe imploded.

CHAPTER 5

Memory

Sasha ran over to the window and flung the shutters wide open, letting in the fresh air and the tentative light. The wooden window ledge hung over the very edge of a bottomless precipice, filled with delicate morning mist that would disperse with the first rays of sunshine, and then the view from the window would extend beyond the gorge to the distant mountain spurs with their covering of pine trees and the green meadows extending between them, the matchbox country houses scattered across the valley and the cartridge cases of the bell towers.

The early morning was her time. She could sense the approach of day and always rose before the sun did, waking half an hour ahead of dawn in order to walk up onto the mountain. Behind their warm, cosy little shack, kept so clean that it positively gleamed, a stony track with yellow flowers along its edges wound its way up the slope. Crumbs of stone scattered downwards from under her feet, and in the few minutes it took to reach the summit Sasha sometimes fell several times, bruising her knees.

Lost in thought, Sasha wiped the damp breath of night off the window ledge with her sleeve. She had been dreaming of something gloomy, dark and bad, something that cancelled out the entire carefree life she had now, but the final traces of her alarming visions evaporated with the first touch of the cool wind on her skin. And now she couldn't be bothered to remember what had distressed her so badly in her dream. She had to hurry to the summit to greet the sun and then hurry home, slithering down the track – to cook breakfast and wake her father, to pack the bundle for his journey. And then, while he was hunting, Sasha would have the whole day to herself, and she could chase the clumsy dragonflies and flying cockroaches through the meadow flowers, as yellow as the patterned panels in the Metro carriages.

She tiptoed across the squeaky floorboards, opened the door a crack and laughed quietly.

It was years since Sasha's father had seen such a happy smile on her face, and he hated the idea of waking her up. His leg had swollen and gone numb. The bleeding hadn't stopped at all. They said that bites from the wandering dogs didn't heal.

Should he call her? But he'd been away from home for more than twenty-four hours – before he went to the garages, he'd decided to visit one of the high-rise, concrete-panel termite nests two blocks away from the station, clambered up to the sixteenth floor and then passed out. And all that time Sasha hadn't slept a wink – his daughter never went to sleep until he came back from his 'stroll'. 'Let her rest,' he thought. 'It's all lies. Nothing's going to happen.' He would have liked to know what she was seeing in her dream right now. He could never completely escape, even in his dreams. Only very rarely did his subconscious release him for a couple of hours for a visit to his carefree youth. Usually he was forced to wander through the familiar dead houses with their scraped-out interiors, and a good dream was one in which he suddenly discovered an untouched apartment full of appliances and books that had somehow miraculously survived intact. As he fell asleep, he always asked to be taken back into the past. He longed most of all to find himself in that time when he had just met Sasha's mother: when he was only twenty years old and already commanded the garrison of the station, which all its inhabitants still thought of as a temporary refuge, not the general barracks for a slave-labour mine in which they were serving a life sentence.

But instead of that he was tossed back into the more recent past, into the thick of those events five years ago. To the day that had sealed his fate and – even more terribly – his daughter's fate. In his rational mind he had accepted his defeat and his exile, but he only had to fall into a doze for his heart to start demanding revenge.

Once again he was standing in front of a line of his soldiers with their Kalashnikovs at the ready – in that situation, the Makarov pistol to which his officer's rank entitled him was worse than useless, except perhaps to shoot himself. Apart from the twenty or so machine-gunners behind his back, there was no one left at the station who was still loyal to him.

The crowd surged and seethed, growing larger and larger, swaying the barrier to and fro with dozens of hands. Then, at a flourish of some invisible conductor's baton, the ragged hubbub swelled into a coordinated chorus. So far they were only demanding his dismissal, but in another minute they would want his head.

This was no spontaneous demonstration: it was the work of provocateurs sent in from the outside. At this stage it was pointless even trying to identify them and liquidate them one by one. The only thing he could do now to halt the rebellion and maintain his grip on power was order his men to open fire on the crowd. It still wasn't too late for that.

His fingers clutched an invisible gun butt, the pupils of his eyes raced about under his swollen eyelids, his lips moved, uttering inaudible orders. The black puddle he was lying in spread wider and wider by the minute, as if it was drawing energy from his departing life.

'Where are they?'

Jerked out of the dark waters of oblivion, Homer started flapping about like a perch caught on a bright spinner, gasping convulsively and gaping at the brigadier with wild, crazy eyes. The massive, cyclopean bulks of the twilight guardians of Nagornaya were still there, crowding together in front of his eyes, reaching out to him with those long, articulated fingers that could easily tear off his leg or crush his ribs. They surrounded the old man every time he closed his eyes, and they melted away slowly and reluctantly when he opened them again. Homer tried to jump to his feet, but the hand that was gently squeezing his shoulder turned back into the steely hook that had dragged him out of his nightmare. Gradually moderating his breathing, he focused on the face furrowed with scars, on the dark eyes that glimmered with an oily mechanical glint... Hunter? Alive? The old man cautiously turned his head to the left, then to the right, afraid of finding himself back at the bewitched station.

No, they were in the middle of a clear, empty tunnel – the fog that blanketed the approaches to Nagornaya was barely even noticeable here. Hunter must have carried him for almost half a kilometre, Homer calculated feverishly. Feeling calmer now, he allowed himself go limp, but still asked again, to make sure:

'Where are they?'

'There's no one here. You're safe.'

'Those creatures... Did they attack me? Knock me out?' The old man grimaced and rubbed the smarting lump on the back of his head.

'I hit you. I had to, to stop your hysterics. You could have shot me, firing like that.'

Hunter finally released his vice-like grip, straightened up stiffly and ran one hand along his broad officer's belt. On the opposite side from the holster with his Stechkin revolver was a leather case, with some purpose that wasn't clear. The brigadier clicked a button and took out a flat copper flask. He shook it, opened it and took a large swallow, without offering Homer any. Then he squeezed his eyes shut for a second, apparently in pleasure. The old man felt a chilly shudder when he saw that the brigadier's left eye couldn't even close properly.

'But where's Ahmed? What happened to Ahmed?' asked Homer, suddenly remembering and starting to shake again.

'He's dead,' the brigadier said indifferently.

'He's dead,' the old man repeated resignedly.

When the monster tore his comrade's hand out of his, Homer had realised no living soul could ever wriggle out of those claws. He'd just been lucky that Nagornaya's choice had not fallen on him. The old man looked round again – somehow he couldn't believe straight away that Ahmed had disappeared forever. Homer looked at his own palm – it was torn and bleeding. He hadn't been able to hold on. He suddenly felt short of air.

'But Ahmed knew he was doomed,' he said quietly. 'Why did they take him, and not me?'

'There was a lot of life in him,' the brigadier replied. 'They feed on human lives.'

'It's not fair,' said the old man, shaking his head. 'He's got little children, he still has so much to live for! He had... And I'm just a wanderer, tumbleweed.'

'Well, would you eat dry moss?' asked Hunter, breaking off the

72

conversation and setting Homer on his feet in one swift movement. 'That's it, let's go. Or we might be too late.'

Trotting awkwardly after Hunter, who had moved up into a jog, the old man racked his brains, trying to figure out how they could have gone back to Nagornaya. The station had drugged them with its narcotic exhalations, like some predatory orchid, luring them back to itself. They hadn't turned back at all – Homer could have sworn to that. He was almost prepared to believe in the spatial distortions that he once loved to tell stories about to his gullible comrades in the watch, but then he realised it was all much simpler than that. The old man stopped and slapped himself on the forehead: the reversing tunnel! A few hundred metres beyond Nagornaya, between the bores of the right and left tunnels, a single-track line branched off, running off to the side at a narrow angle: it was for reversing the direction of trains. Feeling their way along the wall, first they'd got onto the parallel line, and then – when the wall disappeared – they'd turned back towards the station by mistake. 'Nothing mystical about it,' Homer thought uncertainly. But there was something else he wanted to get clear.

'Hey!' he called to Hunter. 'Wait!'

Hunter carried on marching forwards as if he was deaf, and the old man had to fight his breathlessness and pick up his own pace. Drawing level with the brigadier, Homer tried to glance into his eyes and blurted out:

'Why did you abandon us?'

'*I* abandoned *you*?'

The old man thought he heard a note of mockery in the passionless, metallic voice, and he bit his tongue. It was true, he and Ahmed were the ones who had fled from the station, leaving the brigadier to face the demons alone.

Remembering how furiously and yet fruitlessly Hunter had fought at Nagornaya, Homer couldn't rid himself of the impression that the inhabitants of the station had simply rejected the battle that the brigadier tried to impose on them. Were they afraid? Or did they sense a kindred spirit in him? The old man plucked up his courage: there was one question left, the simplest of all.

'Tell me, Hunter, back there in Nagornaya ... Why didn't they touch you?'

Several minutes passed in heavy, painful silence – Homer didn't dare to insist – until the brigadier finally gave him a brief, morose, almost inaudible answer.

'They couldn't stomach me.'

'Beauty will save the world,' her father used to joke.

Sasha would blush and hide the empty plastic packet that once contained powdered tea in the breast pocket of her overalls. This little square of plastic, which, against all the odds, had kept its aroma of green tea, was her greatest treasure. It was also a reminder that the universe was not confined to the headless trunk of their station with its four stumps of tunnel, dug at a depth of twenty metres below the graveyard city of Moscow. It was a magical portal that could transport Sasha through decades of time and across thousands of kilometres. And there was something else, something boundlessly important. In the damp climate here, any paper faded and withered as rapidly as a consumptive. The mould and putrefaction devoured more than just the books and magazines – they exterminated the past itself. Without images or records of events, human memory was left like a lame man without crutches – it stumbled about in confusion and lost its way.

But that little packet was made of plastic impervious to mildew and time. Sasha's father once told her it would be thousands of years before it started to decompose. That meant her descendants would be able to pass it on as an heirloom, she thought. It was an absolutely genuine picture, even if it was a miniature. The golden border, still as bright as the day the little packet came off the production line, framed a view that took Sasha's breath away. Sheer cliff faces submerged in dreamy mist, wide-spreading pine trees clinging to the almost vertical slopes, tumultuous waterfalls crashing down from the heights into the abyss, a scarlet glow in the sky and the sun just on the point of rising... Sasha had never seen anything more beautiful in her life.

She could sit for ages with the packet laid out on her palm, admiring it, and her gaze was drawn right into that early morning mist shrouding the distant mountains. Although she devoured all the books that her father found before she sold them on for cartridges, the words she read in them were not enough to describe the way she felt when she gazed at those centimetre-high cliffs and breathed the scent of those painted pine trees. The impossibility of this dream world – which was also what made it so incredibly attractive... The sweet yearning and eternal anticipation of what the sun would see for the first time... The endless re-examination – what could be hidden behind the idiotic block of colour with the name of the brand of tea on it? An unusual tree? An eagle's nest? A little house clinging to the slope, where she and her father could live?

Her father had brought Sasha the little packet when she was not yet five – and it was full then, a great rarity! He wanted to amaze his daughter with genuine tea. She drank it stoically, like medicine, but she was genuinely astounded by the plastic packet. At the time he had had to explain to her what the naïve picture showed: a generalised landscape from a mountainous Chinese province, perfectly suited for printing on packs of tea. But ten years later Sasha still examined her present just as wonderingly as on the day she first received it.

Her father, however, thought the packet was Sasha's pitiful substitute for the whole world. And when his daughter fell into a blissful trance, contemplating this daubed fantasy by some failed artist, he felt as if she was rebuking him for her own meagre, homeless life. He always tried to repress the impulse, but he could never hold out for long: barely even concealing his irritation, he asked Sasha for the hundredth time what she saw in a scrap of packaging from a gramme of tea dust.

And she hid the little masterpiece in the pocket of her overalls and answered awkwardly: 'Dad... I think it's so beautiful!'

If not for Hunter, who didn't stop for a second all the way to Nagatino, Homer would have taken three times as long to cover the distance. He would never have risked dashing self-assuredly through these tunnels like that.

Their team had paid a terrible toll for the passage through Nagornaya – but two out of three had survived. And all three would have survived, if they hadn't lost their way in the fog. The charge was no higher than usual; nothing had happened to them at Nakhimov Prospect or Nagornaya that hadn't happened there before.

So the problem lay in the stretches of tunnel that led to Tula? They were quiet now, but it was a bad silence, filled with tension. Hunter could sense danger hundreds of metres away, it was true, he could tell what to expect at stations he'd never been to before – but what if his intuition betrayed him down in these tunnels, just as it had betrayed many experienced soldiers before him?

Maybe it was Nagatino, moving closer with every step they took, that held the answer to the riddle? Struggling to restrain his wild thoughts, which were churning rapidly because he was walking too fast, Homer tried to imagine what could be waiting for them at the station he used to love so much. The old man with an unquenchable passion for collecting myths could easily picture the scene if the legendary Embassy of Satan had been set up at Nagatino or it had been gnawed away by rats migrating in search of food through their own tunnels, inaccessible to humans.

Yes, if the old man had found himself in these stretches of tunnel on his own, he would have moved far more slowly, but nothing would have made him turn back. During the years spent at Sebastopol, Homer had forgotten how to fear death. He had set off on this expedition, well aware that it could be his last adventure, and he was prepared to give all the time he had left for it.

But barely half an hour after his encounter with the monsters at Nagornaya, he had already forgotten his terror. And beyond that, he could sense a vague, timid stirring somewhere inside himself, somewhere in the depths of his soul. Something was being born, or awakening – the thing he had been waiting for, asking for. The thing he had sought for in his most dangerous expeditions, the thing he couldn't find at home.

So now he had a cogent reason for struggling with all his might to postpone death for a while. He couldn't allow himself to die before he had completed his work. The Final War had been much fiercer and more violent than any that preceded it – which was why it had been over in a matter of days. Three entire generations had passed since World War Two, and its final veterans had gone to their eternal sleep, leaving the living without any real fear of the memory of war. From being a form of mass insanity that deprived millions of people of everything that was human, it had once again become a standard instrument of politics. The stakes had been raised too fast, there simply wasn't enough time to make correct decisions. The taboo on the use of nuclear weapons had been brushed aside in passing, in the heat of the moment: the shotgun hung on the wall in the first act of the drama had been fired after all in the

76

penultimate act. And it didn't matter any longer who had pressed the fateful button first.

Almost all the major cities on earth had simultaneously been reduced to rubble and ash. Those few cities that were protected by anti-rocket defence shields also gave up the ghost, although at first sight they appeared almost untouched: hard radiation, military poisons and biological weapons wiped out their populations. The fragile radio contact established between the scattered handfuls of survivors was finally broken off only a few years later, and from then on for the inhabitants of the Metro the world ended at the frontier stations on the inhabited lines.

The Earth, which had seemed so thoroughly studied and so small, had once again become the boundless ocean of chaos and obscurity that it used to be in ancient times. One by one, the tiny islands of civilisation sank into its murky depths: deprived of oil and electric power, man rapidly reverted to a wild state. An era of stagnation was beginning.

For centuries scientists had lovingly restored the fabric of history from scraps of papyruses and parchments that they discovered, from fragments of legal codes and old folios. With the invention of printing and the appearance of newspapers, the presses had carried on weaving the fabric out of events covered by the newspapers. There were no gaps in the chronicles of the last two centuries: every gesture and every utterance of the leaders who controlled the destinies of the world had been thoroughly documented. Then suddenly, in a single instant all the world's printing presses had been destroyed or abandoned forever.

The looms of history had stopped weaving. Few had any interest in it, in a world with no future. The broad fabric came to a sudden end, leaving only a slim thread intact.

For the first few years after the catastrophe Homer – who was still Nikolai Ivanovich then – roamed through the overcrowded stations, desperately hoping to find his family in one of them. When hope departed, he carried on wandering, orphaned and lost, through the darkness of the Metro, not knowing what to do with himself in this afterlife. Existence had lost its meaning, the ball of thread that could have shown him, like Ariadne, the right path to follow through the endless labyrinth of tunnels, had fallen from his grasp.

Pining for times gone by, he started collecting magazines that allowed him to remember a bit, to dream a bit. As he pondered the question of whether the apocalypse could have been avoided, he became fascinated by the articles and analyses in newspapers. Then he started writing a bit himself, imitating the news articles, and describing events at the stations where he had been.

And so it happened that Nikolai Ivanovich picked up a new guiding thread to replace the one he had lost: he decided to become a chronicler, the author of a modern history – from the End of the World to his own end. His haphazard and purposeless collecting acquired meaning. Now he had to make a painstaking effort to restore the damaged fabric of time and continue weaving it by hand. Other people regarded Nikolai Ivanovich's passion as harmless eccentricity. He would happily hand over a day's ration for old newspapers, and at every station destiny took him to, he fitted out his own little corner, transforming it into a genuine archive. He joined the watches, because round the campfires at three hundred metres from the station, stern-faced men started telling tall stories, and Nikolai Ivanovich could fish information out of them about what was happening at the far end of the Metro. He collated and compared dozens of rumours in order to sift the facts out of them, then neatly filed the facts away in his school exercise books. The work was a good way of occupying his mind, but Nikolai Ivanovich was always haunted by the feeling that he was doing it in vain. After he died, the terse news reports collected with such loving care in the herbariums of his exercise books would simply crumble into dust without proper care. If he failed to come back from watch duty some day, his newspapers and chronicles would be used for lighting fires, and they wouldn't last long.

Nothing would be left of the pages that had darkened over the years but smoke and soot: the atoms would form new compounds and assume a different form. Matter is almost indestructible. But what he wanted to preserve for posterity, the elusive, ephemeral substance that dwelt on the newspaper pages, would vanish forever, completely. That was the way a man was made: the content of his school textbooks survived in his memory until the final examinations and no longer. And forgetting everything he had learned off by rote gave him a feeling of genuine relief. 'The memory of man is like sand in the desert,' thought Nikolai Ivanovich. 'Numbers, dates and the names of secondary political figures remain in it no longer than notes written on a sand dune with a stick. It all gets swept away and covered over, not a trace is left.'

In some miraculous fashion, the only things that were preserved were those capable of capturing the human imagination, setting the heart beating faster and engaging people's minds and feelings. The gripping story of a great hero and his love could outlive the story of an entire civilisation, infecting the human brain like a virus that was transmitted from fathers to children over hundreds of generations.

It was this realisation that led the old man to his deliberate transformation from a self-styled scholar into an alchemist, from Nikolai Ivanovich into Homer. And now his nights were devoted, not to compiling chronicles, but to searching for the formula of immortality. A storyline that would be as long-lived as the Odyssey, a hero with a lifespan to rival Gilgamesh. Homer would try to thread the knowledge he had accumulated onto this storyline. And in a world where all the paper had been squandered for heat, where the past was gladly sacrificed for a single moment in the present, the legend of a hero like that could infect people and rescue them from mass amnesia.

But the mystical formula wouldn't come to him. The hero refused to be born into the world. Rewriting newspaper articles could not possibly have prepared the old man for making myths. For breathing life into golems, transforming invention into enthralling reality. Torn-out and crumpled sheets of paper filled with uncompleted first chapters of the future saga, with unconvincing characters who lacked life, transformed his desktop into an abortion clinic. The only fruits of his nocturnal vigils were the dark circles under his eyes and the bite marks on his lips.

However, Homer refused to abandon his new destiny. He tried not to think that he was simply not born for this, that creating universes required a talent that he had been denied.

It's just the inspiration that's lacking – that was what he told himself. And where could he draw inspiration from in a stuffy station, locked into the routine of drinking tea at home and agricultural work? Even the watches and patrols were routine, and they took him on them less and less often because of his age. He needed a shake-up, an adventure, intense passions. Perhaps then the pressure would sweep clear the blocked channels in his mind and he would be able to create?

79

Even in the most difficult times people had never completely abandoned Nagatino. It wasn't really fit for habitation: nothing grew here and the exits to the surface were closed off. But many found the station useful for staying out of sight and lying low for a while, for sitting out disgrace or as a secluded spot with a lover. Right now, though, it was empty.

Hunter flew soundlessly up a ladder that should have creaked obstinately and stopped on the platform. Homer followed him, puffing and panting, looking round warily. The hall was dark, and dust hung in the air, shimmering silver in the beams of their flashlights. Scattered sparsely across the floor were the heaps of rags and cardboard on which visitors to Nagatino usually spent the night.

The old man leaned back against a column and slid down it slowly. There was a time when Nagatino, with its elegant coloured panels, assembled out of various kinds of marble, had been one of his favourite stations. But now, dark and lifeless, it resembled its former self no more than a ceramic photo on a gravestone resembles the person who had the photo taken for a passport a hundred years ago, never suspecting that he was not just gazing into a camera lens, but into eternity.

'Not a soul,' Homer murmured disappointedly.

'There is one,' the brigadier objected, pointing at him.

'I meant...' the old man began, but Hunter stopped him with a gesture of his hand.

At the far end of the platform, where the colonnade came to an end and even the brigadier's searchlight could barely reach, something was crawling out slowly onto the platform.

Homer tumbled over onto his side, braced his hands against the platform and got up awkwardly. Hunter's flashlight went out and the brigadier himself seemed to vanish into thin air. Sweating with fear, the old man fumbled at the safety catch and pressed the trembling butt of his automatic hard into his shoulder. He heard the faint pops of two shots in the distance. Feeling bolder, he stuck his head out from behind the column and then hurried forward.

Hunter was standing fully erect in the centre of the platform, with an amorphous, wizened figure squirming pitifully at his feet. It looked as if it had been assembled out of cardboard boxes and rags, and barely even resembled a human being at all, but it was one – ageless and sexless, so dirty that only the eyes could clearly be made out on its face, it whined inarticulately and tried to crawl away from the brigadier towering up over it. It looked as if it had been shot in both legs.

'Where are the people? Why isn't there anyone here?' asked Hunter, setting his boot on the train of tattered, stinking rags trailing after the tramp.

'They've all gone . . . They left me. I'm all alone here,' the tramp hissed, scraping at the slippery granite with his hands, but not moving from the spot.

'Where did they go to?'

'Tula . . .'

'What's happening there?' Homer put in as he came up to them.

'How should I know?' the filthy creature said with a crooked grin. 'Everyone who went there just disappeared. Ask them. But I don't have any strength for staggering through the tunnels. I'll die here.'

'Why did they go?' the brigadier persisted.

'They were frightened, boss. The station's deserted, they decided to break out. No one came back.'

'No one at all?' asked Hunter, raising his gun barrel.

'No one . . . Only one,' said the tramp, correcting himself when he spotted the raised gun and shrivelling up like an ant in the sun's rays under a lens. 'He was going to Nagornaya. I was asleep. Maybe I imagined it.'

'When?'

'I haven't got a watch,' said the tramp, shaking his head. 'Maybe yesterday, maybe a week ago.'

The questions had dried up, but the pistol barrel was still staring into the tramp's eyes. Hunter stopped speaking, as if his spring had suddenly run down. And he was breathing strangely, as if the conversation with the tramp had cost him too much of his strength.

'Can I . . . ?' the tramp began.

'Here, eat that!' the brigadier snarled, and before Homer realised what was happening, he squeezed the trigger twice.

Black blood from the bullet holes in his forehead flooded the unfortunate victim's staring eyes. Flattened against the ground by the bullets, he disintegrated again into a heap of rags and cardboard. Without looking up, Hunter inserted four more cartridges into the clip of his Stechkin and jumped down onto the tracks.

'We'll find out everything for ourselves soon enough,' he shouted to Homer.

Ignoring his feeling of disgust, the old man leaned down over the body, took a scrap of material and covered the tramp's shattered head with it.

'Why did you kill him?' he asked feebly.

'Ask yourself that,' Hunter replied in a hollow voice.

Now, even if he clenched all his willpower into a single tight fist, all he could do was raise and lower his eyelids. It was strange that he'd woken up at all . . . During the hour he'd been oblivious, the numbness had crept across his entire body like a crust of ice. His tongue was stuck to the roof of his mouth, and his chest seemed to be weighed down by something massively heavy. He couldn't even say goodbye to his daughter, and that was the only thing worth coming round for, without following that old battle all the way to the end.

Sasha wasn't smiling any longer. Now she was dreaming of something alarming, curled up tight on her makeshift bed and hugging herself, with a scowl on her face. Ever since she was a little child her father had woken her if he saw she was being tormented by nightmares, but now it took all his strength just to blink slowly.

And then even that became too exhausting.

To hold out until Sasha woke up he would have to carry on fighting. He had never stopped fighting for over twenty years, every day, every minute – and he was deadly tired of it. Tired of battling, tired of hiding, tired of hunting. Arguing, asserting, hoping, lying.

Only two desires remained in his fading consciousness: he wanted to look into Sasha's eyes at least one more time, and he wanted to find peace. But he couldn't manage either. Alternating with reality, images from the past starting flickering in front of his eyes again. He had to take a final decision. Break or be broken. Punish or repent . . . The guardsmen had closed ranks. Every one of them was loyal to him personally. Every one of them was willing to die now, torn to pieces by the mob, or to fire on unarmed people. He was the commander of the last unconquered station, the president of a confederation that no longer existed. For them his authority was indisputable, he was infallible, and any order he gave would be carried out immediately, without a second thought. He would take responsibility for everything, just as he had always done.

If he backed down now, the station would sink into anarchy, and then it would be annexed by the Red Empire that was expanding so fast, frothing over its original boundaries, subjugating more and more new territory. If he ordered his men to open fire on the demonstrators, he would retain his grasp on power – for a while. Or perhaps forever, if he didn't balk at mass executions and torture.

He raised his automatic and a moment later the line of men repeated his movement. Along the line of the gun's sight he saw a raging mob, not hundreds of people who had gathered together, but a faceless jumble of humanity. Grinning teeth, gaping eyes, clenched fists.

He clattered the breech of his gun and the line of men did the same.

It was time at last to take destiny by the scruff of the neck. Pointing the barrel of his gun upward, he pressed the trigger and whitewash showered down from the ceiling. The mob fell silent for a moment. He signalled for the soldiers to lower their weapons and took a step forward. It was his final choice.

And at last memory released him.

Sasha was still sleeping. He drew a final breath and tried to glance at her one last time, but he couldn't even raise his eyelids. And then, instead of imperishable, eternal darkness, he saw before him an impossibly blue sky – as clear and bright as his daughter's eyes.

'Halt!'

Homer was so startled, he almost jumped and raised his hands in the air, but just checked himself in time. He was the only one that nasal yell through a megaphone took by surprise – the brigadier wasn't surprised in the least: huddling down like a cobra before it strikes, he surreptitiously pulled the heavy sub-machine-gun out from behind his back.

Hunter still hadn't replied to the old man's question, in fact he'd stopped talking to him at all. To Homer the one-and-a-half-kilometre journey from Nagatino to Tula had seemed as endless as the road to Golgotha. He knew this stretch of tunnel would almost certainly lead him to his death, and it was hard to force himself to walk more quickly. At least now there was time to prepare, and

Homer had occupied his mind with memories. He thought about Elena, chided himself for his egotism and begged her forgiveness. He recalled with a luminous sadness that magical day on Tver Street under the light summer rain. He regretted not having made any arrangements for his newspapers before he left. He prepared himself to die – to be torn apart by monsters, devoured by immense rats, poisoned by pollution . . . What other explanations could he find for the fact that Tula had been transformed into a black hole that sucked everything into it and let nothing back out?

And now, when he heard a normal human voice as they approached Tula, he didn't know what to think. Had the station simply been captured? But who could grind several assault units from Sebastopol into dust, who would have exterminated all the tramps who converged on the station out of the tunnels and not let even women or old men go?

'Thirty steps forward!' said the distant voice.

It sounded incredibly familiar, so familiar that if Homer only had time, he could have identified who it belonged to. Could it be one of the Sebastopolites?

Cradling his Kalashnikov in his arms, Hunter started meekly counting out the steps: at thirty of the brigadier's steps, the old man had taken fifty. Ahead of him he could vaguely make out a barricade that seemed to be crudely assembled out of random items. And for some reason its defenders weren't using any light.

'Turn out the flashlights!' someone commanded from behind the ragged heap. 'One of you two – another twenty steps forward.'

Hunter clicked the switch of his flashlight and moved on. Left alone again, Homer didn't dare disobey the voice. In the sudden darkness he squatted down on a sleeper, as far out of harm's way as possible, felt warily for the wall and pressed himself against it.

The brigadier's steps fell silent at the measured distance. Homer heard voices: someone interrogating Hunter in a voice he couldn't make out and the brigadier barking abrupt replies. The situation was heating up: tense, but restrained tones were replaced by abuse and threats. Hunter seemed to be demanding something from the invisible guards, and they were refusing to do as he wanted.

Now they were shouting at each other, almost at the top of their voices, and Homer thought he would be able to make out the words any moment now. But he heard just one word clearly, the final one:

'Judgement!'

And then an automatic started stuttering, interrupting the men's argument, followed by the rumble of an army Pecheneg machine-gun, spitting a burst of fire in Homer's direction. The old man threw himself on the ground, jerking back the breech of his gun, not knowing if he ought to fire, and at whom. But it was all over before he could even take aim.

In the short pauses between the chattering of the guns, the depths of the tunnel echoed to a long, drawn-out scraping sound that Homer could never possibly have confused with anything else. The sound of a hermetic door closing. Confirming his guess, a steel slab weighing tons upon tons slammed home into its groove ahead of him, cutting off the shouting and the rumble of shots at a stroke.

Shutting off the only way out into the Greater Metro.

Severing Sebastopol's final hope.

CHAPTER 6

On the Other Side

A moment later Homer was willing to believe he had imagined everything – the amorphous outlines of the barricade at the end of the tunnel and the voice that had seemed so familiar, distorted by the old megaphone. All sounds had been extinguished together with the light, and now he felt like a condemned man with a bag over his head, ready for execution. In the impenetrable darkness and sudden silence, the entire world seemed to have disappeared: Homer reached up and touched his own face, trying to convince himself that he hadn't dissolved into this cosmic blackness.

Then he gathered his wits, fumbled around for his flashlight and launched the trembling beam forward – to where the invisible battle had been played out only minutes earlier. About thirty metres from the spot where he had waited out the fight, the tunnel came to a dead end, cut off by an immense steel shutter that filled its entire height and breadth, like the fallen blade of a guillotine.

His hearing hadn't deceived him: someone really had activated the hermetic door. Although Homer knew about it, he didn't think it could still be used – but apparently it could.

With his eyes weakened by all his paperwork, Homer didn't immediately spot the human figure pressed up against the wall of metal. He held his automatic out in front of him and backed away, thinking it must be one of the men *from the other side* who had been lost overboard, but then he recognised the figure as Hunter.

The brigadier wasn't moving. Streaming with perspiration, the old man hobbled towards him, expecting to see streaks of blood on the rusty metal. But there weren't any. Although he had been fired on by a machine-gun at point blank range in the middle of a bare, empty tunnel, Hunter was unhurt. He had his flattened and mutilated ear pressed up against the metal, sucking in sounds that only he could hear.

'What happened?' Homer asked cautiously as he walked up.

The brigadier didn't even notice him. He was whispering something, but whispering to himself, repeating words spoken by someone who was *there*, behind the closed door. Several minutes went by before he tore himself away from that wall and turned to Homer.

'We're going back.'

'What happened?' Homer asked again.

'There are bandits in there. We must have reinforcements.'

'Bandits?' the old man exclaimed in bewilderment. 'But I thought I heard . . .'

'Tula has been captured by the enemy. We have to take it. We need men with flamethrowers.'

'Why flamethrowers?' asked Homer, completely confused now.

'To make certain. We're going back.' Hunter swung round and strode off.

Before the old man followed him, he inspected the hermetic door carefully and pressed his ear to the cold steel, hoping that he could listen to a snatch of conversation too. Silence . . .

Homer realised he didn't believe the brigadier. Whoever this enemy was that had captured the station, the way he behaved was absolutely inexplicable. Why would anyone think of using hermetic doors to protect themselves against just two men? What kind of bandits would engage in long negotiations with armed men at a border post, instead of simply riddling them with bullets as they approached?

And finally, what was the meaning of that final, sinister word barked by those mysterious sentries? 'Judgement'?

There is nothing more valuable than human life, Sasha's father used to tell her. And for him those were not merely empty words, not just some bland truism. But there was a time when her father didn't think that way at all – there were good reasons why he became the youngest military commander on the entire line.

At the age of twenty years, you take killing and death far less seriously, and life itself seems like a game that you can start all over again if anything happens. It is no coincidence that the armies of the world were always made up of yesterday's schoolboys. And all these youngsters playing at war were commanded by someone who could see thousands of people fighting and being killed as no more than blue and red arrows on maps, someone who could take the decision to sacrifice a company or a regiment without thinking about the torn-off legs, ripped-out intestines and shattered skulls.

There was a time when her father also regarded his enemies and even himself with disdain, when he astounded everyone with his readiness to take on missions that should have cost him his life. But he wasn't reckless, and his actions were always precisely calculated. Intelligent and assiduous, at the same time he was indifferent to life, he had no sense of its reality, he didn't think about consequences and wasn't burdened with a conscience. No, he never fired at women and children, but he executed deserters in person and was always the first to storm the machine-gun nests. He was also almost insensitive to pain. Basically, he couldn't give a damn for anything. Until he met Sasha's mother.

She hooked him, so accustomed to his victories, with her own indifference. His only weakness – his vanity – which had driven him on against the machine-guns, launched him into a new, desperate assault that unexpectedly became a protracted siege.

He had never needed to make any special effort in love before: women themselves cast down their banners at his feet. Debauched by their easy acquiescence, he always sated his appetite for his latest girlfriend before he could fall in love with her and lost all interest in his conquest after the very first night. His relentless insistence and his fame blinded girls' eyes, and very few of them even tried to apply the age-old strategy of making a man wait until they got to know him.

But she found him boring. She wasn't impressed by his decorations and titles, his triumphs in battle and love. She didn't respond to his glances, she shook her head at his jokes. And he started taking the conquest of this young woman as a serious challenge. More serious than subjugating the nearby stations.

She was supposed to be just one more notch on his gun butt, but soon he realised that the prospect of intimacy with her was receding – and also becoming less important. Her attitude made the chance to spend even an hour together during the day feel like a real achievement – and she only went that far in order to torment him a little. She doubted the value of his accomplishments and mocked his principles. She chided him for his heartlessness. She shook his confidence in his strength and his goals.

He put up with all of it. But more than that – he enjoyed it. With her he started reflecting on things, hesitating over decisions. And then he started feeling things: helplessness – because he didn't know how to get close to this girl; regret for every minute not spent with her; and even fear – the fear of losing her, without ever having won her. Love. And she rewarded him with a sign. A silver ring.

Finally, when he had completely forgotten how to manage without her, she yielded to him.

A year later Sasha was born – which meant that now there were two lives he could no longer treat with disdain, and he himself no longer had any right to be killed. At the age of only twenty-five, when you command the most powerful army in the observable part of the world, it's hard to rid yourself of the feeling that your orders can stop the world itself from turning. No tremendous, supernatural might is required for taking away people's lives, but the power to give back life to the dead is granted to no one.

This truth was borne in on him cruelly when his wife died of tuberculosis and he was helpless to save her. After that something in him was broken. Sasha was only four years old at the time, but she remembered her mother very well. And she remembered the terrible, tunnel-black void that was left behind after her mother was gone. A gaping abyss – the closeness of death – opened up in her little world, and she looked down into it often. The edges of the abyss knitted together only very slowly. It was two or three years before Sasha stopped calling out to her mother in her sleep.

Her father still called out to her sometimes, even now.

Maybe Homer was approaching things from the wrong angle. If the hero of his epic refused to reveal himself, maybe he should start with the hero's future beloved? Tempt him out with her beauty and youthful freshness?

If Homer discreetly described her charms first, then maybe the hero would step out of non-existence to meet her. For their love to be perfect, he would have to be her ideal complement, which meant he would have to appear in the epic complete and fully formed.

Their curves and contours, their very thoughts would have to match each other as precisely as fragments of the shattered stained-glass panels at Novoslobodskaya Station. After all, they also were once parts of a single whole, so it was their destiny to be reunited. Homer couldn't see anything wrong in appropriating this effective plotline from the long-departed classics. But although the solution looked simple, there were still problems: sculpting a living girl out of paper and ink proved to be a task beyond Homer's power. And he probably couldn't write convincingly about feelings any longer either.

His present relationship with Elena was filled with the tender feelings of old age, but they had met each other too late to abandon the past completely in their love. At that age people strive to appease their loneliness, not quench their passion.

Nikolai Ivanovich's one true love had been entombed up on the surface. In the decades that had passed since then, all the details of her appearance, apart from one, had faded away, he couldn't have described the affair from life any longer. And in any case, there had been nothing heroic about that relationship.

On the same day when Moscow was hit by the nuclear deluge, Nikolai was offered the chance to become a driver, replacing old Serov, who had been retired. His pay would almost double, and they even gave him a few days off before his promotion took effect. He phoned his wife, who said she would bake an apple cake, and then she went out to buy champagne, taking the children along for the walk.

But he had to finish his shift.

Nikolai Ivanovich climbed into the cabin of the locomotive as its future master, a happily married man right at the very beginning of a tunnel that led off into a miraculously bright future. In the next half hour he aged twenty years in one fell swoop, arriving at the final station a broken man, with no one and nothing. Perhaps that was why every time he came across a train that had survived by some miracle, he was always overwhelmed by the desire to take his legitimate place in the driver's seat, stroke the control panel with a master's hand and glance out through the windscreen at the lacework pattern of tunnel liners. To imagine that the train could still be made to work.

That it could be put into reverse.

No doubt about it, the brigadier definitely created a special kind of field round himself, a field that diverted any kind of danger away from him. And what was more, he seemed to know it. The journey back to Nagornaya took them less than an hour. The line didn't offer them any resistance at all.

Homer had always felt that the scouts and shuttle traders from Sebastopol, and all the other ordinary people who plucked up the courage to enter the tunnels, were alien organisms in the Metro's body, microbes that had infiltrated its circulatory system. The moment they stepped beyond the frontiers of the stations, the air around them became irritated and inflamed, reality ruptured and all the incredible creatures ranged against man by the Metro suddenly appeared out of nowhere.

But Hunter wasn't an extraneous body in the dark stretches of tunnel, he didn't trigger the Leviathan's resentment as he journeyed through its blood vessels. Sometimes he would switch off his flashlight, becoming just another patch of the darkness that filled the tunnel's space, and seemed to be caught up by invisible currents that carried him onward twice as fast. Struggling with all his might to keep up with the brigadier, Homer shouted after him, and then Hunter came to his senses, stopped and waited for the old man.

On the way back they were even allowed to pass through Nagornaya in peace. The murky vapours had dispersed, the station was sleeping. They could see every centimetre of it lying open to view now, and it was impossible to imagine where it could have concealed those spectral giants. Just an ordinary, abandoned station: incrustations of salt on the damp ceiling, a soft, feathery bed of dust spread out across the platform, obscenities scribbled with charcoal on the smoky walls. But then other details caught the eye: strange scrapes left on the floor by some frantic, scrabbling dance, crusty, reddish-brown spots on the columns, ceiling lights that looked scraped and battered, as if someone had rubbed hard against them. Nagornaya flashed by and they went flying on. As long as Homer could keep up with the brigadier, he felt as if he too were enclosed in a magical bubble that rendered him invulnerable. The old man was amazed at himself – where was he getting the energy for such a long forced march?

But he had no breath left for making conversation. And in any case, Hunter no longer condescended to answer his questions. For the hundredth time in that long day Homer wondered why the taciturn and pitiless brigadier needed him at all, if he spent all his time trying to forget about him.

The foul smell of Nakhimov Prospect crept up and enveloped them. This was a station that Homer would gladly have dashed through as quickly as possible, but instead the brigadier slowed down. The old man was almost overcome by the stench, even in his gas mask, but Hunter sniffed it in, as if he could distinguish specific notes in the Prospect's oppressive, choking bouquet of odours.

This time the corpse-eaters dispersed respectfully as they advanced, abandoning half-gnawed bones and dropping scraps of flesh out of their mouths. Hunter walked to the precise centre of the hall and up onto a low heap, sinking calf-deep in flesh. He cast a long, slow glance round the station and then, still dissatisfied, abandoned his suspicions and moved on, without finding what he was looking for.

But Homer found it.

Slipping and falling onto his hands and knees, he startled away a young corpse-eater who was eviscerating a soaking-wet bulletproof vest. Spotting the Sebastopol uniform helmet that went tumbling aside, Homer was blinded by the condensation that instantly coated the lenses of his gas mask on the inside.

Repressing the impulse to gag and puke, Homer crept over to the bones and raked through them, hoping to find the soldier's ID tag. But instead he spotted a little notepad, smeared with thick crimson blood. It opened immediately at the last page, with the words: 'Don't storm the station, no matter what'.

Her father had got her out of the habit of crying when she was still little, but now she had no other answer for fate. The tears streamed down her face of their own accord and a bleak, high-pitched whine rose up from her chest. She realised straight away what had happened, but it took her hours to come to terms with it.

Had he called for her help? Had he tried to tell her something important before he died? She couldn't remember the exact moment when she sank into sleep and wasn't entirely sure that she was awake now. After all, there could be a world where her father hadn't died, couldn't there? Where she hadn't killed him with her weakness and egotism.

Sasha held her father's hand – already cold, but still soft – between her palms, as if she was trying to warm it, trying to persuade him, and herself, that he would find a car, and they would go up onto the surface and get into it, and drive away. And he would laugh like the day when he brought home that radio with the music CDs.

At first her father sat there with his back leaning against the column and his chin braced against his chest – he could have been taken for someone in a doze. But then his body started slowly slipping down into the puddle of congealed blood, as if it was tired of pretending to be alive and didn't want to deceive Sasha any longer.

The wrinkles that always furrowed her father's face had almost completely smoothed out now.

She let go of his hand, helped him lie more comfortably and covered him from head to foot with a tattered blanket. She had no other way of burying him. She would have liked to take her father up onto the surface and leave him lying there, gazing up at the sky that would turn bright and clear again one day. But long before that his body would become the prey of the eternally hungry beasts that roamed about up there.

Here on their station no one would touch him. There was no danger to be expected from the deadly southern tunnels – nothing could survive in there except the winged cockroaches. And to the north the tunnel broke off at a rusty, half-ruined Metro bridge with only a single track still intact.

At the other end of the bridge there were people, but none of them would ever dream of crossing it out of mere curiosity. They all knew what was on the far side: a lookout station on the edge of a scorched wilderness – with two doomed exiles living in it.

Her father wouldn't have allowed her to stay here alone, and there wasn't any point in it anyway. But Sasha also knew that no matter how far she ran, no matter how desperately she tried to break out of the torture cell she had been condemned to, she would never be completely free of it.

'Dad, forgive me, please,' she sobbed, knowing that she could never earn his forgiveness.

Sasha took the silver ring off his finger and put it in the pocket of her overalls. She picked up the cage with the quiet, subdued rat and stumbled off to the north, leaving a trail of bloody footsteps behind her on the granite. When she climbed down onto the rails and walked into the tunnel, an unusual omen occurred at the empty station that was now a funeral bark. A long tongue of flame emerged from the mouth of the opposite tunnel, straining towards her father's body – but it couldn't reach it and retreated back into the dark depths, reluctantly conceding that Sasha's father had a right to his peace now.

'They're coming back! They're coming back!'

Istomin took the telephone receiver away from his ear and gazed at it distrustfully, as if it was some animate creature that had just told him a ridiculous fairytale.

'Who's coming back?'

Denis Mikhailovich jumped up off his chair, spilling his tea, which settled on his trousers in an embarrassing dark stain. He cursed the tea and repeated the question.

'Who's coming back?' Istomin repeated mechanically into the receiver.

'The brigadier and Homer,' the receiver crackled. 'Ahmed was killed.'

Vladimir Ivanovich blotted his bald patch with his handkerchief and wiped his temple under the rubber strap of his piratical eye patch. Reporting soldiers' deaths to relatives was one of his responsibilities. Without waiting for the operator to switch the line, he stuck his head out of the door and shouted to his adjutant:

'Bring both of them to me! And tell the orderlies to set the table!'

He walked across his office, straightened the photos hanging on the wall, whispered something in front of the map and turned to Denis Mikhailovich, who was sitting there with his arms crossed, blatantly grinning.

'Volodya, you're just like some girl before a date,' the colonel chuckled.

'I see you're excited too,' the station commandant snapped back, nodding at the colonel's wet trousers.

'Why should I worry? I've got everything ready. Two assault units assembled, they can be mobilised in twenty-four hours.' Denis Mikhailovich lovingly stroked the light-blue beret lying on the desk, then picked it up and stuck it on his head to make himself look more official.

In the reception office, feet started scurrying about, knives and forks jangled, and an orderly held up a dewy bottle of spirits through the crack of the door. Istomin waved him away – later, all of that later! Then at last he heard a familiar booming voice, the door flew open and the opening was filled by a broad, massive figure. Hovering behind the brigadier's back was that old storyteller he'd dragged along with him for some reason.

'Welcome back!' said Istomin, sitting down in his chair, then getting up and sitting down again.

'What's out there?' snapped the colonel.

The brigadier shifted his dark, heavy gaze from one man to the other and spoke to the station commandant.

'Tula's been occupied by nomads. They've slaughtered everyone.'

'All our men too?' asked Denis Mikhailovich, raising his shaggy eyebrows.

'As far as I can tell. We got as far as the entrance of the station, there was a fight, and they sealed it off.'

'They closed the hermetic door?' said Istomin, half-rising out of his chair and clutching the edge of the desk with his fingers. 'So now what do we do?'

'Storm them,' the brigadier and the colonel rasped simultaneously.

'We can't storm them!' Homer suddenly chimed in from the reception office.

She simply had to wait for the agreed time. If she hadn't got the day wrong, the trolley should appear out of the damp darkness of the night very soon now. Every additional minute spent here on the edge of the cliff, where the tunnel emerged from the thickness of the earth like a vein from a slashed wrist, cost her a year of her life. But the only choice she had now was to wait. At the other end of the interminably long bridge she would run into a locked hermetic door that was only unlocked from the inside – once a week, for market day.

Today Sasha had nothing to sell, but she needed to buy much more than ever before. But she couldn't care less now what the men on the trolley might ask for in exchange for letting her back into the land of the living. Her father's chilly indifference in death had been communicated to her.

Sasha used to dream so much about going to another station some day with her father, to a place where they could be surrounded by people, where she could make friends with someone, meet someone special.... She used to ask her father about his young days, not just because she wanted to revisit her own bright childhood, but because she was secretly setting herself, as she was now, in her mother's place, setting some nebulously handsome man with shifting features in her father's place and awkwardly imagining love to herself. She worried that she wouldn't be able to find any common ground with other people if they really went back to the Greater Metro. What would they have to talk to her about?

But now there were only hours, or perhaps minutes, left to go until the ferry arrived, and she couldn't give a damn for the other people – the women or the men – and even the thought of returning to a human existence seemed like a betrayal of her father. She would have agreed to spend the rest of her life at their station, without hesitating for a single moment, if that could have helped to save him.

The candle stub in the glass jar fluttered in its death agony and she transferred the flame to a new wick. On one of his trips to the surface her father had found an entire crate of wax candles, and Sasha always carried several of them in the pockets of her overalls. She would have liked to think their bodies were like candles, and a little particle of her father had been transferred to her after his light was extinguished.

Would the men on the trolley see her signal in the mist? Before this she had always guessed the time right, so she never had to waste an extra moment lingering outside. He father forbade her do that, and the swollen goitre on his throat was enough of a warning in itself. At the cliff edge Sasha usually felt as agitated as a trapped shrew, gazing around anxiously and only occasionally daring to go as far as the first span of the bridge, in order to look down from it at the black river flowing past below.

But she had too much time. Huddling up and shuddering in the damp, chilly autumn wind, Sasha took several steps forward, and the crumbling summits of high-rise apartment blocks appeared behind the gaunt trees. Something huge splashed in the oily, viscous river, and in the distance unknown monsters groaned in almost human voices.

Then suddenly their wailing was joined by a plaintive, dismal creaking.

Sasha jumped to her feet, raising her lamp high in the air, and they answered from the bridge with a stealthy, slippery beam of light. A decrepit old trolley was moving towards her, barely able to force its way through the dense white gloom, thrusting the wedge of its feeble headlamp into the night and prising its way through. The girl backed away: it wasn't the usual trolley. It strained its way along jerkily, as if every turn of its wheels cost the man working the levers a great effort.

Eventually it shuddered to a halt about ten steps away from Sasha and a tall, fat man wrapped in tarpaulin jumped down off the frame onto the stone chips. Demonic spots of reflected light danced in the lenses of his gas mask, concealing his eyes from Sasha. In one hand the man was clutching an ancient army Kalashnikov with a wooden butt.

'I want to leave here,' Sasha declared, thrusting out her chin.

'Lea-eave,' the tarpaulin scarecrow echoed, drawling the sound in either surprise or mockery. 'And what have you got to sell?'

'I haven't got anything left,' she said, staring hard into those blazing eye sockets bound in iron.

'Everyone has something that can be taken, especially a woman,' the ferryman grunted, then he had a thought. 'Are you going to leave your daddy then?'

'I haven't got anything left,' Sasha repeated, lowering her eyes.

'So he croaked after all,' said the mask, sounding relieved, but also disappointed. 'And he did right. Or he'd have been upset now.' The barrel of the automatic caught the shoulder strap of Sasha's overalls and slowly dragged it downwards.

'Don't you dare,' she shouted hoarsely, jerking back.

The jar with the candle fell, shattering on a rail, and the darkness instantly licked out the flame.

'No one comes back from here, can't you understand that?' The scarecrow gazed at her indifferently with its blank, dead lenses. 'Your body won't even be enough to cover the cost of my journey in one direction. Let's say I accept it in payment of your father's debt.'

The automatic twirled in his hands, swinging round with the butt forward, and struck her on the temple, mercifully snuffing out the light of her consciousness.

*

After Nakhimov Prospect Hunter had kept Homer close beside him, and the old man had no chance to examine the notepad properly. The brigadier was suddenly thoughtful and considerate: not only did he try not to leave his companion too far behind, he actually walked in step with him, although he had to hold himself back to do it. A couple of times he stopped, as if to see whether anyone was dogging their footsteps. But as the glaring beam of his searchlight was turned backwards, it always ran across Homer's face, making the old man feel like he was in a torture chamber. He swore and blinked as he struggled to recover, sensing the brigadier's sharp eyes creeping all over his body, probing him, searching for what he had found at the Prospect. Nonsense! Of course Hunter couldn't have seen anything, he was too far away at that moment. He'd probably simply sensed the change in Homer's mood and suspected him of something. But every time their gazes met, the old man broke out in a sweat. The little bit he had managed to read in the notepad was more than enough to make him feel doubts about the brigadier.

It was a diary.

Some of the pages were stuck together with dried blood and Homer didn't touch them: he was afraid of tearing them with his stiff, tense fingers. The entries on the first pages were incoherent – the author couldn't even keep his letters under control, and his thoughts galloped in a way that made it impossible to keep up with them.

'We got through Nagornaya with no losses,' the diary stated, and then immediately skipped on: 'Tula is in chaos. There's no way out to the Metro, Hansa is blocking it. We can't go back home.'

Homer leafed forward a bit, watching out of the corner of his eye as the brigadier came down off his grave mound and walked towards him. The old man realised that Hunter mustn't be allowed to get his hands on the diary. But just before he thrust the notepad into his knapsack, Homer managed to read: 'We have brought the situation under control and appointed a commandant . . .' And then immediately: 'Who'll be the next to die?'

And another thing: framed in a little square above the dangling question was a date. From the withered state of the notepad's pages, anyone would have thought the events described in the diary must be at least a decade old, but the figures indicated that the entry had been made only a few days ago.

With long-forgotten agility, the old man's ossifying brain fitted together the scattered pieces of the mosaic: the mysterious wanderer seen by the miserable tramp at Nagatino, the guard's voice that seemed familiar at the hermetic door, the words 'We can't go back home...' A complete picture began taking shape in front of his eyes. Maybe the scribble on the stuck-together pages could fill in the meaning of all the other strange events?

What was absolutely certain was that Tula had not been captured by bandits; something far more complicated and mysterious was going on there. And Hunter had spent a quarter of an hour questioning the sentries at the gates of the station – so he knew that just as well as Homer did.

That was precisely why Homer must not show him the notepad.

And it was why Homer dared to oppose him openly at the meeting in Istomin's office.

'We can't do that,' he said.

Hunter turned his head in Homer's direction as slowly as a battleship training its main gun on the target. Istomin shifted his chair backwards, then decided to come out from behind his desk anyway. The colonel screwed his face up wearily.

'We can't blow up the hermetic door, there's ground water all around, the line would be flooded instantly. The whole of Tula Station is held together by no more than a lick and a promise, they're always praying it won't spring a leak anywhere. And the parallel tunnel, you know yourselves... It's ten years since...' Homer went on.

'So do we just knock and wait for them to open up?' Denis Mikhailovich enquired.

'Well, there's always the bypass route,' Istomin reminded him.

Astounded by that suggestion, the colonel started coughing violently and furiously accusing his superior of wanting to cripple and kill his best men. And then the brigadier fired a broadside.

'Tula has to be cleaned out. The situation requires the extermination of everyone there. Not one of your men is left. They've all been finished off. If you don't want to suffer any more losses, it's the only possible decision. I know what I'm talking about. I have information.'

The final words were clearly intended for Homer. They made the old man feel like a naughty little puppy dog being shaken by the scruff of the neck to bring him to his senses.

'Well, since the tunnel is sealed on our side,' said Istomin, tugging down his tunic, 'there is only one way to get into Tula. From the other side, through Hansa. But we can't take armed men through that way, it's out of the question.'

'I'll find men,' Hunter said dismissively, and the colonel started.

'Just to get to Hansa, you have to go through two stretches of tunnel on the Kakhovka Line as far as Kashira Station.'

'What of it?' asked the brigadier, crossing his arms on his chest.

'In the region of Kashira the background radiation shoots off the scale,' the colonel explained. 'A fragment of a warhead fell nearby. It didn't explode, but it's quite bad enough as it is. Every second man who gets a dose of it dies within a month. Even now.'

An ominous silence fell. Homer took advantage of the hitch to initiate a furtive withdrawal – tactical, of course – from Istomin's office. Eventually, Vladimir Ivanovich, apparently afraid that the uncontrollable brigadier would go off to demolish the hermetic door at Tula anyway, made a confession.

'We have protective suits. But only two. You can take the most able-bodied soldier you can find, anyone. We'll wait...' He glanced round at Denis Mikhailovich. 'What else can we do?'

'Let's go over to the lads,' the colonel said with a sigh. 'We'll have a talk with them and you can choose yourself a partner.'

'No need,' said Hunter, with a shake of his head. 'Homer's the one I want.'

CHAPTER 7

The Voyage

As the trolley passed through the long section of tunnel marked with bright-yellow paint on the floor and walls, the helmsman couldn't pretend any longer not to hear the radiation dosimeter clicking faster and faster. He took hold of the brake and muttered apologetically.

'Comrade Colonel, we can't go any further without protection.'

'Let's go just another hundred metres,' Denis Mikhailovich suggested gently, turning to face him. 'I'll release you from watch duty for a week afterwards, as a hazard bonus.'

'But this is the extreme limit, Comrade Colonel,' the helmsman whined, still not daring to reduce speed.

'Stop,' Hunter ordered. 'We'll walk on from here. He's quite right, the radiation level is really getting too high.'

The brake blocks squealed, the lantern hanging on the frame swayed, and the trolley came to a halt. The brigadier and the old man, who were sitting with their legs dangling over the edge, climbed down onto the tracks. The heavy protective suits, made of lead-impregnated fabric, looked like deep-sea divers' outfits. They were incredibly expensive and rare – probably less than two dozen of them could be found in the entire Metro. The two at Sebastopol had almost never been used, they'd just been waiting for their time to come. These suits of armour could absorb the fiercest radiation, but they turned even simple walking into a difficult task – at least they did for Homer.

Denis Mikhailovich left the trolley and walked on with them for a few minutes, swapping phrases with Hunter – snatches of speech that were deliberately clipped and crumpled, so that Homer couldn't unfold and interpret them.

'Where will you get them?' he asked the brigadier gruffly.

'They'll give me them. They won't have any choice,' Hunter boomed, looking straight ahead.

'Everyone stopped expecting you back ages ago. For them you're dead. Dead, you understand?'

Hunter stopped for a moment and spoke in a low voice, as if he were talking to himself, not the perimeter commander.

'If only it was all that simple . . .'

'And desertion from the Order – that means a fate worse than death.'

Without answering, the brigadier swung his hand up, simultaneously saluting the colonel and lopping off an invisible anchor cable. Denis Mikhailovich took the hint and stayed behind on the dockside while the brigadier and the old man moved slowly away from the shore, as if they were fighting a reverse current, and set off on their great voyage across the seas of darkness.

The colonel lowered his hand from his temple and signalled to the helmsman to start the engine. He felt desolate, left with no one to issue ultimatums to and no one to wage battle against. As the military commander of an island lost in one of those dark seas, all he could hope for now was that the little expedition wouldn't get lost out there and would return home some day – from the other side, proving in its own small way that the world really was round.

The final guard post, located in the stretch of tunnel immediately after Kakhovka, had been almost deserted. For as long as the old man could remember, no one had ever attacked Sebastopol from the east.

Now the patch of yellow seemed less like a marker, dividing the endless concrete intestine into arbitrary sections, than a cosmic lift, connecting two planets that were hundreds of light years apart. Beyond it, the inhabitable space of Earth was imperceptibly replaced by a dead lunar landscape, and the apparent resemblance between them was a deception.

As he focused on setting one foot in front of the other in his incredibly heavy boots and listened to his own strenuous breathing, penned into a complex system of fluted tubes and filters, Homer imagined he was an astronaut who had landed on a satellite of some distant star. Indulging in this puerile fantasy made it easier for him to adjust to the weight of his suit – he could explain that by the high gravity – as well as the fact that they would be the only living creatures in the tunnels for kilometres ahead.

All the scientists and science-fiction writers never got their forecasts of the future right, thought the old man. By the year 2034 the human race should have been master of half the galaxy, or at least the solar system, for a long time already – Homer had been promised that when he was a child. But the science-fiction writers and the scientists had both started from the premise that humanity was rational and consistent. As if it didn't consist of several billions of lazy, frivolous individuals who were easily distracted, but was some kind of beehive, endowed with collective reason and a unified will. As if, when it set about conquering space, it had really intended to take the task seriously and not abandon it halfway when the game got boring, turning its attention to electronics and then moving on to biotechnology, without ever achieving any really impressive results in anything. Except, perhaps, for nuclear physics.

So here he was, a wingless astronaut, a nonviable life-form without his cumbersome protective suit, an alien on his own planet, exploring and conquering the tunnels from Kakhovka to Kashira. And he and all the other survivors could simply forget about anything more ambitious than that.

It was strange: here, beyond the yellow marker, his body groaned under the fifty per cent increase in the force of gravity, but his soul was soaring, weightless. The day before, when he said goodbye to Elena before the expedition to Tula, he was still counting on coming back. But when Hunter named Homer again, choosing him as his partner for the second time in a row, the old man had realised there was no way he could weasel out of it. His insistent prayers to be tested and enlightened had finally been heard, and trying to back out now would be stupid and unmanly. He couldn't treat his life's work as a part-time job. It was pointless to play coy with destiny, promising to devote himself to his work wholeheartedly a bit later on, the next time around... There might not be any next time, and if he didn't set his mind to it now, what would he carry on living for afterwards? To end his days as the unknown Nikolai Ivanovich, a local crackpot, a drooling old storyteller with an erratic smile? But to make the transition from a grotesque caricature of Homer to the genuine article, from an obsessive fantasist to a maker of myths, to rise out of the ashes renewed, first he would have to cremate his former self. He realised that if he carried on doubting and started pandering to his yearning for a home and a woman, if he constantly looked back, he was certain to miss something very important up ahead. He had to wield the knife.

It would be difficult for him to return from this new expedition unharmed, or even to return at all. And though he felt terribly sorry for Elena, who couldn't believe at first that Homer had reappeared at the station alive and well after only one day away, and then cried when she failed to change his mind and saw him off again into oblivion, this time he hadn't promised her anything. As he hugged Elena tight against him, he looked over her shoulder at the clock. He had to go. Homer knew it wasn't easy to amputate more than ten years of life just like that, he was bound to suffer phantom pains after the loss. He had expected to feel the urge to look round all the time, but once he stepped beyond that thick yellow boundary marker, it was as if he had really died, and his soul had soared free, breaking out of both of its ponderous, unwieldy, physical shells. He had escaped.

Hunter didn't seem to be hampered at all by his protective suit. The loose clothing bulked out his muscular, wolfish figure, transforming it into an amorphous colossus, but without reducing its agility. He walked along side by side with the panting old man, but only because he was still keeping a close eye on him after Nakhimov Prospect.

After what Homer had seen at Nagatino, Nagornaya and Tula, agreeing to carry on roaming the tunnels with Hunter hadn't been an easy decision. But he had found a way to convince himself: the long-awaited metamorphoses heralding his rebirth had begun while he was with the brigadier. And it didn't matter why Hunter had dragged him along again – to set the old man on the right path or to use him for spare rations. The most important thing for Homer now was not to let this new condition slip away, to exploit it while he still could, to invent things and write them down.

And another thing. When Hunter asked him to come, Homer seemed to sense that the brigadier needed him in almost exactly the same way – not in order to guide him through the tunnels and warn him about the dangers. Perhaps in nourishing the old man's energies, the brigadier was also taking something from Homer, without asking permission. But what could he possibly need?

Hunter's apparent lack of emotion could no longer deceive the old man. Under the crust of that paralysed face, magma was seething, occasionally splashing out through the craters of those smouldering eyes that didn't close. He was in turmoil. He was searching for something too.

Hunter seemed to fit the role of the future book's epic hero. Homer had hesitated for a while and then, after the first few trials, accepted him. But there were many things about the brigadier's character, such as his passion for killing living things, the words he left unspoken, and his miserly gestures, that made the old man wary. Hunter was like those killers who taunted and provoked the police detectives, wanting to be unmasked. Homer didn't know if Hunter saw him as a confessor, a biographer or an organ donor, but he sensed that this strange relationship of dependence was developing into something mutual, growing stronger than fear. And Homer was haunted by the feeling that Hunter was putting off a very important conversation. Sometimes the brigadier turned to him as if he was about to ask something, and never actually spoke. But then, perhaps the old man was merely indulging in wishful thinking and Hunter was leading him on deeper into the tunnels so that he could wring an unwanted witness's neck. More and more often the brigadier's eyes turned to probe the old man's knapsack, with the fateful diary lying in the bottom of it. He couldn't see it, but he seemed to guess that some object hidden in the knapsack attracted Homer's thoughts like a magnet, and he was tracking those thoughts, gradually closing in on the notepad. The old man tried not to think about the diary, but it was futile.

There had been almost no time to pack for the journey, and Homer had only been able to hide away with the diary for a few minutes, not long enough to moisten and unstick the pages fused together with blood. But the old man had leafed rapidly through the other pages, criss-crossed haphazardly with hasty, fragmentary entries. The timeline was disrupted, as if the writer had to struggle to catch the words and had simply set them down on paper wherever he could. To render them meaningful, the old man had to arrange them in the right order.

'We have no lines of communication. The phone is dead. Perhaps it's sabotage. One of the exiles, in revenge? Before we got here.'

'The situation is hopeless. We can't expect help from anywhere. If we ask Sebastopol, we'll be condemning our own men. We have to endure it . . . For how long?'

'They won't let me go . . . They've gone insane. If not me, then who? Make a run for it!'

And there was something else too. Immediately after the final entry, calling for the idea of storming Tula to be abandoned, there was a blurred signature, sealed with a bloody fingerprint, like reddish-brown sealing wax. It was a name that Homer had heard before, one he had often spoken himself. The diary belonged to the signal officer of the team sent to Tula a week before.

They passed the opening of a track leading to an engine depot, which would certainly have been plundered, if not for the intense radiation here. For some reason the black, wilted branch line leading to it had been screened off by someone with sections of steel reinforcement bars, welded together rather clumsily and very clearly in a hurry. A metal plate attached to the bars with wire bore a grinning skull and the remains of a warning written in red paint, but it had either faded with time or been scraped off. Homer's gaze drew him past the barred entrance, deep into this dark well, and he barely managed to scramble back out. The line probably hadn't always been as empty of life as they believed at Sebastopol, he thought to himself.

They passed through Warsaw Station – a terrible, eerie place, rusty and mouldy, like a drowned man fished out of the water. The walls, patterned in squares of tiles, were oozing murky water. Through the half-open lips of the hermetic doors a cold wind blew in from the surface, as if someone huge had set his mouth to them from the outside and was giving the station artificial respiration. Their radiation meters fluttered hysterically, telling them they had to get out of there immediately.

Closer to Kashira one of the instruments broke down, and the figures on the other were jammed against the very edge of the display. Homer felt a bitter taste on his tongue.

'Where's the epicentre?'

It was incredibly difficult to make out the brigadier's voice, as if Homer had his head lowered into a bath full of water. He stopped

– in order to make the best of this short break – and gestured to the south-east with his glove.

'Besides Kantemirovo Station. We think the roof of the entrance pavilion or a ventilation shaft was pierced. No one knows for certain.'

'So Kantemirovo's deserted then?'

'And always has been. After Kolomenskoe the entire line's empty.'

'But I was told . . .' Hunter said, then broke off, gesturing to Homer to be quiet, while he tuned in to his subtle, invisible wavelengths. 'Does anyone know what's happening at Kashira?' he asked eventually.

'How could they?' The old man wasn't sure he'd managed to give an ironic note to the adenoidal boom that emerged from his breathing filters like a trombone snorting.

'I'll tell you. The radiation there's so bad, we'll both be fried to a crisp before we even reach the station. Nothing will do any good. We can't go that way. We're turning back.'

'Back? To Sebastopol?'

'Yes. I'll go up onto the surface and try to get there overland,' Hunter replied thoughtfully, already figuring out his route.

'Are you going to go alone?' Homer asked cautiously.

'I can't keep rescuing you all the time. I'll have enough to do saving my own skin. And two of us wouldn't get through anyway. Even for me there's no guarantee.'

'You don't understand, I need to go with you, I have to . . .' Homer cast around frantically for a reason, a toehold in logic.

'You have to die with meaning?' the brigadier concluded for him indifferently – although Homer knew perfectly well that it was really the filters in the gas mask, screening out any contaminants, letting in only tasteless, sterile air and letting out only soulless, mechanical voices.

The old man squeezed his eyes shut for a moment, trying to recall everything he knew about the contaminated lower end of the Zamoskvorechie branch, about the route from Sebastopol to Serpukhov. Anything at all in order to avoid turning back, to avoid returning to his meagre life, to his false pregnancy with a great novel and timeless legends.

'Follow me!' he wheezed suddenly and set off, hobbling with an agility that surprised even him, to the east – toward Kashira, into the very mouth of hell.

She dreamed she was scraping a file across one loop of the steel shackles chaining her to a wall. The file squealed and kept slipping off, and even when she already thought its blade had bitten half a millimetre into the steel, the moment she stopped working, the shallow, almost invisible groove closed up as she watched. But Sasha didn't despair: she took up her tool again, skinning her palms as she filed away at the unyielding metal, maintaining a strict, regular rhythm. The important thing was not to lose the rhythm, not to stop working even for an instant. In the tight grip of the fetters her ankles had swollen up and gone numb. Sasha realised that even if she could defeat the metal, she still wouldn't be able to run away, because her legs would refuse to obey her.

Sasha woke up and raised her eyelids with a struggle. The shackles had not been a mere dream: her wrists were restrained by handcuffs. She was lying on the dirty floor of an old mining trolley that squealed with excruciating monotony as it crept slowly along. There was a dirty piece of rag stuffed in her mouth and the side of her head was throbbing and bleeding.

'He didn't kill me,' she thought. 'Why not?'

From where she was lying all she could see was a small section of the ceiling – the welded joints of tunnel liners drifting by in an irregular patch of light: the trolley was moving along a tunnel. While she tried to get her shackled hands out from behind her back, the liners were replaced by flaking white paint. That alarmed Sasha: what station was this?

It was a bad place, not just quiet, but desolate; not just deserted, but lifeless, and completely dark. For some reason she had thought every station on the other side of the bridge was full of people and the air everywhere was filled with their shouting and hubbub. So she must have been wrong about that.

The ceiling above Sasha stopped moving. Grunting and swearing, her kidnapper clambered down onto the platform and strolled about with his metal-tipped heels scraping, as if he was studying the surroundings. Then, obviously having removed his gas mask, he growled in a deep, amiable-sounding voice.

'So here we are then. After all these years!'

110

Releasing all the air out of his lungs in a long, lingering sigh, he hit out hard at some bulky inanimate object – no, he kicked it with his boot: it looked like a sack, but what was it stuffed with?

When Sasha realised the answer, she sank her teeth into the stinking rag and started bellowing, arching up her body as if she was having a fit. She knew where the fat man in tarpaulin had brought her and who he was talking to like that.

It was ludicrous even to hope he could get away from Hunter. Moving like a lion, the brigadier overtook the old man in a few long bounds, grabbed hold of his shoulder and shook him painfully.

'What's wrong with you?'

'We only have to go a little bit further,' Homer wheezed. 'I've remembered! There's an access passage from here straight to the Zamoskvorechie Line, just before Kashira Station. We can go through it straight to the tunnel, so we won't have to go into the station. We'll bypass it and come straight out to Kolomenskoe. It shouldn't be very far. Please...'

Seizing his chance, he tried to break free again, but stumbled over the bellbottoms of his trousers and fell flat onto the rails with a crash. He got up again immediately and tried to jerk forward, but Hunter easily held him still on the spot, like a rat on a string, and turned the old man to face him. Leaning down so that the lenses of their gas masks were on the same level, he glanced deep into Homer for a few seconds and then released his grip.

'All right.'

And now the brigadier dragged him along, not halting again for a single moment. The blood pounding in Homer's ears drowned out the frenetic chattering of the dosimeters, his legs turned stiff and numb, almost refusing to obey him, his lungs were straining so hard they smarted painfully and felt as if they were about to burst.

They almost missed the black ink blot of the narrow passage. Squeezing into it, they ran for a few more long minutes, until Hunter galloped out into a new tunnel. The brigadier cast a hasty glance around, dived back into the passage and shouted to the old man.

'Where's this you've brought me to? Have you ever even been here?'

About thirty metres along, to the left of the passage – in the direction they had to follow – the tunnel was blocked from floor to ceiling by a thick curtain of something that looked like cobwebs.

Reluctant to waste his breath on talking, Homer simply shook his head. It was absolutely true, he'd never had any reason to come this way before. And this was hardly the moment to tell Hunter all the things he'd heard about this place.

Throwing his automatic back over his shoulder, the brigadier took a long rectangular hatchet, something like a home-made machete, out of his knapsack and slashed at the sticky white lacework. The dried-out skeletons of flying cockroaches that were stuck in the nets started quivering and rustling like hoarse little bells. The edges of the ragged wound that had been inflicted immediately closed together, as if it was healing up. Turning back the semi-transparent fabric of the web and sticking his flashlight inside, the brigadier lit up the passage. It would take them hours to clear it: the multilayered webbing of sticky threads filled every part of the connecting tunnel for as far as the beam of light could reach

Hunter checked his radiation monitor, made a strange guttural sound and started furiously hacking away the threads stretched between the walls of the tunnel. The cobweb yielded slowly, taking more time than they could afford now. In ten minutes they only managed to move about thirty metres forward, and the threads were woven ever more tightly, choking the passage like a plug of cotton wool.

Finally, at an overgrown ventilation shaft with an ugly two-headed skeleton lying on the sleepers below it, the brigadier flung his hatchet down on the floor. They were stuck in the web, just like the cockroaches, and even if the creature that wove these nets had perished long ago and wouldn't come for them, they would die soon anyway – from the radiation.

In the few moments while Hunter was trying to decide what to do, the old man remembered something else he had once heard about this tunnel. Going down on one knee, he knocked a few cartridges out of his spare clip, twisted the bullets out using a pen-knife and shook the powder into his palm. Hunter didn't need any explanations: a few minutes later, back at the beginning of the connecting tunnel, they tipped a heap of grey granules onto a small pad of cotton wool and held a cigarette lighter to it.

The gunpowder snorted and started smoking, and suddenly

something incredible happened: the flame from the powder spread out in all directions at once, climbing right up the walls to the distant ceiling, invading all the space of the tunnel. It dashed inwards, devouring the cobweb, a roaring, blazing ring of fire, lighting up the grimy tunnel liners and leaving behind only occasional burnt tatters dangling from the ceiling. The hoop of flame moved towards Kolomenskoe, shrinking rapidly and sucking in air like a gigantic piston. Then the tunnel swerved and the flames disappeared round the bend, trailing bright crimson flashes behind them.

And from the far distance, breaking through the regular drone of the fire, came a call that wasn't human, something between a despairing howl and a strident hiss. Although Homer, hypnotised by the spectacle, could easily have imagined it.

Hunter tossed the hatchet back into his knapsack and took out two new, unopened canisters for gas masks.

'I was keeping them for the way back,' he said, changing his own filter and handing the second canister to the old man. 'After that fire, the pollution in there now is like the place had just been bombed.'

The old man nodded. When the flames swirled upwards, they'd stirred up radioactive particles that had been settling into the cobweb for years, eating their way into its threads. The black vacuum of the tunnel was now filled with deadly molecules, suspended in the air like millions of tiny underwater mines, and they had blocked off the voyagers' navigable channel. There was no possible way to avoid them.

They had to break straight through.

'If only your dad could see you now,' the fat man scolded her derisively.

Sasha was sitting directly opposite her father's overturned body, which was lying face down in the blood. Both straps of her overalls had been tugged down off her shoulders, revealing a washed-out singlet with a picture of some jolly little animal. Her kidnapper wouldn't let her see his face, he seared her eyes with a brilliant beam of light every time she tried to look up. He'd taken the rag out of her mouth, but Sasha still had no intention of asking him for anything.

'Not like your mother, unfortunately. And I was really hoping...'

The elephantine legs in the blood-smeared knee boots set off again round the column that Sasha was sitting against. Now his voice came from behind her back.

'Your daddy probably thought that in time everything would be forgotten. But some crimes don't carry a statute of limitation . . . Slander. Betrayal.'

His obese figure emerged from the gloom on the other side of her. He stopped, looking down on her father's body, prodding it contemptuously with his boot. He hacked up spittle and spat out a generous gobbet.

'It's a shame the old fellow snuffed it without my help,' said the fat man, running the beam of his flashlight round the heaps of useless junk that cluttered the bleak, faceless station and halting it on the bicycle with no wheels. 'A cosy little place you have here. I think if it wasn't for you, your daddy would have preferred to hang himself.'

While the flashlight was directed away from her, Sasha tried to crawl off to the side, but a second later the beam picked her out of the darkness again.

'And I can understand him,' said her kidnapper. With a single bound he was there beside her again. 'You've turned out a fine little girl. It's just a shame you're not like your mum. I think he was probably disappointed about that too. Well, never mind,' he said, knocking her to the floor with the toe of his boot. 'At least I didn't waste my time coming all the way through the Metro to get here.'

Sasha shuddered and shook her head.

'See how unpredictable everything is, Pete,' he said, talking to Sasha's father again. 'There was a time when you used to have your rivals in love court-martialled. Thanks, by the way, for not having me executed, merely banished for life. But life is long, and circumstances change. And not always to your advantage. I've come back, even if it has taken me ten years longer than I planned.'

'It's never an accident when someone goes back somewhere,' Sasha whispered, repeating her father's words

'How very true that is,' the fat man jeered. 'Hey, who's there?'

At the far end of the platform something bulky and ponderous rustled and fell, then there was a kind of hissing sound and the stealthy footsteps of a large animal. When silence fell again it was a false silence, frayed and tattered. Like her kidnapper, Sasha could sense something moving towards them out of the tunnel.

The fat man snapped the breech of his gun, went down on one

knee beside the girl, pressed the butt into his shoulder and ran a trembling spot of light over the closest columns. Hearing the southern tunnels come to life after they had been empty for decades was as spine-chilling as seeing the marble statues waking up in one of the central stations of the Metro.

A blurred shadow flitted across the beam of light just as the beam was turning away – it wasn't human, though – the shape was wrong and the movements were too agile. But when the light moved back to the spot where the mysterious creature had just been, there was no trace of it. A minute later the beam, fluttering wildly in panic, caught it again – only twenty steps away from them.

'A bear?' the fat man whispered in disbelief, pressing the trigger.

Bullets lashed into the columns and started rattling against the walls, but the beast seemed to have dematerialised, and not a single shot found its target. Then the fat man suddenly stopped firing senselessly, dropped his automatic and pressed his hands to his stomach. His flashlight rolled off to one side, casting a cone of light that crept across the floor and lighting up his corpulent, hunched-over figure from below.

A man stepped unhurriedly out of the gloom, walking with incredibly soft, almost soundless steps in his heavy boots. In a protective suit that was too large even for a giant like him, he really could have been taken for a bear. He wasn't wearing a gas mask: his scar-furrowed face and shaved head looked like a scorched desert. Part of the face, with hard, coarsely defined, manly features, was even rather handsome, but it looked dead somehow, and Sasha couldn't repress a shudder when she looked at it. The other half was simply repulsive – a complicated tangle of scars transformed it into the half-mask of a folk-tale monster, perfect in its ugly deformity. But even so, apart from the eyes, his appearance was repellent, rather than frightening. A half-crazed, prowling, probing gaze enlivened the stiffened face. Enlivened it, but didn't bring it to life.

The fat man tried to get to his feet, but immediately collapsed on the floor, screaming in pain, shot through both the knees. Then the gunman squatted down beside him, put the silencer on the end of his long pistol barrel against the fat man's head and pulled the trigger. The howling broke off instantly. But for a few seconds the echo wandered under the vaults of the station like a lost spirit, bereft of its body.

The shot had thrown the fat man's chin up, and now Sasha's kidnapper lay there turned towards her. Instead of a face he had a damp, gaping, crimson crater. Sasha huddled back and started whimpering in horror. Slowly and thoughtfully, the terrible gunman turned the gun barrel on her.

Then he looked round and changed his mind: the pistol disappeared into its holster and he stepped back, as if trying to disown what he had done. He opened a flat flask and took a pull from it.

A new character appeared on the small stage illuminated by the dead man's fading flashlight: an old man who was breathing heavily, clutching at his ribs. He was dressed in the same kind of suit as the killer, and looked absolutely absurd in it. When he caught up with his companion, the old man immediately collapsed on the floor in exhaustion, not even noticing that everything around him was awash with blood. It was only later, when he came round and opened his eyes, that he saw the two mutilated bodies and the mute, terrified girl hemmed in between them.

Homer's heart had only just calmed down, but now it leapt again. He couldn't express it in words yet, but he already knew for certain: he had found her. After so many nights spent in fruitless attempts to picture his future heroine, trying to imagine her lips and her wrists, her clothes and her aroma, her movements and her thoughts, he had suddenly met a real person who matched all his requirements perfectly. Of course, until now he had imagined her quite differently... More elegant, more well-rounded and certainly more grown-up. She had turned out to be much more sinewy, she had too many sharp corners and, glancing into her eyes, instead of languorous, enveloping warmth, the old man encountered two cold splinters of ice. She was different, but Homer knew it was his mistake, he had failed to guess what she ought to be like. Her trapped look, her face distorted by fear and her manacled hands intrigued the old man. He might be a master at retelling yarns, but he hadn't been granted the talent to write tragedies of the kind that this girl must have suffered. Her helplessness and hopelessness, her miraculous rescue and the way her destiny had been woven into their story meant that he was on the right track.

And though she hadn't spoken a word yet, he was ready in

advance to believe her. For after all, apart from everything else, this teenage girl, with her white, tousled, carelessly lopped hair, pointed little ears, soot-smeared cheeks and exposed, sculpted collarbones – surprisingly white and vulnerable – with her childishly plump, bitten lower lip, was beautiful in a very special way.

The old man's curiosity was mingled with pity and a surprising tenderness. He moved closer and squatted down beside her. She huddled away and squeezed her eyes shut. 'A little savage,' he thought. He patted her on the shoulder, not knowing what to say.

'Time to go,' Hunter butted in.

'But what about . . . ?' Homer asked with a nod at the girl.

'Never mind. It's none of our business.'

'We can't just abandon her here alone!'

'Simpler to shoot her,' the brigadier snapped.

'I don't want to go with you,' the girl said, suddenly pulling herself together. 'Just take the handcuffs off. He should have the key.' She pointed to the shattered, faceless mannequin.

In three swift movements Hunter frisked the body and pulled a bunch of steel keys out of an inside pocket. He tossed them to the girl and looked round at the old man.

'Is that all?'

Still trying to postpone the parting, Homer spoke to the girl.

'What did that subhuman brute do to you?'

'Nothing,' she said, fiddling with the lock. 'He didn't have time. He's not subhuman. Just an ordinary human being. Cruel, stupid, spiteful. Like all of them.'

'They're not all like that,' the old man objected, but without any real conviction.

'All of them,' the girl said obstinately, wincing as she got up on her numbed legs. 'It's all right. Staying human's not that easy.'

She'd certainly got over her fright very quickly! She didn't lower her eyes any more, now she looked at the men with a lowering, challenging gaze. She walked up to one of the corpses, carefully turned it face up, arranged its arms on its chest and kissed it on the forehead. Narrowing her eyes, she turned to Hunter and the corner of her mouth trembled.

'Thank you.'

Without taking any things or even a weapon, she climbed down onto the tracks and limped off towards the tunnel. The brigadier watched her go with his head lowered, frowning: his hand wandered indecisively along his belt between the knife and the flask. Finally he reached a decision, straightened up and called to her.

'Wait!'

CHAPTER 8

Masks

The cage was still lying where the fat man had knocked it out of her hands. Its little door was slightly open and the rat had fled. 'Let him go,' the girl thought. The rat deserved his freedom too.

There was nothing else for it, so Sasha had put on her kidnapper's gas mask. She thought there were still traces of his stale breath in it, but she could only be glad he'd taken the mask off before he was shot.

Close to the middle of the bridge, the background radiation spiked again

Sasha rattled about in the immense tarpaulin suit like a cockroach larva in a cocoon – it seemed miraculous that it could stay on her. But the gas mask clung firmly to her face, even though it had been stretched across the fat man's broad features and drooping jowls. Sasha tried to blow as hard as she could, in order to drive the air predestined for the dead man out through the tubes and filters. But looking around through the perspiring circular lenses, she had an eerie feeling that she had climbed into someone else's body, not just his protective suit. Only an hour ago the soulless demon who had come for her was in here. And now it was as if, in order to get across the bridge at all, she had been forced to become him and take a look at the world through his eyes. Through the eyes of the men who had banished her and her father to Kolomenskoe and kept them alive there for all these years only because their greed was stronger than their hate. Sasha wondered whether, in order to get lost among people like that, she too would have to wear a black rubber mask and pretend to be someone with no face and no feelings. If only that would help her to change on the inside too, and reset her memories to zero ... To genuinely believe that she hadn't been damaged beyond repair, that she could still start all over again.

Sasha would have liked to think these two men had not picked her up simply by chance, that they had been sent to the station especially for her, but she knew it wasn't true. She found it hard to decide why they had taken her with them – for amusement, out of pity or to prove something to each other. The few words the old man had tossed to her, like a bone to a dog, seemed to hint at sympathy, but he did everything with wary deference to his companion, held his tongue and seemed afraid of being accused of mere common humanity.

And the other one, after giving permission for the girl to go with them as far as the nearest inhabited station, had never even looked in her direction again. Sasha had deliberately hung back and let him go ahead slightly, so she could study him freely from behind. He obviously sensed her gaze on him, immediately tensing up and jerking his head back, but he didn't look round – perhaps out of tolerance for a young girl's curiosity, or perhaps because he didn't want to show that he was paying any attention to her.

From the powerful build and feral agility of the man with the shaved head, which had made the fat man confuse him with a bear, it was obvious that he was a soldier and a solitary. But it wasn't just a matter of his height or his massive shoulders. He radiated energy, and it would have been just as palpable if he were short and skinny. A man like that could make almost anyone submit to his will, and he would eliminate anyone who disobeyed without compunction. And long before the girl finally mastered her fear of this man, before she even started trying to make sense of him and herself, the unfamiliar voice of the woman awakening within her told Sasha that she would submit too.

The trolley moved forward at an incredible pace. Homer could hardly feel the resistance of the levers, all the strain was taken by the brigadier. For form's sake, standing there opposite Hunter, the old man also raised and lowered his hands, but the work cost him no effort at all.

The squat Metro bridge was like a millipede fording the murky, turbid river. The concrete flesh was peeling off its steel bones, its legs were buckling under it, and one of its two backbones had slumped and collapsed. Standard, functional and impermanent, it lacked the slightest trace of elegance – like the residential high-rise developments around it, like all of Moscow's banal, stereotyped suburbs. But gazing round rapturously as he rode across it, Homer recalled the magical movable bridges of St Petersburg and the burnished metal lacework of Moscow's Crimea Bridge.

In the twenty years he had lived in the Metro, the old man had only come up to the surface three times, and each time he had tried to observe more than he could possibly see during his short period of leave. Tried to bring his memories to life, focus the lenses of his eyes, already turning cloudy with age, on the city and click the rusting shutter of his visual memory. Tried to store up memories for the future. He might never be up on the surface again, at Kolomenskoe, Rechnoi Vokzal or Tyoply Stan – in those miraculously beautiful places that he and so many other Muscovites used to regard with such unjustified contempt.

Year by year his Moscow was growing older, falling apart, being eroded away. Homer wanted to stroke the decaying Metro bridge in the same way as the girl at Kolomenskoe caressed the man who had bled to death for the last time. And not just the bridge, but the grey crags of the factory buildings too. He wanted to gaze at them in endless adoration, to touch them, so he could feel that he was really there among them and not just dreaming all this. And also, just in case, to say goodbye to them.

The visibility was atrocious, the silvery moonlight couldn't force its way through the filter of dense clouds, and the old man had to guess at more than he could observe. But that was okay, he was well used to substituting fantasies for reality.

Completely absorbed in his musings, at that moment Homer wasn't thinking of anything else. He forgot about the legends that he was going to compose and the mysterious diary that had been harrowing his imagination without a break for so many hours. He behaved just like a child on a holiday outing, gazing in delight at the blurred silhouettes of the high-rises, turning his head to and fro, talking out loud to himself.

The others got no pleasure from the journey across the bridge. The brigadier, who had taken the forward-facing position, occasionally froze and peered in the direction of sounds that came flying up from below. Apart from that, his attention was riveted to the distant point, still invisible to his companions, where the tracks burrowed back into the earth. The girl sat behind Hunter, for some reason clutching her salvaged gas mask with both hands.

It was very obvious that she felt uncomfortable up on the surface. While the team was walking through the tunnel, the girl had seemed quite tall, but the moment they stepped out into the open she shrank into herself, as if she had withdrawn into an invisible shell, and not even the tarpaulin suit taken from the corpse made her seem any bigger, although it was hideously large for her. She was indifferent to the beautiful views from the bridge and most of the time she looked straight down at the floor in front of her.

They rode through the ruins of Technopark Station, which was being built, with careless haste, just before the war – it had crumbled away, not because of the nuclear strikes, but simply from the passage of time – and finally approached the tunnel. In the pale darkness of the night, its entrance was black with an absolute blackness. For Homer, his suit was transformed into a genuine suit of armour, and he was a medieval knight, riding into a fantastic fairytale cave, straight into the dragon's lair. The noise of the night-time city was left behind on the threshold of the beast's abode, at the point where Hunter ordered them to abandon the trolley. All that could be heard now was the tentative rustling of three travellers' footsteps and their sparse words, fractured by an echo that stumbled across the tunnel liners. But there was something unusual about the quality of sound in this tunnel. Even Homer could clearly sense the enclosed nature of the space, as if they had walked in through the neck of a glass bottle.

'It's closed off ahead,' said Hunter, confirming the old man's fears.

The beam of Hunter's flashlight was the first to find the bottom of the bottle: the closed hermetic door loomed up in front of them, a blank wall. Rails glinted faintly, breaking off at the door, and dollops of brownish lubricant oozed from the bearings. Some old planks, dry broken branches and charred pieces of wood had been dumped right beside the door, as if someone had tried to light a fire there recently. The door was clearly in use, but apparently only for coming out from the inside – there were no bells or any other signalling devices on this side of it.

The brigadier looked at the girl.

'Is it always like this here?'

'They come out sometimes. They come to us on the other side. To trade. I thought . . . today . . .' She seemed to be making excuses. Had she known there was no access, but kept it secret?

Hunter hammered on the door with the handle of his machete, as if it were a huge metal gong. But the steel was too thick and instead of a resonant chime, it gave out only a feeble clang. That sound almost certainly couldn't be heard on the other side of the wall, even if there was anybody alive there.

No miracle happened. There was no answer.

In defiance of common sense, Sasha had been hoping these men would be able to unlock the door. She'd been afraid to warn them that the entrance into the Greater Metro was closed – what if they decided to take a different route and abandoned her where they had found her?

But no one in the Greater Metro was expecting them, and breaking open a hermetic door was beyond the power of any human being. The man with the shaved head examined the massive panel of metal, trying to find a weak point or a secret lock, but Sasha knew there weren't any locks on this side. The door only opened outwards.

'You stay here, I'm going to reconnoitre. I'll check the door in the other tunnel and look for ventilation shafts,' the big man barked. After a short pause he added: 'I'll be back'.

And then he disappeared.

The old man gathered up the branches and planks that were lying around and lit a puny little campfire. He sat down directly on the sleepers, thrust his hands into his knapsack and started rummaging through his belongings. Sasha crouched down quietly beside him, observing. The old man ran through a strange performance – perhaps for her, or perhaps for himself. He fished a filthy, battered notepad out of the knapsack, cast a wary glance at Sasha, shifted sideways away from her as far as he could and hunched over the paper. Then he immediately jumped up with suspicious agility for his age, to check that the man with the shaved head really had gone: he crept awkwardly about ten steps towards the exit of the tunnel, didn't find anyone there and decided that these precautions would be sufficient. Leaning back against the door, he screened himself off from Sasha with a sack and immersed himself in his reading.

He read fretfully, droning something indistinctly to himself, then removed his gloves, took out a flask of water and started sprinkling it on his notepad. He read a bit more, then suddenly started rubbing his hands against his trouser legs, slapped himself fretfully on the forehead, touched his gas mask and plunged back into his reading. Infected by his agitation, Sasha abandoned her musings and crept closer: the old man was too engrossed to notice her cautious movements.

Infused with the light of the campfire, his pale green eyes glinted feverishly even through the lenses of the gas mask. Every now and then he surfaced with an obvious effort – for a gulp of air. In these breaks from reading, the old man peered warily at the distant patch of night sky at the end of the tunnel, but it was clear. The man with the shaved head had disappeared completely. And then the notepad engrossed him entirely again.

Now she realised why he had sprinkled the paper with water: he was trying to separate pages that were stuck together. They obviously resisted and once, when he accidentally tore one of them, he cried out as if he had cut himself. He swore, cursing his own clumsiness, and noticed how inquisitively she was examining him. Embarrassed, he adjusted his gas mask again, but didn't say anything to her until he had read right to the end. Then he skipped over to the fire and flung the notepad into it, without even looking at Sasha, and she sensed that it was pointless to ask any questions now: he would only lie or say nothing. And there were other things that worried her far more just at the moment. Probably an entire hour had passed since the man with the shaved head left. What if he had abandoned them as an unnecessary burden? Sasha moved to sit a bit closer to the old man.

'The other tunnel's closed too,' she said. 'And all the shafts nearby have been blocked off. This is the only way in.'

The old man looked at her absent-mindedly, clearly struggling to concentrate on what he had heard.

'He'll find a way to get inside, he's got intuition,' he said, and a minute later, as if he didn't want to seem impolite, he asked: 'What's your name?'

'Alexandra,' she replied seriously. 'What's yours?'

'Nikolai,' he began, reaching out his hand, and then suddenly jerking it back again before Sasha could touch it, as if he had changed his mind. 'Homer. My name's Homer.'

'Homer. That's a strange nickname,' Sasha said slowly.

'It's just a name,' Homer said firmly.

Should she explain to him that as long as they were with her the door would stay closed? Although it could easily have been standing wide open, if these two had come on their own. This was Kolomenskoe refusing to let Sasha go, punishing her for what she had done to her father. The girl had run off and stretched her chain to its limit, but she still couldn't break it. The station had brought her back to itself once, and it would do it again.

No matter how hard she tried to drive these thoughts and images away, they only flew off to arm's length, like bloodsucking gnats, but always came back, circling round and round her, creeping into her ears and her eyes. The old man was asking Sasha about something else, but she didn't respond: her eyes were veiled by tears and she could hear her father's voice in her ears, repeating: 'Nothing is more precious than human life'. And now the moment had come when she really understood what he meant.

What was going on at Tula was no longer a mystery to Homer. The explanation for everything was simpler and more terrible than he had imagined, but an even more terrible story was only just beginning, now that the notepad had been deciphered. The diary was Homer's black spot; it was a one-way ticket, and once he had held it in his hand, the old man could never be free of it, even if he burned it.

And besides that, his suspicions concerning Hunter had now been confirmed by substantial, unambiguous proof, although Homer didn't have the slightest idea what to do with it. Everything he had read in the diary completely contradicted the brigadier's claims. Hunter was simply lying, and quite deliberately. The old man had to work out what was the motive behind his lies, and if the lies made any kind of sense. The answer to that would determine whether he decided to carry on following Hunter and whether his adventure would turn out to be a heroic epic or a mindless, horrendous bloodbath that left no surviving witnesses.

The first entries in the notepad were dated to the day when the convoy passed through Nagornaya without any casualties and entered Tula without encountering any resistance ...

'The tunnels are quiet and empty almost all the way to Tula. We advance quickly – a good sign. The commander is counting on getting back tomorrow at the latest,' the dead signal officer reported. 'The entrance to Tula is not guarded. We sent in a scout. He disappeared,' he wrote anxiously a few hours later. 'The commander has decided to advance into the station en masse. We are preparing for an assault.' And then again, a little while later: 'We can't understand what's wrong ... We're talking to the locals. Things are bad here. Some kind of disease.' And soon after that he explained: 'Some people at the station are infected with something ... An unknown illness ...' The members of the convoy apparently tried to render assistance to the sick: 'The paramedic hasn't been able to find a cure. He says it's like rabies ... They suffer monstrous pain, they're deranged ... They attack other people'. And straight after that: 'Weakened by the illness, they can't cause any serious harm. That's not the real disaster ...' At this point, as luck would have it, the pages had stuck together, and Homer had to sprinkle water on them from his flask: 'Photophobia, nausea. Blood in the mouth. Coughing. Then they swell up ... They are transformed into ...' – the word had been laboriously crossed out. 'How it's transmitted is not clear. The air? Physical contact?' That entry was made the next day. The detachment had stayed on.

'Why didn't they report this?' the old man thought, and immediately realised that he'd already seen the answer somewhere. He leafed through the pages. 'We have no lines of communication. The phone is dead. Perhaps it's sabotage. One of the exiles, in revenge? They discovered it before we got here, and at first they flung the sick out into the tunnels. One of them? Did he cut the cable?'

At that point Homer looked up from the letters and stared blindly into space. Let's say the cable was cut. But then why didn't they come back to Sebastopol?

'What's worse is that it takes a week to develop. And what if it's longer? And from then to death is another week or two. We can't tell who's sick and who's well. Nothing helps. There's no cure. The death rate is a hundred per cent.' A day later the signal officer made another entry that was already familiar to Homer: 'Tula is in chaos.

There's no way out to the Metro, Hansa is blocking it. We can't go back home.' On the next page he continued: 'The healthy were shooting at the sick, especially the aggressive ones. They've built a pen for infected individuals ... They resist and beg to be let out ...' and after that a brief, terrible phrase: 'They gnaw on each other ...'

The signal officer was frightened too, but the steely discipline in the detachment prevented fear from spilling over into panic. Even at the focus of an epidemic of deadly fever, a Sebastopol brigade remained a Sebastopol brigade. 'We have brought the situation under control, sealed off the station and appointed a commandant,' Homer read. 'All our men are all right, but too little time has gone by.'

The search party dispatched from Sebastopol had reached Tula safely and, of course, got stuck there too. 'We have taken a decision to remain here until the incubation period is over, to avoid endangering ... Or forever,' the signal officer wrote. 'The situation is hopeless. We can't expect help from anywhere. If we ask Sebastopol, we'll be condemning our own men. We have to endure it ... For how long?'

So the mysterious guard by the hermetic door at Tula had been posted by the Sebastopolites. Then it wasn't surprising that their voices had seemed familiar to Homer: the watch was being kept by men with whom he had defended the Chertanovo line of approach against upyrs only a few days ago! By voluntarily deciding not to return, they hoped to protect their home station from being infected.

'Most often from person to person, but it's obviously in the air too. Some men seem to be immune. It started a couple of weeks ago, many have not fallen ill ... But there are more and more dead. We are living in a morgue,' the signal officer scribbled. 'Who'll be the next to die?' he asked, suddenly breaking into a hysterical shriek. But he took himself in hand and continued steadily: 'We have to do something. Warn them. I want to volunteer to go. Not to Sebastopol. To find the point where the cable is damaged. And get through from there. I have to get a call through.'

Then several days passed, filled with invisible conflict with the commander of the convoy, silent arguments with other soldiers and mounting despair. The signal officer gathered his strength and recorded in his diary everything that he tried to make them see.

'They don't understand how things look from Sebastopol. We've been blockaded in for a week now. They'll send another three men, who won't be able to go back either. Then they'll send a large assault team. Declare general mobilisation. Everyone who comes to Tula will be in the risk zone. Someone will get infected and go running home. And that will be the end. I have to prevent an assault! They don't understand...' Then another attempt to get the commandant to see sense, as fruitless as all the others before it. 'They won't let me go... They've gone insane. If not me, then who? Make a run for it!'

'I pretended that I had calmed down, that I was willing to wait,' he wrote a day later. 'I went on duty at the hermetic door. I shouted that I was going to find the break in the cable and ran. They fired on me. A bullet lodged in my back.'

Homer turned the page.

'Not for myself. For Natasha, for little Seryozha. I wasn't thinking of trying to save myself. Let them live. So Seryozha can...' At this point the pen was jerking about in his weakened hand: perhaps he added this later, because there was no more space, or because he no longer cared where he wrote. Then the disrupted chronology was restored: 'Thank God, they let me through Nagornaya. I have no strength left. I walk on and on. Then I faint. How long was I asleep? I don't know. Is there blood in my lung? Is it the bullet or have I got the sickness? I can't...' The curve of the letters straightened out into a slithering line, like a dying man's encephalogram. But then he came round again and finished the sentence: 'I can't find where the damage is.'

'Nakhimov. I made it. I know where the phone is. I'll warn them... They mustn't! Save... My wife, I miss...' He splashed his thoughts out on to the paper less and less coherently, punctuated with scarlet blobs. 'I got through. Did they hear me? I'll die soon. Strange. I'll fall asleep. No more bullets. I want to fall asleep before these... They're standing round me, waiting. I'm still alive, go away.'

The ending of the diary seemed to have been prepared in advance, written in triumphantly vertical handwriting – the appeal not to storm Tula and the name of the man who had given his life to prevent it happening. But Homer could tell that the last thing the signal officer had written before his signal faded away forever was: 'I'm still alive, go away'.

A heavy silence enveloped the two people huddling close to the flames. Homer had stopped trying to lift the girl's mood. He sat there without speaking, stirring the ashes with a stick while the sodden notepad died the stubborn death of a heretic and he tried to ride out the storm that was raging inside him

Fate was mocking him. How he had longed to solve the mystery of Tula! How proud he had been of finding the diary, how it had flattered his vanity to come so close, all on his own, to unravelling all the knots in this story. And now? Now that he had the answers to all the questions in his hands, he cursed himself for his curiosity.

Yes, he was breathing through his respirator when he picked up the diary at Nakhimov Prospect, and he was wearing a full-protection suit now as well. But no one knew exactly how the disease was transmitted!

What a fool he had been to scare himself with not having much time left! Yes, it had spurred him on, helped him to overcome his laziness and conquer his fear. But death was contrary, it didn't like people who tried to dictate to it. And now the diary had set him an absolutely definite deadline: a few weeks from the day of infection to death. Perhaps even an entire month! But there was so much he still had to get done in those pitiful thirty days.

What should he do? Confess to his companions that he was sick and go away to turn up his toes at Kolomenskoe – if not from the sickness, then from hunger and radiation? But if he was already incubating the terrible disease, then Hunter and the girl, with whom he had shared the same air, must be infected too. Especially the brigadier – when he spoke to the sentries on the cordon at Tula, he had come very close to them.

Or should he hope that the sickness would pass him by, just keep his head down and wait? Not simply lie low, of course, but continue this journey with Hunter – so that the swirling tornado of events that had picked the old man up wouldn't drop him again, and he could carry on drawing inspiration from them.

After all, if Nikolai Ivanovich, that decrepit, useless, mediocre citizen of Sebastopol and former engine driver's mate, that caterpillar crushed against the ground by the force of gravity, was dying because he had unsealed that cursed diary, then Homer, the chronicler and myth-maker, the short-lived, bright-winged mayfly, had only just appeared in the world. Perhaps he had been sent a tragedy worthy of the pens of the great, and now it was entirely up to him to see if he could manifest it on paper in the thirty days that had been granted to him.

Did he have any right to ignore this chance?

Did he have any right to become a hermit, forget about his legend, voluntarily abandon genuine immortality and deprive all his contemporaries of it too? Which would be more criminal and more stupid – to carry the blazing torch of the plague through half the Metro or to burn his manuscripts and himself with them?

As a vain and cowardly man, Homer had already made his choice, and now he was only searching for arguments to support it. What would be the point of mummifying himself in the vault at Kolomenskoe in the company of two other corpses? He wasn't cut out for feats of heroism. And if the Sebastopol soldiers at Tula were prepared to enlist in the ranks of the dead, that was their choice and their right. At least they didn't have to die alone. And what good would it do if Homer sacrificed himself? He couldn't stop Hunter in any case. The old man had been spreading the disease without knowing what he was doing, but Hunter had known everything perfectly well since that encounter at Tula. That was why he had insisted on the total extermination of all the station's inhabitants, including the men from the Sebastopolite convoys. That was why he had mentioned flamethrowers.

And if they were both already sick, the epidemic would inevitably affect Sebastopol. In the first instance the people they had been with. Elena. The station commandant. The commander of the perimeter. Their adjutants. Which meant that in three weeks' time the station would first be decapitated and overwhelmed by chaos, and then the pestilence would scythe down everyone else. But how could Hunter expect to avoid infection? Why go back to Sebastopol, even though he realised that the illness could have been transmitted to him as well? It was becoming clear to Homer that the brigadier was not acting on intuition, but implementing some kind of plan, step by step. Until the old man had spoiled his game.

So Sebastopol was doomed in any case, and the expedition was completely meaningless now? But even in order to return home and die quietly beside Elena, Homer would have to complete his round-the-world voyage. The journey from Kakhovka to Kashira had been enough to put their gas masks out of action, and the protective suits had absorbed tens, if not hundreds, of roentgens – they had to be disposed of as soon as possible. He couldn't go back the same way he had come. What should he do?

The girl was sleeping, shrunk up tight into a ball. The fire had finally swallowed the plague-infected diary, consumed the final branches and gone out. To save the batteries of his flashlight, the old man decided to sit in darkness for as long as he could manage it.

No, he had to carry on following the brigadier. He would avoid everyone else, in order to reduce the risk of infection, dump his knapsack here with all his bits and pieces, destroy his clothing... He would hope for mercy, but still count down the thirty days. He would work on his book every day without taking any time to rest. 'It will all work out somehow,' the old man kept telling himself. 'The important thing is to follow Hunter, not to fall behind. That's if he shows up again...'

It was more than an hour since the brigadier had disappeared into the blurred opening at the end of the tunnel. When he reassured the girl, Homer was by no means certain that the brigadier would definitely come back to them.

The more the old man learned about him, the less he understood him. It was impossible to trust the brigadier, but just as impossible to doubt him. He was impossible to analyse, he didn't fit the pattern of normal human emotions. Trusting him was tantamount to surrendering yourself to a force of nature. But Homer had already done it: there was no point in regretting it now, it was too late.

In the pitch darkness the silence didn't seem so dense. Strange mutterings and whispers were hatching through its smooth shell, something howled in the distance, something rustled. In some sounds the old man fancied he heard the shambling, drunken footfalls of the corpse-eaters, in others he heard the slithering of the phantom giants at Nagornaya, and in some the cries of dying men. Before even ten minutes had passed, he surrendered.

He clicked the switch and shuddered.

Hunter was standing two steps away from him with his arms crossed on his chest, staring at the sleeping girl. Blinded by the sudden light, he put his hand over his eyes and said calmly:

'They'll open the door now.'

*

Sasha was dreaming: she was alone at Kolomenskoe again, waiting for her father after one of his 'strolls'. He was late, but she had to wait for him, help him take off his outer clothes, pull off his gas mask, feed him. The table was already laid for lunch and she didn't know what to busy herself with. She wanted to leave the door leading to the surface, but what if he came back at the very moment when she wasn't there? Who would open it for him? And there she was, sitting on the cold floor beside the door, and the hours flew by, the days came and went, and he still didn't return, but she wouldn't leave her place until the door . . . She was woken by the hollow clang of a bolt opening – a bolt exactly like the ones on the door at Kolomenskoe. She woke up with a smile – her father had come back. Then she looked round and remembered everything.

The only real part of her rapidly fading vision was the screeching of the gigantic latches on the metal door. A minute later the immense slab started vibrating and moving slowly. A beam of light poured through the widening crack and diesel fumes seeped out. The entrance to the Greater Metro . . .

The door gently moved aside and slipped into its groove, revealing the insides of the tunnel that led to Avtozavod Station, and then on to the Circle. Standing on the rails, with its engine growling, all ready to go, was a large motor trolley with a front floodlight and several riders. In the hairlines of their machine-gun sight the men on the trolley saw two travellers wincing at the light and covering their eyes.

'Hands!' a voice shouted.

Sasha followed the old man and obediently raised her hands. This time the motor trolley was the same one that used to come out across the bridge on trading days. The team on it knew all about Sasha's story. And now the old man with the strange name would regret taking the shackled girl from the empty station without bothering to ask how she came to be there.

'Take off your gas masks, present your documents,' the voice ordered from the trolley.

As she revealed her face, she castigated herself for being so stupid. Nobody could set her free. No one had annulled the sentence passed on her father – and on Sasha along with him. Why had she believed that these two could take her into the Metro? Did she think she wouldn't be noticed at the frontier?'

132

'Hey, you! You can't come in here!' She had been recognised immediately. 'You've got ten seconds to disappear. And who's this? Is this your...'

'What's going on?' asked the old man, bewildered.

'Don't you dare! Leave him alone! It's not him!' Sasha shouted.

'Clear off!' the man with an automatic told her in an icy voice. 'Or we'll shoot... To kill.'

'At a girl?' a second voice asked uncertainly.

'I told you...' said the first man, snapping the breech of his automatic in anticipation.

Sasha backed away and squeezed her eyes shut, preparing to meet death for the third time in the space of a few hours. Something gave a quiet chirrup and then fell silent. The final order never came: the girl couldn't bear to wait any longer and she half-opened one eye.

The engine was still smoking, with its blue-grey fumes drifting through the torrent of white light pouring out of the projector, which was pointing up at the ceiling.

They were all lying on the trolley or beside it, like gutted dolls: limply dangling arms, unnaturally twisted necks, shattered bodies.

Sasha turned away. The man with the shaved head was standing behind her with his pistol lowered, examining the trolley that had been transformed into a meat chopping board. He raised the barrel and squeezed the trigger again.

'That's all now,' he boomed, satisfied. 'Take off their uniforms and gas masks.'

'What for?' the old man asked with a shudder.

'We're getting changed. We'll drive through Avtozavod on their trolley.'

Sasha froze, gazing dumbfounded at the killer: inside her, fright struggled against admiration, revulsion mingled with gratitude. He had just killed three men as if it was nothing, breaking her father's most important commandment. But he had done it to save her life – and the old man's, of course. Could it be a coincidence that he had saved her for the second time? Was she confusing sternness with cruelty?

She knew one thing for certain: this man's fearlessness made her forget his deformity.

The man with the shaved head went over to the trolley first and started tearing the rubber scalps off his fallen enemies. Then suddenly he staggered back from the motor trolley as if he had seen the devil in person, holding out both arms in front of himself and repeating one word over and over again...

'Black!'

CHAPTER 9

Air

Fear and terror are not the same thing at all. Fear spurs a man on to take action and be creative. Terror paralyses the body and blocks the flow of thought, it makes a man less human. Homer had seen enough in his time to know the difference between them. His brigadier, who was not endowed with the ability to experience fear, had proved surprisingly vulnerable to terror. But the old man was even more amazed by what had reduced Hunter to this state.

The body from which he had removed the gas mask looked unusual. The face that had appeared from under the black rubber had dark, glossy skin, thick lips and a broad, flat nose. Homer hadn't seen any black men since the day the music channels on TV stopped working – more than twenty years ago – but it wasn't hard for him to recognise the dead man as simply a member of a different race. Curious, certainly. But what was so frightening about it?

The brigadier had already taken a grip on himself: his strange fit had lasted less than a minute. He shone his flashlight on the dark face, growled something unintelligible and started roughly undressing the obstinate body, and Homer could have sworn he heard the crunch of fingers being broken.

'It's a mockery... Just to remind me again, right! It's inhuman... A punishment like that...' he wheezed almost inaudibly.

Had he taken the man for someone else? Was he mutilating the body in revenge for his own momentary humiliation or settling some older and much more serious score? The old man suppressed his own revulsion, glancing stealthily at the brigadier as he stripped another body.

The girl didn't take any part in the looting and Hunter didn't try to force her. She walked away, sat down on the rails and lowered her face into her hands. It seemed to Homer that she was crying.

Hunter dragged the bodies out through the door and dumped them in a heap. In less than twenty-four hours there would be nothing left of them. During the day, mastery of the city passed to creatures so appalling that the fearsome predators of the night hid away deep in their burrows, waiting meekly for their hour to come again.

Although the dead man's blood wasn't visible on the dark uniform, it didn't dry out immediately. It felt cold and clammy on Homer's stomach and chest, clinging to him as if it wanted to get back into a living body, causing a horrible itching on his skin and in his mind. He wondered if this masquerade was really necessary, and the only consolation he could find was that it would help them to avoid any more casualties in Avtozavod Station. If Hunter's calculations proved correct, the guards would take them for their own men and let them through unopposed. But what if they didn't? And was the brigadier even trying to reduce the number of deaths that he left in his wake?

Homer found the brigadier's bloodthirstiness repellent, but also intriguing. Self-defence could not justify even a third of all the killings he committed, but it was a matter of something more than plain sadism. What concerned the old man most of all was whether Hunter was heading for Tula simply in order to indulge his craving.

Even if the unfortunate people who were trapped at that station couldn't find a cure for the mysterious fever, it didn't mean that there was no cure, in principle! There were places in the underground world where the embers of scientific thought continued to glow, where research was carried out, new medicines were developed and serums were manufactured. Polis, for example – that confluence of four major arteries, the heart of the Metro, the last remaining simulacrum of a genuine city, that extended through the connecting passages between the Arbat, Borovitskaya, Alexander Garden and Lenin Library stations, where the doctors and scientists who survived had established their base. Or the immense bunker near Taganka Station, the secret technopolis that belonged to Hansa...

And apart from that, Tula might not be the first station where the epidemic had broken out. What if someone had already managed to beat the sickness? 'How could I possibly abandon so easily any hope of being saved?' Homer asked himself. Of course, now that he was carrying the time bomb of the disease in his own body, the old man had a vested interest in this kind of reasoning. In his rational mind Homer had almost accepted the idea that he would die soon. But his instincts rebelled, demanding that he try to find a way out. If he could find a way to save Tula, he would protect his home station from harm and be saved himself...

But Hunter simply didn't believe there was any cure for this disease. After exchanging a few words with the watch at Tula on a single occasion, he had condemned all the inhabitants of the station to death and immediately set about putting the sentence into effect. He had misled the top command of Sebastopol with wild stories about nomads, imposed his own decision on them and was now inexorably approaching the point of making it a reality by committing Tula to the flames.

Or did he know about something happening at the station that turned everything topsy-turvy again? Something that neither Homer nor the man who left his diary at Nakhimov Prospect knew about...

When he was done with the bodies, the brigadier tugged his flask off his belt and sucked out the remains of its contents. What was it? Alcohol? Did he use his hooch as a condiment to help him savour his actions, or was he trying to kill the aftertaste? Was he relishing the moment or trying to escape from it – or perhaps he hoped that with alcohol he could smother something inside himself?

For Sasha, the smoky old motor trolley was a time machine out of the bedtime stories her father once used to amuse her with. It wasn't carrying the girl from Kolomenskoe to Avtozavod, but taking her back from the present into the past – although no one but her could possibly have thought of the stone dungeon where she had spent all these years, that blind alley in space and time, as 'the present'.

She remembered the journey in the other direction very well: she was still only a little girl, her father, tightly bound, with a woolly hat pulled down over his eyes and a gag in his mouth, sat beside her. She cried all the time, and one of the soldiers in the firing squad folded his fingers together and showed her various shadow animals in the little yellow circus ring that was running along the ceiling of the tunnel, racing with the trolley.

The sentence was read out to her father after they crossed the bridge: the revolutionary tribunal commuted his sentence from execution to lifelong banishment.

They pushed him out onto the rails, tossed him a knife, a sub-machine-gun with one clip of cartridges and an old gas mask, then helped Sasha get down. The soldier who had shown the little girl the horsy and the doggy waved to her.

Could he be one of the men who had been shot today?

The feeling of breathing someone else's air grew stronger when she squirmed into a black gas mask taken off one of the bodies by the man with the shaved head. Every tiny little stretch of her journey cost someone's life. The man with the shaved head would probably have shot them anyway, but now that Sasha was here, she was an accomplice.

It wasn't only because he was tired of fighting that her father hadn't wanted to come home. He used to say that all his humiliations and deprivations weighed less than even a single human life. He suffered in order not to cause suffering to others. Sasha knew that the pan of the scales holding all the lives he had taken already hung very, very low, and her father was simply trying to restore the balance.

But the man with the shaved head could have intervened sooner, couldn't he? He could have simply frightened the men on the trolley, just by appearing, and disarmed them without firing a single shot: Sasha was sure of that. None of the dead men was a worthy opponent for him. Why did he have to do that?

The station of her childhood was closer than she thought. In less than ten minutes its lights were glimmering ahead of them. There was no one guarding the approaches to Avtozavod: the station's inhabitants obviously placed too much faith in the locked hermetic doors. Fifty metres before the platform, the man with the shaved head switched the engine to low speed and told Homer to take the helm, while he moved closer to the machine-gun.

The trolley rolled into the station almost without a sound and very, very slowly – or perhaps time was standing still for Sasha, so that she could see everything and remember it all in a few brief moments? On that day her father had left her in the care of his orderly, telling him to hide her until everything was sorted out. The orderly led her deep into the underbelly of the station, to one of the service areas. But even from there they could hear the simultaneous roar of a thousand throats, and he went dashing back to be with his commander. Sasha hurtled along the empty corridor behind him and darted out into the hall...

They drifted along the platform, and Sasha looked at the spacious family tents and the carriages equipped as offices, the little kids playing tag and the old men chatting, the sullen men cleaning their guns...

And she saw her father standing in front of a thin line of angry, frightened men who were trying to enclose and restrain a raging crowd. She ran over to her father and pressed herself against his back. He swung round crazily, shook her off and slapped his adjutant in the face as he came hurrying up. But something had already happened to him. The line of men, which had frozen with its automatic weapons raised in anticipation of the command to open fire, was ordered to stand down. The only shot was one fired into the air. Her father started negotiations on the peaceful handover of the station to the revolutionaries...

Her father believed that a man was given signs. You just had to know how to see them and read them correctly.

No, time hadn't slowed down just so that she could revisit the final day of her childhood. She spotted the armed men rising to meet the trolley before the others did. She saw the man with the shaved head reach the trigger switch with an elusive, fluid movement and start turning the thick, burnished barrel towards the amazed sentries. She heard the hissed command to halt the trolley before the old man did. And Sasha realised so many people would be killed now, that she would feel as if she were breathing someone else's air for the rest of her life. But she could still prevent the massacre, save them and herself and one other man from something more appalling than any words could express.

The sentries were already taking their automatics off the safety catches, but they fiddled with them too long, and were several moves behind the man with the shaved head. She did the first thing that came into her mind – she jumped up and pressed herself against his lumpy, iron-hard back, hugging him from behind and clasping her hands on his chest, which was so still, it didn't seem to be breathing. He shuddered as if she had lashed him with a whip, hesitated ... The sentries, finally ready to fire, were bewildered too.

The old man understood her without any words.

The trolley shot off down the tracks, belching out black clouds of bitter smoke, and Avtozavod Station receded rapidly – back into the past.

All the way to Pavelets Station no one spoke another word. Hunter freed himself from the unexpected embrace, parting the girl's arms as if he were bending open a steel hoop that prevented him from breathing. They slipped past the only guard post at full speed and the spray of bullets directed at them from it bit into the ceiling above their heads. The brigadier managed to pull out his pistol and reply with three soundless flashes of flame. He seemed to have brought one man down, but the others melted into the walls, squeezing themselves in behind the shallow lips of the tunnel liners to save themselves.

'My, my,' thought Homer, glancing at the girl, who was quiet and subdued now. He had assumed the love line would come into play soon after the heroine's appearance, but everything was developing too fast. Faster than he could understand it all, let alone write it down.

They rode into Pavelets Station and stopped.

The old man had been here before, at this station straight out of the mists of Gothic legend. Instead of the plain columns that supported the vaults in all the newer, outlying stations of the Metro, Pavelets Station was supported by a series of airy, rounded arches that were too high for ordinary people. In typical fashion for legends of that kind, Pavelets was the victim of a distinctive curse. At precisely eight o'clock in the evening the hustle and bustle suddenly died away and the thriving station was transformed into its own ghost. Out of its entire dynamic and resourceful population, only a few daredevils were left on the platform. Everyone else disappeared – together with their children, personal effects, trunks stuffed with goods, benches and makeshift beds.

They all crammed into the refuge – the almost kilometre-long connecting passage to the Circle Line – and trembled there through the long night while monstrous creatures who had woken from their sleep prowled around on the surface at the Pavelets railway station. People who ought to know said these creatures were the unchallenged masters of the station building and the adjoining territory, and even while they slept no other beasts would dare to wander in there. The inhabitants of Pavelets had no defences against them: the shutters that cut off the escalators at other stations simply didn't exist here, and the way out to the surface was always open. To Homer's mind, it would have been hard to find anywhere less appropriate for an overnight halt. But Hunter thought differently: when the trolley reached the far end of the hall, it stopped.

'We'll stay here until the morning. Make yourselves at home,' he said, pulling off his gas mask and waving his hand round at the station. And he left them. The girl watched him go, then curled up on the hard floor of the trolley. The old man made himself as comfortable as possible and closed his eyes, trying to doze off, but in vain. He was besieged again by thoughts of the plague that he was carrying round all the stations that were still uninfected. The girl couldn't sleep either.

'Thank you. I thought you were the same as him,' she told Homer.

'I don't think there are any other men like that,' the old man replied.

'Are you two friends?'

'Like a sucker fish and a shark,' he said with a grim smile, thinking that was exactly the way it was: Hunter devoured people, but occasional bloody scraps of human flesh came his way too.

'How do you mean?' she asked, half-sitting up.

'Where he goes, I go. I don't think I could manage without him, and he ... Perhaps he thinks that I'll absolve him somehow. Although no one really knows what he thinks.'

'But why can't you manage without him?' asked the girl, moving to sit closer to the old man.

'I have the feeling that while I'm with him, my inspiration ... won't desert me.' Homer tried to explain.

'Inspiration – I read somewhere that means "breathing in",' said Alexandra. 'But why do you want to breathe that? What good will it do you?'

Homer shrugged.

'It's not what we breathe in, it's what's breathed into us,' he replied. 'I think that as long as you breathe death, no one will kiss your

141

lips. They'll be scared of the rotten corpse smell,' she said, drawing something on the dirty floor with her finger.

'When you see death, it makes you think about many things,' Homer remarked.

'You don't have any right to summon death every time you need to think,' she objected.

'I don't summon it, I just stand there ... and then it hasn't really got anything to do with death ... or not only with death,' the old man countered. 'I wanted a story to happen to me, a story that would change everything. I wanted something to happen in my life. To shake me up. And clear out my head.'

'Did you have a bad life?' the girl asked sympathetically.

'A boring one. You know, when one day's like any other, they fly by so fast and it seems like the last one is really close already,' Homer tried to explain. 'You feel afraid of not getting anything finished. And every one of those days is full of a thousand little things to be done. Do one, take a break, and it's time to start on the next one. You have no time or strength left for what's really important. You think: never mind – I'll start tomorrow. But tomorrow never comes, it's always just one long, endless today.'

'Have you seen many stations?' She didn't seem to be following what the old man was telling her at all.

'I don't know,' he replied, puzzled. 'All of them, probably.'

'And I've seen two,' the girl sighed. 'First my father and I lived at Avtozavod, then we were exiled to Kolomenskoe. I always wanted to see at least one more. It's so strange here ...' She ran her eyes along the line of arches. 'As if there were a thousand gateways, and not even any walls between them. And there they are, all open for me, but I don't want to go through. And I'm afraid.'

'So he was your father? That man, the other one ...' Homer hesitated. 'Did they kill him?'

The girl retreated back into her shell of silence for a long time before she responded.

'Yes.'

'Stay with us,' said the old man, plucking up his nerve. 'I'll have a word with Hunter, I think he'll agree. I'll tell him I need you, for ...' He shrugged, not knowing how to explain to the girl that now she had to inspire him.

'Tell him *he* needs *me*,' said Sasha.

She jumped down onto the platform and wandered away from the trolley, stroking every column as she walked past it.

There was absolutely nothing coy about her, she didn't flirt at all. Along with all kinds of firearms, she seemed to despise the standard female arsenal – those sweet little glances and heart-melting gestures, those fluttering eyelashes that can raise a hurricane and those half-smiles for which a man would sacrifice himself or kill another. Or was it that she simply didn't know yet how to use these weapons?

Whatever the reason, she could manage without them. A single dagger thrust from those eyes of hers had made Hunter reverse a decision, a single movement from her had snared him in a net and kept him from killing. But had that thrust really pierced through his armour into the soft flesh? Or did he need her for something? That was probably it. It seemed strange to Homer even to imagine that the brigadier had any vulnerable spots, that he could even be pricked, let alone wounded.

Homer simply couldn't sleep. Although he had swapped the stifling black gas mask for a light respirator, he still found it just as hard to breathe and the vice that was crushing his head hadn't slackened its grip. Homer had dumped all his old things in the tunnel. He had scrubbed his hands clean with a piece of grey soap, washed off the dirt with greenish water from an old fuel can and made a voluntary decision always to wear a white face mask from now on. What else could the old man do to avoid danger to people he was with?

Nothing. Absolutely nothing at all now, not even going into the tunnel and reducing himself to an abandoned heap of rotten rags would do any good. But today's close brush with death had suddenly taken him back twenty years, to the days when he had just lost everyone he loved. And that had given his plans a new, authentic meaning.

If it was up to Homer, he would have erected a genuine monument to them. But they surely deserved at least a basic headstone. Born decades apart, they had all died on the same day: his wife, his children, his parents.

And there were all his classmates from school and friends from the technical college. His favourite movie actors and musicians.

And all those people who were still at work that day, or had already got home, or were stuck somewhere halfway in the traffic jams.

The ones who died immediately and the ones who tried to survive, lingering for a few more days in the poisoned, half-ruined capital, scraping feebly at the locked hermetic doors of the Metro. The ones who disintegrated instantly into atoms, and the ones who swelled up and crumbled away while still alive, devoured by radiation sickness.

The scouts who went up onto the surface first couldn't get to sleep for days after they returned from their mission. Homer had met some of them round the campfires at transfer stations, he had looked into their eyes and seen streets like frozen rivers swollen with dead fish, imprinted on those eyes forever. Thousands of stalled cars with dead passengers choked the avenues and the highways leading out of Moscow. Dead bodies were lying everywhere. Until the city's new masters arrived, there was no one to clear them away.

To spare themselves, the scouts tried to avoid the schools and kindergartens. But to lose your mind, it was enough to catch a single frozen gaze from the back seat of a family car. Billions of lives were broken off simultaneously. Billions of thoughts were left unspoken, billions of dreams were left unrealised, billions of grievances were left unforgiven. Nikolai's little son had asked him for a big set of coloured felt-tip pens, his daughter had been afraid to go to her figure skating lessons; before she went to sleep, his wife had described in vivid detail how they would spend a short holiday by the sea together, just the two of them. When he thought that these little wishes and desires were the last they had, they suddenly became exceptionally important. Homer would have liked to carve an epitaph for each one of them. But humanity certainly deserved at least one epitaph for its gigantic mass grave. And now, when he himself had almost no time left, Homer felt he could find the right words for it.

He still didn't know what order to arrange them in, what he would use to bind them together, how he would embellish them, but he could already sense that the story unfolding before his very eyes would have a place for every restless, troubled soul, for every single feeling and every crumb of knowledge that he had gathered so painstakingly, and for him too. No plot could have suited his purpose better.

144

When dawn came up on the surface, the rows of market stalls would stir into life down below, and then he would definitely take a walk along them to get himself a clean exercise book and a ballpoint pen. And he had to hurry: if he didn't get down on paper the outlines of the future novel that he could see glimmering like a mirage ahead of him, it could melt away, and who could say how much longer he would have to sit on the summit of his sand dune, gazing into the distance and hoping that his ivory tower would start rising up again out of the fine grains of sand and the shimmering, incandescent air?

There might not be enough time.

'No matter what nonsense the girl might talk, a glance into the empty eye sockets of eternity is certainly a great stimulus to action,' the old man chuckled to himself. And then, recalling the arches of her eyebrows – two flashes of white on the sombre, grimy face – and the bite marks on her lip, and her tousled, straw-blonde hair, he smiled again.

'I'll have to find something else at the market tomorrow as well,' Homer thought as he fell asleep.

Night at Pavelets Station is always restless. Glimmers of light from the smoking torches flicker across the soot-stained marble walls, the tunnels breathe uneasily and the men sitting at the foot of the escalators talk to each other in voices so low, they can hardly be heard. The station pretends to be dead, hoping the predatory beasts from the surface won't be tempted by the smell of meat.

But sometimes the most curious of those beasts discover a passage that leads down deep, start sniffing at it and catch the scent of fresh sweat, the beating of hearts, the murmur of blood coursing through veins. And they set off downwards.

Homer had finally dozed off, and the alarmed voices from the far end of the platform filtered into his awareness as dull, distorted echoes. But then a shot rang out, instantly jerking him out of his hazy half-sleep. The old man jumped up, staring around wildly and groping for his gun on the floor of the trolley.

The deafening, thunderous rumbling of the machine-gun was joined by the stuttering of several sub-machine-guns and the alarm in the sentries' shouts was replaced by genuine terror. Whoever it was they were firing all their weapons at, it wasn't having any effect. This was no longer coordinated fire at a moving target, but the desperate, ragged shooting of men simply trying to save their own skins.

Homer found his automatic, but he couldn't make himself go out into the hall; it took all his willpower to resist the temptation to start the motor and shoot out of the station at top speed – it didn't matter a damn where to. But he stayed in the trolley, craning his neck to make out the battle zone through the crowded line of the columns. Slicing through the yelling and swearing of the sentries trying to defend themselves came a piercing shriek that sounded surprisingly close.

The machine-gun choked and someone gave a terrible scream that was cut short as suddenly as if his head had been torn off. The chatter of sub-machine-guns hammered at Homer's ears again. But now it was sparse and scattered. The shriek was repeated – it sounded a little further away now... And suddenly the creature that made it was answered by an echo – somewhere close to the trolley.

Homer counted to ten and started the motor with trembling hands: any moment now his companions would come back, and they could go racing off immediately – he was doing it for their sake, not his own... The trolley trembled and smoked as the motor warmed up, and then something flickered between the columns at an unbelievable speed, blurring past and slithering out of view faster than his mind could process the image. The old man grabbed hold of the handrail, set his foot on the accelerator pedal and took a deep breath. If they didn't come in the next ten seconds, he'd just drop everything and... And then, without even knowing why he was doing it, Homer stepped out onto the platform, holding his useless automatic out in front of him. Just to make sure that there was nothing more he could still do for either of his companions. He pressed himself tight against a column and glanced out into the hall... He tried to scream, but he didn't have enough air.

Sasha had always known the world wasn't limited to the two stations where she had lived, but she could never have imagined that the world beyond them could be so beautiful. Dull and bleak as Kolomenskoe was, to her it had seemed like a home, cosy and familiar in every little detail. Avtozavod was haughty and spacious, but cold, it had turned its back on her father and her, rejected them, and she couldn't forget that.

But in her relationship with Pavelets she could turn a new leaf, and Sasha's desire to fall in love with this station grew stronger with every minute she spent there. She wanted to fall in love with its light, branching columns, with its huge, inviting arches, with its noble marble covered in darling little veins that made the walls look like someone's delicate skin... Kolomenskoe was ugly, Avtozavod was too severe, but this station seemed to have been built by a woman, it was playful, even frivolous. Even decades on, Pavelets refused to forget its own former glory. The people who lived here couldn't be vicious and cruel, Sasha thought. Did she and her father really only have to get past one hostile station in order to find themselves in this magical land? Would it really have been enough for him to live just one more day, in order to escape from his exile and hard labour and be free again? She would have been able to persuade the man with the shaved head to take both of them...

In the distance a campfire flickered, surrounded by sentries, and the beam of a searchlight probed at the high ceiling, but Sasha didn't want to go that way. For so many years it had seemed to her that once she broke out of Kolomenskoe and met other people, she would be happy! But now Sasha needed only one person – to share her delight and amazement that now the world really was bigger by a whole third and her hope that everything could still be put right. But there probably wasn't anyone at all who needed Sasha, no matter what she might try to make herself and the old man believe.

So the girl wandered off in the opposite direction, to where a dilapidated train stood halfway into the right tunnel, with its windows broken and doors wide open. She walked inside and along through the train, soaring over the gaps between the carriages as she inspected the first, the second, the third... In the last one Sasha found a seat that had miraculously survived and clambered onto it, pulling up her legs. She looked round, trying to imagine that any moment now the train would start moving and carry her on to more stations, brightly lit and vibrant with human voices. But her faith and imagination weren't strong enough to set thousands of tons of scrap iron moving. It had all been so much easier with her bicycle. And her attempt to hide failed: skipping from carriage to carriage in her wake, the noise of the battle unfolding in Pavelets Station finally caught up with her. Again?

She lowered her feet onto the floor and dashed back to the station – to the only place where she could at least do something.

The mutilated bodies of sentries were lying by the glass booth with the frozen searchlight, and in the extinguished campfire, and in the centre of the hall – those men had already abandoned any resistance and were running to seek refuge in the passage, but death had overtaken them halfway there.

A sinister, unnatural figure was doubled up over one of the bodies. From that distance it was hard to make it out clearly, but Homer saw smooth white skin, an immensely powerful, twitching neck, and legs bent at too many joints, with impatiently shuffling feet.

The battle had been lost. But where was Hunter?

The old man peeped again and froze in horror... About ten steps away from him, more than two metres up in the air, a nightmarish face was staring at him, peeping out from behind a column exactly like Homer, as if it was playing peek-a-boo. Something red was dripping from the drooping lower lip, the lower jaw was working incessantly, grinding up its hideous cud, and the space below the sloping forehead was absolutely empty, but the lack of eyes didn't seem to cause the beast any difficulty in moving about and attacking.

Homer pulled back, squeezing the trigger – his automatic didn't make a sound. The monster let out a long, deafening howl and darted into the centre of the hall. The old man started jerking the jammed breech backwards and forwards, realising he didn't have enough time...

But suddenly the monster lost all interest in him: now its attention was riveted to the edge of the platform. Homer swung round sharply, following the line of that blind gaze, and his heart stopped dead. The girl was standing there, gazing round in fright.

'Run!' Homer yelled, his voice instantly breaking into a croak that scraped at his throat.

The white monster sprang forward, covering several metres in a single bound, and stood in front of the girl. She pulled out a knife that was useless for anything but cooking and made a warning lunge. In reply the beast swung one of its front paws and the girl collapsed on the ground; her knife went flying several metres through the air.

The old man was already on the trolley. But he wasn't thinking about running away any more. Puffing and panting, he swung the machine-gun round, trying to catch that white, dancing silhouette in the cobweb lines of the sight. He couldn't: the monster was moving in on Sasha. Homer had the impression that after savaging the sentries, who represented at least some kind of danger to it, the creature was amusing itself by driving two helpless victims into a corner and toying with them before it finished them off.

Now it was hunched over Sasha, screening her from the old man's view. Skinning its prey?

Suddenly it jerked and staggered backwards, scraping with its claws at a dark patch spreading across its back, and swung round with a roar, preparing to devour its attacker.

Treading unsteadily, holding his automatic out in one hand, Hunter walked towards it. His other arm dangled limply at his side and it was clear that every step he took cost him an immense effort and great pain.

The brigadier raked the monster with another burst of fire, but the creature was incredibly tough; it merely swayed, then immediately recovered its balance and came hurtling forward. Hunter had run out of cartridges and he pivoted round in an incredible turn, taking the immense carcass on the blade of his machete as the monster collapsed down onto him, stifling him with its sheer weight and breaking his bones.

The second monster came running up to destroy any remaining hope. It froze over the twitching body of its fellow and plucked at the white skin with its claw, as if trying to wake the other beast up, then slowly raised its eyeless face towards the old man . . .

Homer didn't miss his chance. The heavy calibre bullets shredded the monster's torso and shattered its skull, knocking it to the ground, then continued reducing the marble slabs behind its back to chips and dust. It was some time before the old man could calm his heart and unclasp his cramped fingers.

Then he closed his eyes, took off his respirator and let the frosty air, saturated with the rusty smell of fresh blood, flood into him. All the heroes had fallen, he was left alone on the battlefield.

His book was over before it had even begun.

CHAPTER 10

After Death

What remains after people die? What will remain after each one of us?

Gravestones subside and become overgrown with moss, and it takes only a few decades for the inscriptions on them to become illegible.

Even in former times, when no one was left to take care of graves, the ground in a cemetery was redistributed among the newly deceased. The only people who came to visit the dead were their children or parents; grandchildren came far more rarely, great-grandchildren almost never.

In major cities, what was customarily referred to as 'eternal peace' meant a respite of only half a century before the bones would be disturbed, perhaps so that more remains could be crammed into the cemetery, or perhaps so that it could be ploughed up and a new residential district built on it. The earth was becoming too cramped for both the living and the dead.

Half a century is a luxury that only those who died before Dooms-day could afford. Who can be concerned with a single dead man, when an entire planet dies? None of the inhabitants of the Metro has ever been afforded the honour of being buried, or been able to hope that his body will not be destroyed by rats.

Formerly, remains had the right to exist for exactly as long as the living remembered the people to whom they belonged. A man remembers his relatives, his schoolfellows and his workmates. But his memory is only long enough for three generations – for that same period of fifty-something years.

In the same careless manner as we all discard from our memory the image of our grandfather or school friend, some day someone will discard us into absolute oblivion. The memory of a man can last for longer than his skeleton, but when the last of those who still remember us departs, we dissolve into time with him. Photos? Who still has them made these days? And how many of them were kept, even when everyone used to take them? At one time, at the end of every thick family album there used to be a small reservation for old brownish snapshots, but not many of those who leafed through the albums could say for certain which of his ancestors they depicted. In effect, photographs of the departed can be regarded as death masks, cast from the body, but certainly not life masks cast from the soul. And then, photos decay only slightly more slowly than the bodies of the people they recorded.

So what does remain?

Children?

Homer touched the candle flame with his finger.

It was easy for him to intellectualise; what Ahmed had said was still tormenting him. Condemned to remain childless, deprived of any chance to continue his line, now the old man could only deny the reality of this route to immortality.

He picked up his pen again.

They can look like us. In their features we can see our own features, miraculously fused with the features of those we have loved. Recognising ourselves in their gestures, in the curve of their eyebrows, in their facial expressions, we will be moved to tenderness. Friends might tell us that our sons and daughters are like stencilled copies of us, that they are cast from the same mould. And this supposedly promises us some kind of continuation of ourselves after we cease to exist. But after all, none of us is an initial image from which subsequent copies are made, but merely a phantasmagorical combination, composed half-and-half of the external and internal features of our father and our mother, exactly as they, in turn, consist of halves of their own parents. Does this mean there is nothing unique about us, that there is only an eternal reshuffling of tiny little pieces of the mosaic, which exist in their own right, combining at random into billions of pictures that have no particular value and crumble away before our very eyes? If so, what sense does it make to be so proud of the fact that we see in our children this particular hook of the nose or that particular dimple in the cheek, which we are used to thinking of as our own, but which has really been wandering through thousands of bodies for half a million years already?

Will anything remain after me, in particular?

Homer had a harder time than other people. He genuinely envied those whose faith allowed them to hope for admission into an afterworld. As for him, when he heard it mentioned in conversation, the old man's thoughts immediately flew back to Nakhimov Prospect. Quite possibly Homer did not consist only of the flesh that would be ground up and digested by the corpse-eaters. But even if there was something else in him, that something was not capable of existing apart from the flesh and bone.

What remained after the kings of Egypt? Or after the heroes of Greece? Or after the artists of the Renaissance? Did anything at all remain of them? And did they remain in anything?

But what other immortality is left to man?

Homer reread what he had written, pondered for a moment and then carefully tore the pages out of the exercise book, crumpled them up, put them on a metal plate and set fire to them. A minute later a handful of ash was all that remained of the work on which he had spent the last three hours.

She died.

This was how Sasha had always imagined death: the final ray of light is extinguished, all the voices fall silent, you can't feel your body, and all that's left is eternal darkness. The blackness and silence from out of which people emerge and to which they inevitably return. Sasha had heard stories about heaven and about hell, but the Underworld had always seemed perfectly innocuous to her. Eternity spent in total inactivity, absolutely blind and deaf, seemed a hundred times worse to her than any cauldrons of boiling oil.

And then a tiny, trembling flame appeared ahead of her. Sasha reached out to it, but it was impossible to catch: the dancing firefly ran away from her, moved back closer to tease her, and immediately darted away again, tantalising her, luring her after itself.

She knew what it was: the tunnel spark.

Her father used to say that when someone died in the Metro, their soul wandered in confusion through the pitch-dark tangle of tunnels, and every tunnel ended in a dead end. It didn't understand that it wasn't attached to a body any longer, that its earthly existence was over. It had to carry on wandering until somewhere far ahead it saw the light of a phantom campfire. And when the soul saw the light, it had to hurry towards it, because it was sent for the soul and would run away, leading the soul to a place where peace was waiting. But sometimes it happened that the little light took mercy on a soul and led it back to its lost body. Other people whispered about people like that, saying they had come back from the next world, although it would be more correct to say the darkness had released them.

The spark called for her to follow, it insisted and Sasha gave in. She couldn't feel her legs, but they weren't needed: in order to keep up with the light as it slipped away, all she had to do was not lose sight of it. To keep her eyes fixed on it intently, as if she were trying to win it over, to tame it.

Sasha managed to catch it after all, and the little light dragged the girl through the pitch darkness, through labyrinths of tunnels from which she would never have found a way out, to the final station on the line of her life. Things suddenly started becoming visible up ahead: Sasha fancied her guide was tracing out the contours of some distant room where she was expected.

'Sasha!' a voice called out to her, an amazingly familiar voice, although she couldn't remember who it belonged to.

'Dad?' she asked warily, thinking she could hear a note of affectionate warmth in the other person's voice.

They arrived. The spectral tunnel spark halted, turned into an ordinary flame and hopped onto the wick of a melted, spreading candle, settling down on it comfortably, like a cat that has just come back from a walk.

A cool, calloused palm covered her hand. Hesitantly, afraid of sinking to the bottom again, Sasha detached herself from the little light. Following her into wakefulness, pain stabbed through her torn forearm and her bruised temple started aching. Plain, official furniture surfaced out of the darkness, swaying close by – two chairs, a locker ... Sasha herself was lying on a genuine bed, so soft that she couldn't feel her back at all. As if her body was being returned to her by parts, and some were still waiting for their turn.

'Sasha?' the voice repeated.

She turned her eyes to the speaker and jerked her hand away. Sitting at her bedside was the old man she had travelled with on the trolley. There was nothing intrusive in his touch, it didn't sting or insult her; she took her hand away because she felt ashamed that she could confuse a stranger's voice with her father's, and out of resentment that the tunnel spark had led her to the wrong place.

The old man smiled gently. It seemed to be quite enough for him that she had come round. Looking more closely, Sasha noticed a warm glint in his eyes, the kind of glint she had only ever encountered before in the eyes of one man. It wasn't surprising that she had been deceived. And she suddenly felt awkward in front of the old man.

'Sorry,' she said.

And then, recalling her final minutes at Pavelets, she jerked up. 'What happened to your friend?'

She seemed unable either to laugh or to cry, or perhaps she didn't have enough strength left for either. The girl was lucky, the monster's blade-like claws had missed her: that single blow had landed flat. But even that had been enough to leave her unconscious for twenty-four hours. Her life was in no danger now, the doctor assured Homer. The old man hadn't talked to the doctor about his own troubles. Sasha – while she was unconscious, the old man had got into the habit of calling her that – went limp and slumped back down onto the pillow, and Homer went back to the desk, where the open exercise book, with a full ninety-six pages, was waiting for him. He twirled the pen in his hands and carried on from the place where he had abandoned his newly begun book to go over to the girl when she groaned deliriously.

... the latest convoy had been delayed ... delayed beyond any reasonable limit, long enough for the realisation to dawn that this time something terrible and unforeseen had happened, something against which not even heavily-armed, battle-hardened guards and a relationship built up over the years with the leadership of Hansa had been able to protect it.

And all this would not have been so bad, if only the lines of communication were functioning. But something had happened to the telephone line that led to the Circle: contact had been broken off on Monday, and the team sent out to search for the break had drawn a blank.

Homer looked up and started: the girl was standing behind him, deciphering his scribble over his shoulder. She seemed to be held up by nothing but curiosity. Feeling embarrassed, the old man turned the exercise book face down.

'Is that what you need inspiration for?' she asked him.

'I'm still right at the beginning,' Homer muttered for some reason.

'And what happened to the convoy?'

'I don't know,' he said, starting to draw a frame round the title. 'The story's not finished yet. Lie down, you need to rest.'

'But it's up to you how you finish the book,' she objected, without moving from the spot.

'In this book nothing's up to me.' The old man put his pen down on the table. 'I'm not inventing it, just writing down everything that happens to me.'

'That means everything depends on you even more,' the girl said thoughtfully. 'Will I be in it?'

'I was just going to ask your permission,' Homer chuckled.

'I'll think about it,' she replied seriously. 'But what are you writing it for?'

The old man stood up, so that he wouldn't be looking up at her from below.

After his last conversation with Sasha he'd realised that her youthfulness and inexperience created a false impression; it was as if at the strange station where they had picked her up, every year was worth two normal ones. She had a way of not answering the questions that he asked out loud, but the ones that hadn't been asked. And Sasha only asked Homer about things that he didn't know himself.

And it also seemed to him that if he wanted to rely on her being sincere and open – and how else could she become his heroine? – then he would have to be honest with her himself, not leave things unsaid and tell her everything he would have told himself.

'I want people to remember me. Me and those who were dear to me. I want them to know what the world I loved was like. To hear the most important things that I learned and understood. So that my life won't have been in vain. So that something will be left after me.'

'Are you putting your soul into it?' She leaned her head to one side. 'But it's just an exercise book. It can get burned or lost.'

'An unreliable place for keeping a soul, right?' Homer sighed. 'No,

I need the exercise book to line everything up in the right order, and so I won't forget anything important before the story's been written right to the end. After that it will be enough to tell it to a few people. And if everything goes right for me, I won't need any paper or even a body any more.'

'I suppose you've seen lots of things it would be a shame to forget forever,' the girl said with a shrug. 'But I haven't got anything to write down. And I don't need to be in your exercise book. Don't waste paper on me.'

'Ah, but you're only just beginning...' the old man began, and broke off: he wouldn't be there. The girl didn't respond, and Homer felt frightened that now she would clam up completely. He tried to find the right words to take everything back, but only tangled himself even more tightly in his own doubts.

'And what's the most beautiful thing out of everything you remember?' she suddenly asked. 'The most beautiful, beautiful thing?'

Homer paused, hesitating. Sharing his most intimate thoughts with a person he had known for less than two days felt strange. He hadn't trusted Elena with this – even she thought the picture hanging on the wall in their little room was just an ordinary city view. And how could a young girl who had spent all her life underground possibly understand what he might tell her?

'Summer rain,' he said, deciding to try.

'What's so beautiful about that?' she asked with a funny kind of frown.

'Have you ever seen rain?'

'No.' The girl shook her head. 'My father wouldn't let me go outside. I did go out once or twice anyway, but I felt bad out there. It's frightening without any walls around you. Rain is when water comes falling down,' she said, just to be sure.

But Homer wasn't listening to her any longer. He was suddenly back in that day from the distant past; like a medium who has lent his body to the spirit he has summoned, he stared into empty space and talked, on and on ...

'It was dry and very hot for the whole month. And my wife was pregnant, it was hard enough for her to breathe anyway, and then this blazing heat ... In the maternity home there was just one fan for the entire ward, she kept complaining all the time about how stuffy it was. And because of her I could hardly breathe myself. I was in a terrible state: we'd tried so hard for years, but nothing worked, and now the doctors were frightening us with a miscarriage. And she was supposed to be in there so she could keep the baby, but she would have been better off lying at home. Her time had come and nothing was happening. There were no contractions, and I couldn't keep asking my boss for the day off every day. And someone told me that if a child is carried too long, it can be stillborn. I was beside myself, I dashed straight from work to stand guard under her window. My phone had no signal in the tunnels, and I checked at every station to see if I had any missed calls. And then I got a text message from the doctor: "Call urgently". Like a real fool, before I could find a quiet spot, in my own mind, I had my wife and the child buried already. I dialled the number...'

Homer fell silent, listening to the ringing of the phone, waiting for an answer. The girl didn't interrupt him, saving her questions for later.

'And they tell me: Congratulations, you have a son. It sounds so simple now: You have a son. But at that moment they gave me my wife back, raised her from the dead ... and then there's another miracle ... I go up to the street – and it's raining. Cool rain. And the air was suddenly so light and transparent. As if the city had been wrapped in dusty cellophane, and now it had suddenly been taken off. The leaves started glowing, the sky was moving at last, the houses suddenly got younger. I ran along Tver Street to a flower kiosk, and I was crying from happiness too. I had an umbrella, but I didn't bother to open it, I wanted to get soaked through, I wanted to feel it, that rain. I can't express it properly now. My son had been born, but it was like I'd been born again myself, and I looked at the world as if I was seeing it for the very first time. Now everything was going to be new: if anything wasn't going right, if anything was wrong, I could fix it, everything. Now it was like I had two lives. If I couldn't get something finished, my son would do it.

'We had everything ahead of us. Everyone had everything ahead of them ...'

The old man stopped: he was gazing at Tver Street's ten-storey Stalin-era buildings in the pink evening haze, luxuriating in the businesslike rumble of traffic, breathing in the sweetish, fume-laden air, and he closed his eyes, turning his face to the summer downpour. When he came to his senses the raindrops were still glistening on his cheeks and in the corners of his eyes, proof of his journey back to that day.

He wiped them away quickly with his sleeve.

'You know,' said the girl, seeming just as embarrassed as Homer, 'I suppose rain can be beautiful after all. I don't have any memories like that. Can I remember yours? And if you like,' she smiled at him, 'I'll be in your book. The way it ends has to depend on someone, doesn't it?'

'It's still too soon,' the doctor snapped.

Sasha simply couldn't explain to this dry stick how important her request was to her. She filled her lungs with air for another attack, but didn't use it: instead she just gestured with her healthy arm and turned away.

'Never mind, be patient. But since you're on your feet, you can take a gentle stroll.' He gathered his instruments into a worn plastic bag and shook the old man's hand. 'I'll call back in a couple of hours. My boss told me to keep an eye on things. As you realise, we're in your debt.'

The old man put a soldier's camouflage jacket round Sasha's shoulders and she went out, following the doctor past the other wards of the infirmary, though a string of rooms and cubbyholes crammed with tables and beds, up two flights of stairs and through an inconspicuous low door into the vast, long hall. Sasha froze in the doorway and took a long time to pluck up the courage to step out into it. She had never come across so many people at once before; she could never have imagined that there were so many people alive in the world. Thousands of them – without masks! And all so different from each other ... There were completely decrepit old people and little babies. A huge number of men – men with beards or clean-shaven, tall men and dwarfs, exhausted and drained, red-blooded and muscular. Mutilated in battle or ugly from birth, excessively handsome or attractive for some elusive reason, despite their poor looks. And just as many women – market women with broad backsides and red faces, wearing headscarves and padded jackets; and delicate, pale young women in incredibly bright-coloured clothes and elaborate beads.

Would they see that Sasha was different? Would she be able

to hide in the crowd, pretend to be one of them, or would they attack the outsider, bite the albino to death, like a pack of rats? At first she fancied that everyone's eyes were fixed on her, and every accidentally caught glance threw her into a fever. But after a quarter of an hour she got used to it. The people who looked at her included some who were hostile, or curious, or too insistent, but most of them were indifferent to her. They brushed their eyes gently over Sasha and pushed on through the crowd, taking no notice of her. It occurred to her that these absent-minded glances with nothing jarring about them lubricated the gear wheels of the human bustling, like machine oil. If they took an interest in each other, the friction would be too great and the entire mechanism would be paralysed.

In order to fit in with the crowd, she didn't need to change her clothes or even cut her hair. Instead of that, it was enough to dive into other people's pupils and coldly pull her glance back out after barely dipping it in. Once she had smeared herself with feigned indifference, Sasha could slip between the moving, intermeshing inhabitants of this station without getting stuck at every step.

For the first few minutes her nose was scalded by the simmering brew of human odours, but soon her nose became less sensitive as it learned to pick out the important components and skip all the others.

Weaving their way through the sour smells of stale bodies came the subtle, tantalising aromas of youth. Occasionally the crowd was bathed in waves of fragrance emanating from well-groomed women; and mingling with them was the smoke from meat on braziers, and the stink of the cesspits. In short, for Sasha the passage between the two Pavelets stations smelled of life, and the longer she listened to this deafening smell, the sweeter it seemed.

A full exploration of the boundless passage would probably have taken her an entire month. Everything here was astounding...

Stalls with jewellery woven out of dozens of little yellow metal discs with patterns stamped on them – she wanted to examine them for hours. And immense heaps of books containing more secret knowledge than she could ever master.

A man shouting his wares at a stand that had a sign saying 'Flowers' and a rich collection of greeting cards. The pictures on the cards were faded photographs of all sorts of fancy bouquets.

Sasha had been given a card like that when she was little, but there were so many of them here!

Babies glued to their mothers' breasts, and children a bit older, playing with real cats. Couples still only touching each other with their eyes, and couples already touching each other with their fingers.

And men who tried to touch her.

She might have taken their attention and interest for hospitality or a desire to sell her something, but the way they spoke, in a slippery, breathy kind of tone, gave her an awkward, slightly disgusting feeling. What did they want with her? Weren't there enough local women here for them? And some of them were genuine beauties too, the bright-coloured fabrics they were wrapped in made them look like the half-open flower buds on the cards. Probably they were just laughing at her ... Was she really capable of provoking a man's curiosity anyway? She suddenly felt a prick of unfamiliar doubt – at that spot just below the triangular arch of her interlocking ribs, where the tender hollow began ... Only deeper. In the place she had only discovered a day ago.

Trying to drive away her anxiety, she wandered along the stalls crammed with all sorts of goods – armour plate and trinkets, clothes and tools – but they didn't hold her attention so strongly any more. It turned out that her internal conversation could be louder than the commotion of the crowd, and the human images drawn by her memory could be more vivid than live people

Was she worth his life? Could she condemn him after what had happened? And most important of all, what point was there to her stupid musings now? When she could no longer do anything for him ...

And then, before Sasha even realised why this was happening to her, the doubts receded and her heart calmed down. Listening closely to herself, she caught the notes of a distant melody, seeping into her from the outside, where it was flowing along beside the murky current of the multitude of human voices, without mingling with it.

For Sasha music had begun, as it does for everyone, with her mother's lullabies. But it had also ended with them: her father had no ear for it and he didn't like to sing – wandering musicians and similar buffoons were not welcomed at Avtozavod. And the sentries droning their dolefully hearty soldiers' songs round the campfire were incapable of drawing real music from the drooping strings of their plywood guitars or the taut strings of Sasha's heart.

But what she could hear now wasn't dismal strumming on a guitar . . . It was more like the tender, living voice of a young woman, or even a little girl – but too high, beyond the range of the human larynx, and at the same time unnaturally powerful. But what else did Sasha have to compare this miracle with?

The song of the unknown instrument enchanted the unwary, bearing them off to somewhere infinitely far away, to worlds that no one born in the Metro could know, worlds that were impossible – only they weren't supposed even to suspect that. The song set them dreaming and suggested that any dreams could come true. It aroused a vague, indefinite yearning and immediately promised to satisfy it. It made Sasha feel good, as if she had been lost in an abandoned station, but suddenly found a flashlight and the light of its beam had shown her the way out.

She was standing at a bladesmith's booth, right in front of a tall sheet of plywood with various kinds of knives attached to it – from little baby folding penknives to predatory hunting knives. Sasha froze, gazing spellbound at the blades, with the two halves of her inner self clashing in a frantic struggle. The idea that had come into her head was simple and tempting. The old man had given her a handful of cartridges, and there were just enough of them for a knife with a broad, sharp serrated, burnished blade, which was absolutely perfect for what she had in mind.

A minute later Sasha had made up her mind and smothered her doubts. She hid her purchase in the breast pocket of her overalls – as close as possible to the spot with the pain she wanted to stop. She walked back to the infirmary, no longer feeling the weight of the soldier's jacket and with her aching temples forgotten.

The crowd was a whole head taller than the girl, and the distant musician, breathing out his amazing notes, remained invisible to her. Yet the melody was still trying to overtake her, turn her back, make her change her mind.

But it was futile.

Another knock at the door.

Homer got up off his knees with a grunt, wiped his lips with his sleeve and tugged the chain of the cistern. A short brownish streak was left on the dirty-green fabric of his padded jacket. It was the fifth time he had puked in twenty-four hours, although he hadn't really eaten anything to speak of.

His illness could have several explanations, the old man tried to convince himself. Why did it have to be accelerated development of the disease? It could be something to do with . . .

'How much longer in there?' a woman squealed impatiently in a high falsetto.

Oh God! Had he really been in such a hurry that he'd confused the letters on the doors? Homer blotted his sweaty face with his dirty sleeve, put on an imperturbable air and clicked the latch.

'Drunken lout!' the gaudily dressed floozy exclaimed. She pushed him out of the way and slammed the door shut.

'Never mind,' thought the old man. 'Better for her to think I'm a drunkard . . .' He took a step towards the mirror above the washbasin and leaned his forehead against it. As soon as he re-covered his breath, he noticed the glass was steaming up and realised his respirator had slid down and was dangling under his chin. Homer hastily pulled the mask back up onto his face and closed his eyes again. No, thinking about how he was transmitting death to every person he met on his journey was unbearable. But it was too late to turn back now: if he was infectious, if he wasn't confusing the symptoms, the entire station was already doomed in any case. Starting with this woman, who was guilty of nothing more than getting taken short at the wrong moment. What would she do if he told her now that she would die in a month's time at the latest? How stupid it all was, thought Homer, stupid and tawdry. He was dreaming of immortalising everyone that life and fate brought him into contact with, but instead he had been appointed an absurd, bald, powerless angel of death. His wings had been clipped and he had been ringed, setting him a fixed term of thirty days, and that had galvanised him into action.

Had he been punished for his presumptuousness, for his arrogance?

No, the old man couldn't keep quiet about it any longer. But there was only one person in the world he could make his confession to. Homer wouldn't be able to deceive him for long in any case, and it would make the game simpler for both of them if they showed their cards.

He set off to the hospital wards, walking hesitantly.

The ward he needed was at the very end of the corridor, and usually there was an attendant on duty at the door, but now the post had been abandoned, and staccato wheezing could be heard coming out through the crack. It assumed the rough forms of words, but constructing meaningful phrases out of them was beyond even Homer as he stood there hiding.

'Harder .. Struggle . . . Must . . . Still makes sense . . . Resist . . . Remember . . . Still possible . . . Wrong . . . Condemned . . . But still . . .'

The words merged into a growl, as if the pain had become too intolerable for the man speaking to lasso his scurrying thoughts. Homer stepped inside.

Hunter was lying there unconscious, sprawled across damp, crumpled sheets. The bandages bound tightly round the brigadier's cranium had crept right down over his eyes, his protruding cheek-bones were covered in perspiration and his stubbly lower jaw was hanging open helplessly. His broad chest rose and fell arduously, like a blacksmith's bellows, struggling to maintain the fire in the body that was too large.

The girl was standing at the head of the bed, facing away from Homer with her thin hands clasped behind her back. The old man didn't look closely at first, but then he noticed the black knife that almost merged into the fabric of her overalls – she was clutching the handle tightly in her fingers.

A ringtone beep.

Then another. And another.

One thousand, two hundred and thirty-five. One thousand two hundred and thirty-six. One thousand two hundred and thirty-seven.

Artyom wasn't counting them to impress the commander with his diligence. He had to do it to feel that he was moving in some direction. If he was moving away from the point at which he had begun counting, that meant every beep brought him closer to the point at which this insanity would come to an end. Self-deception? So okay. But listening to those beeps and thinking they would never break off was unbearable. Although at the beginning, on his very first watch, he had actually liked it: the beeps had introduced order into the cacophony of his thoughts, like a metronome, they had emptied his head, subjugating his galloping pulse to their own unhurried rhythm.

But the minutes that they sliced up became exactly like each other, and Artyom had started to feel that it was true, he was stuck in some kind of time trap and he could never get out of it until the beeps stopped. In the Middle Ages there was a torture like that: they shaved the offender's head bare and sat him under a barrel with water dripping out, drop by drop, onto the top of his head, gradually driving the poor victim out of his mind. Where the rack was powerless, ordinary water produced excellent results.

Tethered by the telephone wire, Artyom had no right to leave his post for a second. He tried not to drink at all during his watch, so that the call of nature wouldn't distract him from the beeps. The previous day he'd given in, darted out of the room, rushed to the toilet and then straight back. He paused to listen in the doorway, and his blood ran cold: the speed had changed, the signal was running faster, it had broken away from its usual measured pace. Only one thing could have happened, and he understood that perfectly well. The moment he had been waiting for had arrived when he wasn't there. Glancing back in fright towards the door – had anyone noticed? – Artyom hastily redialled the number and pressed his ear to the receiver.

The phone clicked and the beeps started up in their usual rhythm. Since then it hadn't given the 'engaged' signal even once and no one had answered it. But even so Artyom didn't dare put the receiver down, he just moved it from his sweaty ear to his frozen one, trying not to lose count.

He hadn't told the commander about that incident straight away, and now somehow he didn't really believe the beeps could have sounded any different. He had been ordered to get through, and for a week now that was what he had been living for. If he violated that order, he would end up at a court martial that saw no difference between a blunder and sabotage.

The phone also told him how much time was left to the end of his watch. Artyom didn't have his own wristwatch, but he had checked the time from the commander's when he made his round. The signal was repeated every five seconds. Twelve beeps was a minute. Seven hundred and twenty was an hour. Thirteen thousand, six hundred and eighty was a complete watch. They fell like grains of sand out of one incredibly vast glass flask into another, bottomless one. And Artyom sat in the narrow throat between these two invisible vessels, listening to the time.

The only reason he didn't dare put the phone down was because the commander could show up at any moment to check on him. But otherwise... What he was doing made absolutely no sense. There was definitely not a single living soul left at the other end of the line. When Artyom closed his eyes, he could see the picture in front of him again...

He saw the commandant's office barricaded from the inside and its occupant sitting with his face resting on the desk, clutching a Makarov pistol in his hand. Naturally, with his ears shot to shreds, he can't hear the phone ringing its head off. The men outside haven't managed to force open the door, but the keyhole and the cracks are still open, and the desperate jangling of the old telephone leaks out through them, creeping through the air above the platform that is heaped up with swollen corpses. There was a time when the ringing of the phone couldn't be heard above the incessant hubbub of the crowd, the patter of footsteps and the crying of children, but now it's the only sound that disturbs the dead. The crimson glow of the emergency batteries blinks in its death throes.

A beep.

And another.

One thousand, five hundred and sixty-three. One thousand, five hundred and sixty-four.

No one answers.

CHAPTER 11

Gifts

'Report!'

Whatever else about him, the commander certainly knew how to take a man by surprise. Legends circulated about him in the garrison: supposedly the former mercenary had been famous for his skill in handling cold weapons and his ability to dissolve into the darkness. At one time, before he settled down at Sebastopol, he used to massacre entire enemy guard posts singlehanded if the sentries demonstrated even the slightest carelessness.

Artyom jumped up, squeezed the receiver against his ear with his shoulder, saluted and stopped counting rather regretfully. The commander walked over to the duty roster, checked his watch, made a note of the time – 9:22 – beside the date – 3 November – signed it and turned to Artyom expectantly.

'Silence. I mean, there's no one there.'

'They don't answer?' said the commander, chewing on his lips; he worked his neck muscles and cracked the vertebrae. 'I don't believe it.'

'What don't you believe?' Artyom asked cautiously.

'That Dobrynin's been taken out so fast. Is the epidemic already in Hansa then? Can you imagine the bedlam that must have broken out, if the Ring's infected?'

'But we don't know, do we?' Artyom responded uncertainly. 'Maybe it's started already. We've got no contact with them.'

'What if the lines are damaged?' The commander leaned down and drummed his fingers on the table.

'Then it would be like with base.' Artyom jerked his head in the direction of the tunnel that led to Sebastopol. 'I dial, and it's completely dead. But with them at least I get the signal. The equipment's working.'

'Base clearly doesn't need us, since no one comes to our door any more. Or maybe there simply isn't any base left. And no Dobrynin either,' the commander said flatly. 'Listen, Popov... If there's no one left there, then we'll all croak soon. And that makes our quarantine pointless. Maybe we should just drop it, what do you think?' he asked and chewed on his lips again.

'Definitely not, the quarantine's essential,' said Artyom, crossing himself in fright at his own heresy and recalling the commander's manner of first shooting deserters in the stomach and reading them their sentence afterwards.

'Essential,' the commander repeated thoughtfully. 'Another three feel ill today. Two locals and one of ours. Akopov. And Aksyonov died.'

'Aksyonov?' Artyom gulped hard and squeezed his eyes shut.

'He smashed his head open against a rail. Said the pain was really bad,' the commander went on in the same even tone. 'And he's not the first. It must be one hell of a headache for a man to spend half an hour down on his knees, trying to crack his skull, eh?'

'Yes, sir.' Artyom suddenly felt sick.

'No nausea? No weakness?' the commander asked considerately, pointing his flashlight into Artyom's face. 'Open your mouth. Say "aaaaa". Good man. I tell you what, Popov, you get through to Dobrynin, and get them to tell you Hansa has a vaccine and the medical brigades will be here soon. And they'll save all of us who are healthy. And they'll cure everyone who's sick. And we won't be stuck here in this hell for all eternity. And we'll all go back home to our wives. You'll back to your Galya. And I'll go back to Alyona and Vera. Got that, Popov?'

'Yes, sir,' said Artyom, nodding vehemently.

'At ease.'

His machete had broken off at the handle, unable to support the weight of creature that collapsed onto it. The blade had pierced so deep into the carcass that they didn't even try to extract it. And the man with the shaved head, covered in slashes from the beasts' claws, still hadn't come round after almost three days.

There was nothing Sasha could do to help him, but she had to see him anyway. If only to say thank you. Even if he couldn't hear her. But the doctors wouldn't allow the girl into his ward. They said that all the injured man needed now was peace and quiet

Sasha didn't know for certain why the man with the shaved head had killed those men on the trolley. If he had fired in order to save her, she could absolve him, but although she honestly tried to believe it, she couldn't. Another explanation was more plausible: it was easier for him to kill than to ask for anything.

But at Pavelets everything had been completely different. There was no doubt about it: he had come for Sasha and even been prepared to die for her. Did that mean she hadn't been wrong after all, and some kind of connection really had started developing between them?

When he called to her that time back at Kolomenskoe, she was expecting a bullet, not an invitation to move on together. But when she submitted and looked round, she had noticed the change in him immediately, even though his frightening face was still as impassive as ever: it was in his eyes, as if someone else had suddenly peeped out through the loopholes of those motionless black pupils. Someone who felt curious about her.

Someone to whom she now owed her life. She wondered if she should let him have the silver ring as a hint, the way her mother once did, but she was afraid the man with the shaved head wouldn't understand the sign. How else could she thank him? To give him a knife to replace the one he had broken defending her was the very least that Sasha could do. When she was struck by this simple idea and stopped dead in front of the bladesmith's counter, imagining how she would hand him his new knife, how he would look at her and what he would say, she hadn't forgotten even for a moment that she was planning to buy a killer a weapon that he would use to slit throats and slash open stomachs.

In that moment, for her he wasn't a bandit, but a hero, not a murderer, but a warrior; and above all, he was a man. And there was another thought, unspoken, not even clearly formulated as yet, swirling round in her head: his knife was broken, he was wounded, he couldn't wake up. Perhaps if he had a knife that was whole ... It was like an amulet ... She went ahead and bought it.

So now, standing by his bed, hiding the gift behind her back, Sasha was waiting for him to sense her, or at least sense the presence of the blade. The man with the shaved head twitched and snorted, he started hawking up words, but he didn't come round: the darkness held him too tight in its grip. Until now Sasha had never spoken his name even to herself, let alone out loud. Before she called him in a loud voice, she whispered that name, as if she was trying it out, and finally made up her mind.

'Hunter!'

The man with the shaved head went quiet and listened, as if she was somewhere unimaginably far away, and her voice only reached him as a faint echo, but he still didn't respond. Sasha spoke the name again, louder, more insistently. She wasn't going to back off until he opened his eyes. She wanted to be his tunnel spark.

Someone in the corridor called out in surprise, boots started scraping across the floor out there and Sasha squatted down and put the knife on the locker at the head of the bed, in order not to waste any more time.

'This is for you,' she said.

Steely fingers closed round Sasha's wrist in a grip powerful enough to crush her bones. The injured man managed to raise his eyelids a little, but his gaze wandered about mindlessly without coming to rest on anything.

'Thank you,' said the girl, not even attempting to free her hand from the trap it was clasped in.

'What are you doing here?'

A large, strapping man in a greasy white coat darted up to her and pricked the man with the shaved head in the arm with a syringe. The patient went limp and the orderly tugged Sasha sharply to her feet, hissing through his clenched teeth.

'What's wrong with you, don't you understand? In his condition... The doctor strictly forbade...'

'You're the one who doesn't understand! He has to have something to cling on to, and your jabs only make him loosen his grip.'

He shoved Sasha hard towards the door, but after flying a few metres, she swung round and flashed her eyes at him stubbornly.

'Don't let me see you in here again! And what's this?' he asked, spotting the knife.

'That's his... I brought it for him...' Sasha said and hesitated. 'If not for him... those creatures would have torn me to pieces.'

'The doctor will tear me to pieces if he finds out,' the orderly snarled. 'Come on, get out of here!'

But Sasha lingered for another moment, turning back to Hunter, who was sunk deep in his curative coma, and finished what she was saying anyway.

'Thank you. You saved me.'

She strode out of the ward and suddenly heard a quiet, cracked voice say:

'I only wanted to kill it ... The monster ...'

The door slammed in her face and the key scraped in the lock.

No, that wasn't what the knife was intended for, Homer realised immediately. It was enough just to hear the way the girl called the brigadier's name as he floundered in the quagmire of his delirium – insistently, tenderly, plaintively. On the very point of intervening, the old man halted in confusion and pulled back: he didn't need to save anyone here. The only way he could help was by making himself scarce as quickly as possible, in order not to frighten Sasha off.

Who could say, perhaps she was right? After all, at Nagornaya, Hunter had completely forgotten about his companions, abandoning them to be torn apart by the phantom giants. But in this battle ... Could the girl really mean something to the brigadier after all?

Lost in thought, Homer wandered off along the corridor to his own ward. An orderly tramping in the opposite direction shouldered him aside, but the old man didn't even notice. It was time to give Sasha the little trifle he had bought for her at the market, Homer told himself. It looked as if it might come in useful soon.

He took the little package out of the desk drawer and twirled it in his hands. The girl came bursting into the room a few minutes later – tense, distressed and angry. She clambered onto her bed, pulled her legs up and stared into the corner. Homer waited to see if the storm would break or pass over. Sasha didn't say anything, she just started biting her nails. The time had come for decisive action.

'I've got a present for you,' the old man said, getting up from the desk and putting the package on the blanket beside the girl.

'What for?' she asked clattering her claws without peeping out of her shell.

'What do people generally give each other presents for?'

'To repay them,' Sasha replied confidently. 'For something good they've done for them, or something they're going to ask for later.'

'Then let's just say I'm repaying you for the good things you've already done for me,' Homer said with a smile. 'I don't have anything else to ask you for.'

'I haven't done anything for you,' the girl objected.

'What about my book? I've already put you in it. I have to repay you, I don't want to be in debt. Come on now, open it,' he said, allowing a faint note of humorous irritation into his voice.

'I don't like being in debt either,' said Sasha, tearing open the wrapping. 'What's this? Oh!'

She was holding a red plastic disc, a flat little box that opened into two halves. It had once been a cheap powder compact, only now the two compartments, for powder and rouge, had been empty for a long time. But on the other hand, the little mirror on the inside of the lid was still in perfect condition.

'I can see better in this than in a puddle,' said Sasha gaping at the compact with funny, wide-open, eyes as she studied her own reflection. 'What did you give me it for?'

'Sometimes it can be useful to see yourself from the outside,' Homer chuckled. 'It helps to understand a lot of things about yourself.'

'And what do I need to understand about myself?' she asked warily.

'There are people who've never seen their own reflection and all their lives they think they're someone different. It can often be hard to see clearly from the inside, and there's no one in here to give them a hint . . . So until they stumble across a mirror by accident, they'll carry on making the same mistake. And even when they do look at a reflection, they often can't believe that it's themselves they're seeing.'

'And who do I see in the mirror?' she asked insistently.

'You tell me,' he said, crossing his arms.

'Myself . . . Well . . . a girl.' Just to make sure, she presented first one cheek and then the other to the little mirror.

'A young woman,' Homer corrected her. 'And a rather scruffy one.'

She twisted and turned for a little bit longer, then flashed her eyes at Homer, intending to ask him something, but changed her mind

172

and said nothing, then finally screwed up her courage after all and blurted out something that made the old man gag.

'Am I ugly?'

'It's hard to say,' he said, struggling to prevent the corners of his lips from spreading into a smile. 'I can't see under all the dirt.'

'So that's what's wrong?' Sasha's eyebrows shot up. 'You mean men can't sense a woman's beauty? You need to have everything shown to you and explained?'

'That's probably right. And it's often used to deceive us,' Homer laughed. 'Painting can work genuine miracles with a woman's face. But in your case we're not talking about restoring the portrait, it's more like an archaeological excavation. It's hard to judge how beautiful an antique statue is from a foot sticking up out of the ground. Although it almost certainly is very beautiful,' he added condescendingly.

'What does "antique" mean?' asked Sasha, suspecting a trick.

'Ancient,' said Homer, carrying on with his joke.

'I'm only seventeen!' she protested.

'They'll discover that later. When they dig you up.'

The old man sat back down at the desk with an imperturbable air, opened the exercise book at the last full page and started reading his notes, gradually turning more and more sombre.

If they dug her up. The girl, and him, and everyone else. There was a time when he used to amuse himself with thoughts like that: what if, in thousands of years' time, archaeologists studying the ruins of old Moscow, when even its name had been forgotten, were to come across one of the entrances to the underground labyrinth? They'd probably think they'd found a gigantic mass burial site – it was unlikely to occur to anyone that people could actually have lived in these dark catacombs. A culture that was once highly developed had obviously degenerated in the twilight of its existence, they would decide: these people buried their leaders in vaults, together with all their possessions, weapons, servants and concubines.

He still had eighty-something pages left in his exercise book. Would that be enough to fit both worlds into – the one lying on the surface and the one in the Metro?

'Can't you hear what I'm saying?' said the girl, shaking his arm.

'What? Sorry, I was lost in thought.' He rubbed his forehead.

'Are ancient statues really beautiful? I mean, is what people used to think was beautiful before still beautiful today?'

'Yes,' the old man said with shrug.

'And will it still be tomorrow?'

'Probably. If there's anyone here to appreciate it.'

Sasha started pondering and fell silent. Homer slipped back into the rut of his own grim reflections and didn't try to force the conversation.

'You mean beauty doesn't exist without people?' Sasha asked eventually, puzzled.

'Probably not,' he replied absentmindedly. 'If there's no one to see it... After all, animals aren't capable, are they?'

'And if animals are different from people because they can't see the difference between what's beautiful and what's ugly,' Sasha pondered, 'does that mean people can't exist without beauty either?'

'Oh, yes they can,' said the old man, shaking his head. 'Lots of people don't need it at all.'

The girl put her hand in her pocket and pulled out a strange object: a little square of polythene or plastic with a design on it. Sasha held it out to Homer timidly, and yet somehow proudly, as if she were revealing a great treasure to him.

'What's this?' he asked.

'You tell me,' she said with a sly smile.

'Well now,' he said, carefully taking the little square from her, reading the words on it and handing it back, 'it's the outside package from a tea bag. With a little picture.'

'With a painting,' she corrected him. 'With a beautiful painting. If not for it, I would have... turned into an animal.'

Homer looked at her, feeling his eyes filling up with tears and his breath faltering. You sentimental old fool, he thought, chastising himself. He cleared his throat and sighed.

'Haven't you ever gone up onto the surface, into the city? Apart from this time?'

'Why?' asked Sasha, putting the little packet away. 'Do you want to tell me everything up there isn't like it is in the painting? That things like that don't even exist? I know all that already. I know what the city looks like – the buildings, the bridge, the river. Creepy and empty.'

'On the contrary,' the old man responded. 'I've never seen anything more beautiful than that city. But you... you're judging the entire Metro from a single sleeper. I probably can't even describe it to you. Buildings higher than any cliffs. Broad avenues, teeming like mountain torrents. The sky that's always bright, the glowing mist... A vainglorious city, living for the moment – like every one of its inhabitants. Crazy and chaotic. Made up entirely of contradictory combinations, constructed without any plans. Not eternal, because eternity is too cold and static. But so alive!' He clenched his fist and then waved his arm in the air. 'You can't understand that. You have to see it for yourself...'

And at that moment he really believed that if Sasha went up onto the surface, the ghost of that city would reveal itself to her too; he believed that, completely forgetting that for that to happen, she would have had to know the city when it was still alive.

The old man managed to arrange things somehow, and she was allowed inside the borders of Hansa: they led her right through the station with an armed guard, as if they were taking her to be shot, all the way to the service area, where the local bathhouse was.

The only thing the two Pavelets stations had in common was the name, as if two sisters had been separated at birth and one had ended up in a rich family, and the other had been raised at a hungry way station or in the tunnels. The station on the radial Zamoskvorechie Line had turned out a bit bawdy and frivolous, but light and airy. The station on the Circle Line was low and squat, well lit and polished until it shone, making its house-proud, stingy character obvious from the very first glance. At this time of day there weren't many people about – probably everyone who didn't work there preferred the fairground atmosphere of the radial line station to the grave severity of the one on the Circle.

She was the only person in the changing room. Walls covered in neat yellow tiles, a floor of chipped, multifaceted stoneware slabs, little painted metal lockers for shoes and clothes, electric bulbs dangling on shaggy wires, two benches upholstered with roughly trimmed imitation leather... Everything inside her quivered in delight.

The skinny female attendant with a moustache handed her an incredibly white towel and a hard little brick of grey soap and allowed her to lock the shower cabin with the bolt. The little squares on the waffle towel and the nauseating soapy smell – it all belonged to the far-distant past, when Sasha was a commandant's beloved, pampered little daughter. She had forgotten that all these things still existed somewhere.

Sasha unfastened her overalls that were stiff with dirt and clambered out of them as quickly as she could. She pulled off her singlet, took off her shorts and skipped over to the rust-coated pipe with its improvised showerhead. With a great effort, her fingers slipping over the scorching valve wheel, she released the hot water … It was boiling! Squeezing up against the wall to escape from the scalding spray, she twisted the other wheel. Eventually she managed to mix cold and hot in the right proportions, stopped dancing about and dissolved into the water.

And all the dust, soot, machine oil and blood flowed down through the grille of the drain with the bubbling water, along with Sasha's and other people's weariness and despair, guilt and anxiety. It was quite a while before the water ran clear.

Would this be enough for the old man to stop teasing her, Sasha wondered, examining her pink, steamed feet as if they belonged to someone else and studying her unfamiliar white palms. Would it be enough for men to notice her beauty? Perhaps Homer was right and it was stupid of her to go to the wounded man without tidying herself up first? She would probably have to learn about that kind of thing.

Would he notice how Sasha had changed? She screwed in the valve wheels, shuffled through into the changing room and opened the mirror she had been given … Yes, it was impossible not to notice it.

The hot water had helped her loosen up and overcome her doubts. The man with the shaved head hadn't been trying to rebuff her with his strange words about the monster. He simply hadn't come round yet, and anyway he wasn't talking to her, he was just carrying on a violent quarrel he was having with someone else in his nightmare. She just had to wait until he surfaced, and be there with him when it happened, so that … So that Hunter would see her straight away and understand everything straight away. And what then? She didn't have to think about that. He was experienced enough for her to leave everything up to him. Recalling how the man with the shaved head thrashed about in his delirium, Sasha felt, even though she couldn't explain it, that Hunter was searching for her, because she could calm him, bring him relief from his fever and help him recover his balance. And the more she thought about that, the more feverish she started feeling herself. They took away her filthy overalls, promising to wash them, and gave her a pair of threadbare, light-blue trousers and a sweater with holes in it and a high neck. The new clothes felt tight and awkward – and apart from that, while they were taking her back through the frontier posts to the infirmary, almost every man's eyes were glued to the trousers and the sweater, and when Sasha reached her own bed, she felt like taking another shower. The old man wasn't in the room, but she wasn't left to brood alone for long. A few minutes later the door creaked open and the doctor glanced in.

'Well now, congratulations. You can visit him. He's come round.'

'What date is it?'

The brigadier propped himself up on one elbow, turning his head laboriously to peer at Homer. The old man grabbed at his wrist for some reason, although it was a long time since he had last worn a watch, and shrugged.

'The second. The second of November,' the orderly prompted him.

'Three days,' said Hunter, slipping down onto the pillow. 'Three days I've been lying here. We're behind schedule. We have to go.'

'You won't get very far,' said the orderly, trying to reason with him. 'You've got hardly any blood left in you.'

'We have to go,' the brigadier repeated, ignoring him. 'We're running out of time... The bandits...' He suddenly broke off. 'Why do you need the respirator?'

The old man had been preparing for that question; he'd had three whole days to draw up his lines of defence and plan a counter-offensive. Hunter's unconscious state had spared him the need for superfluous confessions, and now he could replace them with well-considered lies.

'There aren't any bandits,' he whispered, leaning down over the wounded man's bed. 'While you were delirious... You were talking all the time. I know everything.'

'What do you know?' Hunter grabbed Homer by the collar and jerked the old man towards him.

'About the epidemic at Tula ... Everything's all right.' Homer waved his hand imploringly to restrain the orderly, who had come dashing over to drag him off the brigadier. 'I'll manage. We need to have a talk, could I ask you, please ...'

The orderly reluctantly complied, put the cap back over the needle of his syringe and walked out of the ward, leaving them alone.

'About Tula,' said Hunter, still holding the old man in his wild, inflamed stare, but gradually reducing the pressure. 'Nothing else?'

'That's all. The station is the focus of an unidentified airborne infection ... Our men have established a quarantine and they're waiting for help.'

'Right. Right,' said the brigadier, letting go of him. 'Yes. An epidemic. Are you afraid of getting infected?'

'God helps those who help themselves,' Homer replied warily.

'True enough. It's okay ... I didn't go close, the draught was blowing in their direction ... I shouldn't have it.'

'Why that story about the bandits? What are you going to do?' asked the old man, feeling bolder now.

'First go to Dobrynin and reach an agreement. Then clean out Tula. We need flamethrowers. Otherwise there's no way ...'

'Burn everyone at the station alive? What about our men?'

The old man was still hoping the remark the brigadier had passed about flamethrowers had been the same kind of decoy manoeuvre as everything else he told the top command at Sebastopol.

'Why alive? The corpses. There's no other way. Everyone who's infected. Everyone they've been in contact with. All the air. I've heard about this disease ...' Hunter closed his eyes and licked his cracked lips. 'There's no cure. There was an outbreak a couple of years ago ... Two thousand corpses.'

'But it stopped, didn't it?'

'A blockade. Flamethrowers.' The brigadier turned his mutilated face towards the old man. 'There is no other way. If it breaks out ... Just one man. It's the end for everyone. Yes, I lied about the bandits. Otherwise Istomin wouldn't have allowed me to terminate everyone. He's too soft. But I'll take men who don't ask any questions.'

'But what if there are men who are immune?' Homer began timidly. 'What if there are men there who aren't sick? I ... You said ... What if they could still be saved?'

'There is no immunity. All contacts get infected. There aren't any healthy men, only tougher ones,' the brigadier snapped. 'But it's only worse for them. They'll suffer longer. Believe me... It's what they need, for me to... to be terminated.'

'But what do you need that for?' the old man asked, moving back from the bed just to be on the safe side.

Hunter lowered his eyelids wearily, and Homer noticed once again that the eye on the mutilated half of his face didn't close completely. The brigadier's answer took so long to come that the old man was about to run for the doctor. But then, forcing out the words slowly and separately, as if a hypnotist had sent him back into the infinitely distant past for his lost memories, he said through his clenched teeth:

'I must. Protect people. Eliminate any danger. That's all. I'm for.'

Had he found the knife? Had he realised it was for him? What if he didn't guess, or didn't see it was a promise? She flew along the corridor, trying to drive away the thoughts that were tormenting her, still not knowing what she would say to him. What a pity that he had regained consciousness before she was at his bedside!

Sasha heard almost the entire conversation – she froze in the doorway and shrank back when the subject of killings came up. Of course, she couldn't decipher everything, but she didn't need to. She'd already heard all the most important things. There was no point in waiting any longer, and she knocked loudly.

As the old man got up to greet her, his face was a cramped mask of despair. Homer moved as laboriously as if he too had been given a debilitating injection, and the wicks had been unscrewed from the lamps of his eyes. He answered Sasha with a limp nod – as if someone had tugged on a hanged man's rope from above.

The girl sat right on the edge of the still-warm stool, bit her lip and held her breath before stepping into this new, unexplored tunnel.

'Did you like my knife?'

'Knife?' The man with the shaved head looked round and his gaze ran into the burnished black blade: he stared warily at Sasha without touching it. 'What's all this about?'

'It's for you.' She felt as if someone had blown steam into her face. 'Yours got broken. When you... Thank you...'

'A strange present. I'd never accept anything like that from anyone,' he said after a heavy silence. She thought she could hear a half-hint in his words, something important left unsaid, and she accepted the game, but without knowing all the rules, and started groping around for words. It all came out awkward and wrong, but then Sasha's tongue was a completely inadequate tool for describing what was going on inside her.

'Do you feel that I have a piece of you too? The part that was torn out of you ... That you were looking for? That I could give it back to you?'

'What are you babbling about?' he asked. A dash of cold water in her face.

'No, you do feel it,' Sasha insisted, cringing on the stool. 'That you'll be complete with me. That I can be with you and I must. Otherwise why did you take me with you?'

'I gave in to my partner.' His voice was colourless and blank.

'Why did you protect me from the men on the trolley?'

'I would have killed them in any case.'

'Then why did you save me from the beast at the station?'

'I had to wipe them all out.'

'I wish it had eaten me!'

'Are you annoyed because you're still alive?' he asked, puzzled. 'Then take a walk up the escalator, there are plenty more of them up there.'

'I ... You want me to ...'

'I don't want anything from you.'

'I'll help you to stop!'

'You're clinging on to me.'

'Don't you feel that ...?'

'I don't feel anything.' The taste of his words was like rusty water.

Not even the terrible claw of that white monster could have wounded her so badly. Sasha jumped up, cut to the quick, and dashed out of the ward. Luckily her room was empty. She huddled up in the corner, curled into a tight ball. She looked for the mirror in her pocket – she wanted to throw it out – but didn't find it: she must have dropped it beside the bed of the man with the shaved head.

When her tears dried up, she already knew what to do. It didn't take her long to get ready. The old man would forgive her for stealing his gun – he would probably forgive her anything at all. The tarpaulin protective suit, cleaned and decontaminated, was waiting for her in the closet, dangling helplessly from a hook. As if some wizard had disembowelled the dead fat man and cursed him after death to follow Sasha everywhere and do her will. She clambered into it, dashed out into the corridor, rushed along the passage and up onto the platform. Somewhere along the way a rivulet of magical music licked at her, music from the same source that she hadn't identified last time. She didn't have a spare minute to search for it this time either. Halting for only a brief moment, Sasha overcame the temptation and moved on towards the goal of her trek.

In the daytime there was only one sentry on duty at the escalator: the creatures from the surface never bothered the station during daylight hours. It took her less than five minutes to come to an understanding: the way up here was always open, but it was impossible to come down the escalator. Leaving the amenable sentry a half-empty sub-machine-gun clip, Sasha set her foot on the first step of the stairway that led straight up to the sky.

She hitched up her sagging trousers and began her ascent.

CHAPTER 12

Signs

Back home at Kolomenskoe, the surface was very close – only fifty-six shallow steps away. But Pavelets had burrowed much deeper under the ground. As she scrambled up the creaking escalator, mutilated by bursts of machine-gun fire, Sasha could see no end to this climb. All that her feeble flashlight could pick out of the darkness were the shattered glass covers of the lamps along the escalator and the rusty, twisted metal plates on the wall with images of pale, bleary faces and big letters that made up meaningless words.

Why should she go up there? Why should she die?

But who needed her down below? Who really needed her as a person, not as a character in a book that hadn't been written yet?

Why bother trying to deceive herself any longer?

When Sasha walked away from the empty station at Kolomenskoe, leaving her father's body there, it felt as if she was carrying out their old plan of escape, carrying away a little part of him in her and helping him to escape at least in that way. But since then she hadn't dreamed about him even once, and when she tried to summon up his image in her imagination in order to share what she had seen and experienced with him, it came out vague and mute. Her father couldn't forgive her and he didn't want to be rescued like this.

Among the books he had found that Sasha managed to leaf through before exchanging them for food and cartridges, she had special memories of an old reference work on botany. The illustrations in it were strictly conventional: black-and-white photographs that had faded with age and pencil sketches. But in all the other books that came her way she didn't find any pictures at all, and this one was Sasha's favourite. And the plant she liked more than all the others in the book was the bindweed. No, it wasn't even that she liked it – she felt sympathy for the bindweed because she recognised herself in it. She needed support in just the same way, didn't she? In order to grow upwards. In order to reach the light.

And now her instinct demanded that she find a mighty trunk that she could cling to, embracing it and winding herself around it. Not in order to suck the juices out of someone else's body and live on them, not in order to take away his light and warmth. Simply because without him she was too soft, too flexible and flabby to hold out, and on her own she would always have to trail across the ground.

Sasha's father had told her she shouldn't be dependent on anyone or rely on anyone. After all, in their forgotten way station, he was the only one she had to rely on, and he knew he wasn't immortal. Her father wanted her to grow up as a tall, sturdy pine tree, not climbing ivy: he forgot that this contradicted a woman's nature.

Sasha would have survived without him. She would have survived without Hunter too. But to her, fusion with another person seemed like the only reason to think about the future. When she wrapped her arms round him on the hurtling trolley, it felt as if her life had acquired a new core. She remembered that trusting other people was dangerous, and being dependent on them was unworthy, and she had to force herself to try to confess her feelings to the man with the shaved head. Sasha wanted to nestle up to him, and he thought she was clutching at his boots. Left without any support, trampled into the ground, she wasn't going to demean herself by continuing her quest. He had driven her away, banished her to the surface. All right then: if anything happened to her up there, it would be his fault: he was the only one who could prevent it.

The steps finally came to an end and Sasha found herself on the edge of a spacious marble hall with a fluted metal ceiling that had collapsed in places. Incredibly bright beams of greyish-white light were pouring in through the distant gaps, and scattered rays from them even reached as far the nook where she was standing. Sasha switched off the flashlight, held her breath and started furtively creeping forward.

The bullet scars on the walls and marble splinters by the mouth of the escalators testified that human beings had been here at one time. But after only a few dozen steps she reached the domain of different creatures.

The heaps of dried dung, gnawed bones and scraps of skin scattered around the floor indicated that Sasha was at the very heart of the beasts' lair. Covering her eyes so they wouldn't be scorched by the light, she walked towards the exit. And the closer Sasha came to the source of the light, the thicker the darkness became in the secluded corners of the halls she was walking through. As she learned to look at the light, Sasha was losing the ability to sense the darkness.

The halls that followed were filled to overflowing with the skeletons of overturned kiosks, heaps of all sorts of incredible junk and the carcasses of machines that had been picked apart. It gradually dawned on her that people had turned the outer pavilions of Pavelets station into a staging post to which they dragged all the goods from the surrounding area, until more powerful creatures had forced them out of here.

Sometimes Sasha fancied she saw something stirring faintly in the dark corners, but she put it down to her advancing blindness. The darkness huddling there was already too dense for her to distinguish the ugly forms of the sleeping monsters from the mountains of garbage that they merged into.

The monotonous whining of the draught smothered the sound of their heavy, snuffling breathing and Sasha could only make it out when she passed within a few steps of a trembling heap. She listened warily, then froze, gazed hard at the outlines of an overturned kiosk and discovered a strange hump in its jagged profile. She was dumbfounded. The hill that the kiosk was buried in was breathing. And almost all the other mounds surrounding her were breathing as well. In order to make sure, Sasha clicked the switch of her flashlight and pointed it at one of them. The pale little beam landed on fat folds of white skin, ran on across an immense body and disintegrated before reaching the end of it. It was a fellow creature of the monster that had almost killed Sasha on the platform at Pavelets, but it was far bigger than that beast.

In their strange torpid state the creatures didn't seem to notice her. But then the closest one suddenly growled, sucked in air noisily through the angled slits of its nostrils and started stirring restlessly. Coming to her senses, Sasha put the flashlight away and hurried on. Every step she took through this appalling dormitory cost her a greater and greater effort: the further she moved away from the way down into the Metro the more tightly the monsters were packed together, and the harder it became to find a way through between their bodies. It was too late to turn back. Sasha wasn't concerned at all about how she could get back into the Metro. Just as long as she could get past these creatures unheard, without alarming a single one of them, and make her way outside, look around and ... Just as long as they didn't awaken from their dormant state, just as long as they let her out of here: she wouldn't need to look for a way back. Not daring to breathe deeply, trying not even to think – what if they heard her! – she moved slowly towards the way out. A broken tile crunched treacherously under her boots. One more wrong step, an accidental rustle – and they would wake up and tear her to pieces in an instant.

And Sasha couldn't rid herself of the feeling that only very recently – yesterday, or perhaps even today – she had been wandering between sleeping monsters like this ... At least, the strange feeling was familiar to her from somewhere.

She froze on the spot.

Sasha knew that you could sometimes feel someone else's gaze on the back of your head. But these creatures didn't have eyes, and what they used to probe the space around them was far more material and insistent than any gaze.

She didn't need to look round to know that despite all her caution a creature had woken up and was staring hard at her back. But she looked round anyway.

The girl had completely disappeared, but just at that minute Homer didn't have the slightest desire to go dashing off to search for her, just as he didn't have any other desires.

The signal officer's diary might have left the old man a smidgen of hope that the sickness would pass him by, but Hunter had been quite ruthless. In launching into his thoroughly planned conversation with the brigadier, the old man had, in effect, been lodging an appeal against his death sentence. But Hunter hadn't shown him any mercy – and he couldn't have done in any case. Homer alone was to blame for what would inevitably happen to him.

Only a couple of weeks or even less. Only ten pages covered with writing. And all the other things that had to be compressed and squeezed into the remaining clean pages of that exercise book with the oil cloth cover. But quite apart from his own desires, Homer also had a duty, and their enforced halt at Pavelets seemed to be coming to an end.

He smoothed out the paper, intending to pick up the narrative from where he had broken off the last time at the sound of the doctors' shouts. But instead of that his hand traced out the same old question: 'What will be left after me?' And what would be left after the unfortunates locked in at Tula, he thought, perhaps despairing, perhaps still waiting for help, but doomed to a cruel reckoning either way. A memory? But there were so few people who could be found to remember anyone.

And memories were a frail mausoleum anyway. Soon the old man would be gone, and everyone he had known would disappear along with him. His Moscow would disappear into nowhere too. Where was he now, on Pavelets Station? The Garden Ring Road was bare and dead now – during the final hours military vehicles had cleared it and cordoned it off, in order to allow the rescue services to go about their work and give the cortèges of cars with flashing lights freedom to move. The thoroughfares and side streets grinned with their rotten, gap-toothed rows of detached buildings... The old man could easily imagine the local landscape, although he had never gone up out of the Metro at this station.

Before the war he had been here quite often: he used to arrange to meet his future wife for a date in a café beside the station, then they would go to the evening session in the cinema. And not far from here he had gone through the remarkably superficial medical examination that he was obliged to pay for when he was planning to get his driving licence. And this was the station where he had got into a suburban train when he joined an outing into the summer forest with his workmates, to cook kebabs over a campfire... Looking at the paper ruled off into little squares, he saw the square in front of the station, shrouded in autumn mist, and two towers melting into the haze: the pretentious new office block on the Garden Ring Road – one of his friends worked there – and a little further away, the twisted spire of an expensive hotel, tacked on to an expensive concert hall. Nikolai had checked the ticket prices once: they cost slightly more than he earned in two weeks.

He could see and even hear the jangling, angular, white-and-blue trams, packed with dissatisfied passengers whose annoyance at this harmless crush was so touching. And the Garden Ring Road itself, winking festively with tens of thousands of headlights and indicators, all strung out in a single continuous garland. And the timid, incongruous snow, melting before it could even settle on the asphalt. And the crowd – myriads of electrically charged particles, all energised and clashing together as they darted about in apparent chaos, but each one of them actually moving along its own meaningful path. He saw the ravine between the monolithic Stalinist skyscrapers, from which the great river of the Garden Ring flowed out lazily onto the square, with hundreds and hundreds of aquarium-windows lighting up on both sides of it. And the neon flashes of the signs, and the titanic advertising hoardings, shamefacedly concealing the gaping wound in which they were setting a new multi-storey implant...

Which would never be finished.

Watching all this, he understood that he could never express this magnificent picture in words. Would the only things left out of all this really be the subsided, moss-covered, tombstones of the business centre and the fashionable hotel?

She still hadn't shown up an hour later, or even three. Feeling anxious, Homer walked round the entire passage, questioned the traders and musicians and spoke with the leader of the Hansa patrol. Nothing. She'd vanished into thin air.

Not knowing what to do with himself, the old man came to anchor again at the door of the room where the brigadier was lying. The very last man he could ask for advice about the girl's disappearance. But who else did Homer have left now? He cleared his throat and glanced inside.

Hunter was lying there, breathing heavily, gazing fixedly at the ceiling. His right arm – the uninjured one – was lying on top of the blanket and the tightly clenched fist had been grazed on something very recently. The shallow scratches were oozing lymph, staining the bed, but the brigadier didn't notice.

'When are you ready to leave?' he asked Homer, without turning towards him.

'Me, I could go right now,' the old man said and hesitated. 'There's a problem though... I can't find the girl. And how can you go, anyway. You're all...'

'I won't die,' the brigadier replied. 'And there are worse things than death. Get ready. I'll be on my feet in an hour and a half. We'll head for Dobrynin.'

'An hour will be enough, but I need to find her, I want her to go on with us... I really need her to, do you understand?' Homer said hastily.

'I'm leaving in an hour,' Hunter snapped. 'With you or without you... And without her.'

'I can't think where she could have disappeared to!' the old man sighed in frustration. 'If only I knew...'

'I know,' the brigadier said calmly. 'But you can't bring her back from there, that's for sure. Get ready.'

Homer backed away and started blinking. He'd got used to relying on his travelling companion's supernatural intuition, but this time he refused to believe him. What if Hunter was lying again, this time to get rid of an unnecessary burden?

'She told me you need her...'

'I need you,' said Hunter inclining his head slightly towards Homer. 'And you need me.'

'What for?' Homer hissed under his breath, but the brigadier heard him.

'A lot depends on you,' said Hunter, blinking slowly, but the old man suddenly got the impression that the heartless brigadier was winking at him, and he broke out in a cold sweat.

The bed gave a long, drawn-out creak as Hunter gritted his teeth and sat up.

'Leave me,' he told the old man. 'And get ready if you want to be in time.'

But before he cleared out, Homer lingered for a second to pick up the red plastic powder compact lying abandoned in the corner. It had cracks running right across the lid and the hinges had bent open and come apart.

The mirror was shattered to smithereens.

The old man turned back abruptly towards the brigadier.

'I can't go without her.'

*

189

It was almost twice as tall as Sasha; its head touched the ceiling and its sharp-clawed arms hung down to the floor. Sasha had seen the lightning speed with which these beasts moved and the incredible swiftness of their attack. A creature like this could reach the girl and finish her with a single movement, simply by flailing one of its limbs forward. But for some reason it was taking its time.

Shooting at it was pointless, and Sasha wouldn't have had enough time even to raise her automatic. She took a hesitant step backwards, towards the way out. The monster gave a low moan and swayed towards the girl. But nothing happened. The monster stayed where it was, keeping its blind, intent gaze fixed on Sasha. She ventured another step. And another. Without turning her back on the beast, without showing it her fear, she gradually moved closer to the way out. The creature plodded after Sasha as if it were spellbound, hanging back just a little, as if it were seeing her to the door.

It was only when the girl, now only ten metres away from the unbearable glow of that gap, couldn't stand it any more and broke into a run, that the beast roared and dashed forward too. Sasha flew outside, squeezed her eyes shut and dashed on, unable to see anything, until she stumbled and went tumbling across the rough, hard ground. She waited for the monster to overtake her and tear her to shreds, but for some reason her pursuer allowed her to get away. A long, lingering minute passed, and then another. There was silence all around.

Sasha didn't open her eyes until she had fumbled in her bag and found the home-made glasses she had bought from the sentry – two dark glass bottle-bottoms set in metal rings and mounted on a length of twine. The glasses had to be pulled on over a gas mask, so that the transparent green discs sat precisely on top of the peepholes in the rubber. Now she could look. Slowly parting her eyelids and peeping suspiciously out of the corners of her eyes at first, then gazing more boldly, Sasha looked round at the strange place she had ended up in.

Above her head was the sky. The real sky, bright and immense. Giving more light than any searchlight, illuminated in an even green colour all the way across, masked by low clouds in places and in others opening up into a bottomless abyss.

The sun! She saw it through an attenuated veil of cloud: a round disc the size of a detonator cap, polished to a spotless white and so bright that Sasha felt as if it would burn a hole in her glasses in another moment. She turned her eyes away in fright, waited for a little while and then stole another glance at it. She fancied there was something rather disappointing about it: after all, it was just a blinding hole in the sky, why should it be worshipped like a god? And yet it was enchanting, it attracted and excited her. The opening of the exit from the beasts' lair had shone almost as brightly for eyes accustomed to darkness; what if, Sasha suddenly thought, the sun was exactly the same kind of way out, an exit leading to a place where it was never, ever dark ... And if you could fly to it, you could escape from the earth, in exactly the same way as she had just escaped from under the earth? And the sun also gave out a weak, barely perceptible warmth, as if it were alive.

Sasha was standing in the middle of a bare, stony open space, surrounded by ancient, half-ruined buildings, so high that the black gaps of their windows were piled up in almost ten rows. The number of buildings was almost infinite, they crowded together, concealing each another from Sasha as they jostled to get a better look at her. Peeking out from behind the tall buildings were even higher ones, and behind them she could distinguish the vague outlines of absolutely huge buildings. It was incredible, but Sasha could see them all!

It wasn't important that they were tinted a silly-looking green, like the ground under her feet, like the air itself and the insanely glowing, bottomless sky – she could see such unimaginably vast distances now.

No matter how long Sasha had trained her eyes to see in the dark, that was not what they were intended for. At night-time all she could see from the cliff beside the Metro bridge were the ugly structures standing a few hundred metres away from the hermetic door. After that the darkness was laid on too thickly and even though Sasha had been born underground, her gaze couldn't scrape through it.

The girl had never seriously wondered before just how big the world she lived in was. But when she did think about it, Sasha had always imagined a small cocoon of twilight, several hundred metres in each direction, and beyond that a precipice that was final, the edge of the universe, the beginning of absolute darkness.

Although she knew the earth was actually far bigger than that, Sasha couldn't imagine what it looked like. And now she realised there was no way she could have done that anyway – simply because it was impossible to picture it, never having seen anything like it before. And the strange thing was that somehow she didn't feel at all afraid to stand in the middle of this boundless wasteland. Before, when she crept out of the tunnel onto the cliff, she felt as if she had been dragged out of her protective shell, but now it seemed more like an eggshell that she had finally hatched out of. By daylight any danger could be spotted at a great distance, and Sasha would have more than enough time to hide or prepare to defend herself. There was also another timid feeling that she was unfamiliar with – as if she had come home. The draught drove tangles of prickly branches across the barren space, whistled dejectedly in the crevices between the buildings and shoved Sasha in the back, demanding that she be more daring, ordering her to set out and explore this new world.

She really had no choice anyway: to get back down into the Metro, she would have to go back into the building swarming with those fearsome creatures – only they weren't sleeping anymore. Sometimes white bodies flickered momentarily in the dark wells of the entrances and immediately disappeared: they obviously detested the daylight. But what would happen when night fell? She had to get as far away from here as possible before that happened if she intended to see at least something of what the old man had described so vividly, before she died.

And Sasha moved on.

She had never felt so little before. She couldn't believe that these gigantic buildings could have been built by people the same height as she was. Why did they need all this? Probably the final generations before the war had degenerated and shrunk in size... nature had prepared them for a harsh existence in the cramped tunnels and stations. But these buildings had been erected by the present squat human beings' ancestors – as mighty, tall and statuesque as the buildings they lived in.

She came to a broad open patch: the buildings moved apart here and the ground was covered with a cracked grey crust that looked like stone. In a single bound the world became even more immense: from here Sasha had a view of distances that thrilled her heart and set her head spinning.

Squatting down by the mildewed, mossy walls of a castle with a blunt clock tower that propped up the clouds, she tried to picture to herself how this city must have looked before life abandoned it.

Striding along the road – and there was no doubt that it was a road – were tall, beautiful people in bright-patterned clothes that made the most festive costumes of the residents of Pavelets look wretched and stupid. Scurrying along in the vivid crowd were cars, exactly like the carriages of the Metro's trains, but absolutely tiny, only big enough for four passengers. The buildings weren't so sombre: their windows weren't black, gaping holes, they glittered with cleanly washed glass. And Sasha saw light little bridges running between facing houses here and there at various heights. And the sky wasn't so empty – incredibly huge aeroplanes drifted slowly across it, with their bellies almost touching the roofs. Her father had explained to her that they didn't have to flap anything in order to fly, but they appeared to Sasha as lazy behemoths with fluttering dragonfly wings that were almost invisible and only shimmered slightly in the greenish rays of the sun.

And it was raining too.

Supposedly it was just water falling from the sky, but the sensation was absolutely incredible. It didn't just wash away dust and weariness – the jets of hot water from a rusty shower head could do that: the sky water cleaned people on the inside, granting them forgiveness for the mistakes they had made. This magical cleansing washed the grief out of hearts, it renewed and rejuvenated, bringing the desire to carry on living and the strength to do it. Everything was just as the old man had said . . .

Sasha believed so strongly in this world that under the pressure of her childish sorcery it started breaking through into reality around her. She could hear the light chirring of transparent wings high in the air, and the cheerful babble of the crowd, and the regular tapping of wheels and the humming of the warm rain. The melody she had heard in the passage the day before came back to her and wove itself into this chorus . . . She felt a painful pricking in her chest.

She jumped up and ran along the very centre of the road against the stream of people, skirting round the sweet little carriage-cars that were stuck in the throng, holding her face up to the heavy raindrops. The old man was right: this really was a wonderful fairytale place, breathtakingly beautiful. Scrape away the patina and mould of time, and the past started to shine – like the coloured mosaics and bronze panels at abandoned stations.

She stopped on the bank of a green river: the bridge that had once spanned it broke off almost as soon as it began, there was no way she could get across to the other side. The magic had run out. The picture that seemed so real, so vivid only a moment ago, faded and disappeared, and in a second all that was left of the beautiful phantom world were the empty buildings, turned stale and dry by age, the cracked skin of the roads, hemmed in along the margins by grass that was two metres tall, and the wild, impenetrable thickets that had swallowed up the remains of the embankment for as far as the eye could see.

And Sasha suddenly felt so hurt and resentful that she would never see that world with her own eyes, that she would have to choose between dying and going back to the Metro, that there wasn't a single statuesque giant in bright-coloured clothes left anywhere in the world. That apart from her there wasn't a single living soul on that immensely wide road leading away to the distant point where the sky crept down onto the abandoned city.

The weather was fine and settled. With no rain. Sasha didn't even feel like crying. It would be really fine now simply to die.

And as if it had heard her wish, high above her head a huge black shadow spread its wings.

What should he do if he had to choose? Let the brigadier go and abandon his book, stay at the station until he found the missing girl? Or forget about her forever and follow Hunter, erase Sasha from his novel and lurk like a spider in its web, waiting for new heroines to come along?

The old man's rational mind forbade him to separate from the brigadier. If he did, then what sense did his entire expedition make, what sense was there in the deadly danger to which he had exposed the entire Metro? He simply had no right to put his work at risk – it was the only thing that justified all the sacrifices already made and still to come.

But in that moment when he picked the broken mirror up off the floor, Homer had realised that to leave Pavelets without finding out what had happened to the girl would be an act of genuine betrayal.

And sooner or later that betrayal would inevitably poison the old man and his novel. He would never be able to erase Sasha from his memory.

Whatever Hunter might tell him, Homer had to do everything possible to find the girl, or at least make certain that she was no longer alive. And the old man set about the search with renewed vigour, occasionally asking people he met what time it was.

The Circle Line station was out of the question – she couldn't have got into Hansa without any documents. The gallery of rooms and apartments under the connecting passage? The old man searched it from one end to the other, asking everyone he met if they had seen the girl. Eventually someone replied uncertainly that they thought they had run into her, dressed in tarpaulin protective clothing... And from there Homer, unable to believe his ears and his eyes, traced Sasha's route to the gun post at the foot of the escalator.

'So what's it to me? If she wants to go, then let her. I flogged her some good glasses,' the sentry in the booth answered him lethargically. 'But I won't let you through. I've already had an earful from the corporal. The Newcomers' nest is up there. Nobody goes through here. I even thought it was funny when she asked to be let through.' His pupils, as wide a pistol barrels, prodded at space, without hitting the old man at all. 'You'd better get along to the passage, granddad. It'll be getting dark soon.'

Hunter knew! But what did he mean when he said the old man wouldn't be able to bring her back? Perhaps she was still alive?

Stumbling in his agitation, Homer hurried back to the brigadier's ward. He ducked under the low lintel of the little secret door, hobbled down the narrow steps, swung the door open without knocking...

The room was empty: no sign of Hunter or his weapons, nothing but the ribbons of bandages dyed brown with dried blood scattered about on the floor, and the empty flask lying there abandoned. And the perfunctorily decontaminated protective suit had disappeared from the closet too.

The brigadier had simply abandoned the old man, like a dog he was tired of, to punish him for his obstinacy.

Her father had always been convinced that people were given signs. They just had to know how to spot them and read them. Sasha glanced up and froze in astonishment. If someone wanted to send her a sign at this very moment, they couldn't possibly have thought of anything more eloquent.

Not far from the broken-off bridge, an old round tower with an elaborate tip rose up out of the dark thickets; it was the tallest building in the area. The years had not treated it kindly: deep cracks snaked across its walls and the tower was listing dangerously. It would have collapsed long ago, if not for a miracle. Why hadn't she noticed it sooner?

The building was girded round by an absolutely gigantic bindweed plant. Of course, its trunk was many times thinner than the tower, but it was more than thick enough and strong enough to hold up the building that was falling apart. The amazing plant wound round the tower in a spiral: thinner branches ran off from the main trunk, and even thinner ones ran off from them, and all together they formed a net that prevented the building from crumbling.

Of course the bindweed had once been as weak and flexible as the youngest and most tender of its shoots was now. It had once clutched at the ledges and balconies of a tower that seemed eternal and indestructible. If the tower hadn't been so tall, the bindweed wouldn't have grown so large.

As Sasha gazed spellbound at that rescued building, everything acquired meaning for her again and the desire to fight returned. It was strange, after all, absolutely nothing had changed in her life. But suddenly, despite everything, a tiny shoot of that bindweed had broken through the grey crust of despair in her soul – a green shoot of hope. There might be some things that she could never put right, some deeds that were impossible to undo, that could never be retracted. But in this story there were still many things that she could change, even if she didn't yet know how. The important thing was that her strength had come back to her.

And now it seemed to Sasha that she had also guessed the reason why the grim monster had let her get away unharmed: someone invisible had held the ferocious beast back on a chain in order to give the girl another chance.

And she was grateful for that. She was ready to forgive, ready to assert what she believed and fight for it again. And all she needed from Hunter was the very slightest hint. Just one more sign.

The setting sun suddenly went out, but immediately flared up again. Sasha flung her head back just in time to catch a fleeting glimpse of the black silhouette that had hurtled over her head, obscuring the sun's light for an instant and immediately disappearing from view.

A shrill whistling sound and an ear-splitting howl sliced through the air as the massive hulk lunged down at Sasha out of the sky, missing by only a tiny margin. At the last moment, instinct prompted the girl to fling herself full length on the ground, and that was the only thing that saved her. The outlandish monster skidded along the ground on its outstretched leathery wings, then gave a mighty flap to gain height and started turning in a broad half-circle as it moved in for another attack.

Sasha grabbed her automatic, but immediately abandoned the idea as useless. Not even a burst fired pointblank could knock a carcass like that off course, and it was senseless even to think of bringing it down – she would have to hit it in the first place! The girl dashed back towards the open space from which she had set out on her brief journey, without even thinking about how to get back into the Metro.

The flying monster gave its hunting call and came hurtling at her again. Sasha got her feet tangled in the fat man's trousers and tumbled face down onto the road, but squirmed round and fired a short, snarling burst. The bullets discouraged the beast, but they didn't do it any harm at all. In the few seconds she had won herself, the girl managed to get to her feet and dash towards the nearest buildings, realising at last where to find cover from the predator.

There were two shadows circling now, keeping themselves in the air with heavy flaps of broad, webbed wings. Sasha's calculation was simple: to squeeze up against the wall of any building. The flying monsters were too large and unwieldy to get her there: and after that... She had nowhere to run to in any case.

She made it! She pressed herself against the wall, hoping that the beasts would give up on her. But they didn't; they had cornered more inventive prey than this before. First one and then the other of the nightmarish creatures landed on the ground about twenty steps away from the girl and started moving towards her, dragging their folded wings behind them.

A burst of automatic fire didn't frighten, but only infuriated them; the bullets seemed to lodge in their thick, matted fur without reaching the flesh. The beast closer to Sasha snarled balefully, revealing crooked, needle-sharp teeth under the black lip on its upturned snout.

'Get down!'

Sasha didn't even bother wondering where the distant voice had come from, she just flung herself face down on the ground. There was a loud explosion very close to her and she was buffeted and scorched by a blast of hot air. A second blast followed immediately, and that was followed by frenzied squealing and the receding sound of flapping wings.

She raised her head timidly, coughed to force the dust out of her lungs and looked around. Not far away the road was gashed open by a fresh crater and splattered with dark, oily blood. A scorched leathery wing, torn out by the roots, was lying near her, with several more charred, shapeless chunks beside it.

A man with a massive, powerful figure, dressed in a heavy protective suit, was striding steadily across the stony space towards Sasha, holding himself erect.

Hunter!

CHAPTER 13

One Story

He took her by the hand, helped her up and tugged her along after him. Then he let go of her, seeming to come to his senses. His eyes were concealed behind special smoked glass and Sasha couldn't see them.

'Keep up with me! It's getting dark quickly, we have to get out of here in time,' he droned through his filters. Then he rushed on, without even glancing at her again.

'Hunter,' the girl called to him, straining to recognise her rescuer through the steamed-up lenses of her gas mask.

He pretended he couldn't hear her and there was nothing Sasha could do but run after him as fast as her legs would carry her. Of course, he was angry with her: this was the third time he'd had to give the stupid little girl a hand. But he had come up here, come up here for her sake, so how could there be any more doubt...?

The man with the shaved head wasn't planning on going anywhere near the beasts' lair that had been Sasha's way out of the Metro: he knew different paths. He turned right off the main road and ducked into an archway, dashed past the rusty iron skeletons of flat boxes that looked like market kiosks for dwarfs, frightened off a blurred shadow with a shot from his gun and stopped in front of a small brick sentry box with heavy bars over the windows. He turned a key in a massive padlock. A shelter? No, the sentry box turned out to be a blind: inside the door a concrete stairway zigzagged down into the depths.

Hanging the lock back up on the inside, her rescuer switched on his flashlight and tramped down the steps. Time had peeled the green-and-white paint off the walls and they were covered with names and dates: in, out, in, out . . . The man scribbled something illegible of his own. Probably everyone who used the secret way up onto the surface had to write down here when he left and when he came back. Only under many names there was no date of return.

The descent broke off sooner than Sasha was expecting: although the steps ran on downwards, the man with the shaved head halted at a nondescript little cast-iron door, and smashed his fist against it. A few seconds later a bolt grated on the other side and the door was opened by a man with dishevelled hair and a sparse little beard, wearing blue trousers with baggy knees.

'Who's this then?' he asked, looking perplexed.

'Someone I picked up on the Ring,' Hunter boomed. 'He almost got eaten by the birds, I was only just in time with the grenade launcher. Hey kid, how did you get out there?'

He flung back his hood and tugged off his gas mask . . .

The man standing in front of Sasha was a stranger: close-cropped light brown hair, a pale face with grey eyes, a squashed nose that looked as if it had been broken. And she had persuaded herself not to notice anything, telling herself she was wrong when she thought he moved too easily for a wounded man, that his walk was wrong, not feral enough, and the suit looked different . . . She suddenly felt stifled and pulled her own mask off too.

Fifteen minutes later Sasha was already inside the Hansa frontier.

'I'm sorry, I can't let you stay here without any documents.' She could hear a note of genuine regret in her rescuer's voice. 'Maybe this evening . . . you know . . . well, in the passage?'

She shook her head without speaking and smiled.

Where should she go now?

To him? There was still time!

But Sasha couldn't get over her annoyance with Hunter for not saving her this time too . . . And she had something else in mind that she didn't want to put off any longer.

The delicate, enticing cadences of the wonderful music found a way to her through the hubbub of the crowd, the scraping of shoes and the roaring of the traders. She thought it was the same melody that had cast its spell on her the day before. As she stepped towards it, Sasha felt as if she was making her way again towards that opening that radiated an unearthly glow. Only where did it lead to this time?

The musician was surrounded by a tight-packed ring of dozens of listeners. Sasha had to push her way through until the crowd spat her out into the empty circle. The melody drew these people to him and at the same time held them at a distance, as if they too were flying towards the light, but afraid of singeing their wings.

Sasha wasn't afraid.

He was young, slim and incredibly good looking. A little bit fragile, perhaps, but his well-groomed face wasn't soft and his green eyes didn't look naïve. His dark hair was untrimmed, but it lay neatly on his head. His unostentatious clothes looked too clean for this station and made him stand out against the human mishmash of Pavelets. His instrument looked a bit like the kind of whistles that people made for children out of narrow plastic insulation pipes, but it was large and black, with brass keys, imposingly elegant and obviously very expensive. The sounds that the musician drew from it seemed to belong to a different world and a different time. Like the instrument itself... Like its owner.

He caught Sasha's glance in the very first moment, let it go and immediately caught it again. She was embarrassed: she didn't find his attention unpleasant, but it was his music she had come here for.

'Thank God! I've found you...'

Homer pushed his way through to her, sweaty and panting.

'How is he?' Sasha asked immediately.

'Do you really...?' the old man began, then stopped short and said something else instead: 'He's disappeared.'

'What? Where to?' Sasha felt as if her heart was squeezed in someone's fist.

'He left. Took all his things and went. Most likely he's gone to Dobrynin...'

'And he didn't leave anything?' she asked timidly, already guessing what Homer's answer would be.

'Not a thing,' the old man said with a nod.

People started hissing furiously at them and Homer stopped talking. He listened to the melody, all the time glancing suspiciously from the musician to the girl and back again. He needn't have worried: she was thinking about something completely different.

Hunter may have driven her away and run off as soon as he could, but Sasha was starting to grasp the strange rules that he followed. If the man with the shaved head really had taken all his things, absolutely all of them, that meant he simply wanted her to be more tenacious, not to give up and come and find him. And that was what she would do anyway, yes she would. If only . . .

'And the knife?' she whispered to the old man. 'Did he take my knife with him? The black one?'

'It's not in the ward,' Homer said with a shrug.

'That means he took it!'

Even this paltry sign was enough for Sasha.

The flute-player was definitely talented and as skilled in his art as if he had been playing in a conservatory only yesterday. The case of his instrument was lying open for donations, and there were enough cartridges in it to feed the population of a small station – or to slaughter every last one of them. This was genuine recognition, Homer thought with a sad little smile

The melody seemed vaguely familiar to the old man, but try as he might to remember what it was and where he could have heard it – in an old film, in a concert on the radio? – he couldn't recall. There was something unusual about the melody: once you casually tuned in to its wavelength, you couldn't tear yourself away from it; you felt you absolutely had to listen right to the end, and then applaud the musician before he started playing again.

Prokofiev? Shostakovich? In any case Homer's knowledge of music was too meagre for a really serious attempt to guess the composer. But whoever had written down those notes, the flute player was doing more than just perform them, he was filling them with new resonance and new meaning, bringing them to life. Talent. Yes, talent, and for that Homer was prepared to forgive this young lad for the teasing glances that he tossed Sasha's way every now and then, like someone tossing a crumpled paper ball to a kitten.

But now it was time to take the girl away from him. The old man waited until the musical blossom faded and the musician surrendered to the applause of his audience, then grabbed hold of Sasha's damp protective suit that still smelled of bleach and dragged her out of the circle.

'My things are packed, I'm going after him,' he said and paused.

'So am I,' the girl said quickly.

'Do you realise what you're getting involved in?' Homer asked in a low voice.

'I know everything. I overheard it all.' She looked at him defiantly. 'An epidemic, right? And he wants to cremate everyone. Dead or alive. The whole station,' said Sasha, without turning her eyes away.

'And why do you want to go to a man like that?' the old man asked, genuinely curious.

Sasha didn't answer: she carried on walking in silence for a while until they reached an empty, secluded corner of the hall.

'My father died. Because of me. I'm to blame. There's nothing I can do to bring him back to life. But there are people there who are still alive. Who can still be saved. And I have to try. I owe it to him,' she concluded slowly and awkwardly.

'Saved from whom? From what? The sickness is incurable, you heard that,' the old man responded bitterly.

'From our friend. He's more terrible than any sickness. More deadly.' The girl sighed. 'At least diseases leave some hope. Someone always recovers. One in a thousand.'

'How? What makes you think you can do it?' asked Homer, gazing at her intently.

'I've already done it once,' she replied uncertainly.

Was the girl overestimating her strength? Was she deceiving herself by imagining that the callous and relentless brigadier shared her feelings? Homer didn't want to dishearten Sasha, but it was best to warn her now.

'Do you know what I found in his ward?' The old man carefully took the battered compact out of his pocket and handed it to Sasha. 'Did you do that to it?'

'No,' she said, shaking her head.

'That means it was Hunter . . .'

The girl slowly opened the little box and found her reflection in one of the shards of glass. She pondered for a moment, recalling her last conversation with the man with the shaved head and what he said in the dark room when she came to give him the knife. And she recalled Hunter's face, covered in blood, as he took those ponderous steps towards her, so that the monster with its razor-sharp claws already raised to strike would leave Sasha and kill him instead.

'He didn't do it because of me. It's because of the mirror,' she said resolutely.

'What's the mirror got to do with it?' the old man asked, raising one eyebrow.

'It's like you said,' Sasha answered, slamming the lid closed. 'Sometimes it helps to see yourself from the outside. It helps to understand a lot about yourself,' she said, mimicking the old man's tone of voice.

'You think Hunter doesn't know who he is? Or that he's still suffering because of his appearance? And that's why he broke it?' Homer asked with a condescending chuckle.

'It's not a matter of his appearance,' said the girl, leaning back against a column.

'Hunter knows perfectly well who he is. And he obviously doesn't like to be reminded about it,' said the old man, answering his own question.

'Perhaps he'd forgotten?' she objected. 'I sometimes get the feeling that he's always trying to remember something... Or that he's chained to a heavy freight car that's running down a slope into the darkness, and no one will help him to stop it. I can't explain it. I just feel it when I look at him.' Sasha frowned. 'No one else sees it, but I do. That's why I told you that time that he needs me.'

'So that's why he left you,' Homer remarked cruelly.

'I was the one who left him,' the girl said, knitting her brows stubbornly. 'And now I have to catch up with him, before it's too late. They're still alive. They can still be saved,' she repeated insistently. 'And he can still be saved too.'

'Who do you want to save him from?' ask Homer, jerking his head up.

She looked at him mistrustfully – did the old man really still not understand, after she had tried so hard?

'From the man in the mirror.'

'Is this place taken?'

Sasha started and stopped absent-mindedly prodding at her mushroom casserole with her fork. The green-eyed musician was standing beside her with a tray in his hands. The old man had gone off somewhere for a moment, and his place was empty.

'Yes.'

'A solution can always be found!' He put down his tray, jerked across a free stool from the next table and sat down on Sasha's left before she could protest.

'Just remember I didn't invite you,' she warned him.

'Will granddad scold you then?' the musician asked with a knowing wink. 'Allow me to introduce myself. Leonid.'

'He's not my granddad,' said Sasha, feeling the blood rush to her cheeks.

'So that's the way it is?' asked Leonid, stuffing his mouth as full as he could and arching up one eyebrow.

'You're brazen,' she remarked.

'I'm assertive,' he said, raising his fork in the air didactically.

'You're too sure of yourself,' Sasha said with a smile.

'I believe in people in general, and myself in particular,' he mumbled indistinctly as he chewed.

The old man came back, stood behind the intruder and pulled a sour face, but sat down on his own stool anyway.

'Aren't you feeling a bit crowded, Sasha?' he enquired peevishly, looking straight past the musician.

'Sasha!' the musician repeated triumphantly, glancing up from his bowl. 'Pleased to meet you. Let me remind you that my name's Leonid.'

'Nikolai Ivanovich,' Homer introduced himself, squinting at the young man sullenly. 'What was that melody you were playing today? It sounded familiar . . .'

'That's not surprising, this is the third day I've been playing it here,' the young man replied. 'Actually it's my own composition.'

'Yours?' said Sasha, putting down her knife and fork. 'What's it called?'

'It's not called anything,' Leonid said with a shrug. 'I hadn't really thought about a title for it. How can I transcribe it in letters? And what for, anyway?'

'It's very beautiful,' the girl admitted. 'Really incredibly beautiful.'

'Then I can name it in your honour,' the quick-witted musician replied. 'You're worthy of it.'

'No, don't,' she said and shook her head. 'Leave it as it is, without any name. There's a point to that.'

'And there's a definite point in dedicating it to you, too.' He tried to laugh, but choked and started coughing.

'Well, are you ready?' The old man picked up Sasha's tray and stood up. 'It's time. Excuse us, please, young man...'

'That's all right! I've finished eating already. May I see the young lady on her way?'

'We're leaving,' Homer said abruptly.

'Great! So am I. Going to Dobrynin.' The musician put on an innocent air. 'Are you by any chance going my way?'

'Yes we are,' said Sasha, surprising even herself. She tried not to look in Homer's direction and her gaze kept slipping across to Leonid.

There was something light and easy about him, a good-humoured affability. Like a little boy fencing with a twig, he struck with light jabs that didn't hurt and were impossible to feel angry about. And he presented his hints to Sasha so affectedly and amusingly, that she never even thought of taking them seriously. And what was wrong with him liking her?

And then, she had fallen in love with his music long before she met him. And the temptation of taking this magic with her on her journey was simply too great.

It was all down to the music, no doubt about that. Like the Pied Piper of Hamlyn, this damned youth enticed innocent souls with that sleek flute of his and used his gift to debauch all the girls he could get his hands on. Now he was trying to get his hands on Alexandra, and Homer didn't know what to do about it!

The old man found it hard to swallow Leonid's brash jokes, and before long they started sticking in his throat. And Homer was also annoyed by how quickly the musician had managed to reach an agreement with the obstinate Hansa boss for the three of them to be allowed to walk the stretch of the Circle Line to Dobrynin, even without any documents! The musician had walked into the spacious offices of the station commandant – a bald, aging dandy with a moustache like a cockroach's whiskers – with his heavy flute case full of cartridges, and come back out smiling, with his load lightened.

Homer had to admit that Leonid's diplomatic abilities had come in handy at just the right moment for them: the motor trolley on which they had arrived at Pavelets had disappeared from the parking area at the same time as Hunter disappeared, and going the long way round could have taken them up to a week. But what provoked the old man's suspicions most of all was the flippant way the minstrel had uprooted himself from a profitable station and parted with all his savings, just so that he could set off into the tunnels after Homer's Sasha. In different circumstances, this flippancy would have been a sign of being in love, but in this case the old man could see nothing but frivolous intentions and the habit of rapid conquests.

Yes, little by little Homer was turning into a crotchety chaperon. But he had good reasons to be on his guard and grounds for jealousy. The last thing he needed now was for the muse who had been miraculously restored to him to run off with a wandering minstrel! With an absolutely superfluous character, who had no place waiting for him in the novel, but had simply dragged in his own stool and churlishly seated himself right smack in the middle of it.

'Is there really no one left anywhere on Earth?'

The trio was striding towards Dobrynin, accompanied by three guards: the correct use of cartridges could make even the boldest dreams come true.

The girl, who had just given the others a gushing account of her expedition to the surface, broke off and turned sad. Homer and the musician exchanged glances: Who would be first to dash in and console her?

'Is there life beyond the Moscow Orbital Highway?' the old man snorted. 'Does the new generation wonder about that?'

'Of course it does,' Leonid declared confidently. 'The trouble is that no one else survived, there's simply no contact!'

'Well I, for instance, have heard that somewhere beyond Taganka Station there's a secret passage that leads to a certain curious tunnel,' said the old man. 'A normal-enough looking tunnel, six metres in diameter, only without any rails. It lies deep, forty or even fifty metres below ground. And it runs way off to the east . . .'

'Would that be the tunnel that leads to the bunkers in the Urals?' Leonid interrupted. 'And is this the story about the man who wandered into it by accident, then came back with a supply of food and . . .'

'Walked for a week with short halts, then his provisions started to run out and he had to turn back. There was still no sign of the tunnel coming to an end,' Homer concluded scrappily, put off his folk-narrative tone. 'Yes, according to the rumours it leads to the Urals bunkers, where there could still be someone left alive.'

'That's not very likely,' said the musician, yawning.

'And then an acquaintance of mine in Polis told me how one of the local radio operators had established contact with the crew of a tank who had battened down their hatches and withdrawn to somewhere so remote that no one ever even thought of bombing it,' said the old man, ostentatiously speaking to Sasha.

'Yeah, right,' said Leonid, nodding. 'That's a well-known story too. When they ran out of fuel, they buried the tank in the ground on a hill, and laid out a whole farm around it. And for a few more years they talked to Polis on the radio in the evenings.'

'Until the radio broke down,' Homer concluded irritably.

'Right, and what about the submarine?' his rival drawled. 'The nuclear submarine that was on a long-range mission, and when the strikes and counter-strikes began, it simply didn't have enough time to move into battle position. And when it did surface, everything had already been over for ages. So then the crew put it on permanent mooring not far from Vladivostok...'

'And to this day an entire village is powered by its reactor,' the old man put in. 'Six months ago I met a man who claimed to be the first mate of that submarine's captain. He said he'd crossed the entire country on a bicycle, all the way to Moscow. He was travelling for three years.'

'Did you talk to him in person?' Leonid asked in polite surprise.

'In person,' Homer snarled.

Legends had always been his hobbyhorse, and he simply couldn't allow this young smart alec to get the better of him. He had one more story left in reserve, a closely guarded one. He had been intending to tell it on a quite different occasion, not waste it in a pointless argument... But seeing Sasha laughing at this grifter's latest joke, he made up his mind.

'But have you heard about Polar Dawns?'

'What dawns?' asked the musician, turning towards him.

'Oh, come on now!' said the old man said, restraining a smile. 'The Far North, the Kola Peninsula, Polar Dawns City. A God-forsaken place. Fifteen hundred kilometres from Moscow, and at least a thousand to Peter. Nothing anywhere near it except Murmansk, with its navy bases, but even that's a fair distance away.'

'The middle of nowhere, basically,' said Leonid, encouraging him.

'Far away from the big cities, the secret factories and the military bases. Far away from all the main targets. The cities that our anti-rocket shield couldn't defend were reduced to dust and ashes. The ones that had a shield, where the interceptors had time to cut in . . .' The old man looked upwards. 'You know for yourself. But there were other places that no one was aiming at . . . because they didn't represent any kind of threat. Polar Dawns, for instance.'

'No one has any interest in the place now either,' the musician responded.

'But they should,' the old man snapped. 'Because right next to Polar Dawns was the Kola Atomic Power Station, one of the most powerful in the country. It supplied power to almost the entire north of Russia. Millions of people. Hundreds of factories. I come from those parts myself, from Arkhangelsk. I know what I'm talking about. And I visited that station as a school kid, on a guided tour. A genuine fortress, a state within a state. Its own little army, its own agricultural land, its own farm. They could survive autonomously. Even if there was a nuclear war, it wouldn't change anything in their life,' he chuckled darkly.

'So what you're trying to say . . .'

'Petersburg went, Murmansk went, and Arkhangelsk, millions of people perished . . . All the factories, along with the cities . . . reduced to dust and ash. But Polar Dawns City is still there. And the Kola Atomic Power Station wasn't damaged. Nothing but snow for thousands of kilometres on every side, expanses of snow and ice, wolves and polar bears. No contact with the centre. And they have enough fuel to supply a large city for several years, but for them, even including Polar Dawns, it will last for a hundred years. They'll easily make it through the winter.'

'It's a genuine ark,' Leonid whispered. 'And when the flood comes to an end and the waters recede, down from the summit of Mount Ararat . . .'

'Exactly,' the old man said with a nod.

'How do you know about this?' There wasn't a trace of irony or boredom left in the musician's voice now.

'I used to work as a radio operator once,' Homer replied evasively.

'I really wanted to find at least one person alive in my own native parts.'

'Will they hold out for long there, in the north?'

'I'm sure they will. Of course, the last time I was in contact was about two years ago. But can you imagine what that means – another entire century with electricity? In the warmth? With medical equipment, with computers, with electronic libraries on disks? There's no way you could know about that... There are only a couple of computers in the entire Metro, and they're no more than toys. And this is the capital,' the old man laughed bitterly. 'And if there are still people left somewhere – not solitary individuals, I mean, but at least villages... They've been back in the seventeenth century for a long time already, or maybe even the Stone Age. Wooden spills for light, cattle, witchcraft, every third child dying at birth. Abacuses and birch-bark manuscripts. And apart from the two nearest farms, there's nothing else in the world. Empty land and desolation. Wolves, bears, mutants. Why, the whole of modern civilisation is built on electricity. When the power runs out, the stations will die, and that's it. Billions of people took centuries to construct this building, brick by brick, and it's all been reduced to dust. Start all over again. Only can we do it? But there they have a breathing space, a whole century! You were right, it's Noah's Ark. An almost unlimited supply of energy! Oil has to be extracted and processed, gas has to be drilled for and pumped through thousands of kilometres of pipes! Do we have to go back to steam engines, then? Or even further? I'll tell you what,' he said, taking Sasha by the hand. 'People aren't in any danger. People are as resilient as cockroaches. But civilisation – that's what I'd like to preserve.'

'And have they got real civilisation, then?'

'Don't you worry about that. Nuclear engineers, the technical intelligentsia. And their conditions are definitely better than ours are here. Polar Dawns has grown quite a lot in the last twenty years. They set up a transmitter with a repeating message: "Calling all survivors..." and it gives their coordinates. They say people still come crawling in, even now...'

'Why haven't I ever heard about this?' the musician muttered.

'Not many have. It's hard to pick up their wavelength here. But you try it sometime if you've got a couple of years to spare,' the old man chuckled. 'The call sign is "Last Harbour".'

'I'd have known about it,' the young man said seriously, shaking his head. 'I collect cases like that... You really mean there wasn't any war there?'

'How can I put it? Wilderness on all sides, even if there were any villages or small towns nearby, they went wild quickly enough. Sometimes the barbarians attacked. And the animals, of course, if you can call them that. But they had the arsenal to hold them off. All-round defences, a fortified perimeter. Electrified barbed wire, guard towers. A genuine fortress, I tell you. And during the first ten years – the worst time – they put up another barrier, a log stockade. They reconnoitred everything around them, even got as far as Murmansk, two hundred kilometres away. There isn't any more Murmansk, just a fused crater where it used to be. They were even planning to organise an expedition southwards, to Moscow. I tried to talk them out of it. Why cut the umbilical cord? When the background radiation falls, they'll be able to bring more land under cultivation – and then... But in the meantime there's nothing they can do here. This place is just one big graveyard,' Homer sighed.

'That would be amusing, if the human race that destroyed itself with the atom, is saved by the atom too.'

'There's nothing amusing about it,' said the old man, giving him a stern glance.

'It's like the fire that Prometheus stole,' the musician explained. 'The Gods forbade him to give fire to humans. He wanted to drag man out of the mud, the darkness and stagnation...'

'I've read it,' Homer interrupted acidly. '*The Myths and Legends of Ancient Greece*.'

'A prophetic myth,' Leonid remarked. 'The Gods had good reason to be against it. They knew how it would end.'

'But it was fire that made man into man,' Homer objected.

'And you reckon that without electricity he'll turn back into an animal?' the musician asked.

'I reckon that without it we'll be thrown back at least two hundred years. And taking into account that only one in a thousand survived and everything has to be rebuilt, brought back under control and studied all over again – at least five hundred. And maybe we'll never recover. Why, don't you agree?'

'I do,' Leonid replied. 'But is it really just a matter of electricity?'

211

'Well what do you think it is?' Homer erupted, throwing his hands up.

The musician gave him a strange, long, lingering glance and shrugged.

The silence dragged on. Homer could definitely regard this outcome of their conversation as a victory for him: the girl had finally stopped devouring the impertinent rogue with her eyes and started thinking about something else. But just as they were getting very close to the station, Leonid suddenly declared:

'All right. Why don't I tell you a story?'

The old man tried his best to appear exhausted, but he replied with a gracious nod.

'They say that beyond Sport Station and before the ruined Sokolniki Bridge, a dead-end tunnel branches off the main one, running down at a steep angle. It ends at a metal grille, with a tightly closed hermetic door behind it. They've tried to open the door several times, but never got anywhere. And any solitary travellers who set out to find it almost never come back, and their bodies are found over at the far side of the Metro.'

'The Emerald City?' Homer asked, twisting up his face.

'Everybody knows,' Leonid carried on, taking no notice, 'that the Sokolniki Bridge collapsed on the first day and all the stations beyond it were cut off from the Metro. It's usually believed that no one left on the other side of the bridge was saved, although there's absolutely no proof of that.'

'The Emerald City,' Homer said, waving his hand impatiently.

'Everybody also knows that Moscow University was built on unstable ground, which was only able to support the immense building thanks to powerful cold generators working away in its basements, freezing the swampy earth. Without them it would have slid into the river a long time ago.'

'A stale old cliché,' the old man put in, realising where all this was leading.

'More than twenty years have gone by, but for some reason the abandoned building is still standing there ...'

'Because it's hogwash, that's why!'

'Some rumours say that what lies under the University is not just a basement, but a large strategic bomb shelter that goes ten storeys down, and apart from the cold generators, it contains its own nuclear reactor, and living space and connections to the closest Metro stations, and even to Metro-2...' Leonid made terrible eyes at Sasha and she smiled.

'I haven't heard anything new yet,' Homer growled contemptuously.

'They say there's a genuine underground city there,' the musician continued dreamily. 'A city in which the inhabitants – of course they didn't die – have devoted themselves to the collection of lost knowledge, crumb by crumb, and the service of beauty. Sparing no resources, they send out expeditions to the picture galleries, museums and libraries that have survived. And they raise their children so that they don't lose the sense of beauty either. Peace and harmony reign there, and there are no ideologies apart from enlightenment, and no religions apart from art. There are none of those ugly old-style walls, painted in two drab colours with linseed oil paint. Instead of the crudely barked commands and warning sirens, the loudspeakers broadcast Berlioz, Haydn and Tchaikovsky. And absolutely everyone – just imagine it – can quote Dante from memory. And these people have managed to stay the same as they were. Or no, they're not the way they were in the twenty-first century, but like people were in ancient times... Well, you've read about that in *Myths and Legends*...' The musician smiled at the old man as if he was feeble-minded. 'Free, bold, wise and beautiful. Just. Noble.'

'I've never heard anything of the sort!' exclaimed Homer, hoping that the cunning devil wouldn't win the girl over with this.

'In the Metro,' said Leonid, looking intently at the old man, 'this place is known as the Emerald City. But according to the rumours, its inhabitants prefer a different name.'

'And what's that?' Homer erupted.

'The Ark.'

'Drivel. Absolute drivel!' the old man snorted and turned away.

'Of course it's drivel,' the musician responded phlegmatically. 'It's just a story...'

Dobrynin had been overrun by chaos.

Homer looked around, perplexed and frightened. Could he be mistaken? Could something like this be happening at one of the calmer stations of the Circle Line? It looked to him as if someone had declared war on Hansa within the last half-hour. Peeping out of the parallel tunnel was a freight trolley with dead bodies piled up on it higgledy-piggledy. Military medical orderlies in aprons were dragging the bodies onto the platform and laying them out on tarpaulin sheets: one had been separated from its head, another one's face had been reduced to pulp, the intestines were tumbling out of a third...

Homer covered Sasha's eyes. Leonid filled his lungs with air and turned away.

'What happened?' one of the guards assigned to the threesome asked in a frightened voice.

'It's our watch from the large junction, with the Special Service Line. Every last man's here. No one got away. And we don't know who did it.' The medical orderly wiped his hand on his apron. 'Give me a light, will you, brother? My hands are shaking...'

The Special Service Line. A cobweb thread line that ran off behind the Pavelets radial line station, connecting four lines together – Circle, Grey, Orange and Green.

Homer had assumed that Hunter would choose that route, which was the shortest, although it was guarded by reinforced Hansa units.

What was all this bloodshed for? Did they open fire on him first, or did they not even spot him in the gloom of the tunnel? And where was he now? Oh God, another head... How could he do something like this?

Homer remembered the shattered mirror and what Sasha had said. Could she be right after all? Was the brigadier trying to restrain himself, trying to avoid killing unnecessarily, but unable to stop? And when he broke the mirror, was he really trying to strike the hideous, terrifying man that he was gradually turning into...

No, what Hunter had seen in the mirror wasn't a man, but a genuine monster. That was who he had tried to crush. But he had only shattered the glass, transforming one reflection into dozens.

Or perhaps... The old man watched as the orderlies moved from the trolley to the platform... carrying the eighth man, the last... Perhaps it was the man who was still staring bleakly out of the mirror? The old Hunter? And that Other .. was already on the outside?

214

CHAPTER 14

What Else?

Really, what is it that makes man human?

He's been wandering the earth for more than a million years, but the magical transformation that changed a cunning and gregarious animal into something completely different, something absolutely unprecedented, happened to him only about ten thousand years ago. Just imagine, for ninety-nine per cent of his history, he sheltered in caves and chomped on raw meat. Without knowing how to get warm or make tools and genuine weapons, not even knowing how to talk properly! And the range of feelings he was capable of experiencing didn't really differentiate him from monkeys and wolves: cold, fear, attachment, anxiety, gratification.

How was he able, in the space of a few centuries, to learn to build and think and record his own thoughts, to alter the matter around him and invent things, why did he feel the need to draw, and how did he discover music? How was he able to conquer the entire world and restructure it to suit his requirements? What exactly was it that was added to this animal ten thousand years ago?

Fire? The fact that man was given the ability to tame light and warmth, to carry them with him to cold, uninhabited regions, to roast his prey on campfires in order to satisfy his stomach? But what did that change, apart from allowing him to extend his domain? Rats managed to colonise the entire planet without any fire, and they remained what they were to begin with – quick-witted, gregarious mammals. No, it can't have been fire; at least, not only fire – the musician was right. Something else . . . But what? Language? Now there was an undeniable difference from other animals. The precise faceting of rough thoughts into the glittering diamonds of words that can become a universal currency and circulate everywhere. The ability, not so much to express what is going on in your head, as to arrange it in proper sequence: the casting of unstable images, which flow like molten metal, into solid forms. The clarity of mind and coolness of judgement, the ability to transmit orders and knowledge by mouth clearly and unambiguously: which leads to the ability to organise and subordinate, to assemble armies and build states.

But ants manage without words, constructing genuine megalopolises on their own level, inconspicuous though it is to man, and all finding their own places in supremely complicated hierarchies, conveying information and commands to each other with precision, drafting thousands of thousands of soldiers into intrepid legions with iron discipline, which clash head on in the inaudible but remorseless wars of their tiny empires.

Perhaps letters?

Letters, without which the accumulation of knowledge would be impossible? Those bricks out of which the Babylonian Tower of world civilisation, reaching for the heavens, was built? Without which the unbaked clay of the wisdom mastered by one generation would crack and split apart, subside and disintegrate into dust, unable to support its own weight? Without them, every successive generation would have started building the great tower again from the previous level and spent its entire life fumbling with the ruins of the preceding wattle and daub hut before dying in its own turn, without ever erecting the next level. Letters and writing allowed man to export accumulated knowledge beyond the narrow boundaries of his own skull, and so preserve it undistorted for his descendants, relieving them of the need to rediscover what had already been discovered long ago and allowing them to build something of their own on the firm foundation inherited from their ancestors.

But it wasn't only letters, was it?

If wolves could write, would their civilisation be like man's? Would they have a civilisation? When a wolf is sated with food, he falls into a state of blissful prostration, devoting his time to endearments and play, until the griping in his belly drives him on again. But when a man is sated with food, a yearning of a different kind, elusive and inexplicable, awakens within him – the same yearning that makes him gaze at the stars for hours on end, scrape ochre onto the walls of his cave, decorate the bow of his war boat with carved figures,

216

slave for centuries to erect stone colossi instead of reinforcing the walls of his fortress, and spend his life on honing his artistry with words instead of perfecting his mastery of the sword. The same yearning that makes a former engine driver's mate devote the remainder of his life to reading and searching – searching for something and trying to capture it in words ... Something special ... The yearning that drives a dirty, impoverished crowd to listen to wandering fiddlers in an attempt to satisfy it, that makes kings welcome troubadours and patronise artists, and makes a girl who was born underground gaze for hours at a daub on a packet that once held a teabag. A vague but powerful summons that can drown out even the call of hunger – but only in a human being.

Is it not this call that expands man's range of feelings beyond those accessible to other animals, giving him in addition the ability to dream, the audacity to hope, and the courage to show mercy? Love and compassion, which man often regards as his distinctive qualities, were not discovered by him. A dog is capable of loving and being compassionate: when its master is ill, it stays with him and whines. A dog can even suffer boredom and perceive the meaning of its own life in another creature: if its master is dying, it is sometimes prepared to perish, simply to remain with him. But it doesn't have dreams and aspirations.

So it's a yearning for beauty and the ability to appreciate it? The remarkable ability to take pleasure in combinations of colours, sequences of sounds, the angles of lines and the elegance of verbal structures? To extract from them a sweet vibration that wrings the heart and soul. That rouses any soul, whether it is bloated with fat or hard and calloused or seamed with scars, and helps it purge itself of extraneous excrescences.

Perhaps. But not only that.

In order to drown out the stuttering bursts of sub-machine-gun fire and the despairing howls of naked, bound human beings, other human beings played the majestic operas of Wagner at full volume. No contradiction arose: one thing merely emphasised the other. Then what else?

And even if man does survive as a biological species in this present-day hell, will he preserve this fragile, almost impalpable, but undoubtedly real particle of his essential being? The spark that ten thousand years ago transformed a half-starving beast with a dull gaze into a creature of a new order? Into a being tormented more by hunger of the soul than hunger of the flesh? A rebellious being, fluctuating eternally between spiritual grandeur and ignominy, between an inexplicable mercy quite inappropriate for predators and an unjustifiable cruelty unequalled even in the soulless world of insects. Who erects magnificent palaces and paints incredible canvases, rivalling the Creator in his ability to synthesise pure beauty – and invents gas chambers and hydrogen bombs in order to annihilate everything that he himself has created and economically annihilate his own fellows. Who painstakingly builds sandcastles on the beach and blithely destroys them. Did that spark transform him into a being who knows no limits in anything? An irrepressibly restless being who doesn't know how to satisfy his strange hunger, but devotes his entire life to the attempt to do it? Into man? Will this remain in him? Will this remain after him?

Or will it be lost in his past, merely a brief peak in the graph of history, leaving man to revert from this strange one-per-cent deviation to his perennial torpidity, an habitual, customary state of stagnation, in which innumerable generations follow each other, chewing the cud without even raising their eyes from the ground, and the passing of ten years or a hundred or five hundred thousand is equally imperceptible?

What else?

'Is it true?'

'What exactly?' Leonid asked her with a smile.

'About the Emerald City? About the Ark? That there is a place like that in the Metro?' Sasha asked pensively, looking down at her feet.

'There are rumours,' he replied evasively.

'It would be great to get in there someday,' she said slowly. 'You know when I was walking up on the surface, I felt so sad for people. So bitter that they made just one mistake . . . And they'll never be able to put everything back the way it used to be. And it was so good there . . . probably.'

'A mistake? No, it was an absolutely heinous crime,' the musician replied seriously. 'To destroy the entire world, to kill six billion people – is that a mistake?'

'Even so . . . You and I deserve forgiveness, don't we? So does

218

everyone else. Everyone should be given a chance to make himself over and do everything over again, to try again one more time, even if it's the last one...' She paused. 'I'd like so much to see what it's really like up there... I wasn't interested before. I was simply afraid, and everything on the surface seemed ugly to me... But it turns out I just went up in the wrong place. It's so stupid. That city up there is like my life before. There's no future in it. Only memories – and they're not mine... Only ghosts. And I understood something very important while I was there, you know...' Sasha hesitated. 'Hope is like blood. While it still flows through your veins, you're alive. I want to hope.'

'But why do you want to go to the Emerald City?' the musician asked.

'I want to see, to feel what it was like to live before... You said yourself... I suppose the people there really must be very different. People who haven't forgotten yesterday and who will definitely have a tomorrow must be quite, quite different.'

They strolled slowly round the hall of Dobrynin Station, under the watchful eyes of the sentries. Homer had left them alone with obvious reluctance, and now he had been delayed for some reason. Hunter still hadn't put in an appearance.

Sasha saw hints in the marble features of Dobrynin's marble hall. The large, marble-faced arches leading to the tracks alternated with small, decorative, blank arches. Large, small, large again, small again. Like a man and a woman holding hands, a man and a woman... And she suddenly wanted to put her hand into a broad, strong, male palm too. To shelter in it, if only for a short while.

'You can build a new life here too,' Leonid told the girl, winking at her. 'You don't necessarily have to go somewhere and search for something... It can be enough just to look round.'

'And what will I see?'

'Me,' he said, lowering his eyes in theatrical modesty.

'I've already seen you. And heard you,' said Sasha, returning his smile at last. 'I like what I heard, like everyone else... Don't you need your cartridges at all? You gave away so many to get them to let us through here.'

'I only need enough for my food. And I always have enough. It's stupid to play for money.'

'Then what do you play for?'

'For the music.' He laughed. 'For the people. No, that's not right either. For what the music does to the people.'

'And what does it do to them?'

'Well actually – anything at all,' said Leonid, turning serious again. 'I have music that will make people love and music that will make them weep.'

'And the music you were playing the last time...' Sasha looked at him suspiciously. 'The music without a name. What does that make people do?'

'This one?' he asked and whistled the introduction. 'It doesn't make them do anything. It just takes away pain.'

'Hey, mate!'

Homer closed the exercise book and squirmed on the uncomfortable wooden bench. The duty orderly was ensconced behind a little counter with a surface that was almost completely taken up by three old black telephones without buttons or discs. The little red light on one of the phones was winking amicably.

'Andrei Andreevich is free now. He's got two minutes for you from the moment you walk in. Don't mumble, get straight to the point,' the duty orderly admonished the old man strictly.

'Two minutes won't be enough,' Homer sighed.

'I warned you,' the other man said with a shrug.

Even five minutes wasn't enough. He didn't have any real idea of where to start, or how to finish, or what questions to ask and what to ask for, but, apart from the commandant of Dobrynin Station, he had no one else to turn to right now.

But Andrei Andreevich, a large, fat man in a uniform tunic that didn't close across his stomach, was already furious and streaming with sweat, and he didn't listen to the old man for long.

'Don't you understand, or what? I've got a *force majeure* situation here, eight men have been mown down, and you start talking to me about some epidemic or other! There isn't anything here! That's enough, stop wasting my time! Either you clear out of here yourself, or...' Like a sperm whale leaping out of the water, the commandant launched his meaty carcass forward, almost overturning the desk he was sitting at. The duty orderly glanced into the office enquiringly. Homer also got up off the low, hard chair for visitors.

'I'll go. But then why did you send forces into Serpukhov?'

'What business is that of yours?'

'They say in the station...'

'What do they say? What do they say? You know what? To make sure you don't go spreading panic around here... Pasha, come on, stick him in the cage!'

In the twinkling of an eye Homer was tossed out into the reception area and the duty orderly dragged the stubbornly resisting old man into a narrow side corridor, alternating reproaches with slaps to his face.

Between two slaps Homer's respirator came off; he tried to hold his breath, but immediately received a jab to the solar plexus that set him coughing. The sperm whale surfaced in the doorway of his office, filling the opening completely.

'Let him stay there for now, we'll get to the bottom of this later... And who are you? By appointment?' he barked at the next visitor.

Homer had already turned towards him.

Hunter was standing there stock still with his arms crossed, just three steps away from him. He was a wearing somebody else's uniform that was tight on him and hiding his face in the shadow of the raised visor of his helmet. He showed no sign of recognising the old man and no intention of intervening. Homer had expected him to be smeared with blood, like a butcher, but the only crimson spot on the brigadier's clothes was the small stain over his own wound. Hunter shifted his stony gaze to the station commandant, and suddenly started moving towards him slowly, as if he intended to walk straight through the fat man into the office.

The startled commandant started muttering and backed away, opening up the way through. The guard froze expectantly with his arms locked round Homer. Hunter squeezed through the door after the retreating fat man and ended the commandant's resistance with a single lion's roar that reduced him to silence. Then he switched to an imperious whisper.

Letting go of the old man, the orderly stole across to the door and stepped inside. A moment later he was swept back out by a torrent of filthy expletives, during which the commandant's voice broke into a squeal.

'And let that provocateur go!' he shouted at the end, as if he was repeating someone else's order under hypnosis.

Bright red, as if he had been scalded, the orderly closed the door behind him, stomped back to his post at the entrance and stuck his nose into a news flyer printed on wrapping paper. When Homer moved determinedly past his desk in the direction of the commandant's office, he just huddled down even lower behind his little newspaper, to indicate that what happened from now on had nothing to do with him.

Homer glanced triumphantly at the guard covering his shame with the news sheet: at last he could take a proper look at the phones. The one that was winking all the time had a piece of dirty-white plaster stuck to it, on which someone had scrawled a single word with a ballpoint pen:

'Tula'.

'We maintain contact with the Order,' said the commandant of Dobrynin Station, sweating and cracking his fists, but not daring to raise his eyes to the brigadier. 'And no one has warned us about this operation. I can't take this decision on my own.'

'Then call Central,' said Hunter. 'You have time to agree things. But not much.'

'They won't give approval. This will endanger the stability of Hansa . . . Surely you know that comes before anything else for Hansa? And we've got everything under control.'

'What damned stability? If measures aren't taken . . .'

'The situation is stable, I don't understand what you find unsatisfactory,' said Andrei Andreevich, shaking his heavy head obstinately. 'All the exits are covered by guns. A mouse couldn't get through. Let's wait for everything to resolve itself.'

'Nothing will resolve itself!' Hunter bellowed. 'If you wait, all that will happen is that someone will get out and run across the surface or find a roundabout route. The station has to be purged! By the book! I don't understand why you haven't done it yourselves yet!'

'But there could be people there who are still well. How do you imagine it happening? Do I order my lads to shoot everyone in Tula and incinerate them? What about the sectarians' train? And maybe clean out Serpukhov at the same time? Half the men here have kept women there, and illegitimate children . . . No, let me tell you something! We're not fascists here. War's war, but this . . . Killing sick people . . . Even when there was swine fever at Belorussia, they took the pigs into different corners one at a time, so that if one was infected, it died, and if it was healthy, it could live, instead of just slaughtering them all indiscriminately.'

'Those were pigs, these are people,' the brigadier said flatly.

'No, no,' said the commandant and started shaking his head again, splashing sweat about. 'I can't do that... It would be on my conscience afterwards. And I... I don't want the dreams that would come afterwards.'

'You won't have to do it yourself. For that there are men who don't have dreams. All you'll do is let us pass through your station. Nothing more.'

'I sent couriers to Polis, to find out about a vaccine,' said Andrei Andreevich, wiping away his perspiration with his sleeve. 'There is hope that...'

'There is no vaccine! There is no hope! Stop burying your head in the sand! Why don't I see any medical units from Central here? Why do you refuse to call them and ask for the green light to let a cohort of the Order through?'

The commandant remained obstinately silent; for some reason he tried to fasten the buttons on his tunic, fumbling at them with his slippery fingers and then giving up. He walked over to a shabby sideboard, splashed out a glass of some smelly alcoholic infusion for himself and downed it in one.

'Why, you haven't informed them,' Hunter guessed. 'They still don't know anything about it. You've got an epidemic at the next station, and they don't know anything...'

'I answer for something like that with my head,' the commandant said hoarsely. 'An epidemic in the adjacent station means compulsory retirement. I allowed it to happen... Didn't prevent it... Created a threat to the stability of Hansa.'

'In the adjacent station? At Serpukhov?'

'Everything's calm there for the time being, but I caught on too late... Didn't react in time. How could I know?'

'And how did you explain all this to everyone? The forces at an independent station? The cordoning off of the tunnels?'

'Bandits... Rebels. It happens everywhere. It's nothing special.'

'And now it's too late to confess,' the brigadier said with a nod.

'It's not retirement now...' Andrei Andreevich poured himself a second glass and downed it. 'It's the death penalty.'

'And now what?'

'I'm waiting.' The commandant lowered his backside onto his desk. 'I'm waiting. What if...?'

'Why don't you answer their calls?' Homer put in. 'Your phone's blowing its top – they're calling from Tula. What if...?'

'It's not blowing its top,' the commandant replied in a flat, hollow voice. 'I turned the sound off. It's just the light blinking. While it still does that, they're alive.'

'Why don't you answer it?' the old man repeated angrily.

'What can I tell them? To hang on and be patient? To get well soon? That help is near? To put a bullet through their heads? Talking to the refugees was as much as I could take,' the commandant yelled, losing control.

'Shut up immediately,' Hunter told him in a quiet voice. 'And listen. I'll come back in one day with a squadron. I have to be allowed through all the guard posts without hindrance. You will keep Serpukhov Station closed off. We'll move on to Tula and purge it. If necessary, we'll purge Serpukhov too. We'll pretend it's a small war. You don't have to inform Central. You won't have to do anything at all. I'll do it... I'll restore stability.'

The exhausted commandant nodded feebly, as limp as a deflated inner tube from a bicycle tyre. He poured out some more infusion for himself, sniffed at it and, before he drank it, asked quietly:

'But you'll be up to your elbows in blood. Doesn't that bother you?'

'Blood's easy to wash off with cold water,' the brigadier told him.

As they were walking out of the office, Andrei Andreevich filled his lungs with air and summoned the duty orderly in a stentorian voice. The orderly dashed inside and the door slammed shut behind him with a crash. Dropping back a little from Hunter, the old man leaned across the counter, grabbed the black receiver off the phone he'd been watching and pressed it to his ear.

'Hello! Hello! I'm listening!' he exclaimed in a loud whisper into the sieve of the mouthpiece.

Silence. Not blank silence, as if the line had been cut, it was a silence that hummed, as if the phone was off the hook at the other end, but there was no one to answer Homer. As if someone there had been waiting for him to answer for a very long time, but hadn't been able to wait any longer. As if now the other receiver was croaking into the ear of a dead man in the old man's distorted voice.

Hunter glanced ominously at Homer from the doorway and the old man carefully put the phone back down and meekly followed the brigadier out.

'Popov! Popov! Rise and shine! Get up, quick!'

The powerful beam of the commander's flashlight pierced straight though his eyelids, flooding his brain with fire. A strong hand shook him by the shoulder and then the back of it smashed into Artyom's unshaven cheek.

'Where's your gun? Take your automatic and follow me, on the double!' Of course, they dozed with their trousers on, in full gear in fact. Unwinding the tattered rags in which the Kalashnikov that served as his pillow had been wrapped for the night, Artyom tramped off, still swaying, after his commander. How long had he managed to sleep? An hour? Two? His head was buzzing and his throat was dry.

'It's starting,' said the commander, looking back over his shoulder and breathing stale alcohol fumes into Artyom's face.

'What's starting?' he asked in fright.

'You'll see in a moment. Here, take this clip. You'll need it.'

Tula – a spacious station with no columns which looked like merely the top of a single, unbelievably broad tunnel, was enveloped in almost total darkness. In a few places feeble beams of light were darting about, but there was no order or system to their movements, no sense at all, as if the flashlights were in the hands of little children or monkeys. Only where would monkeys come from here?

Waking instantly and feverishly checking his automatic, Artyom suddenly realised what had happened. They hadn't been able to hold them! Or maybe it still wasn't too late?

Another two soldiers, still puffy and hoarse from sleep, darted out of the watch office and joined them. Along the way the commander scraped together the remainder, everyone who could still stand on his feet and hold a gun. Even the ones who were already coughing a bit.

A strange, sinister cry pervaded the thick, stale, expired air. Not a scream, not a howl, not a command... A groan pouring out of hundreds of throats – straining in agony, full of despair and horror. A groan punctuated by a meagre jangling and scraping of iron that came from two, three, ten places at the same time.

The platform was cluttered with torn, sagging tents and capsized kennels for living in, constructed out of sheets of metal and pieces of Metro-carriage cladding, all jumbled together with plywood counters and people's abandoned belongings. The commander strode on, parting the heaps of garbage like an icebreaker moving through icepacks, with Artyom and the other two trotting along in his wake.

A truncated train standing on the right-hand track loomed up out of the darkness: the light in both carriages was off, the open doors had been clumsily blocked with pieces of mobile barriers, and inside ... On the other side of the dark window panes a terrible mishmash of humanity was heaving about, seething and simmering. Dozens of hands had grabbed the bars of the frail barriers and were swaying, shaking and rattling them. Occasionally the machine-gunners in gas masks who were posted at each of the exits skipped up to the black, gaping mouths of the doors and raised their gun butts, but they didn't dare to beat the prisoners, let alone shoot them. In other places, on the contrary, the sentries tried to reason with the raging human sea squeezed into the metal boxes and calm it down.

But did the people in the carriages still understand anything?

They had been herded into the train because they started running away from the special sections of the tunnels, and because there were already too many of them – more than the healthy men.

The commander rushed past the first carriage, and the second, and then Artyom saw where they were going in such a great hurry. The last door, that was where the abscess had ruptured. Strange creatures had flooded out of the carriage – barely able to stand, mutilated beyond recognition by the swellings on their faces, with puffy, appallingly thick arms and legs. No one had managed to get away yet: all the free sub-machine-gunners were converging on the door.

The commander tore through the cordon and walked forward.

'I order all patients to return to their places immediately!' he exclaimed, pulling his officer's Stechkin pistol out of its holster.

The infected man closest to him raised his cumbersome, swollen head with a struggle, in several stages, and licked his cracked lips.

'Why are you treating us like this?'

'You are aware that you are infected with an unknown virus. We're looking for a cure . . . You just have to wait for it.'

'Looking for a cure,' the man repeated after him. 'That's funny.'

'Get back into the carriage immediately.' The commander clicked off the safety catch of his revolver. 'I'll count to ten, then I'll shoot to kill. One . . .'

'You just don't want to leave us without hope, so that you can control us. Until we all die anyway . . .'

'Two.'

'It's a day now since they gave us any water. Why give dead men anything to drink?'

'The sentries are afraid to approach the bars. Two of them have been infected like that. Three.'

'There are lots of bodies in the carriages already. We're trampling on people's faces. Do you know how a nose crunches? If it's a child's, then . . .'

'There's nowhere to put them! We can't burn them. Four.'

'The next carriage is so cramped, the dead are still standing beside the living. Shoulder to shoulder.'

'Five.'

'For God's sake, shoot me, will you? I know there isn't any cure. I'm going to die soon. Then I won't feel my insides being scraped raw with coarse sandpaper and soaked in alcohol . . .'

'Six.'

'And set alight. It feels like my head's full of worms that are eating away my brain and my soul bit by bit from the inside . . . Yum-yum, crunch, crunch, crunch . . .'

'Seven!'

'You idiot! Let us out of here! Let us die like human beings. What makes you think you have the right to torture us like this? You know that you're probably already . . .'

'Eight! This is all a safety measure. So that others can survive. I'm prepared to croak, but not one of you plague dogs is going to leave here. Get ready!'

Artyom flung up his automatic and set the sight on the nearest sick person. Oh God, he thought it was a woman . . . Swollen breasts stuck out under the T-shirt that was dried into a reddish-brown crust. He blinked and turned his gun barrel towards a shambling old man. The crowd of monsters started muttering and pulled back at first, trying to squeeze back in through the door, but it couldn't – more and more infected people were oozing out of the carriage like fresh pus, groaning and weeping.

'You sadist! What are you doing! You're going to shoot living people! We're not zombies!'

'Nine!' The commander's voice turned dull and hollow.

'Just let us go!' the sick man yelled hoarsely, reaching his arms out towards the commander as if he were conducting a choir, and the whole crowd surged forward, following the sweep of his fingers.

'Fire!'

People started flowing towards Leonid immediately, the moment he put his lips to his instrument. The first sounds drawn out of the barrel of his flute were tentative and impure, but still enough to set the people gathered around smiling and clapping in approval, and when the flute's voice grew firmer, the faces of his listeners were transformed, as if the dirt had fallen away from them.

This time Sasha was awarded a place of distinction – beside the musician. Now Leonid was not the only one with dozens of eyes gazing at him intently, some of the admiring stares came her way. At first this made the girl feel awkward – after all, she didn't deserve their attention and gratitude, but then the melody picked her up off the granite floor and carried her along with it, distracting her from her surroundings, in the same way that a good book or a story told by someone can captivate you and make you forget about everything.

The same melody floated through the air again – Leonid's own composition, untitled. He started and ended every one of his performances with it. It could smooth out wrinkles and whisk the dust off the windowpanes of glazed eyes, lighting little icon lamps on the other side of them. Sasha already knew the melody, but Leonid opened up new, mysterious little doors in it, discovering new harmonies, and the music sounded new and different. As if she had been gazing at the sky for a long, long time, and suddenly, through an opening in the white clouds, she had glimpsed a boundless, bottomless, delicate-green expanse.

Suddenly she felt a prick that startled her and brought her back down under the ground ahead of schedule. Sasha spun round in fright. So that was it ... Towering above the crowd, Hunter was standing slightly behind the other listeners with his head thrown back. The sharp, barbed blade of his gaze was thrust into her, and if he released his grip briefly, it was only in order to stab the musician too. Leonid took no notice of the man with the shaved head – or at least, he gave no sign that anything was interfering with his playing.

Strangely enough, Hunter didn't leave, and he didn't make any attempt to take her away or break off the performance. He waited until the final notes, then moved back and disappeared. Abandoning Leonid, Sasha immediately forced her way into the crowd, trying to keep up with the man with the shaved head. He stopped not far away, in front of a bench on which Homer was sitting, looking dejected.

'You heard everything,' he said in a husky voice. 'I'm leaving. Will you go with me?'

'Where to?' asked the old man, smiling as the girl walked up to them. 'She knows everything,' he explained to the man with the shaved head.

Hunter stabbed Sasha again with his barbed gaze, then nodded without saying anything to her.

'Not far,' he said, shifting his head to speak to the old man. 'But I . . . I don't want to be left alone.'

'Take me with you,' said Sasha, seizing her chance.

The man with the shaved head breathed in loudly, clenching his fingers and unclenching them again.

'Thank you for the knife,' he said eventually. 'It came in very useful.'

The girl recoiled, stung, but gathered her courage again immediately.

'You decide what to do with the knife,' she objected.

'I had no choice.'

'But now you do.' She bit on her lower slip and frowned.

'No, I still don't. If you know, then you must understand. If you really . . .'

'Understand what?'

'How important it is to get to Tula. How important it is for me . . . As quickly as possible . . .'

Sasha saw his fingers trembling and a dark patch spreading across his shoulder: she was beginning to feel afraid of this man – and even more afraid for him.

'You have to stop,' she told him gently.

'Out of the question,' he snapped. 'It's not important who does it. So why not me?'

'Because you'll destroy yourself.' The girl touched his hand tentatively and he started, as if he had been stung.

'I have to. Cowards decide everything here as it is. If I delay any longer, I'll destroy the whole Metro.'

'But what if there was another way? If there was a cure? If you didn't have to do it any longer?'

'How many times do I have to say it? There aren't any cures for this fever! Do you really think that I would... That I would...'

'What would you choose?' asked Sasha, not letting go of him.

'There's nothing to choose from!' the man with the shaved head exclaimed, shaking off her hand. 'We're leaving!' he barked to the old man.

'Why don't you want to take me with you?' she protested.

'I'm afraid.' He said it in a very low voice, almost a whisper, so that no one but Sasha could hear him.

He swung round and strode away, growling curtly to the old man that he had ten minutes before they set out.

'Am I mistaken or is someone here a bit feverish?' said a voice behind Sasha's back.

'What?' She spun round and collided with Leonid.

'I thought I heard you talking about a fever,' he said with an innocent smile.

'You misheard.' She didn't intend to discuss anything with him right now.

'And I thought the rumours had been confirmed after all,' the musician said thoughtfully, as if he were talking to himself.

'What rumours?' asked Sasha, frowning.

'About the quarantine at Serpukhov. About some supposedly incurable disease. About an epidemic...' He watched her intently, seizing on every movement of her lips and her eyebrows.

'So how long were you eavesdropping?' she asked, blushing bright red.

'I never do it deliberately. It's just my musical hearing.' He shrugged and spread his hands.

'He's my friend,' she explained for some reason, nodding in the direction Hunter had gone in.

'A classy kind of friend,' he replied enigmatically.

'Why do you say "supposedly" incurable?'

'Sasha!' Homer got up off the bench, keeping a suspicious eye fixed on the musician. 'Can I have a word? We need to discuss what to do from here on...'

'Will you let me have just a second?' said Leonid. Dismissing the old man with a polite smile, he skipped aside and beckoned for the girl to follow him.

Sasha stepped towards him uncertainly: she still had the feeling that the battle with Hunter wasn't lost yet, that if she didn't give up now, Hunter wouldn't have the heart to drive her away again. That she could still help him, even though she didn't have the slightest idea of how to do it.

'Maybe I heard about the epidemic much sooner than you did?' Leonid whispered to her. 'Maybe this isn't the first outbreak of the disease? And what if there are some magical tablets that can cure it?' asked the musician, glancing into her eyes.

'But he says that there is no cure... That they'll all have to be...' Sasha babbled.

'Liquidated?' said Leonid, finishing her sentence for her. 'He... Is that your wonderful friend? Well, that wouldn't surprise me. But what I'm saying is the opinion of a qualified doctor.'

'You mean to say...'

'I mean to say,' said the musician, putting his hand on Sasha's shoulder, leaning down to her and breathing gently into her ear, 'that the illness can be treated. There is a cure.'

CHAPTER 15

By Twos

The old man first cleared his throat irritably, then took a long step towards them.

'Sasha! I need to have a talk with you!'

Leonid winked at the girl and moved away from her a little, relinquishing her to Homer with theatrical submission. But she couldn't think about anything else any longer, and while the old man explained something to her, trying to convince her that Hunter could still be talked round, suggesting and cajoling, the girl looked over his shoulder at the musician. He didn't return her glance, but the faint ironic smile hovering on his lips told Sasha that he saw everything and understood everything. She nodded to Homer, ready to agree with everything he said, just as long as she could be alone with the musician for another minute and hear him finish what he was saying. Just as long as she herself could believe that there was a cure.

'I'll be back in a moment,' she said, running out of patience and interrupting the old man in mid-word. She slipped off and ran over to Leonid.

'Back for a second helping?' he said, welcoming her back.

'You must tell me!' she said, no longer willing to play games with him. 'How?'

'That's a bit more complicated. I know the disease is curable. I know people who have beaten it. I can take you to them.'

'But you said you knew how to fight it.'

'You misinterpreted what I said,' he said with a shrug. 'How would I know? I'm just a flute-player. A wandering musician.'

'Who are these people?'

'If you're interested, I can introduce you to them. We'll have to walk a bit, though.'

'Which station are they at?'

'Not very far from here. You can find out everything. If you want to.'

'I don't trust you.'

'But you want to trust me, don't you?' he remarked. 'I don't trust you yet either, that's why I can't tell you everything.'

'Why do you want me to go with you?' asked Sasha, narrowing her eyes.

'Me?' he shook his head. 'It's all the same to me. It's you who wants to go. I don't have to save anyone and I don't know how to save them. At least, not like that.'

'Do you promise you'll take me to these people? Do you promise they'll be able to help?' she asked after hesitating for a brief moment.

'I'll take you,' Leonid replied firmly.

'What have you decided?' the old man asked insistently, interrupting them again.

'I'm not going with you,' said Sasha, plucking at the strap of her overalls. 'He says there's a cure for the fever,' she added, turning towards the musician.

'He's lying,' Homer said uncertainly.

'I see you know a lot more about viruses than I do,' Leonid said respectfully. 'Have you studied them? Or is it from personal experience? Do you also believe that exterminating everybody is the best way of combating the infection?'

'How do you . . . ?' the old man began, dumbfounded. 'Did you tell him?' he asked, looking round at Sasha.

'Here comes your highly qualified friend,' said the musician, prudently taking a step back as he spotted Hunter approaching. 'Well then, the ambulance brigade is all here, I'm beginning to feel superfluous.'

'He's lying! He just wants to get you to . . . But even if it's true,' Homer whispered fervently to her, 'you won't have time to do anything. Hunter will be back here with reinforcements in a day's time at the latest. If you stay with us, perhaps you'll be able to persuade him . . . But this boy . . .'

'I won't be able to do anything,' Sasha responded gloomily.

'Nobody's going to stop him now, I can sense it. He has to be given a choice. To split him...'

'Split him?' Homer's eyebrows shot up.

'I'll be back here in less than a day,' she promised, stepping away.

Why did he let her go?

Why did he weaken and allow a crazy tramp to abduct his heroine, his muse, his daughter? The more closely the old man studied Leonid, the less he liked him. His big green eyes could suddenly cast surprisingly covetous glances, and obscure shadows skimmed across that angelic face when the young man thought no one was watching him.

What did she want with the musician? At best, that connoisseur of the beautiful would stick a pin through the flower of her innocence and leave it to dry in his memory – crumpled up, with all the charm of youth, which was so impossible to remember or even photograph, lost, scattered like pollen. Deceived and exploited, the girl would take flight, but it would be a long time before she could purge herself and forget, especially since this blasted wandering minstrel wanted to win her by deception.

Then why did he let her go?

Out of cowardice. Because Homer was not just afraid of arguing with Hunter, he was even afraid of asking him the questions that were really worrying him. Because Sasha was in love and her audacity and folly could be forgiven. Would the brigadier have shown him the same indulgence? To himself the old man still called him the brigadier – partly out of habit, but partly because it made Homer feel calmer: there was nothing terrible happening, nothing unusual, he was still the same brigadier of the northern watch from Sebastopol... But he wasn't. The man striding shoulder to shoulder with Homer now was not the same old unsociable soldier of fortune. The old man was beginning to understand: his travelling companion was being transformed before his very eyes... Something terrible was happening to him, and it would have been stupid to deny it, it was pointless trying to persuade himself.

Hunter had taken Homer with him again – this time was it to show him the bloody denouement of the whole drama? Now he was prepared to exterminate not only the whole of Tula, but also the sectarians cooped up in the tunnels and Serpukhov Station too, including all its inhabitants and the soldiers sent there from the Hansa garrison – simply on the suspicion that one of them might have become infected. The same fate could be in store for Sebastopol.

He no longer needed reasons for killing, he was just looking for pretexts.

Homer could only summon up enough strength to trudge after Hunter as if he was mesmerised, contemplating and documenting all the brigadier's crimes like some nightmarish dream. Justifying himself by the fact that they were committed in order to save people, trying to convince himself that this was the lesser of two evils. To Homer, the relentless brigadier seemed like an incarnation of Moloch, and he had never tried to get the better of fate.

But Sasha didn't seem to acknowledge fate at all. And if, in the depths of his heart, the old man had already accepted that Tula and Serpukhov would be turned into Sodom and Gomorrah, the girl was still clutching at the tiniest hope. Homer had stopped trying to convince himself that any pills or vaccine or serum would turn up before Hunter stopped the epidemic with fire and lead. Sasha was prepared to keep searching for the cure right to the end.

Homer wasn't a soldier or a doctor, and above all, he was too old to believe in miracles. But there was still a particle of his soul that passionately desired miracles and dreamed of salvation. He had torn that particle out of himself and let it go with Sasha.

He had simply offloaded onto the girl what he wouldn't have dared to do himself.

And in his resignation he had discovered peace for himself. In twenty-four hours it would all be over. And after that the old man would desert from his post, find himself a monastic cell and finish writing his book. Now he knew what it would be about.

About how a nimble-witted beast found a magical fallen star, a heavenly spark, swallowed it and became a man. About how, after stealing fire from the gods, man hadn't been able to control it and had burnt the world to a cinder. About how, as a punishment, exactly one hundred centuries later, that human spark was taken away from him, but after losing it, he didn't become a beast again – he turned into something far more terrible that didn't even have a name.

*

The head of the sentry squad tipped the handful of cartridges into his pocket and sealed his deal with the musician with a firm handshake.

'For a symbolic additional payment I could put you on a tram,' he said.

'I prefer romantic walks,' Leonid replied.

'Well, look at it this way. I can't let the two of you walk through our tunnels on your own,' said the sentry, trying to reason with him. 'You'll have to go with a guard anyway. Your girl hasn't got any documents... And you could get to where you're going express, in a flash, and there you are, all alone with her,' he whispered loudly.

'We don't need to be all alone!' Sasha declared adamantly.

'We'll consider it a guard of honour. As if we're the Prince and Princes of Monaco out promenading,' said the musician, bowing to the girl.

'What princess?' Sasha asked, overcome by curiosity.

'The Princess of Monaco. There was a principality of that name once. Right on the Côte d'Azur – the Azure Coast...'

'Listen,' the sentry interrupted. 'If you want to walk, come on, get ready will you? A cartridge clip's all very fine, but the lads have got to get back to base before evening. Hey, Kostya!' he called to a soldier. 'See these two to Kiev, tell the patrols it's a deportation. Put them out onto the radial station and get straight back. All correct?' he asked, turning to Leonid.

'Yes, sir,' said Leonid with a humorous salute.

'Come again!' said the sentry, giving him a wink.

How incredibly different Hansa territory really was from all the rest of the Metro! All the way along the stretch of tunnel from Pavelets to October, Sasha hadn't seen a single place that was completely dark. Every fifty steps there were light bulbs hanging from the wire that crept along the wall, and every one of them gave enough light to reach the next one. Even the reserve and secret tunnels branching off from the main line were well lit, and there was nothing frightening about them any longer.

If it had been up to Sasha, she would have gone dashing on ahead, done anything to save the precious minutes, but Leonid persuaded her there was no need to hurry. He flatly refused to say where they would go on to after Kiev Station and strolled along at a leisurely pace with a bored air: she supposed the musician had quite often been in stretches of the tunnels that were barred to ordinary inhabitants of the Metro.

'I'm glad that your friend has his own approach to everything,' he said.

'What do you mean by that?' Sasha asked with a frown.

'If he dreamed as strongly as you do of saving the civilian population, we would have had to take him with us. But this way we've split up into pairs and everyone gets to do what he wants to do. He gets to kill, you get to cure...'

'He doesn't want to kill anyone!' she said in a shrill voice that was much too loud.

'Oh, right, it's just his job, that's all...' He sighed. 'And who am I to judge him?'

'And what are you going to do?' asked Sasha, not attempting to conceal her scorn. 'Play your flute?'

'I'm just going to be with you,' Leonid said with a smile. 'What else do I need for happiness?'

'You're just saying that,' said Sasha, shaking her head. 'You don't even know me at all. How can I make you happy?'

'There are ways. Just to look at a beautiful girl is enough to improve my mood. And then...'

'Do you think you know about beauty?' she asked, squinting sideways at him.

'It's the only thing I do know anything about,' he said with a solemn nod.

'So what's so special about me?' she asked and the wrinkles on her forehead smoothed out at last.

'It's the way you just glow!'

His voice sounded serious, but an instant later the musician dropped back a step and ran his eyes over her.

'It's just a pity you like such crude clothes,' he added.

'What's wrong with them?' she asked, also dropping back, in order to detach his ticklish gaze from her back.

'They don't let the light through. And I'm like a moth ... I always fly towards the flame,' he said, fluttering his hands with a deliberately foolish air.

'Are you afraid of the dark?' she asked, accepting the game.

'Loneliness!' Leonid put on a mask of sadness and folded his arms.

That was his mistake. As he tuned the strings, he misjudged the resistance, and the finest one, the most delicate, which might have started to sing in just another moment, twanged and snapped.

The light tunnel draught, which had blown away Sasha's serious thoughts and made her juggle with the musician's playful hints, instantly died away. She sobered up and rebuked herself for giving way to him. Surely it wasn't for this that she had abandoned Hunter and left the old man behind?

'As if you even knew what that is,' Sasha snapped and turned away.

Serpukhov Station, pale-grey from fear, was dissolving into the darkness. Soldiers in army gas masks had cut it off from the tunnels at both sides and blocked the connecting passage to the Circle Line, and the station was buzzing like a disturbed beehive in anticipation of disaster. Hunter and Homer were led through the hall with an armed escort, like high-ranking officers, and every inhabitant of Serpukhov tried to look into their eyes, to see if they knew what was really happening and if their fate had been decided. Homer stared fixedly at the floor – he didn't want to remember those faces.

The brigadier hadn't informed Homer where he intended to go next, but the old man could guess. Ahead of them lay Polis. Four Metro stations, linked together by passages, a genuine city with thousands of inhabitants. The unofficial capital of the Metro, which was fractured into dozens of warring feudal principalities. A bulwark of science and refuge of culture. A holy sanctuary that no one dared to invade or attack. No one, that is, apart from Homer, the half-crazy messenger of the plague.

But in the last few days he had started feeling better. The nausea had receded, and the consumptive cough that forced him to wash out his bloody respirator had softened a little. Maybe his body had overcome the illness on its own? Or maybe there never was any infection at all? Eh? Maybe he was simply too neurotic about his health; he'd always known he had that tendency, but he had still got so terrified . . .

The stretch of tunnel beyond Serpukhov was dark and remote, it had a bad reputation. As far as Homer was aware, they shouldn't encounter a single soul until they reached Polis, but Polyanka, the way station between inhabited Serpukhov and residential Borovit-skaya, could surprise travellers. There were numerous legends about

239

Polyanka Station circulating in the Metro: if they could be believed, this station rarely threatened the lives of those who walked through it, but it could damage their reason.

The old man had been here several times, but never encountered anything out of the ordinary. The legends had explanations for that too, Homer knew all of them. And now he was hoping as hard as he could that this time the station would remain as dead and abandoned as it had been in better times.

About a hundred metres before Polyanka he suddenly felt strange. With the first distant glints of white electric light on the station's marble walls, and the first echo of fractured sounds coming from it, the old man suspected something was wrong. He could clearly hear human voices... And there was no way that could be right. Even worse, Hunter, who in some mysterious way could sense the presence of any living creatures, remained absolutely deaf and indifferent now.

Completely absorbed in his own thoughts, he didn't respond to the old man's agitated glances, as if he couldn't see the visions being revealed to Homer at that moment... The station was occupied? When had they done that? Homer had often wondered why, despite Polyanka's cramped space, the inhabitants of Polis had never tried to annex and develop the empty station. There was nothing to prevent it but the superstitions – but apparently they had proved a sufficiently weighty reason for this strange way station to be left in peace.

Until, that is, someone overcame their fear of it and set up a tent town here, put in lighting... God, how extravagant they were with electric power here! Even before the two travellers emerged from the tunnel and started walking along beside the platform, the old man had to put his hand over his eyes to avoid being blinded: bright mercury lamps were glaring at full power up under the ceiling of the station.

Astounding... Not even Polis looked so clean and festive. Not a trace of dust or soot was left on the walls, and the marble slabs all gleamed, while the ceiling looked as if it had been whitewashed only yesterday. Homer couldn't spot a single tent through the arches – perhaps they hadn't had time to put them up yet? Or perhaps they were going to make a museum here? That would be just like the eccentric cranks who ran Polis.

The platform gradually filled up with people. They took no interest at all in the cutthroat wearing a titanium helmet who was hung all over with weapons, or the grubby old man hobbling along beside him. Looking closely at them, Homer realised that he didn't have the strength to take another step: his legs had given out.

Everyone who came over to the edge of the platform was dressed up as if someone was shooting a film about the 2000s at Polyanka. Brand new coats and raincoats, bright-coloured down jackets, sky-blue jeans... Where were the old padded jackets, where was the lousy pigskin leather, where was the perpetual reddish-brown of the Metro, the graveyard of all colours? Where had all this wealth come from?

And the faces... They weren't the faces of people who had lost their entire family in a single moment. They were the faces of people who had seen the sun today and who, well, basically, had started the day with a hot shower. The old man would have bet his life on that. And something else... Many of them seemed vaguely familiar to Homer.

More and more of these incredible people appeared, jostling at the edge of the platform, but they didn't get down onto the tracks. Soon the entire station was filled from tunnel to tunnel with the trim, dressy crowd. And still no one looked at Homer. They looked anywhere at all – at the wall, at newspapers, at each other – surreptitiously, lugubriously or curiously, with loathing or sympathy – but not at the old man, as if he were a ghost.

Why had they gathered here? What were they waiting for?

Homer finally recovered his wits. Where was the brigadier? How would he explain the inexplicable? Why hadn't he said anything yet?

Hunter had stopped a little bit further on. He wasn't even slightly interested in the station packed tight with people out of photographs that were a quarter of a century old. He was staring sombrely into empty space, as if he had run into some kind of barrier, as if there was something hanging in the air in front of him, on a level with his eyes... The old man moved closer to the brigadier and peeped warily under his visor.

And then Hunter struck out.

His clenched fist tore through the air, moving from left to right along a strange trajectory, as if the brigadier was trying to slash someone invisible with a non-existent knife. He very nearly caught

Homer, who jumped aside, but Hunter continued his battle. He struck, then moved back, defending himself, tried to restrain someone in a steely clinch, and a second later was wheezing in a stranglehold himself. Barely managing to break free, he flung himself back into the attack. The battle was slipping away from him, his invisible opponent was getting the upper hand. It was harder and harder for Hunter to get to his feet after those silent but crushing blows; his movements became slower and slower, less and less confident.

The old man was haunted by the feeling that he had already seen something like this only very recently. But where and when? And what in hell's name was happening to the brigadier? Homer tried calling to him, but he was possessed, and it was impossible to get him to hear.

The people on the platform took absolutely no notice of Homer; for them he didn't exist, just as they didn't exist for him. They were concerned about something else: they kept glancing with mounting alarm at their wristwatches, puffing out their cheeks in annoyance, talking to the people next to them and checking the red numbers on the electronic clock above the mouth of the tunnel.

Homer screwed up his eyes and looked at it with the others. It was a counter that registered the time since the last train had passed through. But its display seemed unnaturally long, with ten digits: eight digits before the blinking colon and another two – for the seconds – after it. Red dots squirmed, counting off the fleeting seconds and the final digit in the incredibly long number changed: twelve million and something.

There was a scream ... And a sob.

The old man turned away from the mysterious clock. Hunter was lying motionless, face down on the rails. Homer dashed over to him and turned the heavy, lifeless body face up with a struggle. Yes, the brigadier was breathing, although raggedly, and he didn't have any visible injuries, although his eyes had rolled up and back, like a dead man's. His right hand remained clenched, and only now did the old man discover that Hunter had not been fighting this strange duel unarmed. The handle of the black knife was peeping out from his fist.

Homer slapped the brigadier hard across the cheeks and Hunter started blinking, groaning like a man with a hangover; he propped himself up on his elbows and scrutinised the old man with a blurry gaze. Then he jumped to his feet in a single bound and shook himself off.

The mirage dispersed: the people in raincoats and bright jackets disappeared without a trace, the blinding light went out and the dust of decades settled on the walls again. The station was black, empty and lifeless – exactly as Homer remembered it from his previous expeditions.

All the way to October Station neither of them said another word, the only sound came from the guards assigned to them: whispered conversations and puffing and panting when they stumbled over the sleepers. Sasha wasn't even angry with the musician, but with herself. And he... But what about him? He was behaving exactly as he ought to behave. Eventually she even started feeling awkward about what she'd said to Leonid – perhaps she had been too harsh with him?

But then, at October, the wind changed. It was perfectly natural. When Sasha saw this station, she simply forgot about everything else in the world. In the last few days she had been in places that she wouldn't even have believed existed before. But the finery of October eclipsed all of them. The granite floors were covered with carpets, worn completely bald, but still retaining their original patterns. Lamps cast in the form of blazing torches and polished to a high gleam flooded the hall with an even, milky-white glow. People with glossy, gleaming faces were sitting at tables standing here and there, occupied in lazy exchanges of words and pieces of paper.

'It's so... rich here,' Sasha said, bewildered, almost twisting her neck as she gazed around.

'The Circle Line stations remind me of pieces of pork kebab, threaded on a skewer,' Leonid whispered to her. 'They just ooze fat... Yes, by the way! Maybe we could have a bite to eat?'

'We haven't got time,' she said, shaking her head and hoping he wouldn't hear the eager rumbling in her stomach.

'Oh, come on,' said the musician, holding out his hand to her. 'There's a little place here. Nothing you've ever eaten before even comes close... Lads, do you fancy a bit of lunch?' he asked, including the guards in the suggestion. 'Don't you worry, we'll get there in a couple of hours. I didn't mention pork kebabs by accident. The food they make here...'

He started talking about meat in terms that were almost poetry, and Sasha wavered and gave in. If it was only two hours to their destination, a half-hour lunch wouldn't make any difference. They still had almost a whole day in reserve, and who knew when they would next have a chance for a bite to eat?

The kebabs lived up to the poetry too. But things didn't stop there: Leonid ordered a bottle of homebrew as well. Sasha couldn't resist and she gulped down a little glass out of curiosity, the musician and the guards drank the rest.

Later, she came to her senses, jumped up on her limp-feeling legs and told Leonid to get up in a strict voice – all the stricter, because the heady homebrew had made her drowsy, and while they were dining, she had delayed for almost too long before shaking his fingers off her knees. Light, sensitive fingers. Impudent. He had immediately raised his hands in the air – 'I surrender' – but her skin had remembered his touch. Why had she driven him away so quickly, Sasha wondered, punishing herself with a pinch. Now she would have to erase this bitter-sweet lunch scene from her memory, shake it up with some meaningless nonsense and sprinkle words over it.

'The people here are strange,' she said to Leonid.

'How?' he asked, draining his glass in one and finally getting up from the table.

'There's something missing in their eyes.'

'Hunger,' the musician said categorically.

'No, not only that ... It's as if they don't want anything else.'

'That's because they *don't* want anything else,' Leonid snorted. 'They're well fed. Queen Hansa feeds them. And what's wrong with their eyes? Perfectly normal languid, apathetic eyes...'

'When I lived with my father,' she said seriously, 'what we left today would have lasted us for three days ... Maybe we should have taken it and given it to someone?'

'It's okay, they'll feed it to the dogs,' answered the musician. 'They don't keep any beggars here.'

'But it could have been given to the nearby stations! Where there are hungry...'

'Hansa doesn't go in for charity,' put in one of the guards, the one who was called Kostya. 'Let them shift for themselves. We can do without taking on any idlers!'

'Are you a native Circle man yourself?' Leonid enquired.

'I've always lived here! As long as I can remember!'

'Then you may not believe it, but people who weren't born on the Circle have to eat sometimes too,' the musician told him.

'Let them eat each other! Or maybe it would be better to take everything away from us and divide it up, like the Reds say?' the soldier asked aggressively.

'Well, if everything carries on in the same way...' Leonid began.

'Then what? You keep your mouth shut, spindle-legs, you've already said enough to get yourself deported!'

'I arranged to get deported earlier,' the musician responded phlegmatically. 'That's what we're doing now.'

'But I could turn you in to the right people! As a Red spy!' said the guard, getting heated.

'And I could turn you in for drinking on duty...'

'Why you... It was you that got us... And you...'

'No! We're sorry... He didn't mean to say that.' Sasha intervened, clutching the musician's sleeve and pulling him away from Kostya, who had started breathing heavily.

She almost dragged Leonid to the tracks, then looked at the station clock and gasped. Their lunch and the arguments at the station had lasted almost two hours. She had set out to compete against Hunter's speed, and he definitely wouldn't have stopped for a second... The musician laughed drunkenly behind her back.

All the way to Culture Park the guards hissed baleful comments. Every now and then, following his natural impulse, Leonid attempted to answer them, and Sasha had to hold him back or persuade him not to. The alcohol continued swirling round in his brain, making him bolder and more insolent; the girl had to dodge constantly to keep out of reach of his wandering hands.

'Don't you like me at all then?' he asked, offended. 'Not your type, is that it? You don't like them like me, you want muscles... and sca-a-a-ars. Why did you come with me?'

'Because you made me a promise!' She pushed Leonid away. 'Not so that...'

'I'm not like tha-at!' he sighed sadly. 'Always the same old story. If I'd known you were such a prig...'

'How can you? There are people there... Live people... They'll all die if we don't get there in time!'

'What can do about it? I can hardly move my legs. D'you know how heavy they are? Here, feel... And the people... They'll die anyway. Tomorrow or in ten days' time. And me, and you. So what?'

'So you lied? You lied! Homer told me... He warned me... Where are we going?'

'No, I didn't lie! D'you want me to swear I didn't lie? You'll see for yourself! You'll apologise to me. And then I hope you feel ashamed and you tell me: Leonid ! I'm so ash-amed...' He wrinkled up his nose.

'Where are we going?'

'We'll follow the yel-low brick road. Follow the yellow brick, yellow brick, yellow brick...' the musician sang, conducting with his forefinger; then he dropped the case with his flute in it, swore, leaned down to pick it up and almost tumbled over.

'Hey, you drunks! Will you even get to Kiev?' one of the guards called to them.

'Thanks for your concern!' said the musician, bowing to him. 'We'll get there on the yellow brick road... and Dorothy will find her way home.'

Homer had never believed in the legend of Polyanka, and now it had decided to teach him a lesson.

Some called it the Station of Fate and venerated it as an oracle.

Some believed that a pilgrimage here at a critical turning point in life could part the curtains concealing the future a crack and provide a hint or a key, predicting and predetermining the path that remained ahead.

Some... But all sober-minded people knew that discharges of poisonous gases occurred at the station, and they inflamed the imagination, inducing hallucinations.

To hell with the sceptics!

What could his vision mean? The old man felt as if he was just one step away from the answer, but then his thoughts got tangled up and floundered. And he saw Hunter again, slicing the air with his black blade. Homer would have given a lot to know what vision had appeared to the brigadier, who he was fighting with, what duel it was that had ended in his defeat, if not his death...

'What are you thinking about?'

The old man was so surprised, he felt a taut spasm twist his bowels. Hunter had never spoken to him without a compelling reason before. Barked orders, the resentful growling of stingy replies ... How could you expect a soulful heart-to-heart with someone who had no heart or soul?

'Oh, nothing really,' Homer stammered.

'You're thinking. I can hear it,' Hunter said in a flat voice. 'About me. Are you afraid?'

'Not right now,' the old man lied.

'Don't be afraid. I won't touch you. You ... remind me.'

'Of whom?' Homer asked warily after half a minute's silence.

'Of something about me. I'd forgotten there was something like that in me, but you remind me,' said Hunter, looking ahead, into the darkness, as he dragged the heavy words out of himself one by one and set them out.

'So that's what you brought me along for?' asked Homer, simultaneously disappointed and intrigued – he'd been expecting something ...

'It's important for me to keep it in my mind. Very important,' the brigadier responded. 'And it's important for everyone else that I ... Otherwise there could be ... What's already happened.'

'Have you got problems with your memory?' The old man felt as if he was creeping through a mine field. 'Did something happen to you?'

'I remember everything perfectly well!' the brigadier replied sharply. 'It's only myself that I forget. And I'm afraid of forgetting myself completely. You'll remind me, all right?'

'All right,' said Homer and nodded, although Hunter couldn't see him just at that moment.

'It all used to make sense,' the brigadier said with a struggle. 'Everything I did. Defending the Metro, defending people. People. The task was very clear – neutralise any threat. Annihilate it. That was the point, it was!'

'But it is now too ...'

'Now? I don't know what it is now. I want everything to be as clear as before again. I don't do it just for the sake of it, I'm not a bandit. I'm not a murderer! It's for people's good. I tried living without people, to keep them safe ... But I got scared. I was forgetting

247

myself really fast... I had to get back to people. To protect them, to help them... To remember. And then at Sebastopol... They accepted me there. That's my lair. I have to save the station, I have to help them. No matter what price I might have to pay. I think if I can do it... When I neutralise the threat... That's something really big, something genuine. Maybe then I'll remember. I must. That's why I have to move fast, or else... It's moving faster and faster now. I have to get it done in twenty-four hours. Get everything done – reach Polis, collect a squad together and get back... But in the meantime, you remind me, all right?'

Homer nodded stiffly. He was afraid even to imagine what would happen when the brigadier forgot himself completely. Who would remain in his body when the former Hunter fell asleep forever? Would it be that... Would it be whatever he was defeated by in today's phantom combat?'

Polyanka was far behind them now: Hunter was racing on towards Polis like a wolfhound that has scented quarry and been let off its chain. Or like a wolf trying to shake off his pursuers?

Light appeared at the end of the tunnel.

They managed to drag themselves to Culture Park and Leonid tried to make peace with the guards again, inviting them all to 'an excellent restaurant', but the guards were wary now. He almost wasn't even allowed to go off to the privy. After an exchange of whispers, one of the escorts agreed to guard them and the other disappeared.

'Got any money left?' the man on guard at the door asked bluntly.

'A little bit,' said Leonid, setting five cartridges on his outstretched palm.

'Give it here. Kostya's decided to shop you. He thinks you're a Red agent. If he's right – there's a passage through to your line here – well, you should know. If he's wrong, you can wait here for a bit, until counter-intelligence comes for you, and barter with them.'

'Unmasked me, have you?' said Leonid, trying to suppress his hiccups. 'Okay! So be it... We'll be back again! Thanks for the assistance!' He flung his arm up in an unfamiliar greeting. 'Listen... To hell with that passage. Just take us to the tunnel, will you?

The musician grabbed Sasha and set off in front at an amazing pace, even though he was stumbling.

'How kind of him!' he muttered under his breath. 'There's a passage through to your line here... How would you like to go up on the surface? Forty metres down. As if he didn't know everything there was blocked off ages ago...'

'Where are we going?' Sasha didn't understand anything at all now.

'What do you mean, where? To the Red Line! You heard – they've caught an agent provocateur, exposed him...' Leonid muttered.

'Are you a Red?'

'My dear girl! Don't ask me any questions right now! I can either think or run. And running's what we need more... Our friend will raise the alarm any moment now... And he'll shoot us for resisting arrest... Money's not enough for us, we want a medal too...'

They dived into the tunnel, leaving the guard outside. They ran forward towards Kiev Station, hugging the wall. We won't have time to get to the station anyway, thought Sasha. If the musician was right, and the second guard was already pointing out which way the fugitives had gone...

Then suddenly Leonid turned left into a well-lit side tunnel – as confidently as if he was walking home. A few minutes later flags, metal gratings and sandbags heaped up into machine-gun nests appeared ahead in the distance and they heard dogs barking. A frontier post? Had they already been warned about the fugitives? How was he planning to get out of here? And whose territory started on the other side of the barricades?

'I'm from Albert Mikhailovich,' said the musician, thrusting a strange-looking document under the sentry's nose. 'I need to get across to the other side.'

'The usual rate,' said the sentry, glancing inside the hard binding. 'Where are the papers for the young lady?'

'Let's make it double,' said Leonid, turning out his pockets and shaking out the last cartridges. 'And you didn't see the young lady, okay?'

'Let's just do without "let's make it",' said the border guard, putting on a stern air. 'D'you think you're at the market? This is a law-abiding state!'

'Oh don't be like that!' the musician exclaimed in mock fright. 'I just thought, since it's a market economy, we could bargain... I didn't know there was a difference...'

Five minutes later Sasha and Leonid – mauled and dishevelled, with a graze on his cheekbone and a bleeding nose – were tossed into a tiny little room with tiled walls.

The iron door clanged shut.

Darkness fell.

CHAPTER 16

In the Cage

In pitch darkness a person's other senses become more acute. Smells become more vivid, sounds become louder and more three-dimensional. The only sound in the punishment cell was from someone or other scratching at the floor, and there was an unbearable stench of stale urine.

After drinking so much, the musician didn't even seem able to feel his own pain. He carried on muttering something to himself under his breath for a while, then he stopped responding and started snuffling. He wasn't alarmed that their pursuers were bound to catch up with them now. He wasn't bothered about what would happen to Sasha, without any papers or justification for trying to cross the Hansa border. And of course, he was absolutely indifferent to the fate of Tula.

'I hate you,' Sasha said quietly.

He couldn't care less about that either.

Soon a little hole appeared in the absolute gloom enveloping the cell – it was the glass spyhole in the door. Everything else remained invisible, but even this tiny gap was enough for Sasha: carefully groping her way through the blackness, she crept over to the door and unleashed her light little fists on it. The door responded by rumbling, but the moment Sasha stopped hammering it, silence returned. The guards refused to hear the din or Sasha's shouts.

Time flowed on as slow as syrup.

How long would they hold them prisoner? Maybe Leonid had deliberately brought her here? Maybe he wanted to separate her from the old man and from Hunter? Tear her out of the team and lure her into a trap? And all of this only in order to . . .

Sasha started crying, burying her face in her sleeve – it absorbed the moisture and the sounds.

'Have you ever seen the stars?' asked a voice that still wasn't sober.

She didn't answer.

'I've only ever seen them in photographs too,' the musician told her. 'The sun can barely break though the dust and the clouds, and they're not strong enough for that. But your crying woke me up just now and I thought I'd suddenly seen a real star.'

'It's the spyhole,' she answered, after swallowing her tears.

'I know. But here's the interesting thing...' Leonid coughed. 'Who was it that used to watch us from the sky, with a thousand eyes? And why did he turn his back on us?'

'There never was anyone there!' said Sasha, shaking her head abruptly.

'But I've always wanted to believe that someone was keeping an eye on us,' the musician said thoughtfully.

'No one's bothered about us, not even in this cell!' she exclaimed and the tears welled up in her eyes again. 'Did you arrange this specially? So we'd be too late?' She started hammering on the door again.

'If you don't think there's anyone there, why bother knocking?' asked Leonid.

'You couldn't give a damn if all those sick people die!'

'So that's the impression I give, is it? That's a shame,' he sighed. 'But as far as I can see, you're not so desperate to get to those sick people either. You're afraid that if your lover goes off to kill them, he'll get infected himself, and there isn't any cure...'

'That's not true!' Sasha had to stop herself from hitting him.

'It is, it's true...' said Leonid, mimicking her squeaky voice. 'What's so special about him?'

Sasha didn't want to explain anything to him, she didn't want to talk to him at all. But she couldn't hold back.

'He needs me! He really needs me, without me he's doomed. But you don't need me. You just haven't got anyone to play with.'

'Okay, let's suppose he does need you. Not exactly desperately, but he wouldn't say no. But what do you need him for, this ravenous wolf? Do you find villains attractive? Or do you want to save his lost soul?'

Sasha lapsed into silence. She was stung by how easily the musician could read her feelings. Perhaps there was nothing special about them? Or was it because she didn't know how to hide them? That subtle, intangible something that she couldn't even frame in words sounded quite banal, even crass, on his lips.

'I hate you,' she forced out at last.

'That's okay, I'm not so fond of me either,' Leonid chuckled.

Sasha sat down on the floor and her tears started flowing again, first from anger, then from helplessness. She wasn't going to give up, just as long as something still depended on her. But now, isolated in this cell, with a companion who was deaf to her hopes and fears, she had no chance of being heard any longer. Shouting was pointless. Banging on the door was pointless. There was no one she could try to convince. Everything was pointless.

And then suddenly a picture appeared in front of her eyes for a moment: tall buildings, a green sky, clouds scudding along, people laughing. And the hot, wet drops on her cheeks seemed like drops of that summer rain the old man had told her about. A second later the apparition disappeared, leaving only a light, magical mood behind.

'I want a miracle,' Sasha told herself stubbornly, biting on her lower lip.

And immediately a tumbler switch clicked loudly in the corridor, and the cell was flooded with unbearably bright light.

A blissful aura of peace and prosperity extended out for dozens of metres from the entrance to the marble shrine that was the sacred capital of the Metro – together with the white radiance of the mercury lamps. They weren't sparing with light in Polis, because they believed in its magic. An abundance of light reminded people of their former lives, of those distant times when man was not yet a night animal, not yet a predator. And even barbarians from the periphery behaved with restraint here.

The checkpoint on the border of Polis was more like the front entrance of an old Soviet ministry than an armoured guard post: a table, a chair, two officers in clean staff uniforms, wearing their peaked caps. A check of documents, an inspection of personal effects. The old man fished his passport out of his pocket. Visas had supposedly been abolished, so there shouldn't be any problems. He handed the little green folder to an officer and squinted sideways at the brigadier. Absorbed in his own thoughts, Hunter didn't seem to have heard the border guard's question. And did he have passport in any case, Homer wondered doubtfully. But if he didn't, what had he been hoping for, hurrying here so fast?

'I'm asking you for the last time,' said the officer, placing one hand on his gleaming holster, 'present your documents or leave Polis territory immediately!'

Homer wasn't sure if the brigadier still hadn't understood what they wanted from him and simply reacted to the movement of the fingers creeping towards the press stud of the holster. Instantly emerging from his strange dormant state, Hunter flung his open hand forward with lightning speed, staving in the sentry's Adam's apple. The man wheezed, turned blue and collapsed flat on his back, together with his chair. The other man tried to bolt, but the old man knew he wouldn't make it. The implacable burnished pistol appeared in Hunter's hand like an ace out of a cardsharp's sleeve and . . .

'Wait!'

The brigadier hesitated for a second, and that was enough for the fleeing soldier to scramble out onto the platform, go tumbling over and hide from the bullets.

'Leave them! We have to get to Tula! You must . . . You asked me to remind you . . . Wait!' The old man gasped for breath, not knowing what to say.

'To Tula . .' Hunter repeated dully. 'Yes, best to be patient until we get to Tula. You're right.' He sank down heavily onto a chair, put his heavy revolver down beside him and lowered his head. Seizing the moment, Homer raised his hands in the air and ran forward towards the guards who were darting out of the archways.

'Don't shoot! He surrenders! Don't shoot! In the name of all that's holy . .'

But even so they twisted his arms behind his back and hurriedly tore off his respirator before allowing him to explain. The brigadier, who had fallen back into his strange lethargy, didn't interfere. He allowed them to disarm him and walked submissively through into the holding cell. He sat down on a bunk, looked up, found the old man and gasped out:

'You need to find a certain man here. He's called Miller. Bring him here. I'll wait...'

Homer nodded, fastidiously gathered up his things and started squeezing his way through the sentries and curious bystanders crowding round the door, when suddenly he heard his name called.

'Homer!'

The old man froze in astonishment: Hunter had never called him by name before. He walked back to the lengths of reinforcing rods welded into unconvincing prison bars and looked enquiringly at Hunter, who was hugging himself with his massive hands, as if he were shivering with cold. And the brigadier spoke to him in a dull, lifeless voice:

'Not for long.'

The door opened and a soldier looked in timidly – the same one who had lashed the musician across the face several hours earlier. A kick in the backside sent him flying into the cell and he almost tumbled over onto the floor, then straightened up and looked round uncertainly.

A lean-bodied soldier wearing glasses was standing in the doorway. The shoulder tabs on his tunic were covered with stars, his sparse, light-brown hair was sleeked back.

'Gone on, you dumb beast,' he hissed.

'I ... It's ...' the border guard bleated.

'Don't be shy,' the officer encouraged him.

'I apologise for what I did. And you... you... I can't do it.'

'That's an extra ten days.'

'Hit me,' the soldier said to Leonid, not knowing which way to look.

'Ah, Albert Mikhailovich!' said the musician, screwing up his eyes and smiling. 'I was starting to get tired of waiting.'

'Good evening,' said the officer, also hitching up the corners of his lips. 'See, I've come to restore justice. Are we going to take our revenge?'

'I have to take care of my hands,' said the musician, getting up and kneading his waist. 'I think you can punish him.'

'With all due severity,' said Albert Mikhailovich, nodding. 'A month in the guardhouse. And naturally, I add my apologies to this blockhead's.'

'Well, don't get too spiteful with him,' said Leonid, rubbing his bruised jaw.

'Is this going to remain just between the two of us?' The officer's metallic voice grated treacherously, giving him away.

'As you can see, I'm smuggling something out,' the musician said with a brief nod in Sasha's direction. 'Can you relax the rules a bit?'

'We'll arrange it,' Albert Mikhailovich promised.

They left the guilty border guard right there in the cell: after closing the bolt, the officer led them along a narrow corridor.

'I won't go any further with you,' Sasha told the musician in a loud voice.

'What if I told you that we really are going to that Emerald City?' Leonid asked her after a moment's pause, speaking in a voice so low she could barely hear it. 'If I told you it's no accident that I know more about it than your granddad? That I've seen it for myself, and not just seen it? That I've been there, and not just there...'

'You're lying!'

'You know what?' Leonid asked her angrily. 'When you ask for a miracle, you have to be prepared to believe in it. Or you'll miss it when it comes.'

'And you also have to know how to tell miracles from conjuring tricks,' Sasha snarled back. 'You taught me that.'

'I knew from the very beginning that they'd let us go,' he replied. 'It's just that I didn't want to hurry things.'

'You just wanted to drag things out and waste time!'

'But I wasn't lying to you. There is a cure for the disease!'

They reached the frontier post. The officer, who had occasionally looked round at them curiously, handed the musician his belongings and returned his cartridges and documents.

'Right then, Leonid Nikolaevich,' he said, saluting. 'Are we taking the contraband with us or leaving it with the customs?'

'Taking it.'

'In that case, peace and blessings upon you both,' said Albert Mikhailovich. He accompanied them past a triple row of fortifications, past teams of machine-gunners who leapt up off their seats, past metal grilles and tank traps welded together out of rails. 'I suppose no problems will arise with importation?'

'We'll break through,' Leonid told him with a smile. 'I shouldn't say this to you, but honest bureaucrats don't exist, and the harsher the regime, the lower the price. You just have to know who to pay it to.'

'I think the magic word will be enough for you,' the officer chuckled.

'It doesn't work on everyone yet,' said Leonid, touching his cheekbone again. 'As they say, I'm not a magician yet, I'm still studying.'

'It will be a pleasure to do business with you ... When you complete your studies.' Albert Mikhailovich bowed his head, swung round and strode away.

The last soldier opened a small gate through the thick bars of a grille that blocked off the tunnel from top to bottom. The stretch of line that began beyond it was brightly lit, and its walls were scorched in some places and chipped in others, as if from long fire-fights: at the far end of it they could see new bands of fortifications and the broad swathes of banners stretched between the floor and the ceiling. The sight of them was enough to set Sasha's heart pounding.

'Whose frontier post is this?' she asked, coming to a sharp halt.

'What do you mean, whose?' the musician asked, looking at her in amazement. 'The Red Line's, of course.'

Ah, how long Homer had dreamed of being back here again, how long it was since he'd been in these wonderful places ...

At Borovitskaya Station, that residence of the intelligentsia, with its sweet smell of creosote and cosy little apartments, built right there in the arches, and its reading-room for Brahmin monks in the middle of the hall – long wooden tables piled high with books, low-hanging lamps with fabric shades – and its astoundingly precise reproduction of the spirit of the 'debating-hall kitchens' of the crisis period and pre-war years ...

At regal Arbat Station, decked out in white and bronze, almost like the chambers of the Kremlin, with its austere manners and brisk military men, who still puffed out their cheeks, as if they weren't involved at all in the Apocalypse ...

At the old, indeed ancient, Lenin Library Station, which they'd never got round to renaming while it still made any kind of sense to rename it, which was already as old as the world when Kolya first arrived in the Metro as a little kid, the Library, with its connecting passage in the form of a romantic captain's bridge, right in the middle of the platform, with its painstakingly and skilfully restored moulding work on the leaky ceiling . . .

And at Alexander Gardens, with its perpetually dim lighting, long-limbed and angular, in a way that reminded Homer of some weak-sighted gouty pensioner, constantly reminiscing about his young days in the Komsomol.

Homer had always wondered if the stations were like their creators. Could they be thought of as their designers' self-portraits? Had they absorbed particles of the people who built them? One thing he knew for certain: each station left its own imprint on the people who lived in it, sharing its character with them and infecting them with its own moods and ailments. But Homer, with his peculiar cast of mind, his eternal pondering, and his incurable nostalgia, belonged, of course, not to stern Sebastopol, but to Polis, as bright as the past itself.

Only life had dictated otherwise.

And even now, when he had finally got here, he didn't have even a few spare minutes to stroll through these halls, to admire the plaster mouldings and bronze castings, to indulge his fantasies. He had to run. With a struggle, Hunter had managed to muzzle someone inside himself, to cage that terrible creature that he fed from time to time with human flesh. But once it bent apart the bars of that inner cage, a moment later there would be nothing left of the feeble bars on the outside. Homer had to hurry.

Hunter had asked him to find Miller. Was that a real name or a nickname? Or maybe a password? Spoken aloud, it had produced a startling effect on the sentries: talk of a court martial for the arrested brigadier had dried up, and the handcuffs that were about to be clicked onto Homer's wrists were put back in the desk drawer. The pot-bellied head of the watch had volunteered to show the old man the way in person.

Homer and his guide walked up a flight of steps and along the connecting passage to Arbat. They stopped at a door guarded by two men in civilian clothes, with faces that stated very clearly that they were professional killers. Behind them he could see a vista of office rooms. The pot-bellied man asked Homer to wait for a moment and tramped off along the corridor. Less than three minutes later, he came back out, looked the old man over in amazement and invited him to go in.

The cramped corridor led them to a surprisingly spacious room with all its walls hung with maps and diagrams or overgrown with notes and coded messages, photographs and sketches. A bony, elderly man with shoulders as wide as if he was wearing a Caucasian felt cloak was enthroned at a broad oak desk. Only his left arm protruded from the tunic thrown across his shoulders, and when Homer looked closely, he realised why: the man's right arm was almost completely missing. The owner of the office was immensely tall – his eyes were almost on the same level as the eyes of the old man standing facing him.

'Thank you,' he said, dismissing the pot-bellied officer, who closed the door from the other side with obvious regret. 'Who are you?'

'Nikolai Ivanovich Nikolaev,' the old man said, disconcerted.

'Drop the clowning. If you come to me, saying that you're with my very closest comrade, whom I laid to rest a year ago, you must have a reason for it. Who are you?'

'No one...' said Homer, with perfect sincerity. 'But this isn't about me. It's true, he's alive. You just have to come with me, and quickly.'

'So now I'm wondering if this is a trap, an idiotic hoax or simply a mistake.' Miller lit a *papyrosa* and blew smoke into the old man's face. 'If you know his name and you've chosen to come to me with this, you must know his story. You must know that we searched for him every day for more than a year. That we lost several men in the process. You must know, damn you, how much he meant to us. Perhaps even that he was my right hand.' He gave a crooked smile.

'No, none of that. He doesn't tell me anything,' said the old man, pulling his head down into his shoulders. 'Please, let's just go to Borovitskaya. There's not much time.'

'No, I won't go running off anywhere. And I have a good reason for that.'

Miller put his hand under the table, made a strange movement with it and moved back in some incredible fashion, without getting up. It took Homer a few seconds to realise that he was sitting in a wheelchair.

'So let's talk calmly. I want to understand the meaning of your appearance here.'

'Lord,' said the old man, despairing of ever getting through to this blockhead. 'Please, just believe me. He's alive. And he's sitting in the holding cell at Borovitskaya. At least, I hope he's still there...'

'I'd like to believe you,' Miller said and paused to take a deep pull on his *papyrosa* – the old man heard the cigarette paper crackling as it curled up and caught fire. 'Only miracles don't happen. All right. I have my own theories about whose hoax this is. But they'll be tested by specially trained men.' He reached for the phone.

'Why is he so afraid of black men?' Homer asked unexpectedly, surprising even himself.

Miller cautiously put down the receiver without saying a word into it. He dragged the rest of the *papyrosa* into his lungs, right down to the end, and spat out the short cardboard butt into an ashtray.

'Damn you, I'll take a ride to Borovitskaya,' he said.

'I won't go in there! Let me go! I'd rather stay here...'

Sasha wasn't joking or being capricious. It would be hard to think of anyone her father had hated more than the Reds. They had taken away his power, they had broken his back, but instead of simply finishing him off, out of pity or sheer prudishness they had condemned him to years of humiliation and torment. Her father hadn't been able to forgive the people who rebelled against him. He hadn't been able to forgive the men who inspired the traitors and egged them on, or those who supplied them with weapons and leaflets. The very colour red sent him into paroxysms of furious rage. And although at the end of his life he used to say that he bore no grudges against anyone and didn't want revenge, Sasha had had the feeling that he was simply making excuses for his own powerlessness.

'It's the only way to get there,' Leonid said in dismay.

'We were going to Kiev! That's not where you've brought me!'

'Hansa has been fighting the Red Line for decades, I couldn't let just anyone know that we were going to the communists... I had to lie.'

'You can't do anything without lying.'

'The door is on the far side of Sport Station, as I said. And Sport is the last station on the Red Line before the ruined Metro bridge, there's no way to get around that.'

'How will we get in there? I don't have a passport,' she said, keeping her eyes fixed warily on the musician.

'Trust me,' he said with a smile. 'One person can always reach a deal with another. Long live corruption!'

Ignoring Sasha's objections, he grabbed her by the wrist and pulled her after him. Blazing brightly in the glare of the searchlights in the second line of the frontier post, the gigantic red banners hanging from the ceiling rippled in the tunnel draught, making the girl feel as if she was looking at two glittering red waterfalls. A sign?

If what she had heard about the Line was right, the Reds ought to riddle them with bullets on the approaches... But Leonid strode forward calmly, with his lips set in a confident smile. About thirty metres from the frontier post the broad beam of a searchlight struck his chest. The musician simply set his flute case on the ground and raised his hands in the air. Sasha did the same.

The border inspectors walked up to them, looking sleepy and surprised. It seemed as if they had never met anyone from the other side of the border. This time the musician managed to take the senior officer off to one side before he asked for Sasha's documents. Leonid whispered something delicately in his ear, there was a faint jingle of brass and the head of the border unit came back spellbound and pacified. He escorted them past the guard posts in person and even put them on a hand trolley that was waiting, ordering the soldiers to go to Frunze Station.

They started working the levers, puffing and panting, as they got the trolley started. Sasha frowned as she studied the clothes and the faces of these men her father had taught her to call enemies. Nothing unusual. Padded jackets; blotchy, washed-out caps with stars pinned to them, prominent cheekbones, hollow cheeks... No, they didn't have glossy skin, like the Hansa patrolmen, but they were certainly no less human. They had a gleam of absolutely boyish curiosity in their eyes, a feeling that was apparently completely unknown to those who lived on the Circle. These two had almost certainly never heard about what happened at Avtozavod Station almost ten years earlier. Were they Sasha's enemies? Was it even possible to hate people you didn't know, not just formally, but genuinely?

Not daring to strike up a conversation with their passengers, the soldiers merely grunted regularly as they leaned down on the levers.

'How did you manage it?' Sasha asked.

'Hypnosis,' said Leonid, winking at her.

'But what were those documents you showed them?' she asked,

261

looking at the musician suspiciously. 'How can they get you allowed in everywhere?'

'Different passports for different occasions,' he replied evasively.

'Who are you?' So that the others wouldn't hear, Sasha was obliged to sit close beside Leonid.

'An observer,' he said with just his lips.

If Sasha hadn't clamped her mouth shut, the questions would have come pouring out, but the soldiers were too obviously trying to catch the sense of their conversation, even trying to make the levers creak as quietly as possible. She had to wait until Frunze Station – withered, faded and pale, rouged with red flags. Pock-marked mosaics on the walls, columns nibbled on by time . . . Ceiling vaults like dark millponds, with feeble light bulbs dangling from wires stretched between the columns at a height slightly above the heads of the short local inhabitants, in order not to let a single ray of precious light go to waste. It was incredibly clean here: several cleaning ladies were scurrying around the platform at the same time. The station was crowded, but the strange thing was that whichever way Sasha looked, everyone started fidgeting and bustling about, although behind her back all the movement immediately ceased and subdued voices started murmuring. The moment she looked back, the murmuring stopped and people went back to their business. And no one wanted to look into her eyes, as if there was something indecent about it.

'Are strangers unusual here?' she asked, looking at Leonid.

'I'm a stranger here myself,' the musician said with a shrug.

'Where are you at home?'

'Where people aren't so deadly serious,' he laughed. 'Where they understand that a man can't be saved with just food. Where they don't want to forget yesterday, even though the memories are painful.'

'Tell me about the Emerald City,' Sasha said in a quiet voice. 'Why do they . . . Why do you hide?'

'The rulers of the City don't trust the inhabitants of the Metro.'

Leonid broke off to explain himself to the sentries on duty at the entrance to the tunnel and then, as he and Sasha dived into the intense darkness, he set a little light on the wick of an oil lamp with a metal cigarette lighter and continued.

'They don't trust them, because the people in the Metro are gradually losing their human nature. And because they still have

262

among them the people who started that terrible war, although they're afraid to admit it, even to their friends. Because the people in the Metro are beyond redemption. They can only be feared, avoided and observed. If they find out about the Emerald City, they'll just gobble it down and puke it up, the same way they gobble everything they get their hands on. All the canvases of the great artists will be burnt. All the paper, and everything that was on it, will be burnt. The only society that has achieved justice and equality will be annihilated. Drained bloodless, the University building will collapse. The Great Ark will founder and sink. And there'll be nothing left. Vandals...'

'Why do you think we can't change?' asked Sasha, feeling offended.

'Not everyone thinks that,' said Leonid, giving her a sideways glance. 'Some are trying to do something.'

'They're not trying very hard,' Sasha sighed, 'if even my old Homer hasn't heard about them.'

'But then some people have actually heard them,' he remarked suggestively.

'You mean... the music?' Sasha guessed. 'Are you one of those who hope to change us? But how?'

'By coercing you into the love of beauty,' the musician joked.

The wheelchair was pushed by an adjutant, and the old man walked alongside, barely managing to keep up and looking round every now and then at the burly security guard attached to him.

'If you really don't know the whole story,' said Miller, 'then I'm willing to tell you it. You can amuse your cellmates with it, if I see the wrong man at Borovitskaya... Hunter was one of the Order's finest warriors, a genuine hunter, in more than just name. His intuition was positively feral, and he dedicated himself to the cause absolutely. He was the one who sniffed out those Black Ones a year and a half ago... At the Economic Achievements Station. Hasn't anybody heard about that at all?'

'At Achievements...' the old man repeated after him absentmindedly. 'Well yes, invulnerable mutants who could read people's minds and make themselves invisible... I thought they were called the Dark Ones?'

'That's not important,' Miller snapped. 'He was the first to dig up the rumours and sound the alarm, but just then we didn't have the men or the time . . . I told him no. I was busy with other matters . . .' He gestured with his stump. 'Hunter went up there on his own. The last time he was in contact with me, he said that those creatures suppressed people's will and spread terror throughout the district. And Hunter was a simply incredible fighter, a born soldier who was worth an entire platoon all on his own . . .'

'I know,' muttered Homer.

'And he was never afraid of anything. He sent us a boy with a note saying he was going up onto the surface to deal with the Black Ones. If he disappeared, it meant the threat was worse than he had thought. He disappeared. He was killed. We have our own reporting system. Everyone who's alive is obliged to let us know every week. Obliged to do so! He hasn't been in touch for more than a year.'

'And what about the Black Ones?'

'We flattened the entire area thoroughly with Whirlwind rocket salvoes. Since then nothing has been heard of the Black Ones either,' Miller chuckled. 'They don't write, they don't phone in. The exits at Achievements were closed off and life there has returned to normal. That boy also had mental problems, but as far as I know, he's been restored to health. He lives a normal human life, he got married. But Hunter . . . He's on my conscience.'

He trundled down the steel ramp from the steps, startling and scattering the book-loving monks at the bottom of it, then swung round, waited for the panting old man and added:

'Don't tell your cellmates that last part.'

A minute later the entire procession finally reached the holding cell. Miller didn't open the door of the cell: bracing himself on the adjutant, he gritted his teeth, stood up and pressed his eye to the spyhole. A split second was enough.

Absolutely exhausted, as if he had covered the entire distance from Arbat on foot, with his infirmities, Miller fell back into his chair, ran his dead gaze over the old man and pronounced sentence.

'It's not him.'

*

'I don't think my music belongs to me,' Leonid said with sudden seriousness. 'I don't understand where it comes into my head from. It seems to me that I'm just a channel . . . Simply an instrument.

264

In the same way as I put my lips to my flute when I want to play, someone else puts his lips to me – and a melody is born...'

'Inspiration,' Sasha whispered.

'You can call it that.' He spread his arms in a shrug. 'Whatever way it is, it doesn't belong to me. I don't have any right to keep it inside me. It... travels through people. I start playing, and I see these rich people and beggars gather round, all covered in scabs or shiny and greasy, angry ones and wretched ones and great ones. Everyone. And my music does something to them that tunes them all to the same key. I'm like a tuning fork... I can bring them into harmony, if not for long. And they'll chime so pure and clear... They'll sing. How can I explain that?'

'You explain it very well,' Sasha said thoughtfully. 'That's what I felt myself.'

'I have to try to plant this in them,' Leonid added. 'In some of them it will die, in some it will sprout. I don't save anyone. I don't have the authority for that.'

'But why don't the other people who live in the City want to help us? Why are even you afraid to admit that you're doing this?'

He didn't answer, and he remained silent until the tunnel ran into Sport Station, which was just as faded and withered, affectedly triumphant and mournful at the same time, but it was also low and cramped, so that it weighed down heavily, like tight bandages round the head. This place smelled of smoke and sweat, poverty and pride. Sasha and Leonid were immediately assigned a nark, who loitered exactly ten steps away from them, wherever they went. The girl wanted to move on straight away, but the musician threw cold water on the idea.

'We can't go right now. We'll have to wait a bit.' He settled himself comfortably on a stone bench and clicked the locks on his flute case.

'Why?'

'The gates can only be opened at specified times,' said Leonid, looking away.

'When?' Sasha looked round and found a clock. If it was correct, less than half of the time allotted to her was left.

'I'll tell you.'

'You're dragging things out again!' She frowned and pulled back from him. 'First you promise to help, then you try to delay me!'

'Yes,' he said, gathering his courage and catching her eye. 'I want to delay you.'

'Why? What for?'

'I'm not playing games with you. Believe me, I could have found someone to play with, and not many would have refused. I think I've fallen in love. My, my, how clunky that sounds...'

'You think... You don't even think it! You're just saying it, that's all.'

'There is a way to tell love from a game,' he said seriously.

'When you deceive someone in order to get them, is that love?'

'Real love shatters your entire life, it doesn't give a damn for circumstances, including games with all the rest...'

'I take a simpler view,' said Sasha, glowering at him. 'I've never had any life. Take me to the door.'

Leonid stared gravely at the girl, leaned against a column and crossed his arms, fencing himself off from her. He filled his lungs with air several times, as if he was going to rebuke her, but let it back out again without saying anything. Then he wilted, his face darkened and he made a confession:

'I can't go with you. They won't let me back in.'

'What does that mean?' Sasha asked mistrustfully.

'I can't go back into the Ark. I was banished.'

'Banished? What for?'

'For good reason.' He turned away and started speaking very quietly – even standing just one step away from him, Sasha couldn't make it all out. 'I... was insulted by someone. An attendant at a library. He humiliated me in front of witnesses. That night I got drunk and set fire to the library. The attendant and all his family were suffocated by the fumes. It's a pity we don't have capital punishment... I deserved it. I was just banished. For life. There's no way back.'

'Then what did you bring me here for?' Sasha clenched her fists. 'Why did you burn up my time too?'

'You can try to attract their attention,' Leonid muttered. 'The door's in a side tunnel, and there's a mark in white paint twenty metres from it. Directly underneath the mark, at ground level, there's a rubber cover and the button of the bell is underneath that. You have to give three short rings, three long ones and three short ones, that's the code for returning observers.'

266

He really did stay at the station – after helping Sasha to make her way past all three guard posts he strolled back. As they parted, he tried to make her take an old sub-machine-gun that he'd got hold of from somewhere, but Sasha wouldn't have it. Three short rings, three long rings and three short rings – that was all that could be any use to her now. And a lantern.

The tunnels after Sport Station were gloomy and empty. The station was regarded as the last one on the line, and every guard post that the musician showed her through looked more like a small fortress than the one before. But Sasha wasn't afraid, not at all. The only thing she was thinking about was that in an hour, or an hour and a half, she would be on the threshold of the Emerald City.

And if the City didn't exist, there was absolutely no point in being afraid.

The side tunnel was exactly where Leonid had promised it would be, blocked by a badly damaged grille, in which Sasha easily found a gap wide enough to get through. And several hundred steps further on it really did end in the steel wall of a hermetic door – ancient and impregnable. Sasha diligently measured out forty of her own steps from it and spotted a white mark on the wall, which was damp, as if it was sweating. She found the cover immediately. Bending back the rubber, she felt for the bell button and checked the watch that the musician had given her. She was in time! She was in time! She waited for a few more agonisingly long minutes and closed her eyes ...

Three short rings.

Three long rings.

Three short rings.

CHAPTER 17

Who's Speaking?

Artyom lowered his sizzling-hot gun-barrel and tried to wipe away the sweat and tears with the back of his hand, but the hand couldn't reach his face: the gas mask got in the way. Maybe he should just take the damn thing off? What difference did it really make, anyway?

The sick people must be roaring loud enough to drown out the bursts of sub-machine-gun fire. Otherwise, why would more and more of them keep pouring out of the carriage to face the hail of lead? Couldn't they hear the thunderous rumbling, didn't they understand they were being shot at pointblank range? What were they hoping for? Or maybe they couldn't give a damn any more either?

The platform was piled high with swollen bodies for several metres around the exit that had been broken open. Some of the bodies were still twitching, and a groan came from somewhere under the burial mound. The purulent flow from the open abscess of the doorway finally stopped: the people left in the carriage huddled up tightly together in terror, hiding from the bullets.

Artyom glanced round at the other gunners. Was he the only one with shaking hands and trembling knees? None of them said a word. At first even the commander was silent. The only sounds were the wheezing of the overcrowded train trying to suppress a bloody cough and the curse spat out by the last man still dying under the heap of dead.

'Monsters... Bastards... I'm still alive... It's so heavy...'

The commander finally spotted the man, squatted down beside him and emptied the remains of his cartridge clip into the poor wretch, squeezing the trigger until his empty gun started clicking. He got up, looked at his pistol and for some reason wiped it on his trousers.

'Keep calm!' he shouted hoarsely. 'Any further attempts to leave the infirmary without permission will be punished in the same way.'

'What shall we do with the bodies?' the men asked him.

'Put them back in the train. Ivanenko, Aksyonov, see to it!'

Order had been restored. Artyom could go back to his post and try to get some sleep. There were still a couple of hours left until reveille: if he could just get at least an hour of shuteye, so that he wouldn't collapse on duty tomorrow.

It didn't work out like that.

Ivanenko stepped back and started shaking his head, refusing to take hold of the putrescent, disintegrating bodies. Forgetting that he had no cartridges left, the commander hissed in fury and held out the hand with the pistol towards him. The firing pin clattered uselessly. Ivanenko squealed and ran for it.

And then one of the soldiers who was coughing flung up his automatic and stabbed the commander in the back with a crooked, awkward thrust of his bayonet. But the commander didn't fall, he stayed on his feet and slowly looked round over his shoulder at the man who had struck him.

'What are you doing, you bastard?' he asked in quiet amazement.

'You'll do for all of us the same way soon... There's not a healthy man left in the whole station. We shoot them today, and tomorrow you'll drive the rest of us into these carriages,' the man yelled at the commander, trying to tug his bayonet out of him, but not firing for some reason.

No one interfered. Not even Artyom, who took a step towards the two of them, but then froze, waiting. At last the bayonet came out. The commander reached for his wound, as if he was trying to scratch himself, then went down on his knees, braced his hands against the slippery floor and started shaking his head about. Was he trying to come to his senses? Or did he want to fall asleep?

No one could bring himself to finish the commander off. Even the mutineer who had stabbed him with the bayonet recoiled in fright, then tore off his gas mask and shouted loud enough for the whole station to hear.

'Brothers! No more torturing them! Let them out! They're going to die anyway! And so are we! Are we human beings or not?'

'Don't you dare,' the commander wheezed inaudibly, still on his knees.

The gunners started murmuring, conferring with each other. The bars were torn off carriage doors, first in one place and then in another. Then someone shot the instigator in the face and he tumbled over backwards to join the other dead. But it was already too late: with a triumphant roar the crowd of infected people gushed out of the train into the hall, running clumsily on their thick legs. They tore the automatics out of the daunted sentries' hands and wandered off in various directions. The guards faltered too; some were still firing at the sick people, but others mingled with them and wandered out of the station into all the tunnels: some went north, towards Serpukhov and others went south, towards Nagatino.

Artyom stood there, gazing stupidly at the commander, who refused to die. First he crept forward on all fours, then he stood up, slipping repeatedly, and set off to go somewhere.

'And now for your surprise... You didn't think I'd be prepared for this,' he muttered.

The commander's wandering gaze settled on Artyom. He froze for a moment and suddenly spoke in his ordinary voice that brooked no insubordination.

'Popov! Take me to the radio room! I have to order the northern guard post to close the door...'

Artyom lent the commander his shoulder, and they wandered slowly past the empty train, past the fighting men, past the jumbled heaps of lumber, to the radio room, where the phone was. The commander's wound was apparently not fatal, but he had lost a lot of blood and his strength deserted him before they got there: he went limp and slumped into oblivion.

Artyom shoved the desk against the door, grabbed the microphone of the internal switchboard and called the northern guard post. The phone clicked a few times and wheezed as if it was breathing laboriously and then it was silent, with a terrible silence.

If it was too late to close off that direction, Artyom had to warn Dobrynin at least. He dashed over to the phone, pressed one of the two buttons on the panel and waited a few seconds... The phone was still working. At first the only sound in the receiver was a whispered echo, then he heard a rapid clicking, and finally the ringing tone.

One... Two... Three... Four... Five... Six...

Oh God, let them answer. If they're all still alive, if they haven't been infected yet, let them answer, let them give him a chance. Let them answer before the sick people can reach the borders of the station... Artyom would have pawned his very soul now, just for someone to answer at the other end of the line!

And then the impossible happened. The sound broke off midway through the seventh beep, he heard grunting and squabbling in the distance and a cracked, agitated voice gasped through the rustling.

'Dobrynin Station here!'

The cage was shrouded in gloom. But even in that meagre light Homer could see that the prisoner's silhouette was too puny and too lifeless to belong to the brigadier. As if it was a stuffed dummy sitting behind the bars – limp and drooping. It looked like the guard... Dead. But where was Hunter?

'Thanks, I didn't think you'd reach me in time,' said a dull, hollow voice. 'I felt... cramped in there.'

Miller spun his chair faster than Homer could look round. The brigadier was standing in the passage, blocking their way out to the station. His hands were firmly clenched together, as if one didn't trust the other and was afraid to let go of it. He turned his mutilated side towards them.

'Is that you?' asked Miller, and his cheek twitched.

'Yes, for now,' said Hunter, giving a strange little cough. If Homer hadn't known him, he might even have taken the sound for a laugh.

'What's wrong with you? What happened to your face?'

Miller clearly wanted to ask Hunter about something completely different: he gestured with his hand, ordering the guards to go out. They left Homer there.

'You're not exactly in the best shape either.' The brigadier gave that cough again.

'A mere trifle,' said Miller, screwing up his face. 'It's just a shame that I can't give you a hug. Damn you! Where have you...? We searched for you for so long!'

'I know. I needed... to be alone,' Hunter said jerkily. 'I didn't

272

want to come back to people. I wanted to go away forever. But I got scared...'

'But what happened with the Black Ones? Did they do that to you?' asked Miller, nodding at the purple weals.

'Nothing. I wasn't able to destroy them.' The brigadier touched his scar. 'I couldn't do it. They... broke me.'

'You were right,' Miller said with sudden passion. 'Forgive me for taking no notice at first, for not believing. At that time we... Well, you remember... But we found them, we burned out the whole place. We thought you were already dead. That they'd... I wiped them out for you... For you. To the very last one!'

'I know,' Hunter said in a hoarse, distraught voice. 'And they knew that would happen – because of me. They knew everything. They could really see people, and every person's destiny. You have no idea who we dared to raise our hand against... He smiled at us for one last time... He sent them... Gave us one more chance. And we... I condemned them, and you carried out the sentence. Because that's what we're like. Because we're monsters...'

'What...'

'When I came to them... they showed me myself. It was as if I looked at myself in a mirror and saw everything the way it really is. I understood everything about myself. I understood about people. Why it all happened to us...'

'What do you mean?' Miller stared at his comrade anxiously and cast a quick glance at the door – perhaps he regretted having sent the guards away?

'I told you. I saw myself through their eyes, in a mirror. Not the outside, but the inside... behind the screen... They lured me out in front of the mirror in order to show me. A cannibal. A monster. But I didn't see a man. I was terrified at the sight of myself. Something woke up. I'd been lying to myself before. Telling myself I was protecting people, saving... It was lies. I was just a bloody, ravenous beast who tore out throats. Worse than a beast. The mirror disappeared, but it... this thing... stayed. It woke up and refused to sleep anymore. They thought I would kill myself after that. What did I have to live for? But I didn't. I had to fight. At first on my own... So that no one could see. As far away from people as possible. I thought I could punish myself, so that they wouldn't punish me. I thought I could drive it out with pain...'

He touched his scars. 'Then I realised that without people it would defeat me. I was forgetting myself. So I came back.'

'They brainwashed you!' Miller exclaimed in an agonised voice.

'Never mind. It's over and done with now,' said the brigadier. He took his hand away from the weals on his face and his voice became dead and empty again. 'Almost all. That story was finished long ago and what's done is done. We're alone here now. We have to pull through on our own. That's not what I came about. There's an epidemic at Tula. It could break out to Sebastopol and into the Circle. Airborne fever. The same old deadly plague.'

'It hasn't been reported to me,' said Miller, eyeing him suspiciously.

'They haven't reported it to anyone. They're being cowardly. Lying. They don't know what to do.'

'What do you want from me?' asked Miller, sitting up higher in his wheelchair.

'You know that. The danger has to be eliminated. Give me a token. Give me men. Flamethrowers. We have to shut down Tula and purge it. Serpukhov and Sebastopol too, if necessary. I hope it hasn't got any further.'

'Wipe out three stations just in case?' Miller asked.

'To save the rest of them.'

'After a bloodbath like that everyone will hate the Order . . .'

'No one will find out. We won't leave anyone who could have been infected . . . or could have seen anything.'

'It's a huge price to pay!'

'Don't you understand? If we delay just a little bit longer, there'll be no one left to save. We found out about the epidemic too late. There won't be another chance to stop it. In two weeks the entire Metro will be a plague barracks, in a month it will be a graveyard.'

'I have to make sure for myself . . .'

'You don't believe me, do you? You think I've gone crazy? You didn't believe me then and you still doubt me now. Screw it. I'll go on my own. As usual. At least I'll keep my own conscience clear.'

He swung round, pushing aside Homer, who was absolutely stunned, and headed for the exit. But those final words he flung out had sunk deep into Miller's chest, like a harpoon, and they dragged him after the brigadier.

'Wait! Take a token!' He fumbled hastily under his tunic and held out a perfectly ordinary looking flat metal badge to Hunter, who had stopped dead in his tracks. 'I authorise you...' The brigadier raked the token out of the bony fingers, stuck it in his pocket and nodded without speaking, aiming a long, unblinking stare at Miller.

'Come back,' said Miller. 'I'm tired.'

'But I'm just raring to go,' Hunter said, and coughed again.

Then he disappeared.

Sasha didn't dare to ring again for a long time: there was no point in annoying the guards of the Emerald City. They must have heard her, and perhaps they had already taken a good look at her. And if at this stage they still hadn't opened the door that had grown into the ground, it was only because they were consulting, uncertain if they should admit a stranger who had guessed the signal.

What would she say to them when the door finally opened?

Should she tell them about the epidemic raging at Tula? Would they want to intervene? Would they risk it? And what if they could all see straight through people, like Leonid? Perhaps she should tell them straight away about her own, different kind of fever? Confess to someone else what she still hadn't admitted to herself...

And would Sasha even be able to move their hearts? If they had defeated the terrible sickness long ago, why didn't they intervene, why didn't they send a messenger to Tula with the cure? Simply because they were afraid of ordinary people? Or because they hoped the plague would wipe them out? Perhaps it was them who had sent the disease into the Greater Metro?

No! How could she think that? Leonid had said the inhabitants of the Emerald City were just and humane. That they didn't execute anyone or even imprison them. And that no one even dared to think of committing a crime in the midst of the boundless beauty that they had surrounded themselves with. Then why wouldn't they save people who were doomed to die? Why wouldn't they open the door?

Sasha rang again. And again.

The silence behind the steel wall was as impassive as if it were just a fake, concealing nothing but thousands of tons of stony earth.

'They won't open up for you.'

Sasha swung round abruptly. The musician was standing about ten steps away from her, in an awkwardly twisted pose, dishevelled and sad.

275

'Then you try! Maybe they've forgiven you?' said Sasha, giving him a puzzled glance. 'What have you come here for?'

'There isn't anyone to forgive me. It's empty.'

'But you said . . .'

'I lied. This isn't the entrance to the Emerald City.'

'Then where is it?'

'I don't know. No one knows.' He shrugged.

'But why did you let you through everywhere? You're an observer, aren't you? You . . . On the Circle, and with the Reds . . . You're trying to fool me now, right? You blurted out the truth about the City and now you regret it!' She tried to look into his eyes, searching pathetically for confirmation of her own assumptions.

'I used to dream of getting into the City,' said Leonid, gazing stubbornly at the ground. 'I searched for it for years and years. I collected rumours and read old books. I must have come to this spot a hundred times, probably. I found this bell. And I rang it for days on end. But all for nothing.'

'Why did you lie to me?' she asked, walking straight towards him. Her right hand assumed a life of its own and slid towards her knife. 'What did I do to you? Why did you do this?'

'I wanted to steal you from them,' said the musician. Spotting the weapon, he seemed bewildered and instead of running, sat down on the rails. 'I thought that if I was left alone with you . . .'

'But why did you come back?'

'It's hard to say,' he said, looking up at her submissively. 'I suppose I realised I'd crossed some kind of line. After I sent you here . . . After I was left on my own, I started thinking . . . No one's born with a black soul. At first it's transparent, and it darkens gradually, spot by spot, every time you forgive yourself for something wrong and find a justification for it, every time you tell yourself it's only a game. But then the moment comes when there's more black than white. Not many can sense that moment, it's not obvious from the inside. But I suddenly realised that I was crossing that boundary, right here and now, and afterwards I would be different. Forever. And I came to confess. Because you don't deserve this.'

'But why is everyone so afraid of you? Why are they all so spineless with you?'

'It's not me,' Leonid sighed. 'It's my dad.'

'What?'

'Does the name Moskvin mean anything to you?'

'No,' said Sasha, shaking her head.

'Then you're probably the only person in the Metro who doesn't know it,' the musician said with a mirthless chuckle. 'Anyway, my dad's a big boss. The boss of the entire Red Line. He fixed me up with a diplomatic passport. So they let me through. It's an uncommon name, no one takes any risks. Unless they simply don't know.'

'Then what do you . . . ?' Sasha backed away, gazing at him suspiciously. 'Observe? Is that what you were sent out for?'

'They just got rid of me. My dad realised he could never make a man of me, and he gave it up as a bad job. So I just disgrace his name on the quiet,' said Leonid, pulling a wry face.

'Did you have a quarrel with him?' asked the girl, screwing up her eyes.

'How could anyone quarrel with Comrade Moskvin? He's a living monument! I was excommunicated and cursed. You see, even as a kid I was a holy fool. I was always attracted to beautiful pictures, and the piano, and books. My mother spoiled me, she wanted a little girl. When my father realised what was going on, he tried to cultivate a love of firearms and Party intrigues in me. But it was too late. My mother got me addicted to playing the flute, my father tried to break me of the habit with the strap. He banished the professor who was teaching me and replaced him with a political commissar. But it was all a waste of time. I was already rotten. I didn't like the Red Line. I thought it was too grey. I wanted a bright life. I wanted to study music and paint pictures. Dear Papa once sent me to chip off a mosaic, so I would realise that beauty is perishable. And I chipped it off, so that I wouldn't be beaten. But while I was smashing it, I memorised every last detail, and now I could make one exactly like it myself. And ever since then I've hated my father.'

'You mustn't talk about him like that!' Sasha exclaimed indignantly.

'I can,' the musician said with a smile. 'Other people get shot for doing it. And as for the Emerald City . . . My professor told me about it, in a whisper, when I was little. And I decided that when I grew up I was definitely going to find the way in. That there must be a place in the world where what I lived for had some meaning. Where everyone lived for it. Where I wouldn't be a petty little pervert, or a parasitical prince, or a hereditary Dracula, but an equal among equals.'

'And you didn't find it,' said Sasha, putting her knife away. Sifting through the unfamiliar words, she had understood the most important thing. 'Because it doesn't exist.'

Leonid shrugged. He got up, walked over to the button and pressed it.

'It probably doesn't matter if anyone there really can hear me or not. It probably doesn't matter if there really is any such place in the world. What matters is that I think there's a place like that somewhere. And that someone hears me. Only I just don't deserve to have the door opened for me yet.'

'And is that really enough for you?' asked Sasha.

'It's always been enough for the whole human race, it will do for me too,' the musician said with a shrug.

The old man ran out onto the platform after the brigadier and gazed around in confusion: Hunter was nowhere to be seen. Miller trundled out of the cell block, as ashen-faced and desolate as if he had given his soul to the brigadier along with the mysterious token.

Why had Hunter fled and where to? Why had he abandoned Homer? It would be better not to ask Miller: Homer ought to get as far away from that man as possible, before he remembered that the old man even existed. Homer walked away unhurriedly, pretending that he was trying to catch up with the brigadier and expecting to be called from behind at any moment. But Miller didn't seem interested in him any longer.

Hunter had told the old man that he needed him in order not to forget his former self ... Was he lying? Maybe he just hadn't wanted to lose control, go berserk here in Polis and get into a fight that he might lose and so never get to Tula? His instincts and his killing skills were superhuman, but even he wouldn't try to storm an entire station all on his own. If that was it, then the old man had played his role by accompanying him to Polis, and now he had been kicked off the stage.

After all, the final outcome of the whole story depended on him too. And he had done his best to bring about the precise denouement planned by the brigadier – or whoever it was that spoke for him. What was this token? A pass? A badge of authority?

A black spot? An advance indulgence for all the sins that Hunter was so eager to take on his soul? Whatever it was, by extorting the token from Miller, together with his consent, the brigadier had finally given himself a free hand. He wasn't planning to make his confession to anyone. Make his confession! Why, the thing that had taken control inside him, the terrible thing that occasionally came out to look in the mirror, couldn't even talk properly.

What would happen at Tula when Hunter stormed it? Would drowning an entire station – or two or three stations – in blood be enough to quench his thirst? Or would the thing he was carrying inside him simply run riot after sacrifices like that?

Which of the two had asked Homer to follow him? The one who devoured people, or the one who fought with monsters? Which of them had fallen in the phantom battle at Polyanka? And who had spoken to the old man afterwards, asking for help?

And what if... What if Homer was supposed to kill him, what if that was his true mission? What if the final vestiges of the former brigadier, almost completely crushed and suffocated, had dragged the old man into this expedition so that he could see everything for himself, so that he would kill Hunter out of horror or mercy with a treacherous bullet to the back of the head in some dark tunnel somewhere? The brigadier couldn't take his own life, so he was looking for an executioner. An executioner who wouldn't need to be asked, who had to be discerning enough to do everything himself, and deceive that other presence inside Hunter, the one who was swelling, growing stronger by the hour and didn't want to die.

But even if Homer could muster the courage, even if he could seize the right moment and take Hunter by surprise, what good would it do? He couldn't halt the plague all on his own. So was there nothing left for the old man to do in this double-bind but observe and record? Homer could guess where the brigadier was headed. According to rumour, the semi-mythical Order, to which Miller and Hunter apparently both belonged, had established its base at Smolensk Station, in the underbelly of Polis. Its legionaries were called upon to defend the Metro and its inhabitants against dangers that the armies of ordinary stations couldn't cope with. That was all that the Order allowed to be known about itself.

It was absurd for the old man even to think of getting into Smolensk, which was as impregnable as Alamut Castle. And there was no point in any case: in order to meet the brigadier again, all he had to do was go back to Dobrynin... And wait until the groove that Hunter was travelling along inevitably led the brigadier there too, to the scene of his future crime and the final station in this strange story. Should Homer let him deal with the plague-carriers, disinfect Tula and then... Carry out his unspoken will? The old man had thought his role was different: to write, not to shoot, to bestow immortality, not take life. Not to judge or interfere, but to allow the book's heroes to act for themselves. But when the blood is knee-deep all around, it's hard not to get smeared with it. Thank God he had let the girl go with that trickster. At least he had spared Sasha the sight of the appalling bloodbath that she wouldn't have been able to prevent anyway.

He checked the station clock: if the brigadier was on schedule, then Homer still had a little time in hand. A couple of hours to be himself. To invite Polis to one last tango.

'And how were you planning to earn the right to get in?' Sasha asked.

'Well... It's stupid, of course... With my flute. I thought it could put something right. You know, music is the most fleeting and ephemeral of the arts. It exists for exactly as long as the instrument is playing, and then disappears without trace in an instant. But nothing infects people as quickly as music. Nothing else gives them such deep wounds that heal so slowly. Once a melody has moved you, it stays with you forever. It's the distilled essence of beauty. I thought I could heal the soul's deformity with it.'

'You're strange,' she said.

'But now I've realised that a leper can't heal other lepers. That if I don't confess everything to you, the door will never be opened for me.'

'Did you think I'd forgive you? For your lies and your cruelty?' asked Sasha, glancing at him sharply.

'Will you give me one more chance?' Leonid asked and suddenly smiled at her. 'After all, you say we all have the right to that.'

The girl didn't answer, wary of being drawn into his strange games again. A moment ago she had almost believed in the musician's repentance, but now was he starting again?

'In everything I told you, one thing was true,' he said. 'There is a cure for the sickness.'

'A medicine?' Sasha asked with a shiver, willing to be deceived again.

'It's not a medicine. Not tablets and not a serum. A few years ago we had an outbreak of the disease at Preobrazhenskaya Station.'

'But why doesn't even Hunter know about it?'

'There wasn't an epidemic. It fizzled out on its own. These bacteria are very sensitive to radiation. Something happens to them when they're irradiated ... I think they stop dividing. And that stops the disease. It was discovered by chance. The answer lies on the surface, so to speak.'

'Honestly?' She took hold of his hand in her excitement.

'Honestly.' He put his other hand over hers. 'You just need to contact them and explain ...'

'Why didn't you tell me this earlier? It's so simple. All those people who have died in the meantime ...' She freed her hand and her eyes glittered.

'In one day? Hardly ... I didn't want you to stay with that butcher,' he muttered. 'And I was planning to tell you everything right from the start. Only I wanted to swap the secret for you.'

'And swap me for other people's lives!' Sasha said angrily. 'That's not worth a single life!'

'I'd swap mine for it,' said the musician, jiggling his eyebrow.

'It's not for you to decide! Get up! We've got to run back ... Before he reaches Tula.' She jabbed one finger at the watch, whispered as she worked out the time and gasped. 'There's only three hours left!'

'What for? I can use the communications here. They'll call Hansa and explain everything. We don't need to run anywhere. Especially since we might not be in time.'

'No!' said Sasha, shaking her head vehemently. 'No! he won't believe it. He won't want to believe it. I have to tell him myself. Explain to him ...'

'And then what will happen? Are you going to give yourself to him in your joy?'

'What business is that of yours?' she snapped, but then, instinctively sensing the right way to handle a man in love, she added in a gentler voice. 'I don't want anything from him. And now I can't manage without you.'

'You're learning from me how to lie,' the musician said with a sour smile. 'All right,' he sighed helplessly. 'Let's go.'

It took them half an hour to reach Sport Station: the sentries had changed, and Leonid had to drum into their heads all over again how a girl with no passport could cross the borders of the Red Line. Sasha watched the time tensely and the musician watched her – it was very obvious that he was hesitating, struggling with himself.

On the platform, scrawny new conscripts were piling up bales of goods on a stinking old trolley, tipsy workmen were doggedly pretending to caulk the broken veins of pipes and little kids in uniform were learning off a serious adult song. In the space of five minutes two attempts were made to check their documents, and the next check – when they were almost in the tunnel leading to Frunze already – dragged out beyond all endurance.

Time was flying past. And the girl wasn't even sure she still had those pitiful two and a half hours – no one could stop Hunter. The young soldiers had already finished loading the trolley and it was moving towards them, panting as it picked up speed. And Leonid made up his mind.

'I don't want to let you go,' he said. 'But I can't hold you back. I was thinking of making us arrive late, so there'd be nothing left for you to search for. But I realise that still won't make you mine anyway. Being honest is the worst way of all to seduce a girl, but I'm tired of lying. When I'm with you I feel ashamed of myself all the time. Choose for yourself who you want to be with.'

The musician grabbed his miraculous passport out of the dawdling sentry's hands and punched him in the jaw, knocking him to the ground. Then he grabbed Sasha's hand tight and they stepped onto the trolley, which had just drawn level with them. The dumbfounded driver looked round and found himself staring into the barrel of a revolver.

'My father would be proud of me right now!' Leonid laughed. 'The number of times I've heard him say I'm wasting my time on nonsense, that I'll never amount to anything with that blasted whistle of mine! And now at last, here I am behaving like a real man, and he's not here. Jump!' he ordered the driver, who was holding his hands up high.

Although they were travelling at speed, the man obediently stepped off onto the rails, howled as he went tumbling over and over, then fell silent and disappeared into the blackness that was chasing hard after them. Leonid started throwing off the load, and the motor snorted more briskly with every bundle that fell onto the rails. The lethargic headlamp on the bow of the trolley blinked weakly as it peered forward, lighting up only the next few metres. A brood of rats darted out from under the wheels and their squealing was like someone scratching on glass, a startled line walker sprang aside and somewhere far behind them an alarm siren started wailing hysterically. The ribs of the tunnel flickered past faster and faster. The musician was squeezing out every ounce of speed the trolley was capable of.

They flew through Frunze Station: taken by surprise, the sentries scattered like the rats, and the trolley was already hundreds of metres away from Frunze before it started howling furiously in unison with Sport Station.

'Now things will get hot!' Leonid shouted. 'The important thing is to slip past the crossover line to the Circle! There's a large frontier post there... They'll try to intercept us! We'll go straight along the branch line to the centre!'

He knew what to worry about: from out of the side branch that had taken them onto the Red Line a powerful searchlight lashed into their eyes as a heavy freight trolley came rushing towards them. Their tracks would converge in a few dozen metres, it was too late to stop. The musician pressed the worn, shiny pedal to the floor and Sasha squeezed her eyes shut. They could only hope the points were set in the right direction and wouldn't direct them into a head-on collision.

A machine-gun rumbled and bullets whizzed by just centimetres from their ears. There was an acrid smell of burning and heated air, the roar of another motor flared up and faded away, and the trolleys missed each other by a miracle – the battle trolley flew out onto their track only a moment after Sasha's trolley passed the fork before sweeping on, shuddering, towards Culture Park. The battle trolley had been flung in the opposite direction.

Now they had a short lead that would last them until the next station, but what then? The trolley slowed down – the tunnel had started sloping upwards.

'Park's almost at surface level,' the musician explained to her, looking back. 'But Frunze is fifty metres down. We just have to get past the rise, after that we'll pick up speed!'

They even managed to pick up some speed before reaching Culture Park. A proud old station with tall vaults, half-dead and dimly lit, it turned out to be almost uninhabited. A siren started rasping, clearing its rusty throat. Heads appeared above the brick fortifications. Sub-machine-guns started barking after them too late, in helpless fury.

'We might even stay alive!' laughed the musician. 'Just a bit more good luck, and...'

And at that moment a small spark glinted in the darkness astern of them, then blazed up more brightly, becoming blinding as it overhauled them... The battle trolley's searchlight! Thrusting the fierce beam out ahead of it like a lance on which it was straining to impale their ramshackle little vehicle, the battle trolley ate up the distance between them, cutting it back minute by minute. The machine-gun started yammering again and bullets whined through the air.

'Just a bit further! This is Kropotkin already!'

Kropotkin... Ruled off into squares with identical tents set out in them, neglected and unkempt. Someone's rough portraits on the walls, painted a long time ago and already blurred and runny. Flags and more flags, so many that they merged into a single ribbon of crimson, a frozen jet spurting out of a fossilised vein.

Just then an under-barrel grenade launcher barked and fragments of marble showered down onto the trolley: one of them slit Sasha's leg open, but the wound wasn't deep. Ahead of them small young soldiers started lowering a boom, but the trolley had picked up more speed and smashed it aside, almost flying off the rails itself.

The battle trolley was gaining on them implacably: its motor was many times more powerful and easily pushed the steel-clad behemoth along. Sasha and the musician had to lie down and shelter behind the metal frame of their trolley.

But in just a few moments the sides of the two trolleys would touch, and they would be boarded. Leonid suddenly started taking off his clothes, as if he had lost his senses. A frontier post appeared ahead: a parapet built of sandbags, steel tank traps – the end of the journey. Now they'd be jammed between two machine-guns, between the hammer and the anvil.

In a minute it would all be over.

CHAPTER 18

Deliverance

The line of men was several dozen metres long. Only the very finest of Sebastopol's soldiers were in it, each one personally selected by the colonel. Their little helmet lamps twinkled in the gloom of the tunnel, and Denis Mikhailovich suddenly saw the entire combat formation as a swarm of fireflies dashing into the night. Into a warm, fragrant Crimean night, over the cypresses, towards the whispering sea. To where the colonel would like to go when he died.

He shook off the chilly, ticklish sensation, frowned and reprimanded himself severely. He was starting to weaken in his old age after all. He let the last soldier past him, opened a stainless steel cigarette case, took out the one and only hand-rolled cigarette, sniffed at it and struck a flame out of his lighter. It was a good day. Fortune was smiling on the colonel and everything was coming together just as he had planned. They'd got through Nagornaya without any casualties – even the one man who disappeared had caught up with the column again soon afterwards. And everyone was in an excellent mood: going up against bullets was far less frightening to them than floundering in uncertainty and endless waiting. And apart from that, Denis Mikhailovich had let them catch up properly on their sleep just before the expedition. Only he hadn't been able to get to sleep himself: the colonel had always regarded destiny as a simple sequence of fortuitous events and had never understood how it was possible to put any trust in it. There hadn't been any news of the little two-man expedition in all the days that had passed since it set off into the Kakhovka Line tunnels. Anything could have happened, after all, Hunter wasn't immortal.

And what right did Denis Mikhailovich have to rely on just the brigadier, who might have gone totally crazy from all his endless battles, and that old storyteller?

He couldn't wait any longer either.

The plan of action was this: take the main body of Sebastopol's forces through Nakhimov Prospect, Nagornaya and Nagatino to Tula's closed southern hermetic door and send a group of saboteurs over the surface to the sealed-off station. Send the saboteurs down into the tunnel through the ventilation shafts to eliminate the guards, if there still were any, and open the door for the assault brigade. And after that it was a simple, routine job, no matter who had captured the station. It had taken three days to locate and clean out the shafts. All that was left for the stalkers to do today was let the saboteurs in. And that was going to happen in a couple of hours' time. In two hours everything would be decided and Denis Mikhailovich would be able to think about something else again, able to sleep and eat again.

The plan was simple, precise, impeccable. But Denis Mikhailovich had a tense, agitated kind of feeling and his heart was pounding as if he was eighteen years old again, advancing into that mountain village, into his first battle. The colonel cauterised his sense of alarm with the final glow of his cigarette, threw away the tiny butt, pulled his mask on again and strode forward to catch up with the unit.

The brigade soon came up against the steel hermetic door. They could rest here until the assault began and he could run through the carefully spelled out and memorised roles with the section leaders.

Homer had been right about one thing, the colonel thought to himself with a chuckle. It was pointless trying to take a fortress by storm, if you could get it opened up for you from the inside, like the Greeks at Troy. And wasn't it actually Homer who wrote about the Trojan Horse?

Denis Mikhailovich checked his radiation meter: the background level was low, and he pulled off his gas mask. The section leaders did the same, and then so did the other soldiers. That was fine, let them take a breather.

In Polis there were always plenty of people who had struggled to make the journey here from poor, dark, outlying stations, hanging about or wandering through the galleries and halls with their eyes goggling and their jaws hanging open in admiration. And Homer, circling round Borovitskaya, tenderly stroking the elegant columns of Alexander Garden, scrutinising with loving delight the frivolous chandeliers of Arbat that looked like girls' earrings, didn't stand out from them in any way.

His heart had caught a presentiment and wouldn't let go of it: this was the last time he would be in Polis. What was about to happen at Tula in a few hours would cancel out his entire life, and perhaps even cut it short. The old man had decided to do what he had to do. He would let Hunter kill everyone and burn out the station, and then try to kill him. But if the brigadier suspected treachery, he would wring Homer's neck in an instant. And perhaps the old man would be killed in the assault on Tula. If so, his death would come soon. But if everything went well, afterwards Homer would become a hermit, so that he could fill up all the white pages between the already written opening of the book and the final full stop, which he would insert with the shot into the back of Hunter's head.

Would he be able to do it? Would he dare? The mere thought of it was enough to set the old man's hands shaking. But never mind, it would all work out somehow. He didn't need to think about it now, too much thinking led to doubts.

And thank God he'd sent the girl away! Homer understood now why he had got her mixed up in his reckless adventure, why he had allowed her to walk into the lions' cage. He'd got carried away, playing the writer, and forgotten that she wasn't a figment of his imagination.

Homer's novel would turn out different from the way he had thought of it, it would be about something different. But from the very beginning Homer had attempted to shoulder an impossibly heavy burden. How could all the people be fitted into a single book? Even the crowd through which the old man was walking at the moment would be cramped on a book's pages. Homer didn't want to transform his book into a communal grave, with flickering columns of names that dazzled the eyes and bronze letters, behind which it was impossible to glimpse the faces and characters of the fallen.

No, it wouldn't work. Even his memory, so corroded by the passage of time that it had started springing leaks a long time ago, couldn't take all these people on board. The pockmarked face of a sweet seller, and the pale, sharp-nosed face of the little girl handing him a cartridge. And her mother's smile, beaming as bright as the smile of a Madonna, and the lecherous, sticky smile of the soldier walking by. And the harsh wrinkles of the ancient beggars appealing for charity right there, and the laughing wrinkles beside the eyes of a thirty-year-old woman.

Which of them was a rapist, or a money-grubber, or a thief, or a traitor, or a rake, or a prophet, or a righteous man, and which of them still hadn't found themselves yet – Homer didn't know all that. It wasn't revealed to him what the sweet seller was really thinking about when he looked at the little girl, what was really meant by her mother's smile – the smile of someone else's wife ignited by the spark of a soldier's gaze – or how the beggar used to make his living before his legs gave out. And so it wasn't for Homer to decide who deserved immortal fame and who didn't.

Six billion people had simply perished: six billion of them! Was it pure chance that only a few tens of thousands had managed to escape?

The engine driver Serov, whose place Nikolai was to have taken a week after the Apocalypse, was a passionate sports fan, who regarded the whole of life as a football match. 'The whole human race has lost,' he used to tell Nikolai, 'but you and I are still running around, haven't you ever wondered why? It's because our lives don't have a final scoreline yet, and the ref's made us play extra time. And during that time we have to figure out what we're here for and manage to get everything done, set everything straight, and then take a pass and fly with the ball towards that radiant goalmouth...' He was a mystic, that Serov. Homer had never asked him if he managed to score that goal, but Serov's views had certainly convinced Homer that *he* still needed to set his own personal score in order. And it was from Serov that Homer had acquired the certitude that no one in the Metro was there by accident.

But it wasn't possible to write about everything!

Should he even carry on trying?

And then, among a thousand unfamiliar faces, the old man saw what he least of all expected to see at that moment.

Leonid took off his jacket and pulled off his sweater, followed by a relatively white T-shirt, which he flung up over his head like a flag and started waving about, taking no notice of the dense swarm of bullets whizzing through the air around him. And something strange happened: the battle trolley started falling back, and still no one opened fire from the frontier post looming up ahead of them.

'And for that my dear dad would kill me!' the musician told Sasha after they braked with a ferocious grating sound from full speed to a dead halt right in front of the tank traps.

'What are you doing? What are we doing?' Sasha couldn't catch her breath, she couldn't understand how they could have survived the chase.

'We're surrendering!' he laughed. 'This is the entrance to Lenin Library Station, the frontier post of Polis. And you and I are defectors.'

Border guards came running up and took them down off the trolley. When they checked Leonid's passport they exchanged glances, put away the handcuffs they were holding ready and escorted the girl and the musician into the station. They took them into the watch office and went out, whispering among themselves respectfully, to get their commanding officer.

Leonid, who was sprawling haughtily in a threadbare armchair, immediately jumped up, glanced out of the door and beckoned to Sasha.

'They're even worse slackers here than on our line!' he snorted. 'There aren't any guards!'

They slipped out of the room and walked unhurriedly at first, then faster and faster along the passage, finally breaking into a run and holding hands so that the crowd wouldn't separate them. Their backs soon started itching when they heard the trilling of militiamen's whistles behind them, but nothing could have been easier than to lose themselves in this huge station. There were ten times as many people here as at Pavelets. Even when Sasha imagined life as it was before the war, while she was taking her stroll on the surface, she hadn't been able to picture such a huge multitude! And it was almost as bright here as it had been up there. Sasha covered her face with one hand, examining the world through a narrow observation slit between her fingers. Her eyes kept stumbling over things, faces, columns, every one more amazing than the ones that had gone before, and if not for Leonid and his fingers intertwined with hers, she would certainly have stumbled and fallen, completely disoriented. She definitely had to come back here some day, Sasha promised herself. Some day when she had more time.

'Sasha?'

The girl looked back, and her gaze met Homer's: he looked frightened, and angry, and surprised. Sasha smiled: apparently she had missed the old man.

'What are you doing here?' He couldn't have asked two young people trying to make a quick getaway a more stupid question.

'We're going to Dobrynin!' she answered, catching her breath and slowing down slightly so the old man could catch up with them.

'Don't talk nonsense! You mustn't . . . I forbid you to!' But his prohibitions, gasped out through strenuous puffing and panting, made no impression on her.

They reached the check point at Borovitskaya before the border guards had warned it about their getaway.

'I have a warrant from Miller! Let us through, and make it quick!' Homer told the officer on duty coolly.

The soldier opened his mouth, but then without even taking time to gather his thoughts, he saluted the old man and stood aside.

'Did you just lie?' the musician asked Homer politely when the checkpoint was far behind them, lost in the darkness.

'What difference does it make?' the old man snarled angrily.

'The important thing is to do it confidently,' Leonid said appreciatively. 'Then only the professionals will notice.'

'To hell with the lectures!' exclaimed Homer, frowning and clicking the switch of his flashlight, which was already running down. 'We'll go as far as Serpukhov, but I won't let you go any further than that!'

'That's because you don't know!' said Sasha. 'A cure has been found for the sickness!'

'What do you mean, found?' asked the old man, breaking step and starting to cough. He gave Sasha a strange, fearful kind of look.

'Yes, yes! It's radiation!'

'The bacteria are rendered harmless by the effects of radiation,' explained the musician, coming to the rescue.

'But microbes and viruses are hundreds or thousands of times more resistant to radiation than human beings! And radiation impairs the immune response!' the old man shouted, losing control of himself. 'What nonsense have you been telling her? Why are you dragging her off there? Do you have any idea what's going to happen now? None of us can stop him now! Take her away somewhere and hide her! And you...' Homer turned to Sasha. 'How could you believe...a professional?' he said, spitting out the last word contemptuously.

'Don't be afraid for me,' the girl said in a quiet voice. 'I know Hunter can be stopped. He has two halves... I've seen both of them. One wants blood, but the other is trying to save people!'

'What are you talking about?' exclaimed Homer, flinging his arms up in protest. 'There aren't any different parts any more, there's a single whole. A monster locked inside a human body! A year ago...'

But the old man's retelling of the conversation between the man with the shaved head and Miller did nothing to convince Sasha. The longer she listened to Homer, the more certain she became that she was right.

'It's just that the one inside him, who kills, is deceiving the other one,' she said, struggling to find the right words to explain everything to the old man. 'It's telling him there's no choice. One is driven by hunger, and the other by anguish. That's why Hunter's so eager to get to Tula – both halves are dragging him there! They have to be split apart. If he's offered a choice – to save without killing...'

'Oh God... He won't even listen to you! What's pulling you to that place?'

'Your book,' Sasha told him with a gentle smile. 'I know everything in it can still be changed. The ending hasn't been written yet.'

'Nonsense! Gibberish!' Homer babbled in despair. 'Why did I even tell you about it? Young man, you at least...' He grabbed Leonid by the arm. 'I beg you, I believe you're not a bad person and you didn't lie out of spite. Take her. That's what you wanted, isn't it? You're both so young and so beautiful... You have a life to live! She mustn't go there, do you understand? And you mustn't go there. You won't stop anything either, with your little lie...'

'It isn't a lie,' the musician said politely. 'Would you like me to swear to it?'

'All right, all right,' said the old man, brushing aside his protestations. 'I'm prepared to believe you. But Hunter... you've only had a brief glimpse of him, haven't you?'

'But I've heard plenty,' Leonid said with a wry chuckle.

'He's... How are you going to stop him? With that flute of yours? Or do you think he'll listen to the girl? That thing inside him... He can't even hear anything any longer...'

'To be honest,' said the musician, leaning down towards the old man, 'in my heart I agree with you. But it's a young lady's request! And I am a gentleman, after all.' He winked at Sasha.

'Why can't you understand... this isn't a game!' Homer burst out, gazing imploringly at the girl and Leonid by turns.

'I do understand,' Sasha said firmly.

'Everything's a game,' the musician said calmly.

If the musician really was Moskvin's son, he genuinely could know something about the epidemic that even Hunter hadn't heard. Hadn't heard or didn't want to tell? Homer suspected that Leonid was a charlatan, but what if radiation really could destroy the fever? Against his own will and against all common sense the old man started gathering together proofs that he was right. Wasn't this what he had been praying for for the last few days? Then the cough, the bleeding mouth, the nausea – were they merely symptoms of radiation sickness? The dose he had received on the Kakhovka Line must have extinguished the infection.

The devil certainly knew how to tempt the old man! But assuming it was true, then what about Tula, and what about Hunter? Sasha was hoping she could change his mind. And she really did seem to have a strange kind of power over the brigadier. But while one of the parties warring within him might find the bridle the girl was trying to throw over him as soft as silk, it would sear the other like red hot iron. Which of them would be on the outside at the decisive moment?

This time Polyanka chose not to put on a show for him, or for Sasha, or for Leonid. The station appeared to them stark and empty, as if it had given up the ghost long ago. Should Homer take this as a good omen or a bad one? He didn't know. Possibly the draught that had started up in the tunnels – a shadow of the winds rambling about on the surface – had simply swept away all the stupefying vapours. Or was the old man perhaps mistaken about something, and now he didn't have any future for Polyanka to tell him about?

'What does "Emerald" mean?' Sasha asked out of the blue.

'An emerald is a transparent green stone,' Homer explained absent-mindedly. 'So to say something is emerald simply means that it's green.'

'That's funny,' the girl said thoughtfully. 'So it does exist after all . . .'

'What do you mean?' the musician asked with a start.

'Oh, nothing really . . . You know,' she said, looking at Leonid, 'I'm going to search for that city of yours too. And I'll definitely find it someday.'

Homer just shook his head: he still wasn't convinced the musician was sincere in his repentance for filling Sasha's head with nonsense and luring her to Sport Station for nothing.

But the girl was still absorbed in her own thoughts: she whispered something and sighed a couple of times. Then she glanced at the old man quizzically.

'Have you written down everything that happened to me?'

'I'm writing it.'

'Good,' she said and nodded.

Bad things were happening at Serpukhov. The Hansa guard at the entrance had been doubled and the morose, taciturn soldiers flatly refused to let Homer and the others through. Neither the cartridges that the musician jangled under their noses nor his document made the slightest impression on them. The situation was saved by the old man, who demanded to be connected with Andrei Andreevich. A long half-hour later a signal officer arrived, unreeling a thick wire, and Homer menacingly announced into his telephone receiver that the three of them were the advance guard of a cohort of the Order. This half-truth was enough to get them escorted through the hall, which was stuffy, as if all the air had been pumped out of the station, and entirely sleepless, even though it was the middle of the night, to the reception office of the commandant of Dobrynin.

He met them at the door in person, dishevelled and lathered in sweat, with sunken eyes and breath that stank of stale alcohol; the orderly wasn't in the room. Andrei Andreevich looked round nervously and, not seeing Hunter, he snorted impatiently.

'Will they be here soon?'

'Yes, soon,' Homer told him confidently.

'Serpukhov could mutiny at any moment,' said the commandant, wiping his face as he strode round the reception office. 'Someone let the cat out of the bag about the epidemic. No one knows what to be afraid of, they're lying and saying that gas masks won't help.'

'They're not lying,' Leonid put in.

'The guard post in one of the southern tunnels to Tula has mutinied, the entire unit. Mangy cowards... In the other tunnel, where the sectarians are, they're still holding position... Those fanatics have besieged them, howling about Judgement Day... The ruckus is starting up even here, in my own station! And where are our rescuers?'

There was the sound of ranting and swearing in the hall, people yelling and guards blaspheming. Before his question had even been answered, Andrei Andreevich squeezed back into his lair and started clinking the neck of a bottle against a glass in there. On his orderly's counter a little red light lit up on one of the phones, as if it had just been waiting for the commandant to leave the room: it was the phone with the word 'Tula' scrawled on a strip of sticking plaster.

Homer hesitated for a second before stepping towards the desk: he licked his dry lips and took a deep breath...

'Dobrynin Station here!'

'What shall I tell them?' Artyom asked doltishly, looking round at the commander.

The commander was still unconscious: his cloudy eyes looked as if they'd been curtained off and were shifting about restlessly right up under his forehead. Sometimes his body was shaken by a vicious cough. His lung's punctured, thought Artyom.

'Are you alive?' he shouted into the receiver. 'The infected men have broken out!'

Then he remembered they didn't know what was happening at Tula. He had to tell them, explain everything. Out on the platform a woman squealed and a machine-gun rumbled. The sounds slipped in through the crack under the door, and there was nowhere to hide from them. The person at the other end of the line was answering him, asking questions, but he couldn't hear them properly.

'You have to block their way out!' Artyom repeated. 'Shoot to kill. Don't let them get near you!'

He realised they didn't know what the sick people looked like.

How could he describe them? Bloated, with cracked skin, stinking? But then, the ones who had only got infected recently looked like normal people.

'Shoot everyone you see,' he said lifelessly.

But didn't that mean that if he tried to get out of the station, they'd shoot him too, that he'd condemned himself to death? No, he'd never get out. No one healthy was left at the station... Artyom suddenly felt unbearably lonely. And afraid that the man listening to all this at Dobrynin wouldn't have enough time now to talk to him.

'Please don't hang up!' he told him.

Artyom didn't know what to talk about with the stranger, and he started telling him about how long he'd been trying to get through and how he'd thought there wasn't a single station still left alive in the whole Metro. What if he'd been calling into the future, when no one had survived, he thought, and he said that too. He didn't have to be afraid of anything at all now. Just as long as he had someone to talk to.

'Popov!' the commander wheezed behind his back. 'Have you contacted the northern guard post? The hermetic door... Is it closed off?'

Artyom looked round and shook his head.

'Dumb bastard,' the commander barked, hacking up blood. 'Useless jerk... Listen to me. The station's mined. I found these pipes... Up on top... A drain for ground water. I laid charges... we'll set them off and flood the whole damn station. I've got the contacts for the mines here in the radio room. We have to close the northern door... And check if... And check if the southern one's holding. Seal off the station. So the water doesn't spread any further. Close it off, have you got that? When everything's ready, you tell me... Is the line to the guard post working?'

'Yes, sir,' Artyom said and nodded.

'Just don't you forget to stay on this side of the door,' said the commander, stretching his lips into a smile and breaking into furious coughing. 'That wouldn't be a comradely thing to do.'

'But what about you? You'll be here?'

'Don't funk it, Popov,' said the commander, narrowing his eyes. 'Every one of us is born for something. I was born to drown these bastards. You were born to batten down the hatches and die like an honest man. Got that?'

'Yes, sir,' Artyom repeated.

'Get on with it, then!'

The phone went dead.

By some whim of the telephone gods, Homer had heard almost everything the duty officer at Tula said to him quite well. But he hadn't been able to make out the last few phrases, and then the connection had broken down completely.

The old man looked up. Andrei Andreevich's heavy carcass was looming over him; his blue tunic had acquired dark patches under the armpits, his fat hands were trembling.

'What's going on there?' he asked in a hoarse, faint voice.

'Everything's got out of control.' Homer gulped hard. 'Move all your free men to Serpukhov.'

'Can't be done,' said Andrei Andreevich, pulling his Makarov pistol out of his trouser pocket. 'There's panic at the station. I've posted all the loyal men at the entrances to the tunnels on the Circle, to make sure at least that no one disappears from here.'

'You can reassure them!' Homer responded hesitantly. 'We've found out ... The fever can be cured. By radiation. Tell them.'

'Radiation?' The commandant pulled a sour face. 'Do you really believe that? Then fire ahead, you have my blessing!' He saluted the old man buffoonishly, slammed the door shut and locked himself in his own office. What should Homer and the girl and the musician do now? They couldn't even escape from here. But where were the other two? The old man went out into the corridor, pressing his hand against his pounding heart. He ran into the station, calling out her name. He couldn't see them anywhere. Dobrynin was in chaos: women with children and men with bundles were besieging the weakened cordons and looters were darting about among the overturned tents, but no one was paying any attention to them. Homer had seen this kind of thing before: next they'd start trampling on those who had fallen, and then shooting at unarmed people.

And at that very moment the tunnel gave a groan.

The wailing and clamouring stopped, replaced by loud exclamations of surprise. The extraordinary, powerful sound was repeated.

It was like the roaring battle trumpets of a Roman legion that had lost its way in the millennia and was advancing against Dobrynin Station.

Soldiers started scurrying about, moving aside barriers, and something immense emerged from the mouth of the tunnel... A genuine armoured train! The heavy head of the cabin, jacketed in steel that was studded with rivets, with heavy calibre machine-guns protruding from the slits of two gun ports, then a long, lean body and a second horned head, facing in the opposite direction. Not even Homer had ever come across a monster like this.

Sitting on the raven-black armour plating were faceless idols. Indistinguishable from each other in their full-protection suits, Kevlar vests and outlandish gas masks, with backpacks behind their shoulders, they didn't seem to belong to this time or this world at all.

The train stopped. The aliens encased in armour paid no attention to the curious onlookers who came running up: they flew down onto the platform and lined up in three ranks. Swinging round as one man in perfect synchronisation, like a machine, they lumbered off towards the connecting passage to Serpukhov, and their tramping drowned out the awed whispers and the children's crying. The old man hurried after them, trying to spot Hunter among the dozens of warriors. They were all almost the same height, their anonymous bulletproof jumpsuits fitted without a single wrinkle, stretched taut across their massively broad shoulders, and they were all armed in the same menacing fashion: backpack flamethrowers and nine-millimetre sniper's rifles with silencers. No insignia, no coats of arms, no badges of rank. Probably he was one of the three striding along at the front?

The old man ran along the column, waving his hand, glancing into the observation slits of the gas masks and always encountering the same impassive, indifferent gaze. None of the aliens responded, no one recognised Homer. So was Hunter even with them? He had to show up, he had to!

The old man didn't see either Sasha or Leonid on his way through the passage. Could good judgement really have prevailed, and the musician have hidden the girl somewhere out of harm's way? If they would just wait out the bloodbath somewhere, then afterwards

Homer would come to an agreement with Andrei Andreevich, provided the commandant hadn't already blown his brains out.

The formation forged ahead, slicing through the crowd, and no one dared to stand in its way, even the Hansa border guards silently made way for it. Homer decided to follow the column – he had to make sure that Sasha wouldn't try to do anything. No one tried to drive the old man away, they took no more notice of him than of some mutt barking after a hand trolley.

As they stepped into the tunnel, the three men at the head of the column lit up their million-candle-power flashlights, burning out the darkness ahead. None of them spoke and the silence was oppressive and unnatural. It was their training, of course, but the old man couldn't help feeling that in honing the skills of the body, these men had suppressed the skills of the soul. And now he was observing a perfected killing machine, in which none of the elements had a will of its own, and only one, who from the outside was indistinguishable from all the others, carried the programme of action. When he gave the order 'Fire!' the others would commit Tula to the flames, and likewise any other station, together with everything still living in it.

Thank God, they didn't march through the line where the sectarians' train was stuck. The unfortunates had been granted a brief respite before their Day of Judgement: the warriors would annihilate Tula first, and only turn on them afterwards. Obeying some signal that Homer couldn't see, the column suddenly slowed down. A moment later, he realised what was happening: they were already very close to the station. The silence was as transparent as glass, with someone's heartrending howls scraping on it like a nail...

And there was another sound, absolutely incongruous and barely audible. Trickling out drop by drop, making the old man doubt his own reason, miraculous music greeted the alien visitors.

The phone had swallowed up the old man completely and Sasha decided she couldn't find a better moment to run for it. She edged out of the reception room, waited for Leonid outside and led him after her – first to the passage to Serpukhov, and then into the tunnel that would take them to the people who needed them. To the people whose lives she could save.

The tunnel that would also reunite her with Hunter.

'Aren't you afraid?' Sasha asked the musician.

'Yes,' he said with a smile, 'but I suspect that I'm finally doing something worthwhile.'

'You don't have to go with me, you know. What if we die there? You could just stay at the station and not go anywhere!'

'A man's future is concealed from his knowledge,' said Leonid, holding up his finger in a professorial gesture and puffing out his cheeks.

'You decide for yourself what it's going to be,' Sasha retorted.

'Oh, come on,' the musician laughed. 'We're all just rats running through a maze with little sliding doors in the passages. Whoever it is that's studying us sometimes pulls them up and sometimes pushes them down. And if the door at Sport Station is down right now, there's no way you're going to get in there, no matter how hard you scratch at it. And if there's a trap after the next little door, you'll fall into it in any case, even if you can sense that something's wrong, because there isn't any other way to go. The choice is basically keep on running or croak in protest.'

'Don't you resent having a life like this?' asked Sasha, knitting her brows.

'I resent the fact that the way my spine is constructed doesn't allow me to raise my head and look at whoever's running the experiment,' the musician responded.

'There isn't any maze,' said Sasha, biting her lip. 'And rats can even gnaw through cement.'

'You're a rebel,' Leonid laughed. 'And I'm a conformist.'

'That's not true,' she said, shaking her head. 'You believe that people can be changed.'

'I'd *like* to believe it,' the musician objected.

They passed a hastily abandoned guard post. Embers were still glowing in the extinguished campfire with a greasy, crumpled magazine full of pictures of naked people lying beside it and an abandoned Hansa standard dangled forlornly, half-torn off the wall.

Ten minutes later they came across the first body. The corpse was barely recognisable as human. It had flung its arms and legs out wide, as if it was really tired, and the limbs were so bloated that the clothes on them had split. The face was more terrible than any of the monsters Sasha had seen in her short life.

301

'Careful!' said Leonid, catching hold of her hand to stop her going near the corpse. 'It's infectious!'

'So what?' said Sasha asked. 'There's a cure, isn't there? Where we're going, everyone's infectious.' They heard a rumble of shots up ahead and shouting in the distance.

'We're just in time,' the musician remarked. 'It looks like they didn't wait for your friend either...'

Sasha gave him a frightened look, then replied with passionate conviction.

'It's all right, we just have to tell them! They think they're all doomed... We just have to give them hope.'

Another corpse lay right by the door, staring into the ground – this time it was human. Beside it the iron box of a field communications device was spluttering and hissing desperately. Someone was clearly trying to rouse the sentry.

Several men were lying, hidden behind scattered sandbags, at the very exit from the tunnel. There seemed to be one machine-gunner and two men with automatics, and that was the entire blocking unit. Further ahead, where the narrow tunnel walls widened out and the platform of Tula Station began, a terrible crowd was raging and seething, menacing the men under siege. It was a jumble of the sick and seemingly healthy, normal people and monsters mutilated by the illness. Some of them had flashlights, others no longer needed light.

The men lying down were guarding the tunnel. But they were running out of cartridges, shots sounded less and less often and the brazen crowd was creeping closer and closer.

'Reinforcements?' one of the besieged men asked Sasha. 'Guys, they got through to Dobrynin! Reinforcements!'

The multi-headed monster became more agitated and pressed forward.

'People!' shouted Sasha. 'There is a cure. We've found the cure! You're not going to die! Please, just be patient!'

The crowd gobbled down her words, burped irritably and started moving forward again towards the men who were trying to hold it back. The machine-gunner lashed it with a fierce burst of fire and several people sat down on the ground with a groan. The other soldiers' automatics barked briefly. The mass of bodies seethed, advancing implacably, ready to trample the besieged men and Sasha and Leonid, ready to tear them to pieces.

But then something happened.

The flute started to sing, stealthily at first, but then with growing confidence and power. Nothing could have been more stupid and less appropriate in that situation. The soldiers guarding the tunnel gazed at the musician in stupefaction, the crowd roared and laughed and started pressing forward again. Leonid took no notice. Probably he wasn't playing it for them, but for himself – the same amazing melody that had enchanted Sasha, the same one that always captivated dozens of listeners, luring them to him.

Perhaps it was because no worse way to control the rioting and pacify the sick people could possibly be imagined, perhaps it was the touching idiocy of someone who could do something like this, and not the magic of the flute at all, but the crowd relaxed its pressure slightly. Or perhaps the musician really managed to remind these people who had surrounded him, ready to grind him to dust... Remind them of something...

The shooting stopped and Leonid stepped forward, still holding his flute. As if he were facing a normal audience that would burst into applause and shower him with cartridges at any moment.

For a split second the girl thought she could see her father among the listeners – smiling and at peace. So this was where he had been waiting for her... Sasha remembered that Leonid had told her this melody could ease pain.

There was a sudden, premature rumbling in the metal innards of the hermetic door.

Was the advance unit running ahead of schedule? In that case, the situation at Tula couldn't be so very difficult after all! Perhaps the intruders had left the station a long time ago, leaving the door locked?

The group spread out and the soldiers took shelter behind the projecting flanges of the tunnel liners. Only four of them remained beside Denis Mikhailovich, right in front of the door, holding their weapons at the ready.

This was it. Now the massive door would slowly move aside and a couple of minutes later forty heavily armed Sebastopolite assault troops would burst into Tula. Any resistance would be crushed and the station would be taken in an instant. It had all turned out a lot simpler than the colonel expected.

Denis Mikhailovich didn't even have time to give the order to don gas masks.

The column reformed, becoming broader – now it was six men abreast, occupying the whole width of the tunnel. The first rank bristled with the barrels of flamethrowers, the second row held its rifles at the ready. They crept forward like black lava, confident and unhurried.

Peeping out from behind the broad backs of the alien warriors, Homer saw the whole scene in the white light of the searchlights: a handful of soldiers defending the tunnel and two thin figures – Sasha and Leonid – and a host of nightmarish creatures surrounding them. And everything inside the old man seemed to freeze up.

Leonid was playing astoundingly, miraculously, with more compelling inspiration than ever before. The horde of ugly, misshapen creatures was listening to him greedily and the soldiers had half-risen from their lying positions in order to see the musician more clearly. And his melody divided the enemies like a glass wall, keeping them apart, preventing them from grappling with each other in a final, deadly skirmish.

'Stand by!' one of the dozens of black men ordered – but which one?

The entire front rank went down on one knee together and the second row raised its sniper's rifles.

'Sasha!' Homer shouted.

The girl swung round sharply towards him and screwed her eyes up against the blinding brightness. Holding her open hand out in front of her, she walked against the torrent of light flooding out of those flashlights as slowly as if she were fighting a tempestuous wind. Scalded by the bright rays, the crowd grumbled and groaned, bunching tighter together...

The aliens waited.

Sasha walked right up to their formation.

'Where are you? I need to talk to you, please!'

No one answered her.

'We've found a way to cure the disease! It can be cured! You don't have to kill anyone! There's a cure!'

The phalanx of black stone statues remained silent.

'Please! I know you don't want to... You're only trying to save them... And yourself.'

And then a dull voice rang out above the battle formation, as if it wasn't coming from any single individual.

'Stand aside. I don't want to kill you.'

'You don't have to kill anyone! There's a cure!'

'I don't believe it.'

'I beg you!' Sasha shouted, straining her voice into a shriek.

'The station has to be purged.'

'Don't you want to change everything? Why are you doing the same thing you've already done once? That other time, with the Black Ones? Why don't you want forgiveness?'

The idols didn't respond any more; the crowd started creeping closer.

'Sasha!' Homer whispered imploringly to the girl, but she didn't hear him.

'There's no way to change anything. No one to ask forgiveness from.' The painful words finally came. 'I raised my hand against... Against... And I've been punished.'

'It's all inside you!' Sasha shouted, not giving up. 'You can vindicate yourself! Prove your case! Why can't you see that it's the mirror? It's the reflection of what you did then, a year ago! And now you can act differently... Listen to me. Give me a chance... And earn yourself a chance!'

'I have to destroy the monster,' the formation said hoarsely.

'You can't!' Sasha shouted. 'No one can! It's in me, it's sleeping in everyone! It's a part of our soul, a part of our body... And when it wakes up... You can't kill it, you can't slaughter it! You can only lull it back to sleep.'

A grubby soldier slipped through the misshapen creatures and squeezed past the frozen black ranks to the hermetic door and the iron box of a transmitter. He grabbed the microphone and shouted something into it. But then a silencer champed briefly and the soldier fell silent. Sensing blood, the crowd immediately came to life, swelling up and roaring savagely.

The musician put the flute to his lips and started playing, but the magic had dissipated; someone shot at him, he dropped his instrument and grabbed his stomach with both hands.

Fire flickered on the flared muzzles of the flamethrowers. The phalanx sprouted new gun barrels and took a step forward.

Sasha dashed towards Leonid, ready to smash herself against the crowd that had already closed around him where he lay and didn't want to let the girl have him.

'No, no!' she shouted, unable to restrain herself any longer. And then, alone against hundreds of nightmarish monsters, alone against a legion of killers, alone against the whole world, she said stubbornly:

'I want a miracle!'

Thunder rumbled in the distance, the vaults shuddered, the crowd shrank together and retreated, and the aliens also started backing away. Fine rivulets of water ran across the ground, the first drops started falling from the ceiling and the dark streams gurgled louder and louder.

'A breach!' someone howled.

The black men hastily moved away from the station, withdrawing to the hermetic door, and the old man ran with them, looking round at Sasha. She didn't move. The girl held up her palms and her face to the water gushing down on her . . . and laughed.

'It's rain!' she shouted. 'It can do anything! We can start everything all over again!'

The black brigade moved outside the door and Homer went with it. Some of the aliens pushed hard on the door, trying to close off Tula and hold back the water. The slab of metal yielded and started moving slowly. The old man went dashing back to Sasha, left in the drowning station, but he was grabbed and flung out.

And then one of the black figures suddenly darted up to the narrowing gap, thrust his arm through it and shouted to the girl.

'Come on! I need you!'

The water was already waist-deep: the light blonde head suddenly slipped under the surface and disappeared.

The black man jerked his arm back and the door closed.

But the door didn't open. A tremor ran through the tunnel and the echo of an explosion crashed into the other side of the steel barrier and rebounded from it. Denis Mikhailovich pressed himself against the metal and listened. He wiped the dampness off his cheeks and glanced in surprise at the ceiling that was also exuding moisture.

'Pull out!' he ordered 'It's all over here.'

Epilogue

Homer sighed and turned the page. There wasn't much free space left in the exercise book – only a couple of pages. What should he put in, what should he sacrifice? He held his palms out to the campfire, to warm his frozen fingers and comfort them.

The old man had asked to be posted to the southern watch. He worked better here, facing the tunnels, than among the heaps of dead newspapers at home at Sebastopol, no matter how well Elena guarded his peace and quiet.

The brigadier was sitting a little distance away from the others, right on the very boundary of light and darkness. Homer wondered why he had chosen Sebastopol. Evidently there was something about this station after all . . .

Hunter had never told the old man who it was that appeared to him that time at Polyanka, but Homer knew now that what he himself saw wasn't a prophecy, but a warning.

The water receded from flooded Tula Station after a week and what remained was drained out with huge pumps brought in from the Circle. Homer volunteered to go there with the first scouts.

Almost three hundred bodies. Forgetting his revulsion, forgetting absolutely everything, he rummaged through those terrible bodies, searching for her, searching . . .

Afterwards he sat for a long time at the spot where he saw Sasha for the last time. The spot that he had made his dash for, too late to save her . . . or to die with her.

And the sick and the healthy shuffled past him in an endless procession – towards Sebastopol, to the healing tunnels of the Kakhovka Line. The musician hadn't lied: radiation really did halt the disease. Perhaps he hadn't lied at all? Perhaps there was a genuine Emerald City somewhere and it was just a matter of finding the door? Or perhaps he had reached that door, but he still didn't deserve to have it opened for him? 'And when the waters receded...' had turned out to be too late.

But it wasn't the Emerald City that was the Ark. The genuine Ark was the Metro itself. The final haven that gave shelter from the dark, stormy waters to Noah and Shem and Ham: the man of God, the indifferent man and the scoundrel. All the animals two by two. Everyone whose final scoreline hadn't been decided yet, or whose bills still hadn't been paid.

There were too many of them, and they definitely wouldn't fit into this novel. The old man had almost no empty pages left in the exercise book. His book wasn't an ark, it was a little paper boat, it couldn't take all the people on board. But Homer thought that in his tentative lines he had come very close to getting something very important down on those pages. Not about all those people, but about man.

The memory of the departed didn't disappear, thought Homer. Our whole world was woven out of other people's deeds and thoughts, just as each of us was made up of countless little pieces of mosaic, inherited from thousands of ancestors. They had left a trace behind them, they had left a little particle of their soul for their descendants. You just had to look for it.

And his little boat, made out of paper, out of thoughts and memories, could sail the ocean of time endlessly, until someone else picked it up and examined it and realised that man had never changed, that he had remained true to himself, even after the death of the world. And the flames of the celestial fire that was once implanted in him had fluttered in the wind, but not gone out.

His personal score had been amended now.

Closing his eyes, Homer was back in a resplendently bright station, flooded with light. Thousands of people had gathered on the platform, wearing smart clothes that belonged to a time when he was still young, when no one ever thought of calling him Homer, or even addressing him politely as Nikolai Ivanovich, and now they had been joined by people from here, who had lived in the Metro. Neither group was surprised by the other. They all had something in common.

310

They were waiting for something, all gazing anxiously into the dark vaults of the long, long tunnel. The old man recognised those faces now. His wife and children were there, and his workfellows, and his schoolmates, and his neighbours, and his two best friends, and Ahmed, and his favourite movie actors. Everyone he still remembered was there.

And then the tunnel lit up and a Metro train slid soundlessly out of it into the station – with living windows blazing with light, with polished sides, with lubricated wheels. The driver's cabin was empty: hanging inside it was a freshly ironed tunic and a white shirt. That's my uniform, the old man thought. And my seat.

He climbed into the cabin. Opened the doors of the carriages. Tooted the whistle. The crowd flooded inside, occupying the seats. There were places for everyone: the passengers were smiling now, feeling reassured. The old man smiled too. Homer knew that when he wrote the final full stop in his book, this sparkling train, full of happy people, would set off from Sebastopol straight into eternity.

The old man was suddenly jerked out of his magical vision by an inhuman groan somewhere very close. Homer shuddered and grabbed his automatic.

It was Hunter groaning. The old man half-stood, about to go over and check on the brigadier, but then he groaned again... On a slightly higher note... Then again... this time slightly lower...

Homer listened, unable to believe his ears, and shivered.

Hoarsely and clumsily, the brigadier was trying to pick out a melody. When he missed a note, he went back and repeated it stubbornly, trying to get it right. He was tracing out the melody softly. Like a lullaby.

It was the same melody that Leonid had never given a title to.

Homer never did find Sasha's body at Tula.

What else?

311